THE SINGING WINDS

THE SINGING WINDS

Elizabeth Gill

Hodder & Stoughton

First published in Great Britain in 1995
by Hodder and Stoughton
A division of Hodder Headline PLC

10 9 8 7 6 5 4 3 2 1

A CIP catalogue record for this title is available
from the British Library

ISBN: 0 340 62553 8

Typeset by
CBS, Felixstowe, Suffolk

Printed and bound in Great Britain by
Mackays of Chatham, Chatham, Kent

Hodder and Stoughton
A division of Hodder Headline PLC
338 Euston Road
London NW1 3BH

For my daughter, Katharine Elizabeth,
who puts up with me

Oh, the snow it melts the soonest when the winds begin to sing
And the bee that flew when summer shone in winter he won't sing
And all the flowers in all the land so brightly there they be
And the snow it melts the soonest when my true love's for me.

So never say me farewell in a farewell I'll receive,
You can meet me at the stile, you'll kiss and take your leave
And I'll wait here 'til the woodcock crows or the martin takes his leave
Since the snow it melts the soonest when the winds begin to sing.

From *The Snow It Melts the Soonest When the Winds Begin to Sing*

This north-eastern song was contributed to *Blackwood's Magazine* in 1821 by the soap-boiler and Radical agitator, Thomas Doubleday, who collected songs. He got the melody from a Newcastle street singer. In *Northumbrian Ministrelsy* (1882, repr. 1965) the same tune is given as *My Love Is Newly Listed*. I found the song on Anne Briggs' only solo album, Topic Records 12YS 207. Permission to quote was given by Topic Records.

Prologue

*T*he pits are gone now, for the most part. The pit heaps, which in my childhood resembled black mountains, are flattened, are fields. Only the villages remain with their long narrow streets. Many chapels are empty with weeds growing up around the doors for they have long been closed. Some have been sold and converted into houses, others are used for car repair workshops or warehouses. Some of those still open are desperate for money and congregations.

I live in a little pit town very close to where I was born. At least I think of it like that. When I moved here three years ago there was open-cast mining just beyond my house but no pits, though at one time there were three in the small area around my house. Some things haven't changed. There are allotments here and pigeon crees. Sometimes when I walk my spaniel in the afternoons by the river I can see the pigeons flying round and round their crees, their wings silver in the sunshine against the blue sky. People keep greyhounds and join bands, and there are the pubs and workingmen's clubs. During the early autumn there are leek shows where proud gardeners show off shiny bright vegetables. Each year in the newspapers there are stories of leek slashing, of secret recipes for watering, to make the leeks exactly the right size for the shows, and during September broth and leek puddings are made.

The town of which I write still exists. It's a pretty town too, over on the Durham coast, pretty with the kind of emptiness which many of the Durham villages have, a neatness where nothing is disturbed: no pit dirt, no pitmen, no raised voices of a Saturday night, no chapel of a Sunday, no work, no growth. It had three pits in 1880 and three chapels and a church. It had sprung up like a weed from the first few houses until it became a harbour for

1

the export of coal from inland pits, and then one at a time over a period of twenty years the three pits were sunk, houses were built, the trade of the port increased and all the needs of a growing town were met by shopkeepers, tradesmen, anchor manufacturers, brass founders and finishers, iron founders, engineers, even a bottle works. There were three ship-building yards with sail makers, ships chandlers, block and master makers, eight coal fitters. There were fourteen inns and public houses, three breweries. And there were the miners living in houses swiftly built by the mine owners.

Away from the houses there are cliffs to the north and to the south, in places seventy feet high. At intervals there are pleasant sloping grassy banks. A few miles to the north is Sunderland.

Come back with me to the days when the coal industry in Durham was at its height, when the towns which now have boarded up shops and empty streets were busy communities, when the streets of the seaside towns echoed with voices from other countries, to a certain summer afternoon when the shadows were long on the beach and the tide washed the sand just as it had done all that time before and has each day since.

One

*I*t was a rare hot July day. There was on the beach not even the hint of a breeze and the sun beat down on sand, rocks, shingle, gravel and stone, and on the boy and girl who were the only people who walked there. At least he walked. She skipped.

Lizzie was skipping. She was much too old for skipping, she knew, but it was Friday, the tide was down and the day was bright with sunshine. She didn't understand how Sam could walk like that, slowly, as if there was no excitement in him. It was the chapel picnic the following week, something to look forward to. What was he so quiet for?

She glanced sideways at him. His mam was proud of him and she wasn't the only one. Lizzie just had to look at him to be pleased. He was tall and slender and dark, and if his clothes were shabby and had belonged to Alf before him it didn't matter because he was young and held himself high. All the Armstrongs were like that and Sam was the best of them. There had never been a time in her life, good or bad, when he was not with her. They had lived next-door to each other since before she could remember, had played together in the back lane as children, had run together, laughing, along the beach many times. They had shared secrets in their own special sand dune, made plans in his back yard. He had scorned her anniversary pieces, the little poems she had to learn for Sunday School, taught her to play football, and she had helped him with his letters because Sam didn't like school and wouldn't learn.

Now she danced beside him on the beach, just above the slowly spreading waves, but he didn't look up. He kept his hands in his pockets and his head down and she thought that maybe he was thinking about the pit. She wished that she could talk to him about the picnic but she couldn't, close as they were. She had to wait until he asked. He always took her, he had done for years, and Lizzie didn't doubt that he would do so this time but he hadn't asked her yet and she was getting tired of waiting. Something else troubled her too. She hadn't a pretty frock to wear.

They left the beach, Lizzie regretfully, looking over her shoulder as she always did, in promise that she would be back. They walked up to the houses. It wasn't far. Their row was the nearest so they considered the beach their own. They stopped outside Sam's door and he sat down on the low wall there and picked up a stick from the back lane and banged the stick off his knee. His twin sister, May, came out of the house. She was short and dumpy and pale. She came down the yard and said to Lizzie, 'My mam's nearly finished my frock for the picnic. Would you like to come in and see?'

'That would be nice,' Lizzie said. 'Who's taking you?'

'Rob Harvey.'

Rob was three years older than May. He was an only child, a hewer who made good money.

'That's a feather in your cap,' Lizzie said.

'Who's taking you, Lizzie?' May asked.

Her insides felt as though somebody had clouted her in the middle and knocked all the breath out of her.

'What?' she said.

May looked impatiently at her brother but his head was down.

'Hasn't he told you yet?' And there was satisfaction in May's brown eyes that she was giving such important information. Sam looked up then, his own eyes narrowed and his mouth compressed.

'Shut up,' he said.

'He's taking Greta Smith,' May said, and Sam came to his feet, glaring at her. May ran back up the yard and into the house. Sam didn't look at Lizzie even though she waited for him to. She waited for him to say that it wasn't true, and when he didn't and she had gone on waiting and he had neither looked at her nor moved away, her insides took that bitter blow too and she said, 'Are you?'

'Aye.'

'You could have told me.'

'I just have done, haven't I?'

Lizzie could think of nothing to say. When it hadn't mattered, when she was ten and twelve, he had taken her. Now, when she was coming up fifteen and he was almost sixteen, it mattered. And he was taking Greta Smith. Greta had bonny frocks. She had long fair hair and blue eyes and pearly pink cheeks. Suddenly Lizzie hated her.

'I took you last year and the year before,' Sam said. 'I don't have to do it every year, do I?'

Lizzie's cheeks burned.

'Now what's up?' said a voice from the back door, and Jon Armstrong stepped into the yard. Lizzie wished him far enough. Jon was the eldest at nineteen and head of the family since his father had died four years ago. He was taller than most of the pitmen and the only one in the family with blue eyes. Jon's sarcasm could fell you from halfway up the yard and Lizzie didn't want him interfering now. Also half the lasses in the village fancied him. Lizzie didn't, she just wished he would stay out of it. She didn't even look at him.

'Nowt,' Sam said, and Lizzie watched him draw himself up as he spoke, conscious of Jon's height. 'I'm just not taking her to the picnic, that's all. I never said I would.'

Lizzie glared at him.

'You never said you wouldn't neither,' she declared bitterly.

Sam looked sullenly at her.

'I can take who I want, can't I?'

'You could have said,' Jon put in.

Lizzie's eyes filled with tears and her face and throat worked so that she had to look down.

'I'll take you to the picnic, Lizzie,' Jon offered.

'You can't take Lizzie. All the lads'll laugh. Anyroad, you said you weren't going and my mam said she was glad because Mavis Robson's been hanging around the back lane all week, and the lass from the store . . .'

'Why don't you go and have your tea?' Jon said softly and Sam retreated up the yard. Lizzie didn't look up. Her cheeks burned worse than ever. She wanted to go into her own house and have a good cry but she swallowed hard and stood her ground.

'I'm not going to no picnic with you, Jon Armstrong,' she said in a shaky voice. That would learn him, she thought, because any lass in the village would have gone with him.

'What for?' he said.

''Cos for,' Lizzie said, and marched out of his yard.

* * *

It was the first time she had wished that she didn't live so close to Sam. She saw all his comings and goings. She would have to watch him take Greta Smith to the picnic, watch him go out to call for her. Now she felt worse than before; she ached inside. Sam was always there, like her head and arms and legs were always there, her mother and her home. She could not believe that he could prefer another girl to her. It wasn't possible. They had done everything together: gone to school, for walks, sat around the fire. His family were hers: Jon and Alf, the middle brother, and May and their mother. She didn't just like them; she belonged to them and they belonged to her. And even more than that, Sam was special. Left to himself he wasn't bold like the other lads, he was quiet and gentle and often afraid of things, and she wanted to be with him to help and to share and to be a part of everything he did.

Her own household was small with just one brother, Harold, quiet and not very bright. There was no quarrelling, no loud laughter such as the Armstrong family enjoyed next-door. She knew that her mother thought she and Harold were the wrong way round, that Harold should have been clever at his books and that Lizzie should have been content to stay in the house and help. Her father had been hurt down the pit some time back and shortly afterwards had died. Now they had only one pay coming in and the house was much too quiet for Lizzie's liking. Often she'd made excuses to go next-door where it was lively. Now she had no excuse. She knew that her mother dreaded the time when Harold would marry but he had never looked at any lass that Lizzie knew of. She prayed that he never would. To feed a wife and bairns as well as a family on one pay would mean hardship such as they had never known.

Lizzie remembered what life had been like when her father worked. There had been money for material for bonny dresses and her mam and dad had laughed a lot. Then the roof fell in, her father was brought home on a handcart, and after that he was ill and died and there was no more pretty material or special things and her mother went around tight-lipped and Lizzie did not like being in the house.

Now there was just day to day. There was nothing but the different housework on the different days and Harold coming quietly back from work on different shifts. He had gone down the pit at twelve as all the lads did, having finished school at nine and gone to the pit head to screen coal until he was older. Lizzie told herself that she was lucky. Next-door Mrs Armstrong and May would have three men coming in so that there would be another

6

meal and another lot of hot water and another change of clothes all the time. But there was nothing to think about now, nothing to look forward to. No picnic. And worse than that, when Lizzie brought the pictures to the front of her mind, she knew that there had been other things she'd been looking forward to as well. There was the idea that Sam might kiss her. She blushed just thinking about it. She had lain in bed lately thinking of that, not sure whether she ought to think of it, so delicious was the thought. That he might court her as a lad did with a lass and that later they might marry and have a bairn and live with the Armstrongs. She would have liked that. She had hugged to herself the thought of living with them. She would have been happy there, married to Sam, having his bairn, helping his mam with the housework. It had been her biggest dream.

She had tried not to go next-door too often; her mam objected and the objections were sharp-tongued. Lizzie had heard it said that her mother had gypsy blood. Mrs Harton was small, slight, dark-skinned and black-haired with brown eyes and a quick temper and Lizzie had inherited all these things, but her mam was kind too and Lizzie did not want to hurt her feelings by giving the impression that she cared for the Armstrongs so much and wanted to be with them. Now she would have no more reason to go, no excuse. Apart from Sam Armstrong there was nothing but socks to darn and clothes to mend and washing and ironing and cleaning and the hated brasses to be polished.

She tried not to think that she and Sam had been children together and were children no more and that they had both changed. She clung to the memories, paddling in the summer, holly gathering in the winter, games at the Christmas party at the chapel, the secrets they had shared in their favourite sand dune. However, there was one thing to be thankful for. Her only decent dress had been let out until it could be let out no more. It was too tight and too short.

She thought of Jon Armstrong in his Sunday best suit and cap. Fancy, if she had said yes to his invitation and had to go in her ordinary frock. Whatever would he have thought? But then, he hadn't meant it. Part of her wished that he had, part of her wanted to show off such a prize to the other girls, but it was a small part of her. She knew that Jon thought of her just as he thought of May, trotting tame in and out of his house as she did. Could it be that he had felt sorry for her? That made her cross. Maybe that had been the trouble with Sam; he had thought of her the same way, like a sister. Now he wanted to shake her off, like a tree shook off leaves in an autumn wind, shake her off and have her go away. All right then, she would.

She didn't go round to their house or for walks on the beach for fear of seeing Sam there, for fear that he should be with Greta Smith. She stayed at home and got on with her work. But she had to tell her mam.

'We'll have to think what you're going to wear for the picnic, our Lizzie,' she said. 'Your dress won't let out no more. I've got some material . . .'

'It doesn't matter, Mam, I'm not going.'

They were in her bedroom. She and Harold were lucky like that; they had a bedroom each, her mam slept downstairs.

'Not going?' Her mother looked at her from quick dark eyes. 'It's not because of the dress, is it?'

'Sam's not taking me. He's going with Greta Smith.'

Her mother was offended for her, Lizzie could see.

'Well, that's a fine way to carry on, I must say!'

'It's up to him, Mam.'

'What about the other lads?'

'Nobody asked me. They wouldn't, would they? I've always gone with Sam. I thought he would take me, as usual.'

She saw Sam in the lane the next day as he came off the foreshift. She would have ducked into her yard but he saw her too and came across.

'Who's taking you to the picnic then?'

Lizzie said nothing, she was so hurt. She wished that she could have told him somebody was.

'Nobody's taking you, are they?' he insisted. 'And do you know what for? Because you're too clever, that's what for. All the lads wanted Greta.'

Lizzie looked hard into his brown eyes, her ready temper flaring.

'And is that what you wanted?' she said fiercely. 'What *all* the lads wanted? You're daft, that's what you are, Sam Armstrong.'

She thought that he would hit her, as he had done when they had fought as children, but that Alf and Jon, for once on the same shift, were coming down the lane for their dinner.

'Had your gob, our Sam, and howay in,' Jon ordered.

And when Sam stood, glaring, his eldest brother's black fist descended on the back of his collar and hauled him up the yard. Sam twisted, shouting, fists clenched, but Jon only fended him off, threatening, 'You do and I'll bray you.'

8

Sam twisted free and ran away up the lane. Alf turned at the gate. Jon lingered. The blue eyes seemed very bright in his black face, and then he turned and followed Alf in at the gate and up the yard towards the smell of meat and potatoes which was wafting from the open kitchen door.

Lizzie's mother made the dress anyway. It was a dull brown colour which Lizzie thought looked worse against her dark hair and eyes, but her mother was pleased because it fit and because there was plenty to let out across the seams and in the hem so Lizzie pretended that she thought the dress pretty. A new dress was more than plenty of lasses had though she was sure they all had a lad to take them to the picnic. May asked her in again to see her own new dress for the picnic and Mrs Armstrong greeted Lizzie warmly.

Lizzie liked Sam's mother. She was a very big woman, a good cook, and fond of all her family in an affectionate way which was rare in the village. It was rumoured that her family had been Cornish, arriving here when people from other parts of the country came to work in the pits. There was no trace of this in her speech but she had privately told Lizzie that Sam's father's family had thought she was not good enough for their son and there had been trouble between the two families for a long time.

Now she said, 'And just where do you think you've been? You don't have to stop coming, you know, just because you've fallen out with our Sam. I've heard all about it. He's getting a bit too big for his boots is that one. He has no call to be nasty. He's not too big to feel the flat of my hand.'

May proudly showed the new dress. It had lace at the collar and was a pretty blue. Lizzie dutifully admired it.

She knew that Mrs Armstrong had got it secondhand from a stall on the market but the material was good. It must once have belonged to somebody much better off than them. Originally it had had a bustle. Now it was sleek and smooth but not too fitted, cleverly reshaped to suit May's plump figure.

'Have you found a lad to take you to the picnic yet?' May asked.

'She's going with me,' Jon said quietly from the chair beside the window. He was reading a book and had not even lifted his head when Lizzie came in. She saw his mother looking at him in surprise and May's eyes widened.

'You're never,' she said.

Mrs Armstrong laughed.

'I wouldn't go to the foot of the stairs with him if I was you, Lizzie.'

'I'm not,' Lizzie said.

'Oh, go on,' May urged. 'That would fettle our Sam and Greta Smith.'

'No.'

'Does your mam know our Jon's asked you?' Mrs Armstrong said.

'I never told her.'

Jon put down the book, which Lizzie couldn't see the title of and got up.

'So tell her,' he said.

'No. And anyroad, I haven't got a frock to wear.'

'What's that then, your petticoat?'

'Jon!' Mrs Armstrong said.

'Lasses!' he teased. 'Always going on about frocks. Who cares?'

'I do,' Lizzie said, finding the courage to look at him and wishing that she hadn't. Those blue eyes were full of amusement and made her face hot.

'Well, you'd better get your mam told 'cos I'm coming round for you,' he said.

It was easy for him to say but Lizzie didn't know how to tell her mother. She looked for a good time and finally, just the day before, she managed to get the words out.

'Jon's taking me to the picnic, Mam.'

Her mother was baking. She wiped her floury hands and looked even more surprised than Jon's family had. And no wonder, thought Lizzie.

'What, Edie's Jon? What did he ask you for?'

'I don't know. Because Sam didn't.'

Her mother frowned.

'The lad's too old for you, Lizzie, and though he's been good to his mother he's not a good lad. He drinks and swears and fights. Are you sure?'

'He's coming for me at two o'clock. He said so.'

'Does his mother know?'

'Please, Mam. I'm just like May to him.'

'I suppose so then, if you really want to.'

Going to the chapel picnic with the best-looking lad in the village brought Lizzie a rare kind of pleasure which even her awful brown frock did not lessen. There were not many special days like this one. There was the chapel Christmas party, and for the little ones the anniversary where they said their piece. There were weekly Bible classes to which the older ones went mainly so that the lads and lasses could meet up afterwards. There was also the occasional day trip, but the annual picnic was special to Lizzie because she did not think any place could be better than home and it had been the one day in the year when Sam had – apparently unwittingly it seemed to her now – demonstrated to everyone that he was hers.

The day was fine and bright, it being July, and though she had slept badly and was nervous, Lizzie was glad to be there with Jon because his brother looked across and scowled. She also knew very well that several of the other girls were looking across with envy and plenty of others were choosing not to look at all.

Greta Smith had the prettiest dress. It was pink and white and didn't suit her, Lizzie thought. The pink bows looked daft.

The picnic ground had been the same for years – away across the sand dunes and around into the cove where it was sheltered. One or two adults from the chapel went to make sure that everybody behaved as they should but kept close to the younger ones. Lizzie should have enjoyed the freedom of being with Jon and no grown-ups watching but she didn't because he was the wrong lad. She didn't know what to say to him, and when finally they sat down in the warm grass she concentrated on spreading out the food which her mother had carefully wrapped. Sam and Greta were not far away and she glanced across.

'Stop looking at him,' Jon advised.

'I'm not. It's her frock I'm looking at,' Lizzie lied.

'There's nowt between his lugs but fresh air.'

'That's not true,' Lizzie began warmly, and then looked up and saw his eyes laughing. She bit her lip. 'Have a pasty,' she said.

Jon ate and said nothing more. She wasn't surprised. Her mother's baking was always light and good, but today Lizzie couldn't eat.

They went walking on the beach. She didn't think she would ever love anywhere quite as much: the cry of the herring gulls, the swish of the summer waves, the firmness of the baked sand, the spiky grass of the sand dunes, and the never-to-be-forgotten smell of the waves and the grass that was home.

Lizzie kept some way from Jon, aware that it was him beside her and not Sam, bigger than Sam, bolder and more in touch with things. Yet because he was not Sam so she was not happy. They walked back to the top of the dunes, just the two of them, crossing over some way to see a pond where he had said ducks would be swimming, and there in the warmth of a small hollow found Sam and Greta with faces pressed together, kissing inexpertly but with enthusiasm. Lizzie watched them for a second or two and then turned away. She couldn't cry in front of Jon. She walked on further down the dunes and towards the pond. There she sat down in the grass and scanned the expanse of water. It was empty, and there was nobody in sight.

'There are no ducks,' she said as Jon sat down beside her.

'No, I know.'

Lizzie looked at him, not sure now, and she thought that the look in his eyes was not the kind of look that you went to chapel with.

'They come in later, in the dusk.'

'But you said . . .' Lizzie protested, even as he tilted her chin with one effortless finger.

'Did I?'

She watched his eyes close amid a thick dark sweep of lashes and then he was near and his mouth was close against hers. Lizzie had often, and sinfully, she thought, imagined Sam's mouth on hers and had heard the other girls talking of kissing. She had even sometimes pressed her lips to her bare arm to try and imagine what it was like, but her imagination had not taken her half the way to here. No one had touched her like this, not even Sam. Nobody had ever embraced or hit her except during childish squabbles. There had been no kind of physical contact. Even now Jon did not touch her with his hands, as though he sensed that an embrace would be regarded as a kind of invasion. There was nothing but his mouth on hers and that very, very carefully, in the knowledge, she thought later, that she had not been kissed before. It was merely skin to skin, nothing but a soft breath, like the wind across sand. There was nothing clumsy or greedy or inexpert, and Lizzie knew in those seconds that although he treated her so gently, she was not a child now to Jon Armstrong, she was a woman, and wondered for how long he had seen her that way and why it had taken her until now to realise it for herself. He put his fingers under her chin as her eyes closed and her lips parted and gradually his hand gentled its way to her cheek as he kissed her long and slowly.

Lizzie was not even aware by then that he was not Sam. Her mouth began to return the pressure and her fingertips grew bold and edged towards him, touching the front of his shirt where his jacket was open. She had not thought that a man's body was so hard and solid but beneath the crisp clean shirt there was warmth and the kind of muscle which betrayed that Jon Armstrong had not idled away his time in the depths of the Victoria pit. She let the kiss go on and on and gradually it deepened and her lips parted further and her hands began to slide up towards his shoulders and Jon put his other arm about her waist. She tilted up her face more and more until his arm came up from her waist to hold her there and Lizzie became aware of every inch of her body as he gathered the softness of her against him and then some instinct made her press the heel of her hand against his chest in resistance and he sighed and loosed her.

The magic broke. She looked at him and he was not Sam.

'You brought me here on purpose for that, didn't you?' she said.

Jon said nothing. He looked at her and Lizzie found herself unable to look away.

'And you didn't like it?' he said.

She didn't like the way he said that, all sarcastic.

'It was just a kiss,' he said.

That made it worse, it being 'just' something. Lizzie got up.

'I suppose you think I like you,' she said. 'I suppose you think all the girls like you and you can do what you want.'

'Lizzie—'

'Well, I don't like you, so there.'

Jon smiled.

'I'll live,' he said.

Lizzie turned around and walked away and was very glad when he didn't follow her.

Two

K ate blinked hard as she looked out over the square. On the pavement not far away a tabby cat was rolling in the sunshine and at the far end of the street two women were standing talking. Her eyes were so sore from crying and not sleeping that she could scarcely focus and the black dress, hastily made and ill-fitting, was tight under the arms and around the waist and it was too hot for a summer's day.

'So,' her uncle said behind her, 'have you decided what you're going to do?'

'What can I do?' She turned around as she spoke and saw then for the first time how like her father he was and her heart ached. It was a week now since her father had slumped forward over the dinner table and died. He was dead and buried and she was alone except for her Uncle George who had come down to London from the north to be with her. She didn't know him well, she didn't want to. All she wanted was to go back to the day before her father had died, before her world collapsed.

'You can come and live with us,' her Uncle George said now.

'I've lived in London all my life.'

'But you can't stay here. What would you do?' Kate thought that he looked embarrassed, she knew that he disliked having discussions with a young woman. 'Your father had no money. There's nothing for you,' he persisted.

Kate already knew that, she was even a little irritated that he should say it. Her father had been an unworldly man who owned nothing and cared to own nothing. In fact he did not believe in ownership. She parted her lips to tell her uncle this and then closed them again. He would not understand. Her father had not believed in possessions, he had believed in the education of the mind.

15

'I could be a governess,' she said.

Her uncle looked shocked.

'You're very young,' he said, 'I think you must let me decide what's best. Your aunt is fond of you, even though you don't know each other well. You know that we have no children. We'll do our best to make you happy in time. You won't be alone.'

Kate wanted to be alone; it was the only thing she did want now that her father was dead. It was true that a governess's post was not ideal for her. She could not be happy trying to instil knowledge in small stupid minds, and putting up with the humiliation of being a servant.

Her uncle joined her at the window. He was a kind man, she thought. At that moment a carriage turned into the square, and drawing it were matched greys.

'Do you like horses?' he said.

'Yes, I do. The one ambition I have is to learn to ride.'

'Well,' he turned and smiled at her, 'you shall have a horse when you come to live with us.'

The journey out of London held no interest for Kate. With her she carried one small bag. It contained all the clothes she had – which were not many since her father had never deemed such things of any importance – and a few books. She did not look back across the square as she left it for the last time. Her father was not there and the memories would go with her. She could hold those to her now, the happiness of her close relationship with her father. He had loved her when he remembered she was there, she thought with a smile. Between his teaching and his books there was little room for people but she had held a special place in her father's life and she knew it. She thought that she would never love anyone again.

She had not been on a train before and liked the repetitive sound that it made, but rather than make desultory conversation with her uncle she opened a book and took comfort in its words and images and so did not often look out of the window at the changing landscape. She knew that she cared nothing for the country and here it was all fields and cows and deep summer-green grass.

The further north they got the more interesting it became, so that from time to time she looked up from her book in fascinated horror at the dull and dirty towns which were not London. And when she finally reached the north she was sorry to see how ugly it was – just as she had suspected – with its black heaps, its pit heads and general griminess. It seemed to Kate as if summer had made no impression here, that in spite of the warm sunshine it was just as depressingly dirty and black as it would be in bad weather. How could people survive here in such a dark and gloomy place, and how would she ever learn to live here?

Sunderland seemed small but it was apparent that her uncle and aunt lived somewhere even less impressive – and they did. It was a very small town with rows of terraced houses and back lanes, small shops and black ships in the harbour which carried away the coal. Dirty, ill-clad children played in the streets, shouting in their flat, unintelligible voices. Kate could not believe that anyone could live in such a place. Her uncle assured her that there were many things of interest: the library and the reading rooms, the clifftop walks and the amiable people. He told her that the town had its own brass band. Kate disliked brass bands.

She and her uncle were met at the station by a tall silent man with a pony and trap and it was then that Kate realised her uncle kept servants. She did not know why she was so shocked – many people did – but her father believed that men were created equal and should not be required to clear up after one another. She said nothing, but sat and looked about her until the horse and trap stopped outside a square-built brick house, one among a number of such houses, set away from the rest of the town.

As Kate got down from the trap a young woman came out of the house. She wore an apron and was obviously there to help. Nobody introduced them and as Kate walked up the path towards the house another woman came to the door. This was her aunt, Rose Farrer, and Kate remembered then the last time they had met at somebody's wedding. Her aunt had been upset that Kate obviously had not been bought a new dress for the occasion. Rose was short and very plump with pale blonde hair and rather colourless eyes. She smiled as she greeted Kate and ushered her inside and behind them came the maid with Kate's bag. Her aunt chatted on. Kate couldn't get used to her strange flat vowels and her dreadful purple dress which was shiny like satin and extremely vulgar.

The house was quite big inside and vastly overfurnished. No surface existed which was not covered by ornaments of some kind and to Kate's dismay there were no books. Her aunt showed her to her room and when she had done fussing and left, Kate flung wide the window and for the first time saw something which pleased her. It was the sea. On the skyline she thought that she could just make out a ship.

When she had washed her hands and face and tidied herself, Kate went back downstairs to her aunt's dining-room and there she saw why her aunt was as plump as a summer pigeon, because the table was covered with rich food. Kate was urged to eat but couldn't, not just because the food was so plentiful but because she felt sick and full all the time. Her aunt talked about the neighbours, about the doctor and his wife and the people who owned businesses in the town. She talked about going to Sunderland to shop and how Kate needed new dresses and her uncle did not talk much at all. Kate thought about her father who abandoned his books at mealtimes and made conversation. They had talked about London life, about books and politics and lands overseas which Kate had known only in print. Sometimes her father's friends came to the house and they sat over the table for hours arguing in an amicable way about art and literature and philosophy. Even as a little girl she had been allowed to stay and had always liked being in their company. There was no interesting or witty conversation here, only her aunt's chatter and enough food for ten.

Kate was soon desperately tired and longed to escape to her room. There at least she could be herself and not the politely smiling person she had glimpsed in the big mirror on the wall in the dining-room. She hated herself in black, it dulled her dark red hair, made the freckles look even more prominent over her nose and accentuated the thinness which grief had caused. At the table she could not even trust herself to lift her glass, her hands trembled so much, and eventually she found the courage to ask to be allowed to leave.

Her bedroom was pretty and large and smelled of polish. Kate stood by the window and thought about the possibility of having a horse. She had not expected such generosity or kindness. Her uncle and aunt already had one horse which pulled the trap so they could get about. Her horse would be strictly for pleasure.

It was late now, the house quiet. Ellen, the maid who had carried her luggage upstairs, and Mrs O'Connor, the cook, lived in the village, Kate had discovered, and they had gone home. So had Albert, the man who did the garden and drove the pony and trap. Kate dreaded the nights even though the hours of darkness were short. She missed her father so much. Her whole way of life was gone. There was nobody to be with who remembered the life she had led with her father, and though her aunt and uncle were kind they were almost strangers to her. She undressed and got into bed and then she picked up one of the books she'd brought. Reading was her only source of comfort now.

The next day Kate's aunt took her into Sunderland and bought her new clothes: underwear, footwear, dresses. Kate was bored before the morning was half over and was glad to be able to take a walk along the beach that evening. She was only sorry that she chose to walk back through the part of town where the pitmen lived, for there the young pitlads whistled at her and shouted. At first Kate ignored them but then she had to bite at her lip to stop herself from smiling because they were so openly admiring of her. She didn't care for her looks which she thought were ruined by freckles but she knew from some of her father's friends that her green eyes and white skin and red hair were appreciated by men and these seemed no different, but for their accents.

All three pits were just outside what had been a country village before the pits were sunk and the pit rows were built as near as had been decently possible. Between the colliery rows and the mine manager's house were shops, small businesses, and a jumble of other houses. Kate found it interesting. She was not prepared to have her aunt pounce on her when she got back and tell her that she must not go near the pit people or their houses or their work places.

'They're not decent,' she said, 'they're not fit. You're a young lady, Katherine, and we shall find you some fitting company so you can get to know suitable people.'

Kate shuddered over what her aunt's idea of suitable people might be. She was, however, better pleased when her uncle arranged for her to take riding lessons at a small farm just up the road, and soon afterwards the prettiest grey mare in the world was her confidante and greatest source of pleasure. She was so grateful for this that she forgave her aunt the constant chatter and her uncle his lack of conversation other than about work and was happy at least some of the time in the dark house on the edge of the pit town.

Three

*T*he days were turning cooler now with a gentle breeze. Lizzie walked on the beach often. Once, when the day was beginning to lengthen into evening, she ran back up the sand thinking that she would have a few minutes in her favourite sand dune before going back. She stopped as she reached the edge of the dune; someone was there before her. It was Sam Armstrong. He was face down with his head in his arms. Lizzie slid down the dune. He glanced up quickly at the slight noise and hid his face again.

'Why, Sam, whatever's the matter?' Lizzie said.

'Nowt,' said Sam, his voice muffled by his coatsleeve.

Lizzie sat down beside him. The wind was cut off there, down in the dune, and the sunshine had warmed the sand and its grassy sides.

'Is something wrong at your house? Have you been fighting?'

'No.'

'At work then?'

Sam was a pony driver. She knew that he liked it. He was paid for it, proud of it.

'They killed my pony,' he said, voice steady.

'Killed it? What did they do that for?'

'Because it was slow. They ran a full tub into it.'

'But what for?'

Sam sat up slightly on to his elbows.

'So that they could get a younger, faster pony, so that they could make more money. It had pulled too much already.'

Lizzie closed her eyes over the pony. Cheap life. What was it like to be a pony who never saw the light, who spent its time pulling trucks which were too heavy and enduring hurt?

21

'Who did it?'

'Rob Harvey and Ken Smith.'

'Wasn't anybody there to stop them?'

'Our Jon and Alf were on the back shift and your Harold wasn't around.'

'Did you tell May?'

'I didn't tell anybody. What's the good? Our Jon would have hit them, and then what? I hate it.'

'Do you?'

'There's rats down there as big as your arm. An' some of the lads . . . some of them don't have brothers. Some of them . . . have things done to them, but nobody touches me because of our Jon.'

Lizzie frowned. She didn't know what he was talking about.

'Our Jon fights all the time,' Sam said, sitting up. 'My mam complains. I can't tell him about the pony, and anyroad he wouldn't see what it meant.'

'I never thought Rob Harvey was like that,' Lizzie said.

'Don't say nothing to May. You won't, will you?'

Lizzie said that she wouldn't and they got up and walked back to the village. When they got to Sam's house Jon was standing leaning against the wall. Sam turned to Lizzie and smiled.

'We'll go for a walk tomorrow, if you like. When I've had my dinner.'

He didn't expect her to say anything, Lizzie knew, and she didn't, but a little song was beginning inside her. Things were going back to how they had been, how they should be. There had been nothing for her to worry about after all. She sneaked a look at Jon but he wasn't looking up. She could just see the dark bruise on his cheekbone that was evidence of his latest quarrel. Lizzie hadn't seen much of him since the chapel picnic. She turned and went away into her house and she was happy.

The next week Sam was on the foreshift and spent the early evenings with her. Her mother welcomed him back into the house like before and Lizzie thought they would see no more of Greta. It was not to be. Twice that week Greta called of Sam when he was at Lizzie's house. Lizzie herself had begun to go next-door again, just like she always had.

When she called in the middle of the week there was a pile of library books on the seat beside the window. Lizzie loved to read but didn't dare venture as far as the library because of her mother's disapproval. Mrs Harton thought that sewing and mending were much more important. Reading was a waste of time.

Lizzie didn't consider it a waste of time. When she had gone to school, the schoolmaster, Mr Coglan, had made sure that all of his pupils who had enough ability could read, write and add before they left him, and she knew that Mr Coglan had often loaned and sometimes given Jon books and encouraged him because he was clever. Mr Coglan had died shortly after Lizzie left school. She wondered whether Jon missed him and having somebody to talk to about things like that.

She ventured across to the books and turned them over, hoping that there would be something she might borrow and read, but there wasn't a story among them.

'History,' she said in disgust.

'I've told him he'll strain his eyes with all that reading,' Mrs Armstrong said.

It was baking day. She had already done two batches and another lot was on the hearth to rise. The house was full of the wonderful smell of newly baked bread. The door stood open. Mrs Armstrong went down the yard to the gate and came back, looking flustered.

'There she is again,' she said, wiping her hands on her pinny, the sweat standing out on her round red face.

'Who?'

'That lass, hanging round the back lane, waiting of our Jon coming off shift. It isn't nice; her mother should see to her better than that.'

'Which lass? Mavis Robson?'

Mrs Armstrong gave her a glance of mute appeal.

'Oh, Lizzie,' she said, 'you don't think he's done something he shouldn't, do you? She's not a lass I'd want him wed to, and if she's having a bairn . . .'

'I'm sure it'll be all right,' Lizzie soothed.

'It wouldn't be the first time or the last around here but I don't want any of my lads having to get wed. I can hear him.' And Mrs Armstrong, big as she was, shot down the yard and opened the back gate as Alf and Jon walked up the back lane. 'Come on, you're late,' she said, 'the dinner's ready and the water's hot. Hurry up.' She dashed back inside. 'Coming around here and showing her legs. It isn't decent. I wish the rest of my bairns were like Alf. He's the only one . . .'

Jon and Alf came in, black with coaldust.

'Hello, Lizzie,' Jon said. The words were friendly enough but he didn't smile. Alf said nothing but he smiled.

'That lass'll get you into bother,' Mrs Armstrong told her eldest son.

'Why, Lizzie, I didn't know you cared,' he said.

'Not Lizzie, that lass in the back lane, that Mavis Robson.'

'Give over, Mam. I haven't been near enough to see the colour of her eyes yet.'

Harold was different too these days, Lizzie noticed. He took to going out more but didn't come back smelling of beer so Lizzie could see that his mother didn't worry that much and she didn't ask him where he had been. A man's business was just that. But Lizzie knew that it shook her mother something fierce when he asked if he could bring Enid Southern back for tea.

'I knew it wouldn't last five minutes,' her mother said.

'What?'

'The peace.'

'She's a nice enough lass, Mam.'

Her mother looked at her as though she ought to be put away.

'And what if our Harold decides to get wed? Then what?'

'She's just coming for tea, that's all.'

But that wasn't all, Lizzie could see, sitting across from the girl at table that Sunday afternoon. Harold radiated goodwill, like the minister radiated goodness on a Sunday morning. He glowed. He looked like a turnip lantern on Hallowe'en, bulbous and grinning, candlelit. As for the girl, she was the eldest of six. Her mother needed rid of her; she was to feed and clothe or else to send to place, and this girl had been to domestic service in a big house and knew what it was like, how hard the work. This girl was going to have Harold. She was not pretty and not plain. On no money she had done her best. She was clean, and she smiled and grasped Harold's arm, and wore her ill-fitting clothes as well as she could.

'Her mother bred nothing but lasses,' was all Lizzie's mam could say when Enid and Harold had gone.

'If he marries her, Mam, I'll go to place.'

'You will not.'

'I shall have to,' Lizzie said, and her mother did not contradict her.

After evening chapel now there was a lot of standing around and smiling. There was a lot of giggling behind hands, and lads standing awkwardly and looking slyly. More than one lad had asked Lizzie to go for a walk. She had refused them; she only went walking with Sam. May was always with Rob Harvey now even though sometimes he ignored her, turning away as she hung on to his arm. He held important conversations with Ken or another of the older ones. Alf would stay and chat too. Jon never went. In this knowledge, one Sunday evening, even though she and Jon scarcely spoke, Lizzie went next-door. She longed for a book to read and Jon Armstrong was the only person of her acquaintance who had books. She watched the other Armstrongs turn out for chapel and she took her courage and ventured next-door where she found Jon by himself.

'Are you busy?' she asked, lingering on the doorstep.

'No. Come in.'

If he was surprised or annoyed to see her it didn't show but Lizzie didn't pretend that he was glad either. She remembered how he had kissed her and the awful things she had said to him. She couldn't tell him that she hadn't meant them, it was only because of Sam. She would never care for anybody except Sam and because it looked as if it was going to work out she felt softer towards Jon, but still she hesitated before she followed him. She suspected that he had been reading when she knocked on the door and for Lizzie that was as good as being in chapel. Also she had promised herself for weeks that she would talk to him but now she had the chance she didn't know what to say.

'What are you reading?' she asked, going into the kitchen after him.

'Oh, nothing.'

'That's what you always say. Improving yourself, are you?'

He laughed at that. She wished that he wouldn't. Jon was clever enough to make you feel stupid and he owed her back the things she had said to him.

'Think it's an uphill struggle, do you, Lizzie?'

She couldn't get any words out and as he looked at her she began to remember how he had kissed her, how he had made her feel, and how she had resented the fact that Sam had never kissed her like that. She had promised herself that she wouldn't go on remembering, because of Sam, because Jon was the wrong lad, because he should never have kissed her, she should never have let him, and because . . . well just because. And it all made this even harder and it was hard enough on its own.

'Something the matter?' he asked.

'You don't have any stories, do you?'

'Stories?' Jon's eyes were puzzled.

'Yes. I want to read.'

His eyes widened and he smiled a little.

'Oh, I see. Howay.' And Lizzie followed him up the steep narrow stairs and into the bedroom on the right, which had nothing in it but beds. There he got down on the floor and from under the bed slid a box full of books. Lizzie forgot how awkward she felt with him. She gave an exclamation of delight and got down on her knees beside him.

'Are they stories?'

'Nearly all of them. Take what you want.'

'I can only take one,' Lizzie said regretfully. 'My mam mustn't see it.'

'How will you read it then?'

'I don't know.'

'In the light nights you could go for a walk to a sand dune, but the nights are getting shorter now. You could come round here . . . if you want to. Anyway, just take them when you want them.'

Lizzie chose Jane Austen's *Pride and Prejudice* and then walked back down the steep stairs and into the kitchen where the fire was high and the room was warm.

'Your Harold courting, is he?' Jon asked as Lizzie clutched the book to her.

'Looks like it.'

'She's a nice lass.'

'I think he might marry here.'

'That's going to be a bit awkward, isn't it?'

'I'll have to go to place.' There was a pause.

'It's our Sam, isn't it?' Jon said, turning his gaze from the fire to her face.

'It's always been Sam,' she said.

Jon started to say something and then stopped. Lizzie looked hard at him.

'What?' she prompted.

'Nothing. When you want another book, just help yourself.'

'Thanks,' Lizzie said, and went home.

Her mother caught her reading twice and the second time threatened her, so after that she pretended she was going to Bible classes and that autumn she took a candle and huddled in a broken-down shed near the beach. It was very cold and let in the rain.

One evening, lateish, it was dark and bitterly cold and she was in the hut as usual when she heard footsteps outside. She did not even have time to hide the book or extinguish the candle before the door creaked open and somebody big walked quickly inside and closed the door.

'Lizzie?' Jon said.

'Oh, you frightened me. There's nobody out there, is there?'

'In this? It's lashing down with rain. What are you doing here? If I didn't know better I'd think it was some lad.' He walked over and by the light from the flickering candle looked into her face. 'You're blue with cold. What are you doing?'

'Well, I'm not at Bible class,' she said. 'How did you know I was here?'

'I saw you earlier on. What are you doing?'

'Reading. I daren't at home and there's no place else. My mam threatened me with our Harold's belt if I did it again.'

'Your Harold's never going to belt you. You'll get into bother, though, if she finds out you've been telling lies. Somebody's going to tell her, you know.' He got down beside her. 'Give me your hands.'

'What for?'

Jon took each of her hands and rubbed warmth into them with his own long slender fingers. His hands were rough and hard from work but they weren't the kind of square capable hands his brothers had.

'How's the book?' he said.

'Oh, it's wonderful. Do you think it's true?'

'No, it's only a story.'

'I didn't mean that. I mean . . . people living like that, talking to each other that way, like Elizabeth Bennet and Mr Darcy.'

'Shouldn't think so,' Jon said. 'Howay out of here, my feet are numb.'

They walked back slowly because it was a little before the end of the Bible class but Lizzie's mother didn't give her a chance to reach the house. The rain had stopped and she came outside and down the yard into the back lane.

'And just where do you think you've been?' she said. 'Get yourself in here.'

Jon followed them without invitation and her mother turned on him, white-faced to Lizzie's astonishment, as he closed the door.

'So it's Bible class now, is it? They didn't used to call it that when I was young and they didn't used to tell lies about it neither. You'd go behind my back, would you, Jon Armstrong?'

Lizzie stared at her mother and her mouth went dry. Didn't her mother know that it was Sam she cared for and would only ever care for? Jon said nothing. Was he going to give her away and save himself or let her mother think . . .? Her mother didn't give him a chance to reply.

'I don't want you near my Lizzie, do you hear? You drink and fight and swear – don't think I don't know – and you read too many of them books. I don't know where you think it's going to get you but I'll tell you: it's going to get you into bother. You stay away from her.'

In the lamplight Lizzie thought that Jon's blue eyes had darkened so much that they were almost black.

'I never touched her,' he said.

'That's a likely tale, lad. She's got no father to see to her so I'm telling you – don't you come round here again. As for you, Miss, you just wait until our Harold comes back.'

Lizzie went upstairs, crying, as Jon left. She was lying on her bed when Harold came home and once again her mother's voice rose and fell for a long time and then Harold's slow footsteps came up the stairs and he pushed open the thin wooden door. When Lizzie looked up he went to her and sat on the edge of the bed, gazing anxiously at her.

'What have you been doing?' he asked. 'My mother's in a right state and Jon Armstrong met me in the back lane and said he'd knock my block off if I brayed you. As if I would!'

The room was full of shadows from its single candle and it was cold but Lizzie didn't notice.

'We weren't doing nothing,' she said, exasperated at her mother's, and Harold's, lack of understanding.

'Well what then?'

'He's been lending me books, that's all. Mam doesn't like books. I've been reading them in that hut near the beach.'

'Dad always liked books,' Harold said. 'When you were little he went on and on about being something different, something important, not like this. He told her we'd have money and fine things. We never did. Don't you think Mam's had enough in her life without you going on the same? Anyway, he isn't to come into the house and you aren't to go next-door, so now you know.'

'But it's Sam I go next-door to see, you know that.'

'That's what I tried to tell my mam,' Harold said, shaking his head.

After that Lizzie didn't speak to Jon even if she met him outside but she looked for Sam everywhere. She wasn't allowed out much, her mother found her sewing to do in the evenings and kept her at home, but as the time went on she relented a little because she liked Sam and so Lizzie was allowed out occasionally to see him. Her mother also made Lizzie a pretty dress in a wine colour which suited her dark looks.

Christmas was coming. Lizzie became excited at the idea. Sam hinted that Christmas would be extra good this year. He was earning more money, had been promoted and was a putter now, putting the tubs of coal from the thin narrow seams to the main seams and, with the aid of a pony, taking the tubs to the bottom of the shaft. He had grown tall and he talked about the pit more like the other lads did. Lizzie began to go next door again. She and Sam and Alf played noisy games at the kitchen table. May joined in.

Lizzie felt happiness like a spiral inside her that was growing bigger. Her dream was about to come true. She was going to have Sam Armstrong all to herself. Sometimes when May was not out with Rob but playing at the table or giggling with Lizzie by the fire, with Rob sitting by the window talking softly to Alf, they could look into each other's eyes and know the same things, the things that women knew. Lizzie thought that maybe she and May would get married to their lads and live next-door and have their babies together. It was possible, she thought. It was possible to be happy like this, to wake up in the mornings and turn over slowly in your bed and smile and be pleased at the day.

One Sunday, just before Christmas, when the weather was as fine and warm as September, she and Sam went walking on the beach and when they had walked a long way and turned back, the sun bright on the sea, the gulls low over the waves, they sat in their favourite sand dune and he took from his pocket a little box and handed it to her.

'It's your Christmas present,' he said.

Lizzie looked down at the square gift in her hand, wrapped in paper, and then she tore at the paper and took the lid off the tiny box and inside it was a gold locket on a chain in the shape of a heart.

'I was going to keep it until next week but I couldn't wait,' he said. 'I got it from Sunderland.

'Oh, Sam!' Lizzie said, and threw her arms around his neck, and as she did so he got hold of her and began to kiss her.

It wasn't like she had imagined. It wasn't anything like her only previous experience of intimacy. It was knowing and hot and too fast, and so disappointing. Lizzie remembered in detail the one time that Jon Armstrong had kissed her. It had felt so right, so gentle and safe and special. Her only response now was to try and stop Sam because she was frightened by what he was doing. There was no magic here. All she wanted to do was get away but she didn't know how and he didn't expect her to and he was so much bigger than she was. She reminded herself that he was Sam and she loved him so that it must be right, and she would like it soon but she didn't. She pushed vainly at him with her hands while his urgent mouth assaulted hers and then it seemed that her pushing at him had worked because he suddenly wasn't there and when she had regained her senses she saw that Sam had been pulled away from her by his brother.

Lizzie blinked. She didn't understand what was happening, or why, and then she was treated to her first glimpse of Jon's temper given free rein. She retreated against the sand dune and watched, horrified, as he knocked the boy down into the sand with three or four blows, well-aimed and effective. Sam didn't get up. Lizzie wished that he would. She wished that he would get up and kill his brother. She wished that she could do it herself. Sam lay there, panting hard, while Jon glared down at him.

'You bastard!' he said.

Lizzie winced. She wasn't used to bad language. She was a good chapel lass and Harold never swore.

'You rotten little bugger,' said Jon. 'Get yourself home.'

To Lizzie's amazement Sam got painfully to his feet and staggered off towards the village. Jon turned to her.

'Give it to me,' he said.

At first she didn't know what he meant and then she remembered the locket still held tightly in her hand. She put both hands behind her back and then thought of what he had just done to his brother and bit her lip.

'Give it to me or I'll take it from you.' And Jon held out his hand.

Lizzie hadn't known how the temper would rise up in her, red hot and fast. She put up her chin.

'Come and take it then.'

She even thought she might stop him that way, that she had enough hold on Jon, but he tried to pull her hands from behind her back. She kicked him and thumped him, tears welling up in her eyes at his treatment of her. They fought and she retreated as Jon got nearer, and then lost her balance and they went back into the sand. Lizzie was so horrified at what was happening that the temper gave way to tears but she went on fighting with him. Nothing like this had ever happened to her before. It took Jon time to stop her from kicking and thumping him but there came a point where he had her pinned helplessly. It was one of the worst moments of her life, being held down, even though he was not hurting her. It was the feeling that somebody so much bigger and stronger would use that strength against her and for no reason that she could understand. It was small relief to see that she had actually done him damage where her fingernails had met his face. She had not known she was scratching him but the blood on his face was too obvious to be denied. Jon got hold of her hand where the locket was still tightly clasped and he forced open her fingers. Then he got up and threw the locket as far as he could and it went a long, long way, glinting all the time in the sunshine, over the edge of the dunes and across the narrowing strip of beach and way into the water.

When the locket had stopped being a shiny golden missile in the cold December afternoon Lizzie got slowly to her feet. She had never felt hatred before; there had even been times when she had liked Jon a lot. She could have kicked him or thumped him some more but she didn't, she hit him open-handed across the face, and when the flat of her hand stung crazily from the impact of his cheek the books that he had loaned to her came in handy. She remembered the kind of words that people said to one another.

'You had no right to do any of that. I'll never talk to you any more.'

Jon laughed. Lizzie didn't like him laughing. She hadn't seen that look in his eyes before. It was bitter.

'That'll be some loss,' he said. 'You never talk to me anyroad. You don't see nobody except him.'

Lizzie had to swallow tears before she could talk back.

'He's nice,' she said, 'he's not like you. He wouldn't have treated me like that. When he's older he'll be a better man than you'll ever be.'

Jon went back and picked up Sam's cap which had fallen off and not been retrieved. He shot her one brief sideways look and then walked back across the dunes towards the village. Lizzie stayed where she was, shaking now and crying, the tears running because everything was spoiled, but later when she awoke in the darkness there was a small part of her which admitted that things were not like they had been with Sam, that they never would be like that again and that she had pretended to herself, the illusion had been inside her, in her head and in her mind, because she wanted to go back and couldn't, she couldn't ever go back there again.

31

Four

Kate ran up the back stairs and across the landing into her bedroom. Ellen was waiting there. Her clothes, including her new green dress which had just been made for her, were laid across the bed and the fire burned brightly because the evening was bitterly cold.

'You're late, Miss,' she said. 'They'll be here soon. The missus is cross.'

'I'm sorry, Ellen.'

'Where have you been?'

'On the beach.'

'I don't know what you get up to on that beach all day. There's nothing there that I know of and it's been dark for hours.'

'I rode and read and then I had a sandwich.'

Kate did not go on. Ellen would not have understood. All Ellen knew was the work at Mrs Farrer's house, and her family. She had a family. It had made Kate's heart ache to hear about Ellen's father and mother, her small sisters and brothers. How could it be, she wondered, that Ellen should have so many people and she should have no one? In her uncle's house there was nobody she could talk to about the things which interested her, but she had found a friend in the sea. She thought that it was exciting, especially at this time of the year when there were huge tides. She had stayed late, growing uncomfortably chilled, to see it at full tide, roaring its way up the beach with nothing to stop it and she sitting on the top of a dune in the cold darkness watching its momentous progress. The horse was with her, munching happily at the long grass of the dunes. The mare was her other friend. Dolly could be talked to. Granted, she wasn't a great conversationalist but she could be hugged, she could be cried and laughed over, and she asked for no explanation.

'Mrs Farrer wanted you here to help,' Ellen said.

'I expect she managed with you and Mrs O'Connor.'

Mrs O'Connor had driven Kate wild with her preparations for the party, her talk of food and organising. Kate had tried to explain to her uncle and aunt that she didn't want a party to introduce her to the people of the area, she wasn't used to things like that and didn't need anybody.

'There was a lot to do,' Ellen said reprovingly. 'You'd better have a good wash before you put your dress on. And whatever have you done with your hair?'

She went on scolding as Kate got ready for her aunt's party and when she ventured down the stairs – guiltily because she knew that the party was for her so that she could meet what her aunt called 'people your own age' – there were already a number of people gathered in the drawing-room. Kate wished that she could have stayed upstairs, said that she wasn't well, or at least retreated to the kitchen with Ellen.

'You wouldn't want to if you knew how much work we'd put in today while you was gallivanting,' Ellen had said severely when she'd voiced this desire, so now Kate went down the stairs. Her aunt greeted her without a smile.

'You knew I wanted you back here early. The Nelsons said that they might come.'

Kate knew that her aunt was impressed by wealth and position and the Nelsons had both. They owned the three pits in the area, including the Victoria where Mr Farrer was manager. They had a big house four miles from the village, a house with huge grounds and gates. They were the important family in the area and they had a son, Charles, whom Kate had not met.

'And have they come?' she asked, not in the least curious but feeling guilty that she had not helped.

'Not yet. We'll be very lucky if they do.' Her aunt stared at her and the stare turned into a frown. 'I thought you were going to wear the new green dress.'

As her final act of defiance before facing an evening she dreaded Kate had refused to wear the new dress. She pretended now that Ellen had not tried all her persuasion to get her to wear the green. She did not want to appear before these self-important people in something which flattered her looks. She didn't know quite why, but maybe it was because she remembered sitting down to a late supper with some of the most respected people in London and they had cared nothing for how she dressed, only for who she was herself.

'What's wrong with this one?' she asked, looking down at herself.

'It's mended and it's brown. You know that I had the green one made especially. Look at all the other girls in their pretty colours.'

Kate glanced around. They were like a flock of peacocks, she thought. They stood around in twos and threes, giggling stupidly. The young men stood back from them, looking awkward.

Her aunt introduced her to a good many people in the next hour and it was then that she made the discovery that Kate could not dance. Kate knew that it had not occurred to her aunt that any young lady did not know how. It was a fresh source of disappointment to her so while other people shuffled about the small area which was reserved for dancing and the musicians did their best, Kate, who had a taste for music and could stand this vile noise no longer, went out to the stableyard and caressed her horse's velvet nose and talked quietly to her about how horrible the party was and how she wished that they had not had to come back. She was eventually obliged to go back inside and found her aunt gushing over a brown-haired young man in a brightly coloured waistcoat. This, Kate guessed, was Charles Nelson. Her aunt saw her and insisted on making them known to one another. Kate only wished that she had stayed outside even though her bare arms had been freezing. She was determined not to be impressed and could only be relieved that Charles was not especially tall or good-looking and had eyes which were rather small.

'I've been here for half an hour and haven't seen you,' he said. 'Where have you been?'

'Talking to my horse,' Kate said.

Charles laughed.

'It must have been an interesting conversation.'

Kate didn't spare him.

'The best of the evening so far,' she said. Charles, she thought, was too intelligent to misunderstand her. 'Have you ever been down the mines?' she asked him.

'What a very odd question. No, of course I haven't. My father employs people like your uncle to do that.'

'Haven't you ever wanted to?'

'Certainly not.'

'But you own them.'

'My father does, and other people look after them. I know nothing about the subject, nor should I want to.'

'Then what do you do?'

'I'm at Oxford. After that I'll do what gentlemen do. Shoot, fish and hunt.'

Charles, Kate concluded, was not worth her time.

'My mother is having a dance at Christmas,' he said. 'I could ask her to send you an invitation.'

'I shouldn't bother,' Kate said smiling. 'I don't dance.'

She would have been glad when the evening was over but for the fact that her Aunt Rose bemoaned the way that Mr and Mrs Nelson had not come and that Kate had been unable to accept numerous invitations to take a turn about the floor. She questioned Kate closely about Charles, asked what they had talked about. Kate returned satisfactory answers just so that she could escape to bed. She thought that most young men were dull but Charles was the dullest she had ever met.

The following morning two young women and their mothers turned up to discuss the party and Kate had to sit through tea and cake while the talk went on about who had been there and who hadn't, the different dresses dwelt on at great length and the arrival of Charles Nelson, whom the two girls obviously admired. Kate could only think that it was his name and his fortune they liked, it could hardly have been his looks, wit or conversation. Charles had made one remark during the evening which evoked a response in Kate, and then she had wished to kill him. It had started with a question about her father and what he had done. Charles, Kate had swiftly concluded, was a snob.

'He was a scholar,' she had said.

'Did he have money?'

'No.'

'Doesn't that worry you?'

'Why should it?'

'With freckles like yours?' Charles said.

Kate knew that it was meant to hurt and she should not be bothered about it but she was. She looked long at her hated face in the mirror in her bedroom. Why couldn't she have been fair-haired and blue-eyed and pale-skinned?

When the morning visitors had gone her aunt insisted that Kate should take an interest in what they were eating that evening, in the new linen and various other matters. Her aunt was trying to teach her household management. Kate loathed it, the more especially because she knew her aunt expected that in time she would marry and have a similar house of her own. In the afternoon there was mending to do. She pricked her finger several times until her aunt complained that there was blood on the material for the new sheets and said that she despaired of her. She let her go and Kate quickly changed and went down to the stables for Dolly.

It was a bright winter's day and quite warm. The tide was down and the beach empty except for one person walking some distance away down by the water. A tall man, Kate estimated. The waves broke as small as a summer sea's and she was happy there, cantering along on Dolly, until for some reason the mare suddenly came to an abrupt halt and to her dismay Kate went clean over her head and landed in what wasn't as soft a beach as she had thought. The wind knocked from her, bruises hurting, Kate couldn't get up to begin with and the horse, startled, set off at a gallop. She watched helplessly as her only means of transport careered away along the beach and then at the person who set off towards her at a run and didn't stop until he reached her. Kate could see that he was young, tall and neatly dressed, an off duty pitlad. She had wanted very much to meet one but she hadn't thought that when she did he would make her feel embarrassed and stupid and inept. She didn't know quite why she felt like that because his face was all concern as he got down beside her, squatting pitman fashion on his toes, asking urgently, 'Are you hurt?'

'I thought I was a horsewoman. Now I know I'm not,' she said ruefully, and then he smiled and the whole world changed. There had not been at her aunt's supposedly fashionable party a young man one-quarter so elegant. She thought he was graceful and handsome. He had straight black hair, shiny clean, and blue eyes almost as dark as the navy suit he wore. If only, Kate thought, there had been someone like that at the party. He wasn't awkward and coltish or given to making unamusing jokes so that she felt superior and bored. He looked her over carefully for damage, helped her to her feet, and when she gazed anxiously after the mare he said, 'She'll stop shortly and I'll go and have a look.'

'Do you know about horses?'

'Only pit ponies,' he said, and they set off walking in the direction in which Dolly had gone.

Although she was anxious about the horse Kate had no desire to hasten her departure from him. She liked how tall he was beside her. He didn't worry about entertaining her or talking to her but was somehow easy to be with. Kate gathered her courage.

'Where do you work?'

'Down the Vic.'

'The Victoria? What do you do?'

'I'm a hewer.'

'Aren't you young for that?' After several failed attempts, she had finally persuaded her uncle to talk to her over dinner about the pits and she knew that the men who hewed the coal with a pick and shovel worked in seams as low as two or three feet high, crawling on hands and knees and often lying on their backs. It had been difficult at first, her aunt protesting that such talk was unsuitable for Kate's ears, but Kate had persisted and her uncle, seeing her enthusiasm, finally gave in and told her a bit about mining. Now each evening she dragged from him every detail of what had happened that day. She even knew, by proxy, the names and the jobs of the men in the office, of the overmen, the troublemakers, the ones who fought, the ones who drank, those who were absent often. She knew quite a lot.

'I've been down there seven years,' he said.

'That's a long time. Did you ever go to school?'

He smiled at that.

'On and off. There's your horse.'

Kate was rather disappointed that Dolly had run such a short way but glad that the mare wasn't lathered in cold water. He went up to her slowly, talking softly, and was able to take the reins and put them back over the mare's head and to stroke her neck.

'Shall I put you back up?' he offered.

Kate didn't know what to say. Usually Albert cupped his hands and she got up that way, or there was a mounting block or steps, but the young pitman put both hands around her waist and lifted her up. Kate thought it was the nicest thing that had ever happened to her but he did it so impersonally, saying to her, 'Are you sure you're all right?' when she was up on Dolly.

She assured him that she was, and thanked him, and then she rode away. It wasn't until she was most of the way home that she realised they hadn't even exchanged names.

At dinner that night her uncle was talking about a clerk in the office he had had to get rid of because the man wasn't up to the job.

'Stupid. Couldn't add up. I'll have to find somebody else, and quickly. There's a lot of work to be done.'

It was then that the idea was born in Kate's mind.

'I could do it,' she said.

Her aunt put down her knife and fork. It was a shame, too, because it was a good beef dinner. Her uncle stared.

'Eat your dinner, Katherine, and try not to be foolish,' he said.

'It isn't foolish,' she said. 'I'm very good at figures and all the other things involved. I did mathematics with my father for years. My writing's good too. You could give me a chance.'

'Young women don't go into mine offices, Katherine, and even if they did it would be beneath my position to let you.'

'Oh, but I want to. I'd be so good at it. Please let me try. I want so badly to do something useful and I'm no good in a house, am I, Aunt Rose?'

'It's a woman's job to learn how to run a house,' her aunt said. 'You'll learn in time.'

'Please let me try. I know I could do it. I'd love to come to the office.'

Her uncle would not be persuaded but Kate was not about to give in. The following day she told her aunt that she was going for a walk and went for the first time to the Victoria. It was in some way like meeting the young pitman had been. There at the pit head amongst the big wheel, the buildings, the offices and the dirt, Kate felt more excited than she had ever felt in her life. And to one side, just away from the pit, something was going on. There was a big crowd of men gathered and a lot of shouting.

As she stood watching a door opened and her uncle rushed out with another man. The crowd parted and Kate could see two men fighting. She had never seen such a thing in her life. The men of her acquaintance in London used their minds to settle their differences. There was a part of her that was worried they might hurt themselves or each other, but there was another part that thrilled. She strove to subdue the feeling while the man with her uncle pulled them apart, and as he did so she recognised, in spite of the coal-dust and the circumstances, the young man who had helped her on the beach. She couldn't believe that someone so polite and friendly could do such a thing. The other young man stood with his head down as her uncle delivered a lecture, but her rescuer stood and looked straight into her uncle's face though he said nothing. The crowd dispersed, the men gone, her uncle walked back to the office and there noticed Kate.

'What are you doing here?'

'Why were they fighting?'

'This is no place for a woman, Katherine, I told you last night. Now get yourself home.'

She went but the following day was down at the office again early in the morning just after her uncle had gone down the pit. She made herself useful to the head clerk, telling him that her uncle would not mind, and by the time he got back at almost midday he had to listen to the man saying how good she was and what a difference it made to the place to have her there. Uncle George told her that she could stay for the rest of the day but no longer, and the following day Kate was missed in the office. Her uncle took on a new clerk and had to listen to the head man saying he was nowhere near as sharp as his niece. By the end of the week he was without a clerk again. By the Monday Kate had a job. Her aunt, she knew, was disappointed but secretly relieved since Kate showed no talent for anything in the house or for anything to do with a woman's place. She hated shopping, visiting and social events of any kind. Kate knew that on the Monday morning when she went off to work with her uncle, her aunt looked forward to a day of untroubled domesticity, and was only glad that she did not have to share it.

Five

'**S**he's expecting,' Mrs Armstrong said flatly.

Mrs Harton and Mrs Armstrong were sharing a cup of tea in the kitchen of Lizzie's house. They didn't know that she was about to walk down the stairs. She stopped short, something inside of her suddenly hurting badly with the knowledge, she didn't quite know why. Jon and Mavis Robson. It didn't seem possible, it didn't feel right. He couldn't have, could he? Not that she cared. She hadn't spoken to him for weeks. He could have been hurt down the pit and she wouldn't have cared. And yet in those cold silent hours of the night it occurred to her more than once that something could happen to Jon Armstrong down the Victoria, he could be injured or even worse he could die, and she would be left with the sound of that slap under her hand, the feel of his lean cheek, the bitter look that he had given her and the silence between them. For days she had wanted to make peace with him and now suddenly it seemed too late.

She had tried to think of why he had knocked Sam down and thrown the pretty gold locket far off into the sea, why he had treated her so badly and spoiled her happiness. She wondered if perhaps it had something to do with the day of the chapel picnic, if he thought he had some claim on her; she could think of no other reason – yet Jon had kissed plenty of other girls, and obviously that and more with Mavis Robson. Lizzie couldn't take it in. She stood there chilled to the bone. For weeks she had ignored him, and during those weeks had seen nothing more of Sam though she had longed to. She had wanted to go round to their house but her pride wouldn't let her and in that time Greta had been there often.

Lizzie didn't understand. Everything was going wrong. She tried to picture Jon married to Mavis Robson, because he would have to marry her now. He would go and live with Mavis Robson in another house in another row because Jon was a good worker and could have his own house. His mam would have to get by without him and so would everybody else. Mavis was a bonny lass with dark brown hair and matching brown eyes, and she had run about after Jon for months. Now it looked as though she had caught him.

'You mean Mavis Robson?' she heard her mother say.

'No.' Mrs Armstrong sighed and lowered her voice but it was difficult to discuss anything quietly in a miner's thin-walled house. 'Our Sam's lass, Greta.'

'Greta?' Lizzie's mam sounded shocked, and worse. 'Oh, dear,' she said.

'I know. Whatever will Lizzie say?'

At the top of the stairs in the winter gloom Lizzie sat down heavily. This was worse, this was the worst ever, and in a split second she remembered again the gold locket shining as it spun through the air. Her cheeks went hot and her stomach felt sick. Sam couldn't have done such a thing. He couldn't have done that to Greta and then made up to her.

'A baby in the house,' Mrs Armstrong said. 'She's more than four months gone now.'

'Are they going to live with you?'

'I want them to live with her folk but Sam won't.' Lizzie thought of Greta Smith living next-door, taking Lizzie's dream away. Greta growing big with Sam's baby. She sat there in the cold until Mrs Armstrong left and then her mother came to the bottom of the stairs.

'Are you there, Lizzie? I didn't hear you go out so you must be. Come down and I'll make you a cup of tea.'

She went off back into the kitchen and Lizzie slowly followed. She felt ill. Every bone ached and she was tired and the thumping in her head made a pain over her eyes and the fact that she wanted to cry and wouldn't let herself made it worse. She sat by the kitchen fire with the hot cup comfortingly in her hands and her mam sat down with her.

'The Armstrongs aren't the only lads in the village, you know. There are plenty of others.'

Lizzie didn't trust her voice for a few moments and then she managed to get out, 'I cared about him.'

'I know you did, but look at how he turned out. You're a bonny, good lass, you could have anybody you wanted. And it might be much better than that.

You never know. You're young yet, there's plenty of time. They're a bad lot, you know, Sam doing that and their Jon fighting. There's only Alf left and he's so quiet you wouldn't know he was there. They're just like their dad was.'

That spring, when Sam and Greta had been married for less than five months, she had a baby, a little boy. Lizzie didn't go next-door again and Mrs Armstrong had more sense than to ask her. Harold and his lass were courting and were always sitting about in Lizzie's house so that she was glad when the fine weather came and she could go outside. She often heard the baby screaming through the thin walls, and Sam and Greta shouting at one another which they seemed to do a lot of, and Mrs Armstrong complained to Lizzie's mother about how much work there was to do because Greta was no housekeeper.

'Her mother's mucky so it isn't surprising,' she said.

Lizzie wished that she didn't enjoy hearing how mucky Greta was, what a bad mother Greta was, and how often Sam and Greta had rows. She had cried a lot over Sam Armstrong and had told herself that she would never bother with another lad. She stayed at home and helped her mam. Rob and May were to be married that summer and May didn't have much time for Lizzie so she went off walking by herself on the beach as the nights grew lighter and the flowers began to show like yellow stars in the grass. She would lie in their sand dune and wish things were different. One night Sam was lying there when she reached the dune and she hesitated and would have turned but he said, 'Don't go.'

Lizzie hadn't realised until then that it was Sam she hated now and not his brother but she sat down, some way from him.

'How's Greta and the bairn?'

'Fine. It's a bit cramped.'

'Yes, it will be.' Talking to him was impossible for the first time. Lizzie could think of nothing to say, she didn't even want to be there.

'Is that a new frock? It's bonny. You're bonny.'

'Don't say things like that to me. You didn't want me. You wanted Greta.'

'I didn't know.' Sam looked at her with warm brown eyes. 'I didn't think you'd turn out so bonny. Being married's awful. Greta whinges all the time and the baby cries all night. I can't stand it. I never wanted to marry her. I didn't. I wish it was like before.'

It was exactly what Lizzie had wished so many times and then all of a sudden she didn't. She looked at Sam Armstrong and knew that he was the worst thing that a man could be in a pit village. He was soft. And to think she had cared for him. However could that have been? She didn't care about him now. She got up and left him there in the sand dune and gave him no more thought as she made her way home.

May was married to Rob Harvey in June. The days were hot and long and the nights short and sticky. They were married in the chapel and the Armstrongs had a meal which was going to be in their house but the weather being so warm they put the borrowed tables outside. Mrs Armstrong had baked and cooked until she couldn't see the top of her kitchen table and it was a fine spread. Lizzie thought that May had never looked bonnier in her new blue dress.

That week Lizzie had been in the Armstrong house several times helping May and her mother with the preparations, and she was excited about the wedding. Her mother had made for her a light summer dress, the prettiest she had ever had. It was a deep rose pink and when she looked into the mirror that morning she was surprised at the girl who looked back at her. The large dark eyes were bright and clear, she had pretty blushed cheeks, creamy skin, her black hair was held back with ribbons and had its own sheen to it, and she had the dress. Lizzie was almost satisfied.

May had been round to Lizzie's house more than once that week and they'd talked in whispers. May was glad to be leaving. Rob didn't want a house of his own. They were going to live with his parents. Next-door Greta was in the way and Jon and Greta didn't get on, May said.

Jon Armstrong was behaving like the lad Lizzie's mother thought him, coming home drunk and bruised on Saturday nights and never speaking to Lizzie until she didn't know what she'd say to him if he ever did. Jon never saw the inside of chapel and when Lizzie ventured to his house there were no more books. He had taken to going walking with Mavis Robson and the lass from the store and one or two others. His mother was less than happy with him and told Lizzie's mother that Alf was the only good son she had.

It being a chapel wedding there was no drink. Lizzie thought that the only reason for Jon Armstrong's scowl. Everybody else seemed happy enough, sampling the sausage rolls and the sweet cakes and drinking tea and talking and laughing.

The afternoon grew hot and some of the lads and lasses made that their excuse to leave the tables. Some of them wandered away down to the beach; even Sam and Greta left the baby with her mother and disappeared. The women fussed and stood about, the men gathered to smoke and talk, and the children played ring games in spite of the heat. The lass from the store was there because she was a friend of May's, and she was almost as fair and pretty as Greta. Lizzie watched her talking and looking up at Jon, and he was smiling then, but when he looked at his sister there was no pleasure in his face. Later he walked away by himself in the direction of the beach and after a good five minutes' hesitation, Lizzie followed him.

It wasn't nearly as warm there with the breeze coming off the sea. There was nobody about but Jon. She wondered what had happened to all the others. The sea was deep blue, the waves making barely a splash as they broke. He lay down at the top of the beach and by the time Lizzie reached him, silently, because of the soft sand there, he had closed his eyes. She didn't know what to say.

'Jon?' He opened his eyes quickly. 'I'm sorry,' Lizzie said. 'You could have told me.'

'About what?' he said.

'About your Sam and Greta.'

'I didn't know what there was to tell.'

'You must have had a fair idea.'

'I didn't know she was having a bairn. You can sit down, I don't own the beach.'

Lizzie promptly sat.

'He says he didn't want to marry her,' she said shyly.

'No, well, if you don't want to get your feet wet, you don't go and paddle in the water, do you?'

'Don't you like weddings?'

'What?'

'You've only smiled once all day and that was at Annie. Maybe it's this type of wedding you don't like?'

'What's that?'

'No beer.'

'Aye, maybe that's it.'

'But May's your sister and Rob's your friend–'

'He's not my friend!' Jon cut in, and Lizzie sat back a little.

45

'You go drinking with him,' she said.

'I go drinking with a lot of lads.'

'Don't you like him then?'

'No, I don't.'

'Couldn't you have stopped her?'

'I did try. Do you listen to your Harold?'

'Not a lot.'

'Well, then.'

Lizzie remembered what Sam had said about Rob killing the pony.

'He's not soft,' she said.

'He isn't that,' Jon said grimly. 'If he lays one finger on her, I'll kill him.'

'He won't do that, Jon,' Lizzie said.

She went down to the water to paddle. She took off her shoes and stockings and left them a little way up from the waves and then walked through the shallow water before standing letting it wash over her ankles and the sand sink through her toes. It was wonderfully cold.

'Come out,' he said from behind her.

Lizzie hadn't seen him or heard him approach. She turned around.

'What?' she said.

Jon lifted her out by the waist. To her own astonishment, instead of protesting at this treatment she let him hold on to her and she stood on tiptoe and put her arms up around his neck and let him kiss her. It didn't matter to Lizzie that she was only one of three or four girls whom Jon had kissed that summer, neither did she mind that he kissed her now as fiercely as his brother had done because although the kiss was hot and deep it was nothing like kissing Sam. She didn't know why it didn't worry her, and when he didn't let her go she was quite happy there with her arms around his neck and her toes in the sand and his body close to hers and his mouth so sweet.

Lizzie did a twirl in front of her tiny bedroom mirror and laughed at herself, reliving for the thousandth time the afternoon of May's wedding day. The cool water running under her toes, the sun warm on her body, and his mouth on hers. They had walked back up the beach together and Jon had put his arm around her waist and she had liked the possessiveness of the action. She did another twirl and then ran out of the door and down the stairs.

'You'll break your neck coming down them stairs like that,' her mother said, looking up from the kitchen table where she was baking. She looked

46

Lizzie over carefully. 'And just where do you think you're going?' she said.

Lizzie faltered.

'For a walk?'

'Oh, yes, and what about that pile of mending there is in the kitchen?'

'I'll do it when I come back.'

'I suppose Jon Armstrong's going for a walk too, is he?' her mother queried, looking at her.

Lizzie hesitated.

'He's waiting for me at the gate.'

'No.'

'Oh, Mam, please.'

'I thought there was something,' her mother said, wiping floury hands. 'I saw you on Saturday afternoon, sneaking off.'

'We weren't.'

'Lizzie, I've told you before and I'll say it again. That lad is going to make some poor lass the worst husband in the world.'

Lizzie stood at the foot of the stairs, hesitating, her eyes full of tears. Her mother sighed.

'What do you want, Lizzie, a baby a year and a husband who drinks? Because that's the kind he is. He's got a temper too. He'd knock you about when you crossed him. His father was like that, just the same, big and good-looking. Every lass in the village wanted him, and poor Flo thought she'd got a catch. Tom used to come back on a Saturday night full of beer and leather her, and the bairns and all, Jon especially because he stood up to him. That lad's been brought up with fighting, he knows nothing else. And Tom . . .' Lizzie watched her mother's cheeks go pink. 'He was always interfering with her, gave her no peace. That sort of thing . . . it isn't nice, you know, Lizzie.'

'Isn't it?' she said softly, not wanting to break her mother's train of thought and thinking back to the way that Jon's kisses made her feel, like she wanted to lean all over him and give in.

Her mother wrinkled her nose.

'When the candle's out men are different. Mucky. Then you get a big belly.'

'Jon wouldn't do that.'

Her mother laughed harshly.

'Wouldn't he? You just give him half a chance, my lass. Them Armstrongs, they're all alike. Look at Sam. Jon Armstrong'll be a hard man, Lizzie, you mark my words. He'll lead some woman a pretty dance.'

'Can I go, Mam?'

'You haven't listened to a word I've said, have you?'

'Please.'

Her mother sighed and relented and she skipped out of the house and down the yard. They went walking on the beach and she thought about what her mother had said. She knew that Jon had a temper, a slow heavy kind of temper which left you breathless, but she didn't think he was like his dad. Tom Armstrong had been the sort who shouted and hit out. Jon was at his most dangerous when he talked soft and pleasant and sarcastic at you like you were daft. Then she remembered him shouting and swearing at Sam and knocking him down. She would have thought that having a father like Tom would have put him off beer and fighting but it hadn't.

He was nothing like that now. He laughed and chatted and they walked a long way because the tide was well out and the sands went on for miles that way without a break and the evening was fine and still, and then they ran up the beach and collapsed, exhausted, at the top of the dunes, breathing heavily and laughing. And then he asked her softly, 'You were late coming out. Was that because of your mam?'

Lizzie looked respectfully at him. You couldn't put one over on him.

'She doesn't want me to see you. She doesn't like you.'

'The thing is, do you like me?'

'I've always liked you.'

'No, you haven't. You always liked our Sam.'

'That was different.' It wasn't the answer Jon wanted to hear, she knew as she said it.

'You chase half the lasses in the village,' she said.

It had come as a surprise to Lizzie to find that this mattered to her. Her feelings had changed. She didn't know when or how but the brothers had changed places in her mind. At first she was disgusted with herself, behaving like the other lasses did just because Jon was big and good-looking and had kissed her down by the water's edge. She'd relived that kiss so often that she thought she might die for the lack of another.

Jon didn't look at her now as he said softly, 'You do want me here, don't you?'

'Yes.'

He kissed her, gently and deliberately, and she reached up with both hands to draw him nearer. Her fingers were in his hair, her eyes closed, her lips parted, and a sweet warmth stole over her body. He put both arms around her so that the top of her was crushed against him. She couldn't have got away, so fierce was the hold, but Lizzie didn't want to get away, she wanted to get nearer, to have more of the kisses that were making her feel this wonderful and new sensation. When he released her she made a little noise of disappointment in her throat. She sat back and blinked and looked at him. Jon was frowning. Had she done something wrong? The rejection so soon after the pleasure brought tears into her eyes and she had to blink several times to get rid of them and swallow hard and clear her throat.

'Will you be my lass?'

Lizzie met his gaze, unbelieving.

'I thought . . . you didn't like it.'

He smiled and then it was all right, she knew it was.

'I like it, Lizzie. So, will you?'

'Oh, yes.' And since she didn't dare throw herself at him, in the strange daft way that she immediately wanted to, she smiled brilliantly at him. As she stifled the desire to hurl herself at him he smiled back at her, his eyes very blue and warm.

'Howay then.'

Lizzie shook her head.

'Come on. I won't hurt you and I won't get you like our Sam got Greta.'

Lizzie had never been cuddled before in her life and it was as wondrous an experience as the kissing had been. She flung herself at him and he laughed and caught her into his arms. She buried her face against his chest and put both arms around the solid warmth of him. Eyes closed there against his shirt, she was happier now than she had ever been. Jon Armstrong was the whole world to her now.

'Oh, Lizzie,' he said, burying his face in her hair, 'I've thought about you a lot. You always were the bonniest little lass in the world, running after our Sam and now I'm going to make you all mine. You won't go with no other lad, will you?'

'No,' Lizzie said, smiling with delight.

He crushed her nearer.

'I'm never going to let go of you, never ever,' he said.

Six

L izzie knew that May was visiting her mother that afternoon and she and her mam went around for tea and scones because for once all the men were out together and Greta and the baby had gone to her own mother's for the day. Not that she was much help when she was there, Mrs Armstrong said.

'More of a hindrance than anything else.'

The talk was all about the girl in the office at the Victoria.

'Mr Farrer's niece,' Lizzie's mam said disapprovingly. 'Whatever is he thinking about? I wouldn't let any lass of mine around all them men. Some of them aren't nice, spitting and saying things they shouldn't and doing goodness knows what.'

'She's a bonny lass too,' Mrs Armstrong said. 'I had to go up about our Alf's pay the other morning and there she was – hair you could warm your hands against and a posh accent. They say she comes from London.'

'Whatever is she doing here?'

'Her father died and she didn't have no mother and Mr and Mrs Farrer took her in.'

'Well, it must be bad enough for her here after a place like London without them making her work. I think it's disgraceful,' Lizzie's mother said.

'Maybe she likes it, Mam,' Lizzie put in.

Her mother looked at her as though she was daft.

'Coming from a nice home like that?'

'She even has a horse, I hear,' Mrs Armstrong said. 'They get invited up to the big house, you know.'

'What, the Farrers?'

The house was the mineowner's house belonging to the Nelsons. It was four miles away. Lizzie had never seen the mineowner or his family except at a distance. As the mine manager, and therefore the boss, Mr Farrer was the person the pitmen dealt with, and Mr Nelson had an agent called Mr Forrester who sometimes came to the Victoria, but the Nelsons didn't.

'There's going to be a dance. I expect little Miss Farrer will be there. She'd look lovely in green.'

Later Lizzie and May went off on their own for a walk. The woods were full of flowers. May was quiet.

'Is everything all right?' Lizzie asked as they sat down in the sunlight where the trees were well spaced.

May shook her head.

'Oh, Lizzie, the things he does to me.'

'What does he do?' Lizzie asked in fascinated horror.

'It isn't nice to talk about it. Do you think men are all alike?'

'Well, I suppose they must be generally.' Lizzie thought back to what Jon had said about Rob mistreating his new wife. 'Does he hit you?'

May shook her head. Lizzie was relieved about that. It meant that she didn't have to make a decision about whether to tell Jon that Rob was knocking May about.

'What does he do?'

'Don't get married, Lizzie, it's awful,' May confided. 'It hurts and it's so . . . it's so . . .'

'I thought you liked him kissing you and so on.'

'It's nothing to do with kissing,' May said.

Lizzie was worried about this information and the very next time that she was alone with Jon she wouldn't let him touch her.

'Summat the matter?' he asked.

They were sitting in what had been Sam and Lizzie's dune and she claimed it now for her own. It was warm and sheltered there, down away from the wind.

'Do you think getting married hurts?'

Jon looked guilelessly into her eyes and then said, 'Getting married?'

'Yes. You know.'

'Oh.'

'You do know about it?'

Jon looked away for a few moments and Lizzie didn't know whether to ask any more.

'People aren't supposed to do it until they're married,' she said.

Jon laughed shortly.

'Unless they're our Sam and Greta Smith, you mean?'

'Do you think it hurts?' Lizzie said again.

She hadn't seen Jon embarrassed before. She would have laughed if she hadn't been so concerned about the topic of conversation.

'Maybe a little bit at first because . . . well, because it's new, but I don't think it should much because otherwise people wouldn't do it.'

Jon, Lizzie concluded gratefully, had a good share of common sense. It left the question of Rob and May. Was he hurting May on purpose and should she tell Jon? She decided not to. May was a married woman now and her business, unless Rob was hitting her, was nothing to do with anybody but her husband. Jon couldn't go interfering.

To Lizzie's relief May became pregnant early that autumn and she seemed so pleased about it that Lizzie thought everything must be all right again. Perhaps May and Rob had got past the hurting part and when the baby was born Rob would be so pleased that he wouldn't ever hit May anyroad.

Harold and Enid decided to get married some time before Christmas. Lizzie had been waiting for weeks to hear them say so. She knew how Enid felt. Enid had been brought up in a house full of women, had seen the other village lads and known that she didn't want a hard-drinking pitlad yelling at her and leaving her every time to go out with his mates, or a Methodist type who spent all his time being good. Harold was gentle and quiet and a good worker. Lizzie knew that was what Enid saw in her brother.

When they told his mam that they wanted to get married it was money that came first into Lizzie's mind. She would have no choice now, she would have to go into domestic service like so many other lasses had to. It didn't make her happy.

'They're looking for a kitchen maid up at the house,' Lizzie's mother said. 'When Harold and Enid are wed we'll need the money. There'll be babbies in no time if Enid's owt like her mother.'

Lizzie said nothing. She was going for a walk with Jon that evening. Up on top of the sand dunes, the tide way out and the gulls calling, she poured out the story to him.

'I'll get to come home once a fortnight for half a day, I expect.'

'That's nice.'

That was all he said. Lizzie couldn't believe it, and then she thought. She was very young. Why should Jon think of marrying her? Because it was the only alternative? She was being silly. Jon didn't like the idea, he didn't want to marry her or anybody, why should he? Marriage was bairns and being grown up and Jon had worked hard to keep his mother and his brothers. He might not want to work hard to keep a family just yet.

She went to bed that night and thought of the things he had said to her about being his lass and how much he cared for her, and decided uncomfortably that maybe he had just said such things so that she would let him kiss her and put his hands on her. And then she knew that wasn't fair. Jon hadn't done anything he shouldn't have done and yet he could have. He was a true Armstrong. She had heard her mother say that Mrs Armstrong had been expecting Jon when she married Tom. Sam and Greta had had to get married. Lizzie could understand why now. Jon could have persuaded her into anything. Only he hadn't. Was that because he'd never intended to marry her and didn't want to get caught?

Lizzie thought about what work would be like up at the house, not seeing her family and not seeing Jon, and not being with him and laughing with him and having him take her into his arms, the comfort and the pleasure. After that it was hard to think about Harold and be pleased that he and Enid would be happy.

Seven

*I*t was not the first time that Kate had seen Jon at the office. Her uncle didn't like people fighting and since Jon was constantly in trouble he was occasionally brought in and told off. It hadn't happened much lately though and although Kate didn't want Jon to get into trouble she missed seeing him.

She knew a good many of the pitmen by now but to her Jon was special, not just because he had been kind to her and helped her the day that she fell off Dolly but because he made her feel like no one else had ever done before. He made her nervous; she couldn't remember what she was supposed to be doing when he was there, and couldn't think about anything else in his presence. To her dismay she found herself closing her eyes at night thinking what fine eyes Jon had and how tall and slender he was. In vain did she give herself lectures on the subject. She liked him and there was no way past it.

At the end of the foreshift on that particular day Jon had walked across to the office and asked if he could see Mr Farrer. Kate remembered well the last time that Jon had been fighting and in trouble. She had sympathised with him.

'Don't worry,' she had told him, 'he feels as if he ought to shout but it doesn't mean anything.'

Jon smiled and Kate felt an inexplicable happiness.

'Thanks, bonny lass,' he said.

'I'm not a bonny lass,' she said seriously. 'I have too many freckles.'

'Sun-kisses,' he said.

Kate had been happy for days afterwards.

Now she greeted him with a smile and tried to be sober.

'You haven't been fighting again, have you?' she said reprovingly. 'He didn't send for you?' She looked all over his face for evidence.

'No, I just wanted a word with him. Is he in?'

'He was a minute ago. I'll ask.' And Kate went beyond the half-glassed door into the inner office where her uncle said that he would see Jon. She was desperate with curiosity, but she tried to keep busy. She had her own tiny office outside her uncle's. It made her feel important; she was not just a clerk like the others were but she made her uncle's life easier by arranging his appointments and seeing to the people who came in and opening his post and making sure he got to where he had to go at the right time and a hundred other things. She loved being there.

After a few minutes her uncle called her in.

'Young Armstrong's getting married. He needs a house.'

Kate felt as if someone had poured a bucket of cold water over her. She did nothing for what seemed to her like a very long time but was in fact only a few seconds. She stared at Jon. He couldn't possibly be getting married. He was too young. And then she remembered what her aunt had said about the pitmen having to get married, some of them. Her aunt spoke scathingly and said they were like animals. Had Jon got some girl into trouble? Was he like that? There was another reason that he couldn't get married. Kate didn't quite understand but it was all to do with the fact that she thought she would have known if he had had a girl, that he wouldn't have flirted with her like he did, that he wouldn't have put his hands on her waist, that somehow she would have known there was someone he cared for. It wasn't possible. Jon couldn't get married. She would lose him then and she had not recovered from losing her father yet.

Prompted by her uncle she found a house for Jon but she was so pale that her uncle sent her home early, and it was the first time that she had been glad to do so.

The pit had been a shock to her at first. The pitmen seemed to have no respect. They were not like other men. When she ventured out of the office at the end or beginning of shifts some of the young ones whistled and laughed and brought the blood rushing into her face and the desire to run back into the office to her feet, but she soon learned that there was another side to them. When she spoke to them singly they called her 'pet' or 'flower' or 'sweetheart', and although Kate knew this wasn't respectful either it was kindly meant. She had learned to decipher their rough words. They often teased her. Kate had never been teased before, her father had always been serious. She found that she liked being among these men and they were not so different from the intellectuals of London. The old men who sorted the coal in the shed near her office were happy to talk. They told her stories of pit disasters and holidays and their families. When she rode her horse through the village they waved at her and if she stopped on the way to work or back to admire babies or speak to children she soon found herself invited into tiny spotless cottages where the kettle appeared to be always on the boil for a pot of tea. The women talked about their men and their families and their neighbours and Kate learned a great deal about them.

She grew to like her way of life. She grew to love the pit and all the comings and goings. She loved to discuss the problems and the work. Her aunt despaired of her at mealtimes, and at social events she was bored. Her ears strained for talk of work among the young men she met. She asked them questions but was rewarded with laughter or strange looks.

She knew that her uncle and aunt looked on her differently now. She knew that her aunt was disappointed, that she had wanted Kate to be a daughter to her, but it was no use, she couldn't be. She knew that they were determined that she should have the best. She was sure that they had spent money which they should not have spent, on her horse and on small parties at the house and on expensive material which her aunt had made into dresses. Kate cared nothing for any of it. She tried to please her aunt because they had taken her in but the truth was that Aunt Rose bored her. Other women, except the pitwives, bored her. She hated their inactivity and their frivolous minds. She hated the talk of domestic things. They did not read or care about politics or what went on in the world. Kate found men's conversation much more interesting but she was not invited to join in. If she ventured near they stopped talking or made pretty remarks for her benefit. She thought she was likely to die of boredom.

After she'd started work at the office she had been happy, and caught up in that happiness was Jon Armstrong. Kate did not realise until the day she learned that he was to marry how much he meant to her. She knew that it was foolish but when she reached her bedroom she sat down on the bed and wept so much that her aunt suggested they should send for the doctor. When Kate refused, her aunt insisted that she should undress and get into bed. A fire was lit and the bed was warmed. Her aunt brought her a hot drink and Kate lay and watched the day turn into dusk and wished more than she had ever wished anything in her life that Jon Armstrong should not get married. She saw with a new and stunning clarity that he could not marry anybody else. It was not possible, it could not happen. God would not let it happen.

Eight

*L*izzie didn't wait for Jon that evening, even though he had been on the foreshift and was quite free to go walking with her as usual. She rushed out of their gate before the time he would meet her and sat in the sand dune. Some time later when he jumped down into the sand she didn't get up. She didn't look up either. She'd had a lot of time since yesterday evening in which to think and she had decided that Jon didn't really care for her and that the best thing was for them not to see each other again, but she didn't know how she was going to say it.

'You could have waited for me,' he said now, sitting down beside her.

Lizzie took a deep breath.

'I didn't think you'd be there,' she said.

'I said I would.'

'I think it's time we parted,' she said, but the tears would fill her eyes.

'Do you?' It was all he said. Lizzie could have hit him.

'I don't think I like you no more.'

'What a fib,' he said mildly.

The tears receded. Lizzie felt more in control because she was cross with him.

''Tisn't a fib. It's best.'

'If you stop crying I'll tell you what's best.'

'I'm not crying, and you don't know.'

'Oh, I know all right. Come on, Lizzie, there's nowt to cry for. I'll stop the tears, I promise.'

She turned straight into his arms, sobbing out against his shoulder.

'I thought you liked me. I should've known. My mam tried to tell me . . .'

'Hush. Listen. I went to see Farrer today and he says that we can have old Turner's house.'

Lizzie stopped crying. She drew back from his shoulder and looked at him.

'What?'

'Have you washed your ears this week, Lizzie Harton? Mr Farrer says we can have old Turner's house.'

'Can we?' She smiled brilliantly at him.

'Aye, we can. So, when will you marry me?'

Lizzie flung herself at him and Jon pulled her down on top of him into the sand and grass, and he laughed and hugged her.

'Oh, Jon, Jon! Did Mr Farrer really say it?'

'He really said it.'

'Our own house. How did you manage that?'

'I don't know,' he confessed.

Lizzie had expected her own mother would be ill-pleased but was surprised that Mrs Armstrong also objected. Her mother said that she was too young, that Jon had bad blood, that she would regret it. Mrs Armstrong said nothing. That upset Lizzie much more than her own mother's ranting and raving, though it was her mother she talked to.

'At least I won't have to go to place now,' she said.

'And is that what you're marrying him for?' her mother said sharply. 'Well, it's a poor reason, Lizzie.'

'That isn't the reason, you know it isn't. I just thought you might think of it like that.'

'I'd rather have you slave in somebody's kitchen all your days than marry him.'

Lizzie felt anger rise within her.

'He's done nothing,' she said.

'It's not what he's done, it's what he will do that bothers me. You could have anybody you wanted.'

'I want him.'

'Aye, that's the trouble.'

'What is?'

'I've seen the way you look at him. He's laid hands on you, and maybe more.'

'He's never,' Lizzie said, her throat almost stopped.

'You'll rue the day you marry him. I'd have almost anything happen rather than see it. You, so bonny and good. You're fit to marry a lord.' And her mother strangled a sob and turned away.

They had hardly any furniture for their new house which looked so big and bare but was of more interest to Lizzie than a palace and when her mother got used to the idea, she decided that she was glad Lizzie was marrying rather than going to place. She even spoke to Jon sometimes. Harold was pleased because she would not be his to keep and Lizzie thought of how rich they would be on Jon's pay. Her mother gave her her own bed which was big, and helped her to make curtains. Jon set to and made a table and Alf, who was good at woodwork, made chairs. They spent all their free time at the house and once, in the late evening, when the sun had set blood red over the houses and Alf had gone back home for his supper, Jon pulled Lizzie down on to the bed and kissed her hard.

They were a week away from the wedding and Lizzie was sleeping downstairs with her mother just for those few days. The little house was spotlessly clean, right to its shiny windows.

'I'll never care for another lass like I care for you,' Jon told her.

'I should hope not,' she teased.

'And I'll be kind to you.'

'You always are.'

'And gentle. I won't drink and I won't hurt you. I'll be good to you always. Oh, Lizzie, Lizzie, I never thought to be like this.'

He kissed her again and she returned the kiss, eagerly pressing against him, and gradually he brought his hands from her back around to the sides of her body as though he was going to slide them the full length of her which he never had done and didn't now. His hands and mouth tantalised and she felt the way that she was not sure decent women should feel, with his mouth sweet on hers and the heel of his hands in slow caress just this side of where they should be. She would have nothing to be ashamed of on her wedding day, nothing at all.

It was the next day, Monday. Lizzie had congratulated the weather, bright sunshine and a good breeze, because it was washing day. She liked washing day, even though it was hard work. She liked the smell of the clean clothes, the sight of them blowing so brightly in the back lane. She liked the pegging out of them, the line getting longer and longer to show the work done, and the ironing of them too while they were still damp, the smell of drying, the creases smoothed away.

Mrs Armstrong had come in earlier, grumbling because Greta had chosen to go to her mam's that day rather than help with the washing, so Lizzie divided her time between her own house and next-door's. Her mam didn't mind, she didn't have so much to do and knew that Lizzie was trying to please Jon's mother.

Greta came back when a lot of the hard work had been done. Lizzie was in her own house at the time but she came out to find Greta and Mrs Armstrong shouting and the next thing Greta was in the back lane, the baby screaming indoors, and she had the clothes poles out of the washing and was just about to pull it down and trample it into the thick dust of the back lane when Lizzie arrived.

'You do, Greta Smith,' she warned, 'you just do when his mam and me have spent all morning getting it clean, and I'll smack your face.'

'Trying to get in with the old biddy, are you?' Greta retorted. 'It won't do you no good. That's a fat paypacket you're pinching.'

'It's no more than you did.'

Greta laughed. 'You what? Sam doesn't make the half of that and at least he gives her some. You're lucky. You won't have to live like Sam and me, their Alf snoring and his mother moaning over you like she's moaning over me.' The tears stood out in Greta's pretty blue eyes. 'I'm expecting. She says it's my fault. She doesn't know him. You wait until Saturday. You'll wish you hadn't when he puts a bairn into you. You'll be sorry then. And all she can say is that it's *my* fault!' And Greta turned in fury, pulling on a shirt and the line and the washing came down on top of them, the greys and browns and whites of socks and skirts and stockings all in a muddle in the dirt of the back lane.

Lizzie got hold of Greta and slapped her and the other girl squealed and retaliated. They got hold of each other's hair and went down into the dirt amongst the clothes, fighting. Mrs Armstrong and Lizzie's mam came out and rescued the washing, and Mrs Armstrong pulled Greta up and took her into the house. Lizzie's clothes were dirty where she had fallen and a clothes prop had hit her on the head and made a bump.

'I needn't ask what all that was about,' her mother said. 'Them Armstrong lads is nothing but trouble. You go next-door and help with that wash.'

So Lizzie and Greta, not speaking, began the washing again. Lizzie was pegging out the first lot when she heard the siren that came from the pit. She dropped the pegs into the clothes basket and started down the lane, and Greta and Mrs Armstrong and Lizzie's mother and all the women from their row came out of their houses. Jon and Alf were supposed to be on backshift but things had been changed around. For once, all the Armstrong boys were down together and so was Harold and so was Greta's father.

The Victoria was on the seashore and the pit extended under the sea, large pillars of coal left to support the land so there was no reason for that particular roof fall. Sometimes it just did that: the awful rumbling sound, the thick black dust and the breaking rock, men running from the coal face, and all around them the black storm and the dust that set you choking, and everybody trying to get out of the way. The earth was like an outraged animal determined on revenge for the invasion of its body, for the black gold hewn from it. It seemed to the men's ears as though the rumbling would never stop and they fled, timber groaning and breaking around them and the suffocating blackness descending in a gritty foulness that clogged eyes and mouth and nose and throat, working its way into sweat and skin. They only stopped when the noise had stopped and they were well clear, and then it was to find out who was missing, and there were several, and by then a wall of stone stood between them and the face.

Jon knew exactly where he was as he opened his eyes. It was like that moment when you were having a bad dream, the moment before you woke up from the nightmare and found that you were in your own bed with the summer sunshine coming in through the curtains. Alf would be lying on his back, snoring, and his mother would already be clattering about down in the kitchen.

It was the moment before that, the moment of terror, and in just another second he would wake up in his own bed. But the moment passed and his eyes would not open any further, in fact for some time he didn't know whether they were open or closed, and after that it was as he'd suspected all along it might have been. His brain was too good for him, it would not tell him lies even for a second or two's illusion of peace. He had known where he was from the beginning. His brain was issuing other unwelcome messages. His eyes saw the blackness just as if they had been shut, except that it was some comfort to close his eyes. His body was very hot and sweaty, he could smell the sweat, could smell the thick choking dust and taste it too, and there was something else, something that he would not, could not acknowledge just then.

He was not hurt, there was just nowhere to go, nowhere to move to. The rock covered him, held him close like a black embrace above and below and all around, and it was heavy. Its flatness was smooth against him, its jagged edges bruised him. And he was not alone. Not far away someone was groaning, very faintly. The groaning was a horror and a comfort for a little while and then there was silence and Jon knew what that silence meant.

No one was breathing near him. He was quite alone now and there was hardly any air, his lungs told him that. There was also all around him the smell of death, of men broken and crushed, like chickens with their entrails being taken out, the warm sweet stench of ripped bowels and of blood. He let himself acknowledge all these things very slowly indeed because there was no point in panicking, he couldn't move and hoped, selfishly, that the others had got out, that the men who were lying here weren't his brothers, though he knew as he thought it that they had been right there with him, that the tubs were full of coal and Sam was busy with them, that he and Alf had just completed their task. It seemed to him now that Alf had been near enough to feel the warmth of his breath and that the last words he had heard screamed were from his young brother's mouth.

It couldn't be. It couldn't be, even God couldn't be so cruel. But he knew otherwise. And if they were dead then at least they wouldn't have to lie here and die slowly of thirst because it was possible, it was quite possible. He could feel the tears at the back of his eyes and in his throat and he told himself that crying was a waste of air and there wasn't any of it to waste. In fact there didn't seem to be any at all, his lungs were so tight. He tried to think of something pleasant.

He thought of Lizzie in her rose-coloured dress, of how he had kissed her on the bed the day before, he thought of the wedding to come and the plans they had made and of taking Lizzie to bed after the wedding. He thought of her sweet lips and her beautiful eyes and he thought that he might never see her again, that he might never come out of this grave, never smell fresh air or touch the grass or see the sky, and his mind began to do strange things.

He thought he could feel sand trickling down his back, hear the sea that was four hundred feet above him. The tide was coming in and the waves were crashing over the rocks on the point, spraying themselves across the harbour wall. He thought that he could feel the warmth of the sun, that he was lying on top of the sand dunes with Lizzie. But the images didn't last. He was hot and thirsty and alone with not enough air to breathe in. Breathing was such an effort, breathing was all there was, and soon that would become too much in the thick darkness, in the silence entombed.

Kate ran out of the office and watched the women as they streamed past. She saw Lizzie and her mother and knew very well by now that Lizzie was the girl Jon intended marrying. Kate didn't hate people naturally so she couldn't hate Lizzie Harton, she'd just felt miserable when she'd seen her for the first time walking through the town. Lizzie was so beautiful and Kate had never been so conscious of her own freckled face and unaccomplished ways. She'd seen the thick black hair and the deep brown eyes and Lizzie's brown skin, tanned deep golden from the summer sun. She was laughing and had very white teeth and she was rounder than Kate, with a curved perfection which Kate envied. Since her father had died Kate had lost a lot of weight and it had not come back. Lizzie looked to her like somebody who had everything. Kate thought that this girl would probably make Jon Armstrong the perfect wife; she would have been trained by her family how to look after a man, she would know the mysteries of cooking and cleaning and comfort, all things which Kate knew little of because her father had despised everything which was not completely of the intellect. Never before had she wished she had paid attention to her aunt's instructions.

Now, as the women gathered by the pit head, Kate saw her again and hurried across. The women looked at her, not as though she had no place there but as though she belonged. Kate warmed, feeling that she had a place here, and the miserable dislike which she had so far felt for Lizzie Harton dissolved as she reached her. Lizzie had put on a brave face, Kate thought, such as she could not have managed and she turned to Kate and smiled.

'Miss Farrer,' she said.

'Are your – are your men down?' This should perhaps have been apparent but it wasn't always so, Kate knew. Those who could help would come and do so, even if it was just to give comfort.

'All of them,' Lizzie said. 'Jon, Sam, Alf, Greta's dad, and my brother, Harold.'

Greta began to cry, standing there. Mrs Armstrong put an arm around

65

her, and May, Jon's sister, whom Kate knew was pregnant, now plump and pretty, ran to meet them.

'Don't run, May,' Lizzie said. 'You shouldn't.'

'I'm all right, really.'

Kate stood with them and as she did so she thought back to how she had wished that Jon wouldn't marry Lizzie, of how she had hoped he wouldn't be able to marry. If he was dead he wouldn't be able to marry anybody, she thought, and the tears sprang into her eyes. Lizzie squeezed her arm.

'Don't worry,' she said. 'Sometimes it's nothing.'

They both knew this for a lie and for the first time Kate said the other girl's name.

'Oh, Lizzie,' she said.

Men were brought up and their women went to claim them. Kate thought that May's face only changed fractionally when she saw Rob and his father stepping into the warm sun. More and more were brought up but none of them were Armstrongs, and then Greta cried, but Mrs Armstrong stood there still and white-faced. Lizzie's mother went forward when Harold came out, and the doctor was brought, and the boss came to Mrs Armstrong and Greta's mother to tell them that their men were still in the pit and that they were trapped by a rock fall. He said that volunteers would go down and dig. He said he didn't know how badly hurt the men were, and Lizzie turned away and put her hands over her face, and to Kate's own surprise she took the girl into her arms and held her.

Other people went away. Lizzie's mother went back with Harold and Enid and took Greta's baby with her, and Mrs Armstrong and Lizzie and Greta and her mother and Kate waited at the pit head while the shadows lengthened and fell across the pit head buildings and the wheel.

After a long while Harold came to Lizzie and tried to persuade her to go home for a little while and have a cup of tea. He told her that it might take all night, but she wouldn't budge and Kate didn't blame her. No power on earth would have moved either of them. Kate stood there and prayed. She made bargains with God for Jon Armstrong's life, said how sorry she was to have thought and wished such things; that God would not make them come true because it was too awful, that if Jon was saved she would never ask to be his wife. She would not dislike Lizzie, she would be glad to see them married, she would never ask for another thing so long as she lived. She prayed and prayed and tried to contain her tears because she knew that she had no right to cry for him here. She tried not to give vent to her worst fears. She tried not to think that Lizzie and Jon might not be married that week, tried not to think about the possibility of a life without him. There was no life without him, there was nothing worthy of the name.

It wasn't much longer before they brought Jon, exhausted but alive, to the surface. It was the longest wait of Kate's life and even then she was not allowed to go to him. She had to watch Lizzie go forward and claim him, she even tried to be glad. God had answered her real prayers after all, he had not listened to her selfish and unthinking rantings. They would be married now and everything would be all right.

Jon was bruised and bleeding and his eyes were blank and after him they brought up the lifeless bodies of Sam and Alf and Greta's father. Harold came and took Lizzie home and Mrs Armstrong went back with Jon. Kate's uncle came to her. He draped a shawl around her shoulders, she didn't know where it had come from, and he put her up into the pony and trap which somehow miraculously had appeared complete with Albert and he took her home. Kate was just so glad. She knew that as long as Jon was alive she would be able to stand anything, that she had done the right thing. She was so weary that she could hardly eat the dinner her aunt had made and afterwards she fell into bed and slept the clock round – at least that was what her aunt said.

Nine

M rs Harton wouldn't let Lizzie go next-door where the curtains and doors were closed for days. On the day of his brothers' funeral Jon didn't even look up to see Lizzie, never mind speak to her. She tried to be patient but he didn't come to her. She had a great desire to dash out of her house and up their back yard and hammer on the door and throw herself into his arms. But she didn't. She waited.

Kate had just as little comfort. Her uncle for some reason didn't shut his door when he saw Jon and she was forced to endure the interview.

The autumn sun shone through her grimy office window like a mockery.

'The company . . .' Her uncle paused. Kate had seen him and heard him at home, calling the company names which she had thought would never pass his lips, and it came to her then that her uncle's work was a necessity not a luxury like hers. He managed the Victoria because he was paid to. He liked the Nelsons no better than anybody else. 'The company accepts no responsibility for what happened. You know as well as I do that the Victoria is as safe as we can make her. Some . . . man must have removed a vital support by mistake, that's all I can think. We're very careful, Armstrong, very careful indeed.'

Kate sat hunched behind her desk holding on to her breath. She knew that Jon had a ready temper. Any display of it here and he would lose his job and his house and any chance of working in the Durham coalfield again. He had to accept now that there would be no compensation of any kind from the company. Kate sat there listening to his silence. She had heard her uncle say at home that there wouldn't be a penny because if the company offered money it would mean that they acknowledged blame, and if they did that there would be a case to answer and as far as anybody knew there was not and he doubted whether anything could be proved. Her uncle did not fear the union who had apparently already turned down Jon's request for help. One man had even blamed Sam and there had been a fight. The rumour was that Jon Armstrong had almost killed him.

After the silence had gone on for so long that Kate didn't dare to breathe, her uncle said, 'You won't be eligible for another house now, Armstrong. One man, one house. And your brother's widow and her mother will have to be out of their house by the end of the week.'

Jon walked out without a word. He brushed past Kate and didn't even look at her. When he had gone she went through into her uncle's office.

'I should've sacked him as well,' George Farrer said.

Kate looked levelly at him. Her uncle snapped a pencil in two and threw both halves on the desk.

'I thought he'd give me reason to. I couldn't even find out about the fight. They closed ranks. He'll cause trouble before he's through will that lad, real trouble.'

That evening Lizzie was sitting at the table with her mother and Harold and Enid when Jon arrived. They had just finished their tea. She was so relieved to see him that she got up and went to him, but he didn't encourage or touch her. He looked past her to her mother.

'How's your mam?' asked Lizzie's as though they didn't live next-door and meet every day.

'Grand. Mrs Harton, I cannot marry Lizzie.'

The words came out in such a rush that Lizzie stared at him.

'Aye, I know,' her mother said.

'Greta's expecting another bairn and her mam'll be put out of her house on Friday.'

Lizzie couldn't believe what she was hearing. 'It isn't true,' she said. 'Because of Greta.'

Jon looked at her then. His eyes hadn't lost the blankness that they had held ever since he'd been brought up out of the pit with his dead brothers.

'I can't let our Sam's bairns starve.'

'Isn't there anybody else to take them?' Lizzie said, and she heard her voice wobble. He didn't have to answer the question because as they stood there in silence, not touching each other, her eyes filled with tears and her lips quivered. Her face worked and then she broke down and turned towards her mother in a storm of weeping, and for the first time ever her mother took her into her arms. Harold and Enid got up and went into the other room.

Jon would have left but as he tried to she pulled away from her mother and flew to him and put herself into his arms, clutching at the lapels of his jacket, her slim fingers white at the knuckles. The tears brimmed and fell and she heard the front room door click as her mother went out. Lizzie said his name over and over until he pulled her to him and kissed her mouth sweetly to bruising and all over her face, kissing away the tears, and then he held her from him and Lizzie stood back and let him walk out.

After that there was silence except for the fire crackling. Lizzie stood in the middle of the room where he had left her, seeing nothing, feeling nothing, unable to believe what was happening to her. Everything was finished, the happiness was all gone, and there was nothing but a great big hole. There was nothing to replace it. How frightening, she thought, like a cliff edge. She had done that once when she went away for the day down the coast. She had stood on the edge of a very high cliff, the sea way way below and the jagged rocks, knowing that if her feet slipped or if she stepped forward or if she was given even a small shove she would fall, lose her footing and fall, with nothing to clutch on to. It was like that now. It was like dying.

Her mother came back into the room.

'You have what you wanted now,' Lizzie said.

Her mother threw her such a look but the words tumbled out regardless.

'You never wanted me to marry him. You said you'd rather I slaved in somebody's house all my life . . .'

'Oh, lass, I wouldn't have had it be like this.'

'Jon won't ever be able to marry anybody now. He'll have to keep all those people for always.'

'Greta's a bonny lass. Somebody'll take her on. Even with her mother, maybe.'

Her own mother was trying to make a joke, Lizzie thought in surprise. She never made jokes.

'Do you think they might?'

'I'm sure of it.' And Lizzie's mother cuddled her again. That was another surprise. 'Just give it a little time. It'll all come right in the end. Things always do.'

Jon walked quickly up the yard and down the row and through the village. He didn't stop. He wanted to but there were people about and he knew that they pitied him, that either they would avoid him or come over to say something meaningless that he had heard a dozen times already. He couldn't stand that. If he stopped he would run all the way back to Lizzie and get hold of her and never let her go again, but as long as he kept walking there was a part of him which didn't believe that life could be so bad. It wasn't possible that he could lose her.

He stopped outside Greta's mother's house. The evening was not over yet but the rest wouldn't be as hard as that.

Greta's mother, Nellie, was sitting over a meagre fire as though she had a cold. The kitchen was already stripped bare leaving only the basics as they had been. She managed a smile for him as he walked in. She was a small faded version of Greta with silver-gold hair and tired eyes, a sharp, bitter woman whom Jon had never liked. Greta looked up too. She was a different kind of lass from Lizzie though she too had been crying, and there were dark shadows under her bonny eyes.

Her hair was the colour of ripe wheat and for all her grieving her body was ripe and rounded and her cheeks like peaches, but Jon didn't care for any of that. He didn't like her and he knew very well that she didn't like him. He blamed her for seducing Sam, thought that she had deliberately given herself to him because her father was a bully and she wanted to get out of the house. And although Jon knew that she was not to be blamed for wanting to get away from a man like that, Sam was gentle and vulnerable and she had seen that and played on it. She had made him miserable both before and after their marriage. Greta was the kind of lass who didn't like to be touched except when it suited her.

Right now Jon just wished that she had never existed. She was his burden now, she was the weight for his back. Her body was not yet showing the second child, it was early in her pregnancy and the first baby was crying in her arms. In similar circumstances Jon thought he could have felt sympathy for any woman but Greta didn't give him the chance. She looked at him without pleasure and her eyes were dull. In two days she and her mother would be on the streets and she could expect no help when people's initial sympathy had gone. She would have to find work where she could and keep her mother and two bairns somehow. The child, a little boy called Tommy, stopped crying now and she put him down into his wooden cradle, the cradle which Alf's clever fingers had made. Jon tried not to think about Alf. He missed Sam it was true and that hurt, but he missed Alf with the numbness of disbelief.

'What do you want?' Greta said.

'I want to talk to you, in the other room.'

'Don't trouble yourselves,' her mother said, getting up wearily. 'I'm going to my bed while I still have one. Is your mother all right, Jon?'

'Aye, she's fine.' People had been asking for days and he had been answering the same way. They had to ask, to show they cared, and he had to answer. His mother had to be all right, there was nothing anybody could do about it even if she wasn't.

'What do you want to talk to me about?' Greta demanded, and her chin came up in the same way as it had done when they were having an argument.

Jon took badly to being defied. He hadn't known that he would because he had for some reason assumed that grief and fright would have made her pliable. They hadn't, and somehow it pleased him and annoyed him all at the same time.

'You have to be out of here by Friday.'

'I know.'

'You can come to us.'

'We will not.'

Jon sighed inwardly. Why did she have to argue and make this worse than it was? He didn't want her there any more than she wanted to come.

'You don't have a choice.'

Greta fairly spat.

'It's nowt to do with you!'

'They're Sam's bairns.'

'He's dead,' Greta said harshly. 'Anyroad, you're daft. You can't keep me and my mam and two bairns, and your mam and you and Lizzie and whatever bairns come.'

Jon held her gaze.

'I'll not be keeping Lizzie,' he said.

Greta stared at him. Tears drenched her eyes like a sudden rain shower and she backed away.

'You can't do that,' she said. 'I'm going away from here. I've got the money from the union. I'll take in mending. I'll find a place for us and . . .'

'You won't. They're Sam's bairns and they're going no place. Tell your mam she can't bring the furniture, there isn't room. Tomorrow.'

'No. Not tomorrow and not any day.'

Jon looked hard at her.

'Do you think I'm like Sam, Greta, to be mucked about by you? If you aren't down our house by the time I come off shift tomorrow, I'll come up here and fetch you. Now, I'll organise your things to be brought. You just bring your mam and yourself and the bairn. And don't go being stupid and thinking there's any other way.'

He waited for the argument but nothing happened. Greta stood with her head down, well backed off, and said nothing. Jon went out, slamming the door, letting go of his breath as soon as he got outside, and he thought that if she caused trouble tomorrow he would kill her.

But she was there the next day. Her mother looked gratefully at him and the two older women, to his relief, got on much better than he had thought they would. He had explained to his mother that it was necessary but had thought she would not want her house invaded in this way. He had not thought of how lonely she was with only himself for company, and he was not there most of the time. He had also reckoned without the attraction of her grandson. She loved babies and children and this was a part of Sam that she could never lose. He came back to the usual spotless house and a fine dinner and the sound of his mother laughing, which made him feel better. She was sitting by the fire with the baby in her arms, Greta's mother opposite. They were drinking tea and gossiping. But from the beginning Greta was sullen and silent.

She and her baby had the room next to his and the two women slept downstairs in the front room. They got on with the housework and saw to the baby, but Greta did nothing and never spoke to him.

Jon was on the backshift that fortnight, forcing himself to go, telling himself that there was no choice, coming back when the light was gone, hoping that he might sleep for what was left of the night, sleep and not dream.

Greta and her mother had been there for more than a week before he had the dream. Eight days of Greta's sullen silence and him holding back his temper, eight days of resenting that she was not Lizzie, and the wanting of Lizzie so bad, and the waiting for his brothers to come home from the pit each day like they never would. That night it all jumbled up in his head and it was the worst dream he had ever had.

The roof fell in and he didn't waken, he couldn't. He tried and tried but he couldn't wake up. He wasn't ever going to waken again and there was no air and he couldn't breathe. He couldn't breathe and his lungs were bursting and then there was this awful screaming, and when he came to he didn't know where he was. The shaking was uncontrollable, the sweat was running off him, and worst of all a gold and white vision was there among the wrecked sheets and pillows, taking him in her arms. Nasty sullen Greta, all white nightgown and golden hair, drew him against her.

'Go away,' Jon managed.

'Shh. It's all right now. You're at home.'

He wanted to move away, felt that he would never again have any credibility whatsoever with Greta. She would have the loan of him forever. His mind told him that but his body was still stuck in that black hell and shook and sweated and grieved and couldn't move from her. She drew him closer and he kept his eyes shut against her shoulder. She smelled all clean and normal and now she was stroking his hair. Jon took several deep breaths and then moved back.

'Did I wake you up?'

'I wasn't asleep. I was awake with the bairn. Bairns never sleep much. When the baby's born I'll maybe be able to find somebody to marry me out of your road. Then you and Lizzie can get wed.'

There was a strange guilty look on her face.

'It's not your fault,' he said.

'You don't understand. I should never have married Sam. I didn't make him happy and he didn't make me happy neither. I'm not going to be the cause of making you unhappy and all. I won't do it.'

'Don't you miss him?'

'No. Isn't that awful?' And Greta shuddered. In the next room the baby began to cry and she slid off the bed. As the crying turned into a wail she hurried out. Jon lay back down again in the peaceful silence which followed.

It wasn't dark in the room at all, it had just been his nightmare. The curtains were half-open and the dawn had broken. The room was bathed in light from the new day. Within a minute or two he had closed his eyes and gone to sleep and didn't dream any more.

Ten

*L*izzie walked the four miles for her interview on a cold and windy day. The waves broke hard up the beach. The house was on the coast, not inland, and its gardens went down to the sea. It looked very big to her. There were two sets of gates. Lizzie went in at the second set as instructed by her mother. At the back of the house was a chapel with a small graveyard. There were fields and roads and gates, but Lizzie went over a little bridge and through the trees. She thought that they made the back of the house very dark and gave it a strange feeling. Ahead of her was an archway which led into a big square yard around which stood various buildings.

She knocked on the back door. A young man opened it and Lizzie was ushered inside, through a narrow hallway and up some narrower stairs into a great wide hall which had thick carpets in the middle of it, then up again, up a great wide staircase with the same brightly coloured carpet. The staircase divided into two at a landing halfway up. She followed the left side and went along a hall where there were grand mirrors and further along lots of dark paintings.

The young man opened double doors and Lizzie walked behind him into the biggest room she had ever seen. It seemed to her as big as a whole row of pitmen's cottages. It had cream walls, and rugs on the polished wooden floor. There were oil paintings on every wall and various seats. Two dozen people could have sat there. The chairs were grouped at the fire and around small tables, and there were ornaments and vases of flowers.

A lady was sitting on a sofa, and she smiled and spoke softly and looked so unlike Lizzie's idea of what the mineowner's wife would look like that she had to remind herself not to stare but there was a numbness anyway about her feelings, as if she was not quite there, removed from it all. She had cried herself sick over Jon Armstrong and there had also arisen in her an anger against him, a resentment which she knew was misdirected.

Since he had called off their wedding he had not spoken to her or seen her, in spite of the fact that he and Harold worked together. When they had set off for work one day that week she had actually heard Jon whistling and she had hardened her heart against him. If he didn't care then neither would she but it was not that easy. Living next-door to him, hearing his voice from time to time, from the yard or the kitchen when the door was open, was very hard to bear. And hearing Greta too. And worst of all Greta was determined to be nice to her. Lizzie could have stood anything but that Greta should be nice. First she had stolen Sam and now she had been the cause of Lizzie's complete misery, and it was too much. Lizzie couldn't be nice back and she began to be glad of the numbness. It stopped her thinking of how her wedding should have been. And of the house they would have had, and of being Jon Armstrong's wife. If it had not been for the numbness Lizzie thought that she would have died. And now her mother had made her come here because Harold and Enid were to be married on Saturday and after that there was no reason for Harold to keep his sister. Her mother had also sent her for another reason and that was to get her away from Jon, Lizzie knew.

The lady wore such a bonny frock; it was the kind of material that made you want to reach out and touch it, and she had large green eyes and pretty white teeth and long slender hands which she used when talking. She was older than Lizzie, could even have been as old as Lizzie's mother except that she didn't look it. She asked several questions about Lizzie's family and then she was sent to the housekeeper, which was where she thought she had been going at first. The woman was quite intimidatingly large, dressed entirely in black and with cold round all-seeing eyes. She had a small sitting-room, comfortable enough but quite a contrast to the drawing-room where Lizzie had just been. She told Lizzie that she was to start the following Monday, that she would have one day a fortnight free, and Lizzie trudged all the way home again.

Saturday was the wedding. Lizzie dreaded it. Jon turned up at the chapel with Greta, her mam and his mam, and Greta carried the child. They were all wearing new, albeit sober clothes which Greta's nimble fingers had sewn. Jon looked smarter than Lizzie had ever seen him. And Greta, she thought bitterly, had never looked bonnier than she did in dark colours. No widow had ever looked less distraught than she did that day, the dark-coloured clothes contrasting with her pink and white cheeks, sparkling blue eyes and shiny golden hair.

It was a sweet late-autumn day, the seagulls circling the harbour, the sea blue with a gentle tide as it had been in summer. Lizzie had gone early to the beach, reassuring herself that she would see Jon and feel nothing, but the moment she walked into the chapel with her mam the numbness fell away. The wound was raw and aching and it grew worse, seeing him sitting there next to Greta. He was so tall and fine. Lizzie felt like somebody seeing him for the first time: the long slender hands which had held her to him, the heavily lashed blue eyes, the dark hair, and worst of all he didn't look unhappy. That was the hard part. She suddenly wanted him to look unhappy because Harold and Enid were going to be married today and he and Lizzie couldn't be.

They had a do in the hall which church and chapel shared. A posh do, Lizzie's mam said in disapproval, Enid's mother pretending that she could afford such things. But both mothers had made the food and so there was plenty and good to eat, and Lizzie could not help but watch how often Greta and Jon talked together, and smiled so it seemed at each other, and how he actually took the child from her when it cried, which men never did and which would have occasioned any number of remarks usually but for the way things were. But the child was not his so that when he took Sam's son on to his knee the men pretended they were invisible and the women talked about him in soft tones, and later when Greta went past with the bairn in her arms, Lizzie's mother stopped her and took the baby and said, 'He's a fine bairn.'

Greta smiled but her mouth trembled.

'Hello, Lizzie.'

'Hello.'

'I hear you're starting work at the house on Monday.'

'Well, there's nowt wrong with your hearing, Greta,' Lizzie said, and when her mother's mouth dropped open she got up and walked out of the hall and into the cool of the afternoon. Greta followed her out. Lizzie had walked a little way into the thick long grass beside the hall so Greta went after her and said softly, 'I lost my dad and my husband. I'm as bad off as you.'

'Are you?' Lizzie turned around and watched the barb reach home as she encountered Greta's burning cheeks and guilty eyes.

'It's not my fault,' she said.

'No, it's not your fault that you look so happy, orphaned and widowed. First you took Sam and now it's Jon.'

'He's not – he's not mine.'

'No, he's not yours, he just keeps you and works for you. And your mam and his mam mind the bairn and do the house. You were singing yesterday when you were out the back. You didn't sing when you were Sam's wife.'

Greta's cheeks burned scarlet. Jon walked out of the church hall and said softly, 'The bairn's crying,' and she hurried back inside.

He held Lizzie's eyes with his own.

'So you're leaving tomorrow?'

'I'll be back once a fortnight for my dinner but if you stay inside long enough you won't have to see me,' she said, and would have marched off but that he got hold of her arm, none too gently.

'What?'

Just that, nothing else, but it was the way he looked at her that made Lizzie wish herself out of his sight, out of the way of that severe blue gaze.

'Nothing,' she said, and then she would have gone but that he had so tight a grip on her arm.

'I suppose you think there's something we can do?'

'I didn't say so.'

'You maybe thought it?' His voice was quiet and dangerous.

'No.' Lizzie looked down.

'You just want us all to go around looking miserable, is that it?'

'Greta's not miserable.'

'Greta's not a lot of things.'

'You whistled when you went to work the other day,' Lizzie said, lifting her eyes, finding some anger.

'Oh, I see. I'm meant to go down the road with your Harold blaring my eyes out, am I? The other lads would just love that, wouldn't they? Jon Armstrong's gone soft, they'd say. And do you know what would happen then? They'd eat me alive. I can't afford to have that happen. I have a lot of people to look after.'

'I know that, Jon.'

'There's something you want me to do then? Maybe go on as if there was nothing any different, talk nice to you and put my hands on you and get you like Sam got Greta? Well, that's fine. Just say because that's what I want to do.'

Lizzie was shaking her head.

'No,' she said. 'No, you know I don't. I just . . . I just want you to be sorry.'

'I haven't got any room to be sorry. Alf and Sam are dead and I have to work. I've got Sam's bairns to think about and my mam. I don't want you to go but you don't have any choice now.'

When Lizzie was at the house in her narrow lumpy bed, when she had worked so hard that her legs ached and stopped her from sleeping, she didn't think of how she hadn't married Jon, she didn't think of how she had been made to leave him, she thought of what he had said to her then, the last conversation they had had before she left. Jon had given her no hope because there was none.

Eleven

K ate's aunt had insisted on her learning to dance so that she could go to the New Year's Ball at the Nelsons' house. Her aunt made it a condition of her staying on at the office because Kate hadn't been too well. She caught cold and had a cough for weeks afterwards. Her aunt blamed the office but said if Kate could work she could learn to dance and had a man come out from Sunderland every week to show her the steps.

She had no natural talent for dancing. Mr Withers, the teacher, told her in a frank moment that if her aunt hadn't been paying for her he wouldn't have bothered but there was a twinkle in his eyes when he said it so he and Kate persevered.

She was having to make herself go to work each day. She was heavy-hearted and blamed herself for what had happened to Jon and Lizzie. She told herself the things her father would have said, that God did not take notice of self-centred little fools, but she could not rid herself of the feeling that she was at least partly to blame. She knew that Lizzie had gone off to the Nelson house. Kate had been there for the summer ball and shuddered to think what it must be like to have to work there. It was the gloomiest house she thought she had ever seen and had a strange atmosphere which she could not like. The housekeeper reminded Kate of a dissatisfied crow. She did not know how Lizzie could endure it, but of course Lizzie had no choice. Kate was very sorry too that Jon was so hard-worked to look after a family his brother had – according to gossip – produced because he had not the sense to do anything better, and Lizzie was up at the house in a situation so bad that Kate awoke at three in the morning shuddering to think of it.

Kate saw Jon at least from a distance almost every day. She could pick him out and to her surprise he did not look any different. He had not lost the energy in his stride or the way that he talked and laughed with his friends. He was just the same, tall and slender against Harold who was getting quite fat. Perhaps Harold's new wife was too good a cook, Kate thought. And Jon had a new friend, a man called Eddie Bitten, who had come over from the far side of Durham to live with his aunt, in her house two doors away from Jon's after her husband died.

Kate had seen him when he first came to the office and had thought at the time that he was rather like Jon, tall and slim and good-looking. There the resemblance ended. Eddie was a big Methodist, her uncle had said in relieved tones, he did not drink or swear or fight. He went to chapel twice on Sundays and to Bible class and to other chapel social events, but somehow he and Jon became friends and she saw them laughing together and arguing amiably as they went home. Her uncle hoped that Eddie might have some influence on Jon though he had bigger things to worry about.

There was throughout the county the threat of strike action by the miners. Kate was very well-informed. She knew Mr Pearson of the Durham Miners' Association, a neat little man in a suit who, according to her uncle, was trying to remedy the situation by persuading the miners at various lodge meetings that it was the wrong time of the year for a strike but there was unrest and you could see it in the men's faces.

Life at the house was every bit as bad as Lizzie had thought it would be. She had to work very hard indeed. She carried huge buckets of coal up to the various rooms every day because the weather was cold and the rooms were big and there were lots of fires to be fuelled and fireplaces to be cleaned and grates to be blacked and ashes to be taken out. There was other cleaning to be done too, and beds to make, and so much clearing away and clearing up after people. If there was a special occasion there were chandeliers to be taken down, every piece of glass washed and dried and polished, and there was also the never-ending laundry, the ladies' underthings to be rinsed in lavender. There was furniture to be polished and crockery to be washed and silver to be cleaned. Worst of all there were dinner parties, when the clearing and washing up and other work went on until the early hours of the morning so that sometimes Lizzie was hardly in bed before she had to get up and see to the kitchen fire which had to be lit before the cook descended.

The kitchen was huge. It was cold when the weather was cold and sweltering when the fires were on, and it had different little rooms going off it in which different tasks were performed. The little rooms were dark from the trees outside which prevented the light getting in and during the winter knocked their branches against the windows. The rooms had no heating and during that winter they were at iceberg temperature.

In the arctic-desert regions Lizzie slaved. The other side of the house was like a palace to her at first but on the servants' side of the door there was always the smell of stale vegetables and rancid fat. The servants' quarters had dark poky rooms and the bedroom where Lizzie slept on the first floor was occupied by a fat rosy girl called Madge, the other kitchen maid. She snored and kept Lizzie awake until she was too tired by her sixteen-hour day to be kept awake any longer.

Officially Lizzie was a kitchen maid who peeled vegetables and assisted the cook and got shouted at a lot for not getting things right, but she found herself doing the housemaid's job just as often.

She hated dinner parties most of all because of the vegetables. Spinach was the worst. It was grown in the big hot glass house so there was always spinach, so much of it, to be washed and washed in icy water – and after all that effort it went to nothing by the time it was cooked and sieved and buttered. During the autumn there was grouse. The smell of it cooking was, Lizzie thought, somewhere between turpentine and burned heather and it went into the dining-room and came back picked at or untouched. Lizzie got to eat a lot of grouse because the servants were given the left-overs. When the dinners were good and there was not much left, which happened often, Lizzie ate badly or not at all and thought with longing of her mother's cooking. When she went home her mother would give her food to take back with her and feed her a proper Sunday dinner. Going home was wonderful.

On the first Sunday she dropped down on to the beach to walk home because it was the quickest way and the tide was well out, and saw somebody tall in dark Sunday best waiting for her. Her heart soared like a bird. Jon had walked the four miles, bridged the gap between their lives, and the misery slid away from her. Her smile nearly split her face though she tried not to show it.

'Jon!'

'Now.'

Lizzie pushed on her hat.

'I didn't think you'd come all this way.'

'All what way?' His eyes danced.

'Well . . . my, you're a picture.'

Jon laughed and they set off. He asked her if she was all right and Lizzie swallowed the complaints that were on her tongue's edge. They talked all the way back, lightly, easily. He told her everything that had happened in the village that fortnight that she might want to know about. Lizzie made it funny when she told him about the house, Fat Madge snoring and the housekeeper with her keys and pompous face.

He left her at the back gate and Lizzie's mother fed her the best Sunday dinner of her whole life, and over the meal she told them all about the big house and what happened there. Her mam wouldn't let her wash up, Enid did the clearing away. Lizzie sat by the fire with Harold and drank tea. Before she went back her mother made her up a package of pies and scones and cake to keep her going. At the end of the afternoon when she set off back Jon was waiting for her. The tide was in but they could walk across the top of the dunes.

'You can't go back with me,' she said.

'What for?'

'That's sixteen miles, Jon.'

'And me so old and little and all. Howay.'

Still Lizzie hesitated.

'What's the book?' she asked, regarding the small volume in his hand.

'It's for you.' And he handed it to her.

'I don't have much time to read,' she said.

Jon looked anxiously at her.

'Take it anyroad.'

Lizzie took it.

'Poetry? Wherever did you have it?'

'Just sort of . . . came by it.'

Lizzie laughed.

'Jon Armstrong. If the other lads ever knew you read poetry . . .'

'I don't,' he said hastily, 'I just thought you might.'

Lizzie looked down at the book.

'You know I still can't tell when you're fibbing. I bet you could reel off pages of it.'

'I don't know what makes you think so. Howay, or you'll be late.'

Lizzie followed him on to the beach. The tide was well up and the day was icy. Jon walked without talking.

'Our Harold says there's going to be trouble,' Lizzie announced. 'Do you think he's right, Jon?'

'Trouble?'

'Yes.' Jon didn't answer. 'Well?' she prompted.

'Your Harold talks too much.'

'Nobody could accuse you of that. Tell me about it. I don't know what our Harold's talking about.'

'Nothing's happened yet. It probably won't either. You don't need to worry.'

'I worry more when nobody tells me. Is our Harold right or not?'

'Maybe,' Jon said finally. 'The price of coal's gone down.'

'What for?'

'Because there's a lot of it about, there's less demand. It works on a sliding scale. Less profit is made and wages go down accordingly.'

'How far is accordingly?'

'We don't know yet.'

'Harold says fifteen percent, maybe twenty. Isn't that an awful lot?'

'It's a lot,' Jon said, setting off to walk again.

'A fifth,' Lizzie said. 'Can we live on a fifth less?'

'We might have to.'

'But the coalowners are rich. You should see Mr Nelson's house, Jon. Carpets made 'specially in bright colours, and a library. Walls and walls of books – and paintings of people. They have people to dinner all the time, and the food . . . there are chandeliers and great long tables. They can't do it, Jon.'

'That's the trouble,' he said smoothly. 'They can do it. They've picked the right time of year, they're so cunning. Anyway, nowt's decided yet so don't worry about it. It might never happen.'

Twelve

C hristmas at the house meant more work than ever but there was a kind of excitement. In the first place Charles Nelson was coming home. Madge and the other young ones among the maids had told Lizzie that he was a handsome young gentleman. He had gone to Oxford and afterwards had been abroad and now was due home for the festivities.

A huge Christmas tree was put up in the front hall. Lizzie helped decorate it and it was the first time that she had enjoyed any of her duties. Things had been a lot worse lately. She didn't know quite why because the work had not become any harder. It was, she thought, just the going on of it all, the endless monotonous day after day. The only pleasure was when she went home once a fortnight, but lately the pleasure had gone from that too. Jon was starting to treat her just like he treated everybody else and that meant he no longer came to meet her. She understood, at least she thought she did, why he didn't walk backwards and forwards with her. People would talk, think that they were still a couple, and they themselves might believe it too. Usually she didn't see him at all on her day off and when she made careful enquiries about next-door it seemed that Greta never went out so that she could make known to the local lads she wanted to remarry. At first Lizzie thought this might be some kind of delicacy on Greta's part because she was pregnant and then she dismissed this thought. Greta hadn't a delicate bone in her body. She was sitting pretty next-door.

When Lizzie did come home it was not to a happy house. Harold was more talkative than he had ever been, telling high tales of Jon and himself drinking, so that Enid and Lizzie's mother were silent – no doubt, Lizzie imagined, thinking of the money that Harold would spend. He also talked of work and of the threat of a strike, but not of saving a little in case the worst happened.

On the Sunday after Charles had arrived Lizzie thought about him and had to admit that she had been rather disappointed. He was well enough. He was educated, rich, well-spoken, expensively dressed, and he greeted the housekeeper with charm. The house could be a better, lighter place with him in it but there was something about Charles which she did not care for, and after a few days she knew that it was his indolence.

At Christmas there was no time off for her, just more work, with the cook in a bad mood because all the meals had to be special, and the housekeeper in a bad mood because there were guests. Lizzie never stopped. Young ladies and gentlemen came to stay and more of them came for the parties and the dancing. The house was suddenly full of laughter. It made Lizzie feel more lonely than ever. The young ladies got up late because they had danced most of the night; spent a lot of time over breakfast, not eating much but talking and giggling. In the afternoons, after a huge luncheon during which there were more guests, they went riding or walking if the day was crisp and fine, which the days over Christmas were, and in the evenings they romped as much as their parents would allow.

If there was no entertainment at the house there was something organised elsewhere and they went off early and came back very late. Lizzie had never seen such idle people, nor such pretty dresses – prettier by far than the rose pink dress which she had worn at May's wedding when she had first thought that she and Jon might be together.

One day she turned when she had been cleaning out grates and saw her own reflection in the mirror in the dining-room; she thought that she looked like a crow, thin and in black and with smudges under her eyes because she was so tired. If she hadn't been so tired she would have cried in her bed but she never did.

Sometimes before her candle went out she took from beneath her pillow the one book which she had in her possession. It was a selection of nineteenth-century poets. She wondered what Jon was doing with such a book and why on earth he had given it to her, but lacking anything else to read, she had looked at it and found that it was the perfect book for somebody with very little time. She could even read just a couple of lines and be comforted and find pleasure in the rhythm of the words. It didn't always make sense the first or the second time she read but mostly after a while it did and she had even memorised some of it. It was like carrying a cushion about with her, easing things for herself as she went about her hardest tasks.

And yet if anybody had told her that she would do such a thing she would have laughed and said they were daft. At night she clutched the book to her. It was all she seemed to have left of Jon, that and his silence. He had inscribed it too, in flowing black letters: 'To Lizzie, with love from Jon', and the date. Quite simple. Lizzie thought it was the most wonderful book in the world. It was her private world which no one could barge into and damage. Not this time.

For the night of the servants' dance Lizzie had brought from home the rose pink dress. That evening also the servants were to be given presents from the big tree in the hall and she was quite excited. She had never spent a Christmas entirely without presents and when she was called, after Madge, to the tree and given a good-sized heavy package by Mrs Nelson she went back to the tiny freezing bedroom and tore open the paper. She kept her eyes closed until she could see what was in the package the moment that she opened them and could look down upon her Christmas present. It felt like material. She remembered all the pretty colours, the pastel shades and rich satins which the girls had worn, and grew very excited indeed. Then she opened her eyes and could not believe what she saw. It was indeed material. It was the coarsest, ugliest, sickly yellow-green that with her looks she could never have worn. She put it back into the paper and slid it under the bed and then she washed in cold water and put on her dress and brushed out her hair and went downstairs to the dance only because she knew that she had to.

Lizzie didn't know how to dance; chapel and dancing did not mix and she had not been taught. So it was lucky that nobody asked her. The butler danced with the housekeeper and then with the cook, and the chauffeur danced with Mrs Nelson's personal maid, and Mr Nelson's man danced with every woman except Madge and Lizzie because although they did all kinds of work they were after all the kitchen maids when it came to everyone knowing their place. Only the stable lad asked her to dance and she pretended that she didn't hear him.

That was the night she went to bed and for the first time let herself remember how she had felt when Jon Armstrong pulled her down on to a bed beside him, and kissed her, and told her how good he would be to her and that he would never care for another lass like he cared for her. She was not going home for another week and even then it was unlikely that she would see him and even if she did she couldn't say anything to him. She couldn't touch him.

All she had was the memory of his sweet mouth and hard young body, of his promises and his bitterness and his love for her. She lay awake with her eyes closed and listened to Madge snoring.

Thirteen

*T*he strike began after Christmas. The union had tried to persuade the
men to accept the cut but, when it became obvious that they were all
solidly behind the idea of strike, urged them out. Kate sat in her office late
and watched them streaming out of the lodge meeting. She should have been
at home long since but she ran out after Jon, causing some of the men to stop
and stare, though nobody made funny remarks, their mood was too depressed
for that. Jon didn't look too pleased when she caught hold of his sleeve or
when she called him by his name.

'Jon! What's happened?'

He frowned but stopped. Eddie Bitten was with him, and Harold, behind
them Rob, May's husband, and his friend Ken.

'What's happened?' she said again, and heard Rob say in an undertone,
'Don't tell her owt, she'll tell Farrer.'

'It doesn't make any difference,' Jon said. 'We're out.'

'Oh, Jon, no.'

As he stood with her the other men streamed past; even Eddie went though
she doubted he was going off as the others were to the pub.

'You shouldn't be here at this time of night,' Jon said.

'I couldn't go home. What will happen now?'

'I don't know.'

'There's all the winter,' she said, 'and the children to think about.' She
looked sharply at him. 'Did you vote to go out?'

'I suppose it's your business, Miss Farrer?'

'You did. How could you?'

'The whole county's going out,' he said.

'Oh, yes. That's probably what Pearson went around telling everybody,'

93

she said bitterly, and then saw the way Jon looked at her.

The other men were all gone now.

'I didn't want to go out,' Jon said, 'it's the wrong time. We've let them choose the weapons and the timing. If it was me I'd wait. I'd let them think they'd won, wait until they needed us, until we were in a position of power.'

'And if the price of coal goes down further?'

'Aye, well, you pays your money and you takes your chances. Nobody's listening. But this isn't just for now, it's about everything that went before. They get to you if you live long enough. The men only want to hear one kind of talk and it isn't the kind you and me are thinking about. They've run out of patience. You can't ask them to wait any more, so really it isn't a question of wanting to.'

Kate was quite excited. She had never heard Jon talk like this before. Usually he talked to her like she was certain he talked to other women, all soft-voiced and flirtatious.

'What is it a question of?' she said.

'They own it. They own the whole bloody earth as far as we're concerned, and they'll go on owning it as long as we go on letting them because they're cleverer than we are and because we let them – but we are as entitled to it as they are and either way they're trying to starve us.' He seemed to remember who he was talking to at that point and stopped. 'Have you got somebody to see you home?'

Kate was terribly disappointed.

'I don't want to go,' she said.

'It's late. What's your uncle thinking about, letting you come out?'

'He doesn't know I'm here,' she said.

'Oh, I see. It's a down the drainpipe job, is it?'

'No. I sneaked out of the back door.'

'And what if it's locked when you get back?'

'It won't be yet.'

'Go and get your coat and I'll see you home.'

She was uncomfortably cold without it but didn't want to go.

'I'm not going,' she said flatly, and that spoiled it. Jon stopped talking to her like they were friends, and begged her pardon, Miss Farrer. She winced under the sarcasm and ran to the office. She hastily put on and buttoned her coat, thinking that he might have gone off and left her, but he was waiting outside. He didn't say anything though, for so long that Kate stopped so far through the streets and said, 'Talk to me.'

'What about?'

'Like before. About things.'

'I don't know owt.'

'You mean "I know nowt",' said Kate, trying to imitate a northern accent. She won from Jon what was just a smile.

'Aye.'

'But you do. You should have been at Oxford by now, Jon.'

He laughed.

'I can just see it,' he said.

'But you should,' she insisted. 'If you had some kind of an education you could do much more.'

'Are we talking power here?'

'Education is power,' she said.

Jon didn't reply for a few moments as they walked and then he said, 'Did you never hear the story about the local lad who was caught trespassing on the lord's land?'

'No. Tell me.'

'Well, the lord told him to get off and the lad said, "How did you come by the land then?" And Lordy said, "My ancestors fought for it," and the lad said, "Take thy coat off then and let's thou and me fight for it." The coalowners aren't daft. They timed it and gambled that we'd maybe give in without a fight—'

'Some fight,' Kate said, 'with children involved.'

'Maybe, but it has to be because there isn't any other road left for us.'

When they reached her house Jon said only, 'Are you sure you can get in?'

'I think so.'

'I'll wait a few minutes, and then if you can't we'll think of something else.'

'My bedroom window's unlatched.'

'I can just see you shinning up a drainpipe.'

'I can though,' she said.

'You surprise me.'

'Thank you, Jon. Goodnight.'

'Goodnight, Miss Farrer.'

'Don't "Miss Farrer" me. My aunt and uncle call me Katherine but my father called me Kate and so can you if you want.' And she ran off around to the back before he could think of a suitable reply.

Kate was obliged to attend the New Year's party at the Nelsons' house. Her aunt had had made for her a lovely dress in amber satin which flattered her creamy skin. Kate hated it.

'I don't see why I should be taken out and paraded like a doll,' she fumed as Ellen helped her to pack. Ellen said nothing and Kate wished that she had held her tongue. Ellen would have given a lot for a dress like that, for a party and well-to-do young men. It would not have surprised Kate if Ellen had thought she was a spoiled stupid female. She and Ellen were too far apart to have even a thought in common, not like she and Lizzie. She hoped to see Lizzie that night, to speak to her. It was the only thing she was looking forward to.

They were going early and staying overnight; the horse would be stabled because the nights were dark and long. Kate well knew that her uncle and aunt were considered nobodies in society and wondered whether they were asked because of Charles. At the summer party he had spent a lot of time with her, more than he should have, so that she was singled out. Kate could not but think that his parents would have liked not to invite her again – she had neither money nor position and was hardly the kind of girl whom Charles would have been encouraged to be with – but the invitation had come and her aunt was flattered to be asked to spend the night and to go to a ball where they would be totally outclassed. It made Kate shudder to think about it. She thought about the night when Jon had walked her home, and cared more for that than for any number of young men at social events like this. No one but her father and recently her uncle had ever talked sensibly to her, no young man but Jon had taken her seriously. Unfortunately Kate had dreamed about Jon's kissing her so perhaps it wasn't altogether the elevated talk which had impressed her.

She was given a pretty room with a big fire and a view of the sea and was about to begin unpacking her bag when there was a knock on the door. When she said 'come in', the door opened and Lizzie appeared.

The sight of her was a shock to Kate. She was now as thin as Kate herself, and nobody looking at her could have pretended that she was anything but very unhappy. She also looked tired. This did not stop her from smiling broadly, and saying as though delighted, 'Miss Farrer. It's you.'

'Yes, it's me,' Kate said, and was instantly ashamed, firstly of having dreamed about Jon – though what she could have done to prevent this was not immediately apparent to her – and secondly that she had ever grumbled about her life. She was a girl about to go to a party, and another girl had been sent to wait on her.

'I'm so glad to see you, Miss. How are you?'

'I'm very well.'

'They sent me to look after you, though I'm not sure what to do. I'm better with pots and pans.'

Her chapped red hands gave evidence of this.

'I don't need looking after. Sit down.' And Kate urged her to have a seat by the fire.

Lizzie had brought with her a tea tray and they settled by the fire and Kate poured Lizzie two big cupfuls and gave her two large pieces of spice cake.

'Don't you want any?' Lizzie said through a mouthful of crumbs.

'No, I'm fine. Don't they feed you?'

'Not if they can help it and I haven't been home for weeks. My mam usually stocks me up.' And Lizzie laughed. 'I'm supposed to do your unpacking.'

'There's nothing to do, and I took out my dress so that it wouldn't crease.'

'Oh, let's have a look at it,' Lizzie said, and Kate got up obligingly and showed her the dress. 'It's beautiful,' Lizzie sighed.

Kate amused her with tales of the dancing teacher and her own clumsiness but what she really wanted to do was to grab Lizzie's hand and run down the stairs and out of the front door. After that Lizzie had to go but she would be back to do Kate's hair and help her to dress. Kate had nothing to do but read by the fire or lie on the bed. Lizzie had to help with the dinner.

Later, when Kate stood in front of the full-length mirror in the bedroom, ready to go down to the dance, she could see Lizzie's thin face behind her.

'You look a treat, Miss, you really do.'

Kate turned to her impulsively.

'I wish we weren't here. I wish we could be friends.'

'I thought we were friends, sort of.'

'Did you? I like to think of us like that too. I must go down. Don't wait up for me, Lizzie.'

'I'm supposed to.'

'I'll help myself out of this wretched outfit. You look as though you could sleep for a week.' Kate went to the door and there she paused again. 'Are you worried about the strike?'

'Yes, are you?'

'I hate the Nelsons,' said Kate before she opened the door.

When the celebrations were over and the house was back to normal it snowed so much that Lizzie feared she would not get home. She confided this worry to Madge but the other girl scorned her fears.

'It could be all gone by then,' she said. 'You never get a lot of snow at the seaside, now do you?'

Charles and his father had a disagreement that morning. Lizzie didn't hear them, she was too busy in the kitchen, but when the servants sat down to eat their main meal in the middle of the day, Tammy the parlourmaid told her that Mr Nelson had shouted so much he could be heard all over the top of the house and it was not for the first time either. Lately there had been other rows. Tammy said that it had been all about Master Charles's work.

Lizzie finished her lumpy custard and stale cake and went back to her own work, but later that day when she was attending to the neglected library fire – neglected because nobody but Charles ever went in there – he and one of his friends were in the room. Lizzie was about to bob back out when he called to her to attend to the fire, and then they both ignored her and went on talking.

'He wants me to learn about the mines, go into the office like any clerk. That's what he has mine managers for, so that *he* doesn't have to do that, but he expects *me* to. I've slaved for three years at college. I think he might give me a little time now.'

His friend murmured agreement. Lizzie stacked up the fire and left. There was further trouble the next day and Charles flung out of the house and went riding until dark.

The strike was now in its third week against the twenty per cent wage cut. She couldn't imagine that people didn't need coal in this weather but it seemed that there was much more stored than was needed, the price had dropped, and Mr Nelson, according to servants' gossip, was pleased that the men had come out because now he wouldn't have to pay them during the bad weather. By Lizzie's day off there was twice as much snow and she didn't get to go home, which Cook said was just as well because there was plenty of work to do. She spent her day off in a freezing little room with her hands in cold water, peeling potatoes.

The weather grew steadily worse. Lizzie didn't get home inside a month and during that time Charles Nelson found every opportunity to speak to her. In her heart Lizzie knew why. In spite of her thinness and the hurt that wouldn't heal she was now the way that she thought Jon had known she would be. Her skin and teeth were good, her black hair was thick, her lips were scarlet without any help. Her lashes were long and her cheeks slightly flushed when she had had a decent night's sleep. She was taller than most girls, her hands and feet were long and slender. Her breasts and hips strained against the now too small dresses. She kept her eyes lowered, did her work so that no one could complain, but the harder she tried the more people complained about what she did and Lizzie knew that she was no longer seen as an asset to the household.

She didn't know when Charles Nelson first noticed her. It was days before she saw that where she was he contrived to be and she was not so much in the kitchen now since one of the housemaids had left and had not been replaced. Lizzie had the kind of promotion which meant that she constantly carried huge buckets of coal to every room in the house and spent a great deal of time taking the ashes out of the grates and building up the fires. It was hard dirty work and she thought it no better than the kitchen but at least a new kitchen maid was taken on so she did not have to fit in both. Where she was, Charles appeared. At first he didn't talk to her. He had more sense than to do that; he was just around.

The last Sunday in February the weather was bright and cold but the snow was deep and Lizzie had been given the day off. She thought that she would not live another day unless she went home, it had been so long. She *had* to get there. She had not gone far from the house, the wind raging its bitter way across the icy beach, when she heard the horse behind her and the rider was Charles.

Inwardly she argued with herself. She had no liking for him but knew that she would not make the distance to the village if he did not take her up on to his horse as he suggested. She didn't want to turn back so she agreed and he helped her. She climbed clumsily and then clung to his back because she had not been so near to a horse before and was quite terrified. It was much quicker than walking though and she was grateful to him. She thought she would burst if she didn't see her mam.

When they reached the outskirts of the village she thanked him and slid down and ran up the beach and into her house. He hadn't offered to come back for her and Lizzie was grateful. She prayed that it would snow more so that she could not possibly go back, but she knew that if that happened she would lose her position and though not to go back would have been the nearest thing to heaven she was ashamed of such thoughts when she went into the house.

The fire was low in the grate because there was not much coal and what there was had to be eked out, and the meal was as frugal as any she had had that week. The house was chilly and the family were quiet. Harold went to bed as he usually did on Sundays to sleep for a couple of hours and Enid and Lizzie's mother popped next-door to hear if there had been any news of May's baby which was due at any time. Only five minutes had gone by before Jon walked in and Lizzie, who had been hoping for some quiet, just half an hour to read, put down her book with some reluctance until she saw who it was and got to her feet. They hadn't been alone together for weeks.

'Jon.'

He didn't say hello, he didn't say that it was nice to see her, that he had missed her, that he was glad she had come home, or ask if Christmas had been all right at the house and how she was getting on. He closed the door.

'Your mam says somebody brought you.'

Lizzie had been vague on purpose. Her mother would not accept that she could have walked and had wanted an explanation. Silently she cursed Jon's active mind.

'Turned the carriage out for you, did they?' His voice was soft but Lizzie wasn't deceived. It was a long time since she had been on the heavy end of Jon's temper and it wasn't pleasant.

'No.'

'What then?'

Like it was his business, Lizzie thought, fuming.

'Master Charles brought me. On his horse.'

Jon's blue eyes snapped.

'Charles Nelson brought you here?'

'What did you think I did? Flew?' Lizzie said, her own temper getting the better of her. 'You don't know what it's like there and not being able to come home at all.'

Jon's face was dark.

'His father's starving us.'

She glared at him. There was silence. Lizzie prayed that Harold would wake up and bluster his way downstairs and into the room but nothing happened. She felt awful. He was treating her as though she didn't know she was doing wrong.

'I wanted to come home bad. I wanted to see my mam.'

'What did he do it for?'

'What?'

'You heard me,' Jon said loudly, making her jump. 'What did he do it for?'

'He did it for nothing,' Lizzie retaliated though her hands shook.

'Well,' she hated the sarcasm in his voice, 'he must be the first lad that ever did owt for a lass for nowt back! This strike's not over yet, it's nowhere near over. Don't you do things like that.'

'I'll do what I like,' Lizzie said between clenched teeth. 'Charles Nelson is a gentleman. He's no ignorant pitlad.'

She could have bitten her tongue out. He said nothing. He said nothing for so long that Lizzie wrapped her arms across her front and stilled her quivering bottom lip. And he didn't look at her when he finally said softly, 'If it wasn't for ignorant pitlads he wouldn't be a gentleman, Lizzie.'

'No, I know.'

'And you are a pitlass. Don't forget it. He won't.' And Jon walked out.

The strike went on. The pitmen and their families stole from the pit heaps to keep their fires going. By the time it was Lizzie's day to go home again Charles offered to take her to the village. The snow was trodden but deep in places so she agreed. He also carried a big sack on the horse and when he let her down some way from the village – it was a big tide that day, they had come by road which was much further than the beach or walking across the dunes – he gave the sack into her hands.

'What is it?'

'It's for you. A present. Courtesy of my dear father.'

He rode off. Lizzie opened the bag. It was full of dead rabbits. Jon was in the back lane as she struggled along. It looked as though he had walked May to their house for dinner. She carried in her arms the new baby girl. Lizzie smiled over the baby and said all the right things and then May went to take the child out of the cold.

'Do you want a hand with that?' Jon asked.

'I can manage,' Lizzie said, but she couldn't and as Jon turned to go into his own yard she tripped over and some of the contents spilled. He glanced across and then stared.

'Wherever did you get those?' he said softly, and fastened the bag up tightly.

'You'd better take them into your house,' Lizzie declared, 'my mam would have a fit.'

She would have left him there with them but that he gripped her arm and when she looked at him his eyes were dark with concern.

'Come in here,' he said, and dragged her up the yard and into the house, past the women in the kitchen. He took no notice of their stares but pushed her into the chilly front room and shut the door. It was so cold in there that Lizzie could see her breath but the room was shining clean.

'What have you done?' he said.

'I haven't done nothing. He gave them to me.'

'What?'

Lizzie glanced at him, at his furious expression. He didn't let go of her either and his was a grip that bruised.

'Have you let him bring you on that horse again? Don't you ever listen?'

Lizzie tried to pull free but couldn't. 'You're hurting my arm.'

Jon let go and she rubbed it and then said, 'It's nowt to do with the strike or with me. It's him and his dad. They fight.'

'They do what?'

'His dad wants him to work in the offices,' Lizzie explained. 'They don't get on.'

'And he gets back at his father through us? What is he, a bairn?'

'What's it matter? It's food, isn't it?'

Jon hesitated but only for a second and then he sighed.

'Sometimes I think you're as daft as any of them. What when they find out these have gone? What if they find out it was you?'

'How will they find out?'

Jon was quiet for a moment or two and then he spoke slowly as though addressing a child.

'It only takes one person to see, one person to think something is happening. It's not just one or two rabbits, it's a whole sackful. If they find out you'll go to prison. You, not him. Are you listening?'

'I would still have done it,' she said, 'the village is hungry.'

'They made the choice, not you. You're out there working to keep your family and nobody thinks it's easy. You're doing everything you should be, and more.'

'Sam's dead, and Alf. My dad and yours. I'd do it again.'

'No, please, Lizzie, I'm asking you. You're putting the wind up me.'

In the end she promised but the following fortnight the same thing happened except that Charles didn't let her straight down, he kissed her, briefly and for the first time, on the lips. Lizzie let him but only because she knew it for payment. She didn't want Charles to kiss her and she didn't kiss him back in case he was encouraged and might want to do it again.

She slid down and took the sack from him and it was only after she had stepped back and he had ridden away and she had started up the path from the freezing beach that she stopped short. Jon was standing against the edge of the gable end of the first house, watching her, and his eyes were as warm as a snow storm.

Lizzie wanted to defend herself but she couldn't think how to explain away a kiss with Jon knowing that she had never let anybody else near her. She wanted to tell him that she loved him but she couldn't while he was looking at her like that.

'You promised,' he said.

Lizzie's cheeks burned but she lifted her chin and answered stoutly, 'You didn't think much of my promise. You're here.'

'Aye, I'm here.'

He didn't move and he was so thin that Lizzie was worried. After a long silence she said, 'Things bad?'

'May's baby died Thursday.'

'Oh, Jon, no.' But she knew that his silence wasn't for May's baby or for the bad way that things were in the village, it was for the kiss that he had seen an educated young man bestow upon her apparently eager lips and that he would die rather than ask about.

'Will you carry it for me?' she said.

'You carry it. You earned it.' And he walked away, up the row and in by his back gate.

Lizzie called his name twice but it made no difference, and then she was so frightened that she was going to cry that she stayed out there for some time wishing things otherwise.

The snow began to melt that day and a pale sun crept into the sky. Later the wind sang around the houses in the village, a good strong biting wind to help shift the snow away. The softer weather when it came was too late – the men had given in and gone back, and for the twenty per cent cut. They were saying that it had all been for nothing. Kate knew that several old people had died with the cold weather and lack of decent food, but she didn't feel that the men had been wrong to try, and as for May's baby, Mrs Armstrong said that she thought there had been something wrong from the beginning. Kate could see the relief on the men's faces their first day back at work. Even the low seams – as little as two to three feet high where the men hewed the coal – the darkness and the bad wages were better than watching your family starve. It was a heavy defeat but it was better than nothing.

The best thing to come out of the strike from Kate's point of view was that she had gone over one day to see how they were coping and had been so warmly received by Jon's mother that from time to time she visited again and heard all the local gossip.

Greta's baby was almost due. Kate was fascinated. She had never had anything to do with babies and was looking forward to seeing it while it was small. She liked Tommy, Greta and Sam's son, and that winter spent several happy hours on a Sunday afternoon, sitting by the fire with the Armstrongs, showing Tommy his few toys and eating the cakes which came magically wonderful from Mrs Armstrong's oven. Sometimes she went next-door as well to see Lizzie. She thought that Lizzie's mother looked suspiciously at her at first but it didn't last. She never told her aunt where she was going, just that she went walking, because she knew that her aunt and uncle would have disapproved and might even have forbidden her this new and interesting company.

The Armstrongs were open and kind people. Since leaving London Kate had not met such hospitality, though she thought that Mrs Armstrong looked hard at her when she argued with Jon – which she did all the time about books and politics and anything else he cared to express an opinion about. She thought also that Greta didn't like her. She and Greta somehow crowded one another. It seemed to Kate that Greta liked Jon more than she should have liked her brother-in-law, and Kate wondered whether he noticed. She herself heartily disliked Greta, not just because Greta was blonde and blue-eyed as Kate had wanted to be herself but because Jon treated her like a piece of Sunday best china, as his mother would have said. Greta's mother was a skinny little woman for whom nothing was ever right. Kate could not have imagined that anyone could be so miserable. She told Jon that it was probably because her husband had died, but he said they never got on, so it couldn't have been that.

The day that Greta went into labour Jon called at the office to tell Kate. At mid-day when she rushed across to the Armstrong house the downstairs was empty. Mrs Armstrong came down the stairs slowly.

'Oh, Kate,' she said.

'Is Greta all right?'

Jon's mother paused.

'We've had to send for the doctor.'

Kate knew how serious things must be. The doctor was expensive and the Armstrongs were poor. She had to go back to work then. When the day was over she longed to go back and find out what had happened but was obliged to go home with her uncle and endure a meal and worry. The following day she had to wait until Jon came on shift, and then he popped into her tiny office and his face told her that he had nothing good to say. She shut the door after him.

'What happened?'

'Greta lost the bairn.'

'I'm so sorry. Will she be all right?'

'I don't know. She'll need a lot of care. The doctor says she won't have any more.'

Kate stared at him. She knew as well as he did what this meant. He would never be able to marry Lizzie now. No man would take on a woman who couldn't have sons to keep their parents in old age. He would always have to keep Greta and her son and her mother and his own.

'There must be something you can do,' she said fiercely.

'Like what?'

'You must go to college.'

Jon didn't even laugh at her like he had before when she had suggested it.

'You're dreaming, Kit,' he said. Lately he had started calling her by this shortened version of her name. Kate liked it so much she didn't know how to think, but today was different.

'Sunderland is near enough. You could go to classes.'

'In my sleep,' he said, turning to the door. 'I'm going to be late.'

'You could learn mining engineering.'

'I know enough about mining to last me.'

'No, you don't, not really. You could if you really wanted to.'

'Maybe I don't really want to then,' Jon said wearily.

'What are you going to do – keep on like this?'

'I have to go to work. I have the doctor to pay.'

'My uncle did it and he's not as clever as you.'

Jon looked at her. 'When I come out of that pit, I haven't got anything left but I have to keep doing it. I have five people to support. You maybe think I like it?'

'It isn't fair,' she said bitterly.

'Come on, Kit, grow up,' he said, and went to work.

Greta was very ill. She didn't leave her bed for several weeks. Jon would carry her up and downstairs. Every time Kate ventured to the house when Jon was at home he was sitting with her. She was very sorry to discover that she was the kind of person who could be jealous of a girl who was ill. Greta was almost transparent. She looked to Kate like pictures she had seen of The Lady of the Lake, with her long blonde hair and frail limbs, lying on the sofa when she was a little better. Jon tried to teach her to play chess. Kate could have told him that Greta was too stupid to be any good at such things but he persevered and was a good enough teacher that she learned the moves and even a little bit of skill. It seemed to Kate that Greta was forever smiling into Jon's eyes during those days and she couldn't think why he put up with such a dull girl, but of course Greta was ethereally beautiful. She made Kate feel as clumsy as a carthorse.

The warm weather came and Greta got better so that now when Kate called they were out walking on the beach and sometimes she saw them, Greta with her shoes and stockings off walking in the shallow water and Jon beside her just above the waterline, walking slowly with their heads down, talking. Whatever did they find to talk about, the girl whose empty-headedness meant that she could not master a game and the young man who loved books? And then it came to Kate. Jon had been frightened when Greta almost died, that God had made an unbearable decision and was going to kill her so that Jon could have his dearest wish – and so now he had to treat her with great care.

Fourteen

*L*izzie was sent home that summer. No explanations were given. She was told by the housekeeper that she wasn't needed. She knew why. Charles was the reason. In fact she had done all that she could to discourage him but even she could see through the little cracked glass in her bedroom that she was now prettier than she had ever been and no uniform could disguise the fact that if she had regular good food she would be beautiful.

The young men who visited the house tried all ways to be alone with her but she avoided them. She also avoided Charles, but it was not enough. He wanted to be with her and since she could not be rude to him he did not understand her refusals. He wanted to spend her free Sundays with her when all the time she was longing to go home, and in the end his father and mother saw what was about and got rid of her.

She knew that she must look for another post and dreaded it. She could not believe that first day, waking up in her own house, small and shabby though it was. She turned over. The bed was clean and comfortable and her mother had gone downstairs and was singing hymns in the kitchen in a clear voice. Harold and Enid had the other room upstairs but no child was in evidence so nobody had accused her of being one too many mouths to feed or taking up room when there wasn't any. And how could they, she thought, when she had kept them all winter? She told them earnestly that she would find work soon and Harold had smiled and her mother had told her that it was good to have her home.

She luxuriated in her bed for a moment or two longer. If she had still been at the house she would have been up hours earlier than this and would be toiling up the stairs with breakfast trays by now. She glanced out of the window. They sky was very blue and she thought of the sea and wondered whether her mother would allow her half an hour to go to the beach as she longed to do. She got up and poured water into the bowl and washed thoroughly – it was nice to have the time and the chance – and then she put on an old dress and ran down the stairs.

In the kitchen the fire was burning brightly and her mother was cooking eggs. Harold's hens were laying well. Eggs for breakfast. There was fresh bread too and a big pot of tea. Lizzie smiled at her mother. Harold, who was on the backshift, was still in bed.

'Our Harold's different, you know, Mam,' she said, in the knowledge that Enid was upstairs.

'Aye, I know. Goes drinking now he does with that wrong one from next-door. Came back rolling the other night, and singing songs – and they weren't hymns neither, I can tell you.'

'Is Jon drinking a lot?' Lizzie asked softly.

'He's swimming in it,' her mother said. 'Things aren't right next-door, Lizzie. They haven't been right since Greta lost that bairn.'

Lizzie's mother encouraged her from the beginning to go out, not to places like the beach, walking, but to Bible classes and to the chapel teas and to chapel twice on Sundays, and she knew what her mother's idea was. That she would marry. There were plenty of young pitmen looking for a wife and most of them looked at Lizzie. Unlike Greta, she had plenty of offers to walk her home. Lizzie felt sorry for Greta. Nobody but the minister looked her way – not even now that she was better and prettier than she had ever been. The minister sometimes walked Greta back from chapel. He was a fat bald little widower of forty with five unruly children.

The only lad that Lizzie took a slight fancy to was Eddie Bitten. Maybe, she thought, because he was Jon's friend. Her mother had told her that they didn't go around together much when Jon was drinking but Eddie would talk about Jon on the way back from Bible class – quite unwittingly, she thought, since he didn't know that she and Jon had been almost married. To Eddie she was new to the village because she had been in service when he first arrived. He was a nice lad, if a bit keen on chapel goings-on. He was also respectable and hard-working and had his own house on the other side of Lizzie to Jon where he had once lodged with his aunty. The old woman had died recently and Lizzie knew that Eddie would have to go and lodge with somebody else soon if he didn't marry. Single men weren't allowed company houses. She didn't go to his house, that wouldn't have been right, but she knew that to the other village girls Eddie was a catch and it was always nice to be envied so sometimes she let him walk her home.

One evening after she had been at home for several weeks her mother sent her next-door to give Mrs Armstrong her eggs. Lizzie ventured in at the back door. It was a cool rainy evening. The firelight danced against the black fireplace in the kitchen and at first she thought that the house was empty. There was no noise. Only one lamp burned, hissing in the silence. And then she saw Jon. He was lying on the rug in front of the fire and he was asleep. The rug was all kinds of different coloured squares and Jon was in dark clean neat clothes. He was always better turned out than anybody else, Lizzie thought wryly. It came of having three women to look after him. He was lying on his side sound asleep, black hair shiny in the firelight, eyelashes as thickly fringed as the special tablecloth her mother used on Sunday afternoons when the white cloth had been taken off. He didn't look very old like that. She ventured to the kitchen table and as she did so he stirred and opened his eyes.

'It's just me,' she said softly. 'My mam sent your eggs.'

He sat up slowly and then stood up. It was the first time they had been together since she had come home. They had not even spoken.

'Greta out?' Lizzie said brightly because he didn't talk to her and she didn't know what to say to him.

'Yes, they're all out. Gossiping, I expect.' He looked properly at her for the first time and smiled. It wasn't a real smile, it didn't reach his eyes. He stopped it before it got that far. Lizzie knew why that was; it was for Charles Nelson. There had been various rumours in the village as to why she had been sent home. Several women had looked hard at her slender waistline and flat stomach. As for Jon, she knew that he had thought she fancied a gentleman for herself.

'I hear you're going to Bible classes and study group,' he said. 'Getting religious, are you? They say the minister's looking for a wife.'

Lizzie didn't think he was funny.

'Bible classes are all right,' she said. 'Eddie Bitten's there. He's a nice lad. He doesn't drink his pay and he's got a house all to himself.'

'You mean to tell me that a pit lad'll do after Charles Nelson?'

Lizzie glared at him.

'Charles Nelson is a gentleman,' she said, 'and so's Eddie. You wouldn't understand, not being one yourself.' This was such a good exit line that

Lizzie started to leave but he got hold of her, something that nobody else in the whole world would have dared to do. He put one hand around her waist and the other around her shoulders and he pulled her to him and kissed her hard on the mouth. Lizzie had been wanting him to do just that for so many months now that she got a shock and thumped him. When this had no effect she pulled her mouth free and said, 'No, Jon, don't.'

'Why not? You did as much for Charles Nelson. More maybe.'

'I didn't!'

'And Eddie?'

'No. Nobody. Just that once, and never anybody else.'

Jon kissed her again. The kisses hadn't changed, they were still exactly right. She pushed against him and Jon caught her hands behind her back, and he kissed her eyes and her cheeks and her throat and her neck. He slid one hand on to the buttons at the top of her dress and undid them and kissed the hollow at the base of her throat.

'Stop it, Jon.' This because he pulled her down with him on to the kitchen settle and kissed her until she didn't know where she was.

She heard the sneck on the back door, though she hadn't heard anybody come up the yard. When Greta walked into the room with Tommy in her arms Jon didn't hear anything, Lizzie knew. He was far too absorbed in what he was doing. Lizzie pushed at him and spoke to him and when he could hear her she managed to disentangle herself from him but Greta's eyes reflected the mess of her hair where the pins had come out, her bare neck where the buttons had been undone, and she realised for the first time as Greta's face paled how Greta felt about Jon. Greta held the child up against her for a few seconds and then she went away up the dark stairs as quickly as she could with the child impeding her.

It was a joke in the village that the minister had asked Greta Armstrong to marry him. Lizzie didn't think it was very funny. She was still looking for work. She had been to four different places to try out for the post of kitchenmaid but wasn't taken on at any of them. All that time when Harold was on the foreshift he would go drinking every night. Lizzie thought that her mother was being less than kind to Jon because it was only Saturday nights when he and Harold were together, though she could see her mother's point. On weekdays Harold had a couple of pints and came home. On Saturdays she would hear him from her bed, singing when he came down the back lane.

Then he would stagger into the house, clashing the back door, and clatter about downstairs before either sleeping it off on the settee because he couldn't reach the stairs or getting halfway up and shouting for Enid. He disturbed them all. Harold's Sundays were spent in bed except for mealtimes.

Enid was, to her joy, expecting by this time and Lizzie was more desperate than ever. She had outstayed her welcome at home where Harold seemed to drink more and more of his pay each week and there was not enough work to keep three women busy.

One late-autumn night Harold drank so much that he couldn't walk and Jon had to support him all the way down the back lane and up the yard into the house. Lizzie had waited up. She thought it was time that somebody had a word with Harold but it became obvious to her that she would have no word with him tonight. Jon let him slide on to the settee in the front room and then he went back into the kitchen with her. She thought that he looked remarkably sober for somebody who'd spent the entire evening in some stuffy little room, drinking beer.

'What do you mean, bringing him back like that?'

'It's nowt to do with me,' he said. 'I wasn't even with him. I just picked him up on the way out.'

'Likely,' Lizzie said. 'He's a changed lad is our Harold since he started going drinking with you.'

'Yes, well, he's got three women in the house and a bairn on the way. It's enough to get anybody like that.'

Lizzie tried to control her temper. She could see now that Jon was not drunk and neither was he sober, he had had just enough to argue. His eyes were clear and there was a gleam of anger in them. They were dark too by the one lamp and the glow of the fire which she stood with her back to. The kitchen was in shadow. Harold didn't move in the front room and there was not a sound from upstairs.

'There's hardly enough for us to live on, what with the cut and all, and now thanks to you he's drinking most of it. We're worse off that we've ever been. I don't understand why you do it. You sit there, the lot of you, telling tales about how clever you are, drinking your fortnight's pay, all that mucky smoke and beer fumes—'

Jon's eyes were narrowed and almost black.

'We've been down the pit all week, that's why, and it gets us away from the likes of you whose gobs never stop!'

Lizzie would have hit him if she had been a bit quicker but he got hold of her before she managed to and then he got her chin in his fingers and kissed her. He kissed all the temper out of her and the beer tasted good, warm and nutty on his breath.

'Is that better?' he asked eventually.

Lizzie would have given anything not to let go. She buried her face in his shoulder and closed her eyes and wondered like she had never wondered in her life why you could never relive the best moments like this one whereas the horrible things that had happened were replayed over and over again to you, sleeping and waking.

'I'm sorry, Jon, I didn't mean to shout at you.'

'It's all right.'

Lizzie smiled weakly against him, she was so relieved to be there.

'I even wish Greta had married the minister. Isn't that awful of me?'

'She would have too,' Jon said. 'That mucky little bugger. I wouldn't let him marry Greta's mother.'

'Oh, I don't know. I would say they're a matched pair.'

Jon laughed and she looked into his eyes while trying not to let go even an inch, one hand in the thickness of his hair. But then the laughter went from his eyes and he said, 'We're never going to be able to get married. You do know that, don't you? It isn't going to make any difference that we want things otherwise. It's not going to be.'

She went back to hiding at his shoulder.

'That's not true,' she said.

'Look at me.'

'No. Something will happen. We're going to get married.'

'Nobody is ever going to marry Greta,' Jon said slowly as though trying to make himself believe it.

'I hate Greta.'

'No, you don't. It's not her fault.'

'Yes, it is.' Lizzie could hear her own voice, much too loud, but only the anger was keeping her from crying now. 'If she hadn't been so daft in the first place none of this would have happened. Greta and your Sam–'

'He's dead,' Jon said shortly. 'Is that how you want her?'

'No, but . . . no.' Her fingers were crushing the front of his jacket. 'It isn't right. There's no reason why we should pay for their mistakes, for their daftness. I can't manage any longer without you, Jon. I love you.'

'We can't get married. You know we can't. And it's time for you to have a house of your own and some bairns.'

Lizzie was so horrified at the idea that she let go completely and moved back.

'No. No.'

Jon got hold of her by both arms as though he was going to shake her, but he didn't. He just stood there and closed his eyes for a second and then looked at her.

'You don't have any choice. You can't find work, your Harold can't go on keeping you. What are you going to do?'

'I can't marry somebody else, Jon.'

'You have to. Do you think I want you to waste your life waiting around when I'm never going to be able to marry you?'

'I want you. I'm never going to want anybody else as long as I live. How can you think so?'

'There's nothing else to do,' he said slowly. 'If we don't do something about this, one of these days we're going to ruin everything. We can't stay here and go on like this.'

Lizzie was suddenly so angry that she pushed away from him.

'I suppose you're going to come to my wedding,' she said bitterly.

'It's all there is.'

'All right then. You'll come and watch me marry Eddie?'

'Eddie?' Jon stared at her.

'Yes, Eddie.' Lizzie tossed her head. 'He likes me. He's nice is Eddie. He has his own house, he doesn't drink. You'll come and watch me marry him then?'

'Yes.'

'Liar, Jon Armstrong.'

Jon didn't say anything for a few moments and then he looked down at his hands.

'Eddie's like Alf,' he said. 'I miss Alf.'

He looked up and Lizzie didn't know how it happened but one minute she felt like she was going to start and cry and the next she was in his arms being held so close that she couldn't breathe and didn't want to. She didn't know how she had got there, whether Jon had grabbed hold of her or she had gone to him, but she had her arms around his neck and her eyes closed against him.

'There's only you. There's only ever been you. Please, Jon, you must know it.'

'I thought after all this time that maybe those feelings had changed?'

'They haven't, and they won't.'

Jon hesitated and then eased her from him.

'I love you. I'm always going to love you. But it isn't any good me wishing things differently and getting myself worked up when I see you with another lad, never mind who it is. Just tell me again that you care about me and I'll go.'

'There's only you,' she said, 'there only ever will be you I love. Whatever happens, remember it.'

'I will,' Jon said, and he kissed her and went home.

After that, for days and days, Lizzie scarcely went beyond the doors fearing that something incomprehensible might happen. She tried to make herself invaluable around the house but the truth was that her mother and Enid could do everything more than adequately. Enid got on with her mother far better than she herself had ever done, and Enid was a good cook. This endeared her to Lizzie's mother more than she could have known. There was nothing Lizzie's mother admired quite so much as the ability to make perfect bread, pastries, cakes, and a good meal for a man coming in hungry from work. Enid did not sneak off to read. She was always there to chat. She had a good nose for gossip, and most of all she cared deeply for Harold. Lizzie thought that she must be blind. Apart from the fact that he never fought, Harold was now as bad as any man in the village for drinking and neglecting his wife. Enid didn't seem to notice or care. She helped with the cleaning and the polishing and was like Greta for singing as she hung out the clothes. Lizzie hated Greta. She now looked happier than ever before and more beautiful. Greta with her so pretty clothes and her perfect face, her shining eyes and smiling mouth. Greta who had so little to do and was so well kept.

Lizzie's mother began to make plain to her in many ways that her help was not needed. She encouraged her even more to go out. She talked of how little money there would be when the baby was born. After a month of almost begging to be given work in the house so that she could feel less uncomfortable, after days and days of wanting so badly to see Jon that she cried herself to sleep every night, Lizzie went out as her mother wanted her to. Outside Jon's house she listened hard for the sound of his voice. She had nightly, with her tears, hugged to her the remembrance of his kisses, his body, his words.

At the modest social events the village allowed Lizzie was quietly swamped with young men. There she found herself ticking them off mentally. One had lots of sisters, another a bad-tempered mother or no father to help bring in money. She whittled them down to the ones who had no obvious faults or problems, to those who could afford to keep her, and then she whittled them down even further past stupid, fat, ugly, hardly-ever-takes-a-bath, doesn't read, drinks heavily, has an awful laugh and so on. Even then there were half a dozen or so very nice lads in the village, lads who were hard workers and good fun. She felt nothing for any of them except the one she couldn't have.

Eddie Bitten went on walking her home on Thursday nights. She knew and liked him. He was built rather like Jon and was a year or two older. She could find little in Eddie to object to. He was religious but didn't talk about it, he worked hard but didn't moan. He wasn't boring or stupid or ugly. Eddie liked her a lot. She knew he did.

One evening in late-autumn he asked her to his house for a cup of tea after the class. She knew that she shouldn't go and it wasn't as if she wanted to but she felt that she would be safe with him. Eddie was kind and gentle. And when she saw his house everything changed.

Eddie's aunty had had good taste in furniture and there was plenty of solid stuff, all brought to a high shine by the woman whom Eddie paid to do his housekeeping. The house smelled of polish. It was neat and tidy and the fire was on in the front room – much to Lizzie's surprise because the front room in her house was kept for occasions. Or was it that Eddie considered this an occasion and had lit the fire on purpose? It had been banked down but he soon brought it back to a blaze. And there in the front room was a bookcase with four shelves packed with the kind of books she liked.

'I didn't know you read like that,' she said, delighted.

'Sometimes. Some of them belong to Jon. The others were either mine or my aunty's.'

He made tea on a tray: biscuits, cake and teacups with fluted gold edgings. Lizzie listened to the silence of the house. There was nobody else, nobody to disturb them, no one to get in the way. Eddie, she knew, was the most fortunate young man in the village so far as the lasses were concerned. His house was all his.

'You're so lucky,' she said, sighing. 'All this to yourself.'

'Not much longer, the way things are going.'

'What for?' Lizzie asked, searching Eddie's kind face for clues.

'They overlooked me for a while but now they've noticed I'm an unmarried man and there's a shortage. I might have to give it up.'

'But you're used to this. You wouldn't like lodging with other people.'

'Like it or not . . .' Eddie said, and offered her more tea.

'But what would you do with the furniture?'

'I don't know.'

He asked if she would go for a walk with him on Sunday afternoon and Lizzie knew that she ought to ask him for Sunday dinner so she did. She told her mother the next day and thought that she had never looked more pleased. Everybody liked Eddie. The women liked him because he didn't drink and went to chapel and was good-natured and honest, the men liked him because he was a good worker. Her mother also, she knew, thought of Eddie's house and Eddie's pay and Eddie's lack of dependants. Her mother was so pleased that it was difficult for Lizzie to remain unmoved.

The dinner was one of the best they had ever had in spite of the lack of money. Eddie was more than courteous, he was entertaining. He talked to her mother and Enid, and so easily, as Jon had never bothered to do. Harold grudgingly said afterwards that she could do worse. Lizzie ignored him but when she went to bed that night the tears poured down her face. She catalogued to herself how tall and fine Eddie was, his lovely house and the books and the pretty furniture, thought about how he had no disgusting habits and would never come back drunk and start on her. And he cared. He looked at her a lot when he thought she didn't see. Now he walked her home two nights a week when he was on the shift that allowed him, and he saw her on Sunday afternoons.

Every time they went out she wondered how it would be if they met Jon and then they did, one cold dull winter afternoon when Eddie had said that it was too frosty for a walk and she had insisted on some fresh air. She wondered then why it was that they had not met him before like that with Jon just next-door to her. Eddie presented Lizzie to Jon as his, just by a hand on her arm, a soft word, and Lizzie wondered whether their friends had deliberately said nothing to Eddie and made such mischief. When she ventured to look at Jon there was nothing in his face to give him away but she knew. His expression was the same as when he had told her mother that he could not marry her and she knew that only endurance was keeping him there with a half smile on his lips. As for Lizzie, she could have stood there for the rest of her life, looking into Jon Armstrong's hard blue eyes. It didn't have to be more than that and she didn't think she could stand less. When Eddie urged her away she wanted to turn around and strain her eyes for a glimpse of Jon.

The following Thursday Eddie did not turn up for Bible class. Lizzie wondered whether he was ill. He had been on the foreshift with Harold but her brother had said nothing and she thought that he would have. When she came out, however, he was standing waiting for her. Lizzie went over to him. Eddie didn't smile.

'I want to talk to you,' he said. 'Will you come back to my house?'

'I shouldn't.'

'We can't talk any place else, it's too cold outside, and this is private.'

They walked there in silence and Lizzie thought that she knew what it was about and her feet dragged. When they got there Eddie took off his coat but didn't offer to take hers.

'Why didn't you tell me about Jon?'

No front room this time, just Eddie's clean kitchen with the shiny kitchen range.

'What did you want to know?' Lizzie said.

'Well, it might not seem important to you but since you nearly married him I would have thought it was worth a mention.'

'Who told you?'

'Rob and Ken.'

Who else? Lizzie thought.

'And what makes you think you have the right to know?'

'I was going to ask you to marry me.'

Talk about to the point, she thought.

'What is it that you want to know? What we said, what we did?'

'I want to know whether you still care about him?'

Lizzie got stuck over that. Should she lie to Eddie and say that Jon didn't matter to her now, because that way Eddie would probably ask her to marry him, or should she tell the truth – and if she did what would happen? She thought of her life at home where she wasn't wanted, of her future as a servant, but when she looked into Eddie's honest grey eyes she couldn't lie to him.

'I still care about him,' she said.

'And would you have told me that if I'd asked you to marry me?'

Lizzie went on looking steadily at him.

'I wouldn't hurt you on purpose. If I could change things I would. Jon can't marry me and . . .'

'You have to marry somebody?' he guessed.

'I don't have any choice. I can't stay at home with Enid pregnant and I've done my best to find work. I would have gone if I could have. There are plenty of lads in the village who'd take me and not care.'

'I don't want anybody in my bed who doesn't want to be there.'

Lizzie blushed at his bluntness.

'I don't know anything about that,' she said. 'And if that's something else you're worried about . . .'

'It isn't.'

'No. Well. I think I ought to go unless there's anything else you want to know?'

Eddie said nothing. Lizzie left. She didn't go home. She didn't want anybody to see her upset. The cold air was welcome. It dried the tears at first, but before she reached the end of the street there were too many of them and by then she couldn't see where she was going and had to stop. She didn't even know who they were for and was forced to conclude they were selfish. Eddie was never going to marry her now and perversely she wanted him. She didn't want to go for the rest of her life never kissing anybody, never being held, never having a home of her own or a bairn. Eddie was the only man in the village other than Jon for whom she felt anything and when she examined the feeling it was affection. She didn't want to hurt him, she should have told him before but she had been frightened that this would happen and now it had. Maybe if she had been honest with him and said something sooner it would have been all right. Now it would never be all right again. She stood against the end of the row and gave in to her tears and as she did so he found her.

'There's nothing to cry for.'

'Yes, there is. I wanted to tell you but I didn't want you to know.'

Eddie chuckled. Lizzie couldn't think why it was funny.

'I like you a lot,' she said. 'I know it isn't the same thing, and now I'll have to marry somebody fat who drinks or – or . . .'

Eddie seemed to think that was even funnier and when he had stopped laughing he drew her away from the wall and kissed her. Lizzie thought it must have been the saltiest kiss ever, she had cried so hard, and it was a shock too. Nobody, discounting the brief touch of Charles Nelson, had ever really kissed her except Jon, and kissing Eddie was so different. She had also thought that she would never want anybody else to kiss her, but that was not true either. She suspected that she had a need now to be kissed, that Jon had created that need and Eddie was supplying it, and thought that her mother was right. It was time for her to marry and Eddie's timing was excellent, just like his kisses. When he stopped and released her it took her a moment or two to remember where they were and the circumstances, and he looked surprised and a lot more pleased than she had thought he could.

'I want you to marry me,' he said. 'Will you?'

Lizzie looked hard at him.

'Are you sure?'

'No, but I'm prepared to take the risk. You were honest with me and it's a start.'

'I might not make you happy.'

'I'm not very happy now and I can't watch you marry another lad. If you're willing to try and do the best you can, I think that's good enough.'

Lizzie nodded. 'There's only one real problem.'

'What's that?'

'I didn't plan to live next-door to my mam when I married.'

That made Eddie laugh and Lizzie liked the sound. In fact it was what she had planned when she was younger, she and Sam. What a long time ago that seemed now, and how different. Whether she would ever be able to love Eddie was doubtful but he was her only real option. She would try hard to make him happy. She thought back to being in service in the big house. Eddie had saved her from that, and from the fate of being unwanted in her own home. She would have to be grateful and make the best of her opportunity.

Fifteen

*I*t was Sunday afternoon and such a bitterly cold day that Kate's aunt could not understand why she had wanted to go out. But she went out every Sunday afternoon to the Armstrongs. She ought to have gone home by now, it was almost dark, but she lingered there by the fire with Tommy, playing draughts with Jon and wishing that every day could be like this. Greta was in the kitchen and had been baking. Kate could smell fresh scones.

Mrs Armstrong came in from next-door where she had been gossiping to Lizzie's mother. She came into the front room now just as Kate said to Jon, 'You're cheating.'

'No, I'm not. You said we could jump over our own men.'

'I never did.'

Kate had Tommy on her lap, her feet under her. Nellie, Greta's mother, was dozing by the fire. The bottle tops on the checker board reflected the firelight. It was almost teatime.

'Some news from next-door,' Jon's mother said. 'Their Lizzie's getting married.'

Jon didn't look up.

Nellie opened her eyes.

'What's that?'

'She's marrying Eddie Bitten.'

Nellie sniffed.

'He's been trying to get his feet under the table for months.'

'You can't move there,' Jon said to Kate.

'What?' Her startled gaze met his calm one.

'You can't move back. It's not allowed.'

'You make up the rules as you go along,' she accused him. 'I'm going to go and help Greta.' And she went off to the kitchen.

Greta was not there. Kate waited about for a short while and then found her standing in the back yard, crying.

'Greta,' she said, shocked, 'whatever's wrong?'

Kate had never liked her much but when the other girl sobbed and said, 'Lizzie's getting married. I wish I could get married,' Kate felt so sorry for her. She hadn't thought about Greta, just about how awful it was for Jon. 'Eddie Bitten's the nicest lad in the village. She won't have to live with his mother and her mother and never be able to touch anybody.'

'I thought you were happy?'

'I was, but I'm the reason Jon can't marry Lizzie. How would you like it? Being the cause of somebody's unhappiness when you care about them isn't very nice.'

Kate didn't have time to reply. Jon came out to them.

'I suppose you want us to butter our own scones now?' he said.

Kate went back inside and as she did so, said, 'You're not a lad, Jon Armstrong, you're a brick wall.'

'It's just as well I am.'

But it was not like that, she knew. He insisted on walking her home through the icy darkness. Kate loved being out when it was so starry.

'Doesn't your aunty ask where you've been?' he said.

'Yes. I tell lies.'

'You aren't a good lass,' he said severely.

'I can't afford to be. I'd never get what I wanted that way. So, are you going to go and dance at Lizzie's wedding, metaphorically speaking of course?'

'It's summat to look forward to.'

'Greta cried.'

'She's cousin to a watering-can,' he said.

Kate stopped and looked at him.

'Why will nobody marry Greta when she's so beautiful?'

'They're that bloody daft around here they think you have to want to put a bairn into a lass before you bed her,' Jon said.

It was a rather more frank answer than she had expected from him.

'You could at least stop pretending that you don't mind about Lizzie marrying Eddie,' she said.

'My minding isn't the point.'

'Then what is?'

'The point is, Little Miss Cleverclogs, that Eddie can marry her and look after her and she has a chance of being happy. And if I didn't want that for her there wouldn't be much good in my caring for her, would there?'

'That's extremely noble of you, Jon, but it makes you the biggest liar in the county.'

'Well, you know what they say, bonny lass. It takes one to know one,' he said.

Lizzie Harton was married in white; it was the talk of the village, the dress which her mother had sewn for her. It made her the prettiest bride for a long time, her hair free, the first of the spring flowers in her hands and Eddie was in his best dark suit, as were all the men. Kate's triumph was that she had been allowed to go. Her aunt would have refused but her uncle intervened. He said that Eddie was a thoroughly respectable young man and that Lizzie came from a decent family and since she had been asked there was no reason why Kate should not go. Indeed it would have been an insult to have refused. She wore cream and green. Jon told her that she looked like a sand dune. Kate wondered how he could sit there and watch the girl he loved get married, and wondered how on earth Lizzie would marry a man she didn't love, though for her part Kate liked Eddie Bitten. He was in fact a much better bet than Jon, being sober, even-tempered and clean-mouthed. He was not pious or boring, and on that day he looked very happy. Kate saw how the bride avoided looking in Jon's direction and wondered how long it would last.

Throughout the ceremony Jon sat with Tommy on his knee. Children, Kate thought, were so useful on these occasions, and afterwards at the meal Jon sat with his arms around the child reminding Kate rather awkwardly of a doll she had clutched to her when first starting school.

Greta cried throughout the ceremony, though not audibly – apart from the occasional sniff – and Lizzie's mother wore a new blue hat and looked very satisfied, as well she might, thought Kate, Lizzie having landed the most eligible pitman in the village. She knew that generally the bride was regarded as a very lucky girl. Lizzie herself smiled a great deal as though she had to keep on reminding herself to do so. Kate wondered whether the friendship between Eddie and Jon would survive the ceremony.

That morning Lizzie had got up at an early hour. Several weeks since her mother had suggested to her that she might have a new dress for the occasion.

Lizzie had looked at her old rose pink and decided that if she wore that Jon would probably run away with her out of the chapel and down the lane. It had been altered to suit her size and shape and still fitted, but it would not do.

White would not have been her choice. She knew that posh people were married that way but she was not posh, and besides, when she saw herself in the mirror in the white she felt like some kind of sacrifice. There was something so untouched about it, which of course was how brides were meant to be. Lizzie didn't feel untouched. She felt as though every part of her belonged to Jon Armstrong. Marrying Eddie seemed somehow adulterous.

She went through the day feeling strange, as though somebody else was getting married. From time to time she thought that she saw a smiling girl in white being married to a man who was almost a stranger to her. She felt as though she was sitting next to Jon where she should be and was nothing to do with the actual ceremony. She remembered nothing of the wedding itself, the responses or the words. She remembered coming out of the chapel into bright sunshine and various people congratulating Eddie and talking about how bonny she looked, but there was a cold part of her deep inside which remained aloof. She could eat and drink nothing. She saw Jon sitting with other people, talking with them and behaving quite normally, and that should have made her feel better but she knew him too well by now to think that the way he behaved had anything to do with the way that he felt. And when she and Eddie went over to where he was sitting, as they did with everybody at some time during that afternoon, she only had to look into Jon's eyes to know the truth. Smiling at him and trying to go on as if there was nothing the matter exhausted her. It was a good thing that Eddie had hold of her arm. She did not think she could ever have moved away otherwise.

The day seemed like a mountain she was climbing which kept getting bigger and bigger no matter how hard she tried. By the time the wedding was over all she wanted to do was cry, and still, she thought, there would be no let up. There was the evening to be got through with no one but Eddie, and then there was the night, and to make it worse Eddie's house was next-door so she had her mother near and Jon too, so near, and yet he was lost to her now for good and always. She stood in the sunshine in Eddie's front room and shook and shook. He was in the kitchen, doing she didn't know what; she was just glad that he was out of the room. He came back before long and pushed a glass into her hands. Lizzie looked down at the golden liquid which smelled strange.

'What is it?' she said.

'Brandy. Drink it.'

Lizzie looked at him. And him a good Methodist, she thought.

'I think I'd rather have a cup of tea.'

'I've put the kettle on. Drink that anyway.'

Lizzie swallowed it in three gulps. It bit the back of her throat and went down warmly on to her empty stomach, making her feel much better. She was surprised. Eddie made tea and sandwiches and she was suddenly hungry and ate and had two cups of tea and then fell asleep on the sofa.

When she woke up she could tell by the light that it was late-evening. She was stiff from lying down and her dress was so crumpled that she was only glad her mother wasn't there to see it. Eddie came to the doorway as she got up.

'Feeling any better?'

'Lots.'

'How about a walk on the beach?'

It seemed so normal, something she always did and not the kind of thing new husbands usually asked, Lizzie felt.

'Just give me a minute. I'm not going like this.' And she went upstairs to find an old dress. The covered buttons on the back of her wedding dress defeated her and she hovered, too embarrassed to ask Eddie to help, but he came upstairs after a little while.

'I thought you were getting changed?' he said.

'I can't unfasten it.'

'You should have shouted.'

'I couldn't.'

Eddie undid the buttons for her and then went off downstairs again, saying, 'Don't be too long.' She pulled off the dress, left it in a heap on the floor and found her oldest, most washed out frock and put that on.

Being on the beach made her feel even better. It was late now and almost dark and there was nobody around. The tide was halfway down. Eddie put an arm around her just as he always did when they went walking and they set off slowly along the beach. It was so much like those evenings with Jon had been when they had gone walking in the summer and planned their marriage that Lizzie forgot to be unhappy. By the time it was dark they had walked all the way back and sat down in the sand dune which had been hers and Sam's. That seemed like such a long time ago now.

Jon had taken her into his arms so often in that sand dune that when Eddie did it didn't feel wrong. She was also used to his kisses now. She didn't remember who he was, or care, just that she had waited so long. And she thought of what her mam had said: 'He's put his hands on you and more.'

Now he did. It was just as well, Lizzie thought, that she was not wearing the awful white dress because those covered buttons down the back would have created problems, but her old dress had its buttons at the front. She thought afterwards that if she had been less in shock she would have known right then that the man was not Jon because Eddie Bitten, serious young Methodist that he was, had obviously not always been the God-fearing lad he was now. At some time in his life there had been other women. He knew how and where to touch her, and exactly what to do, and although Lizzie thought that perhaps instinct might take you to there it would not have done quite so surely. Eddie seduced her. He did it so well that there was no awkwardness and no pain. Also, Lizzie had always imagined that whatever happened happened in bed, and yet they were outside in her favourite place in the whole world, dark and secluded, so that they couldn't be seen. There had been no lead up as there would have been at home, worrying about undressing and facing one another. It felt so natural. This was how she would have been with Jon if she could have chosen. Afterwards Lizzie's first reaction was that her mother had been wrong about it, that she felt sorry for women who had not been sent out of their minds with pleasure, but that was just her first reaction. Beyond that was the knowledge that he was not Jon, that she did not love this man, and that somehow, somewhere she would be made to pay for having taken part in such an act without love.

When they got home Lizzie took herself off to bed and lay there in the not quite darkness, thinking about what May had said about Rob hurting her. Eddie came upstairs and the candle threw shadows against the wall. Lizzie turned away from him and as she did so the tears ran so fast that she could not stifle a sob.

Eddie sat down on the bed and turned her over towards him and took her into his arms. He held her there against him, stroking her hair and saying, 'It's all right, it's all right,' while she cried.

Kate went back with the Armstrongs to their house after the wedding. It was a mistake. Mrs Armstrong made tea and talked brightly and Greta's mother drank her tea and said what a lucky lass Lizzie was to have such a husband.

They talked about how beautiful she had looked in her white dress and what a lovely mother she would make and Kate was not surprised when Jon got up in the middle of tea and walked out. She went after him. It was early evening. She caught him up at the end of the lane. He was walking very fast.

'Jon!'

He didn't take any notice of her, just increased his pace. Kate nearly fell over trying to keep up.

'Jon–'

'Go away.'

'If you go and get drunk it'll only make things worse.'

'Things couldn't be any worse,' he said.

'Yes, they could. Jon, please. Will you slow down?'

He didn't. Kate ran after him and grabbed his arm and he stopped and turned on her.

'I suppose you think it's summat to do with you like, is it?'

'You're ruining your life.'

'You should be writing books.'

'I wish you wouldn't be so sarcastic.'

'Look, Kit, I'm going to the pub. Women aren't allowed in pubs around here, so stop following me, all right?'

'It isn't right.'

'It's the only place I get any peace. Go home.'

'Jon–'

'Kit, you don't have any place here. Go home.' And he walked off fast and left her standing there.

Watching Lizzie being married was to Jon like being given a good hiding. He tried to think of something else but he couldn't, and afterwards he went off to the pub. He stayed there until late, not drinking much because somehow the beer wouldn't go down just when he needed it to, listening to the other men talking. There was a great gaping nothingness between himself and the world. When it was dark and late he went to the beach and sat down on top of a dune and let the darkness surround him until the night grew cold and the weather turned stormy.

Everybody was in bed. He walked quietly into the house and tiptoed up the stairs. He took one candle with him and was shrugging off his jacket when he heard the door click. He looked up. Through the small mirror which stood on the dressing table he could see Greta standing just inside the door. She was wearing a long pale blue nightdress and her hair was braided.

'Where have you been?' she asked, watching him through the mirror as he pulled off his tie and hauled at his collar.

'Nowhere.'

'I thought maybe you'd gone to the pub.'

'I did earlier and then I went for a walk.'

'You must be wet through. It's raining and it's cold.' And Greta shivered visibly.

The wind tore around the outside of the house.

'Go to bed then,' Jon suggested, but she didn't move and he turned around and looked hard at her. 'Go on, it's late.'

'Lizzie made a lovely bride.'

'Aye.' Jon hesitated over his shirt. 'Are you going or aren't you?'

She didn't say anything, she stood there against the door, and gradually her head lowered. Jon went to her and then he said softly, 'Summat the matter?'

Greta raised drenched cornflower blue eyes and a tremulous mouth.

'I want you to kiss me,' she said.

Jon stared at her.

'What? No, you don't. Come on, Greta, don't play up to me. I'm tired.'

'Just once.'

'Will you go back to bed? You'll catch your death wandering around like that.' When she didn't move he said, 'I'll talk to you tomorrow.'

He tried to open the door and Greta, who had been standing near it, moved back against it. Jon's control started to slip.

'Don't do this to me,' he said. 'I've had a bad day.'

'Do what?'

'You don't want me to kiss you, not really. You don't like being touched, you never did. And besides, I couldn't kiss anybody right now.'

'Is it because I'm not Lizzie?'

'Greta,' Jon sighed and sat down on the bed, 'you don't owe me nothing. It wasn't owt to do with you. Just accept that it's the way that it is. I will.'

'Will you?'

'Yes. In time.'

'And until then?'

When Jon didn't answer she started over the room up to him.

'Will you go away?' he said.

She went to him. She got down on the bed and slid her arms up around his neck and she kissed him. Her mouth was soft and warm and her lips were parted. Jon couldn't believe it. This was Greta. This was the lass who had lain silently under his brother, the chapel lass who didn't want a lad anywhere near her. She had never liked it, he knew she hadn't. She was doing him the favour for what she thought she had stolen away. He pushed her from him.

'Right, now go to bed.'

'No.'

He was aware of her now, the young rounded body beneath the material, the sweetness of her lips, the feel of her fingers against him, her warmth beneath his hands.

'Greta, you're going to be good and sorry about this.'

She reached up and would have fastened her hands round his neck but Jon caught at both her wrists.

'I'm all right,' he said. 'Don't feel sorry for me, I'm fine.'

'Are you?' she said, and when Jon let go she started to take down her hair. It made him think of the story of the girl in the tower and it mesmerised him. When the hair was loose it was almost to her waist and as bonny as gold. Then she started to undo the buttons on her nightdress. They went all the way down past her waist. By then Jon couldn't think what he was trying to say. She took hold of his hands and guided them inside to the warmth of her bare skin. Her breasts were more generous than he had thought they would be, warm and round and soft, filling his hands, hard-tipped under his palms. He got hold of her and put her down on to the bed. Her mouth was sweet and willingly parted and when he lifted her nightdress she let him put his hands all over her. He took the nightdress off her and she was beautiful, neat-waisted and slender-thighed, her stomach still flat and her hips with exactly the right curve for his hands. The candlelight gave her body a glow which it didn't need. She even helped him off with his clothes. Jon didn't think about her with his brother. She let him take her, naked by candlelight. To him it was wonderful, like nothing before, her body yielding more and more to him, so soft and fluid. It was as though she drew him into her, further and further, right into the very centre of her. At some time he pushed a pillow under her arched back and went on until their bodies were slick with sweat and Greta was making helpless little whimpering sounds in her throat. At the finish she gave a sharp cry which Jon tried to smother with his hand for fear of

131

somebody hearing. Under his fingers she gave another. He thought that it was the sweetest sound he had ever heard in his life.

'Are you sorry?' she looked over the white pillow at him a few minutes later and Jon saw her differently than he had ever seen her before, her eyes as blue as a summer sea, her mouth like crushed raspberries. He got hold of her quite ungently but she only laughed and gave him her lips and then her body, down across the narrow width of the bed.

Sixteen

*E*nid had had twin girls that winter. Mrs Harton had not been very pleased and had confided to Lizzie that it would have been bad enough if she had produced one girl at once, but two. Enid was just like her mother. Was that all she could turn out? Girls were to keep. Now if just one of them had been a boy their Harold would have been better pleased. As it was he went on just like he had. If the babies woke in the night he never heard them, he was always full of beer.

Lizzie said nothing. She knew what was coming next. Enquiries about whether she was feeling all right. After six months of marriage Lizzie was not pregnant. She knew very well what this meant, that the other lads at the pit would tease Eddie and ask whether he needed any help, and she would have to put up with persistent enquiries from her mother and friends. Eddie had come home with a black eye the week before, evidence that he was not taking the teasing very well, and she was not pleased to think that he might be fighting. Was this Jon's influence?

She was doing her best. She never mentioned Jon's name. Not once since the day of the wedding had it crossed her lips and Eddie had nothing to complain about. His house was spotless, the sheets smelled of lavender. The place shone, the meals were perfect, the baking was light. She didn't waste a penny. She didn't argue with him. She was always there when he went out and when he came home. She never complained or crossed him and never once denied him her body. She could not understand why he had become so tight-lipped and awkward.

One cold day in November Eddie came home to his neat house where the brasses shone and the water was ready and the dinner was timed to perfection, and his neatly dressed wife made the usual polite enquiries about

133

his day. He was going to a meeting at the chapel. Lizzie would stay at home and sew or read.

He was quiet. He answered her enquiries with either 'yes' or 'no'. When he was washed and changed and as clean and tidy as the house, he sat down and waited for her to bring the dinner from the oven. The potatoes and vegetables were already on the table, it was only the meat which had been done slowly in the oven and was now producing the most wonderful smell of onions and gravy. Somehow between the oven and the table Lizzie managed to slip and the best part of Eddie's dinner went up into the air, parted company with its dish and then both lay in ruins on the floor. It was a mess. The dish clattered, bounced, turned over. The meat and gravy and onions spattered everywhere.

Eddie pushed back his chair and got up. He didn't even give her a chance to say anything. He went to her. He said, 'You clumsy little bitch!' and smacked her hard round the ear.

For a few moments Lizzie was too shocked to do anything, she just stared at him, and then she burst into tears and ran for the stairs. She sat down on the edge of the bed and cried and cried. Seconds later Eddie came into the room and Lizzie, who was no longer sure who she was dealing with, looked at him to see whether there was more to come. He didn't move any nearer than the door.

'I'm sorry. Will you forgive me?'

'No.'

'You'd forgive me if I was Jon though, wouldn't you?'

'Jon wouldn't do such a thing.'

'Wouldn't he? With a temper like his? Jon wouldn't have put up with the half! I'm sick of this. I'm sick of coming home to a perfect house and a wife who thinks that Jon Armstrong's name is a sacred thing. I should give you a bloody good hiding and then you could hate me properly.'

'I don't hate you,' Lizzie managed between sobs.

'And am I supposed to be glad about that? If I broke my neck down that pit tomorrow you'd say, "Oh, dear. What a pity. Now I'll have to marry somebody else."'

'That's not fair. I do everything.'

Eddie came over to the bed and turned her to face him.

'You never make a sound. Never. Even when I know from the way your body reacts that you want me, you never tell me. You never tell me anything, no matter what I do or how much I give. You never touch me first or kiss me and you turn your face away. All the time that you're here I'm just not Jon to you. You're like a little machine that never breaks down and never feels anything.'

Lizzie's whole body shook with fright, and her cheek burned where he had hit her. He let her go and he went out. He went, she presumed, to his meeting though how he could she didn't know. Eddie was a changed man. He had had a fight last week, he had sworn at her tonight and now he had hit her. She just hoped that he had gone to his meeting and not drinking as she suspected.

After the night that Eddie hit his wife there was silence. They spoke to one another only about ordinary things but everything changed. The first thing was that Eddie turned away from her in bed and didn't turn back, and the days became a week and two weeks and a month. The year turned, the spring came, the weather warmed and Lizzie gave up trying to be any kind of wife because Eddie rarely came home. As the weather warmed she began to go out. She spent a lot of time at the beach. She got books from anywhere she could and spent full days down there as the summer advanced. She lay in her sand dune and considered the blue sky. She took a sandwich and a drink and had solitary picnics, and there she sometimes met Kate who would get down from her horse and stop to chat.

It was the only time they saw one another. Kate had stopped coming to the village on Sunday afternoons. For one thing the Armstrongs had made it plain she was not wanted and her aunt often had visitors on Sunday. Also Charles Nelson occasionally came to call so her aunt had forbidden her to go further than the garden.

'Does he fancy you, Kate?' Lizzie asked her one day when she was paddling at the water's edge and Kate was walking Dolly through the waves.

'Yes, I think so.'

'He'll own the pits one day and have lots of money.'

'I don't care about things like that. I don't like him,' Kate said.

'I don't like him much myself,' Lizzie might have added or anybody else but she didn't. Her house had become dusty and neglected. She didn't cook. They lived on bread and cheese and jam. Eddie ventured to the pub on Saturday nights. Lizzie tried never to get home first but it was a contest since neither of them wanted to be there. She was not home until dark and would come in tanned and tired. She rarely went to her mother's since she was always asking things Lizzie didn't want to talk about. She couldn't tell her mother that there was no likelihood of her conceiving since her husband wouldn't have anything to do with her.

One Sunday afternoon she went for a long walk on the beach and then climbed up the dunes and lay down on the top. The beach was deserted. She lay there with her eyes closed against the sun and after a little while she heard voices from the beach. They sounded familiar and they were laughing. Lizzie turned on to her stomach and lifted her head just a little way so that they couldn't see her and then she opened her eyes wide. It was Jon and Greta. They were facing one another; Greta was walking backwards, almost dancing, and she was giggling. Then he caught hold of her with both hands around her waist and she stopped.

To Lizzie's horror he brought her to him and started to kiss her and it was obviously not the first time and it was not brief. Greta stood on tiptoe and linked her arms up behind his neck. She lifted her face and he held her against him so that there wasn't an inch of space between their bodies.

Lizzie's first instinct was to run away but she couldn't. There was no road behind the dunes here and no way through the tall grass. The only way back was by the beach and they would see her. She lay down and closed her eyes and put her hands over her ears and when she looked up again after a long time they were walking on even further away from the village. She waited until they were out of sight around the corner and then she got up and ran.

Eddie wasn't at their house. He didn't come back. When it was very late and she was worried there was a banging on the back door and to Lizzie's amazement Jon was standing there, propping up Eddie. She didn't say a word.

'He can't be drunk,' she said finally as Jon helped him up the stairs. 'He's too heavy, Jon, don't take him up there.'

'It's all right.'

Jon dumped Eddie on the bed and Lizzie took off his shoes and they left him.

'He's unconscious. Will he be all right?'

'In the morning.'

'But he's on the foreshift.'

'He can't go to work in that state. Nobody'll say anything. Half the place is missing on a Monday.'

Lizzie followed him down the stairs.

136

'Eddie's never missed a day.'

'Well, he's going to now. When did he start drinking?'

'Months since. Didn't you know?'

'Haven't seen him. If you must know he turned up at my door trying to tell me that something was all my fault.'

Lizzie went off into the kitchen and when he went after her she said, 'I saw you today.'

'Is that summat fresh?'

'With Greta along the beach. You were kissing her, just like you used to kiss me.'

'So?'

'Oh, Jon, you mustn't. It's not right. You know it isn't. She's your sister-in-law.'

'Don't you kiss Eddie?'

Lizzie stared at him.

'I'm married to Eddie. Besides . . . Eddie and I . . .'

'What's Eddie drinking for?'

'We had an argument. He said that the house was too clean.'

Jon glanced around distastefully.

'If my house was as dirty as this there'd be some sorting out done.'

'Awful, isn't it?'

'What did he do?'

'He hit me.'

Jon stared.

'Did he? What for?'

'Because . . . I dropped the dinner all over the floor. He's not you.'

'No, he's not,' Jon said, with a touch of humour. 'He was a nice lad when you got married. Now he's nearly as bad as the rest.'

'You can't marry Greta so why do you kiss her?'

'Did you think I was never going to kiss nobody again?'

'But you shouldn't. You don't have any right to do it.'

'That's why I do it,' Jon said with a grin. 'It's like drinking. If it was the right thing to do nobody would do it.'

'But you can't marry Greta, you can't . . . you can't touch her.'

'Why can't I?'

'Because it's a sin. Jon. You wouldn't, you mustn't.'

'I don't care,' he said.

Lizzie shook her head.

'No,' she said.

'What did you think I did the night you got married?'

'I don't know.' Lizzie's voice was down to a whisper.

'Did you think about me?'

'I didn't think about anything else, that was the trouble. It wasn't fair to Eddie but I couldn't help it.'

'And that was why he hit you, in the end?'

Lizzie put both hands over her face.

'That was months and months ago and since then . . . It's my fault, Jon.'

'You could try and change it. He's a nice lad is Eddie. If you–'

'I don't want a nice lad. I want you.'

Jon smiled a little bit over that even though she was almost in tears.

'I can't do that. Eddie would kill me.'

'No, you'd rather do it to Greta. How could you? I hate you!'

'Well, that's a step up,' he said.

The tears were running down Lizzie's face now.

'You said there'd only be us. Now there isn't.'

'You married him.'

'I had to. I had to marry somebody. Eddie was the nicest lad in the village.'

'Yes, *was*,' Jon said. 'Now he drinks, doesn't go to chapel and hits you. It was only once, wasn't it?'

'He gets into fights too sometimes.'

'Yes, I know.'

'With you?'

'No, not with me. At least not yet. He's good.'

'At fighting?' Lizzie stared through her tears.

'Really good.'

'I don't understand it.'

'You could try cleaning the house and making the odd meal and being nice to him. You never know.'

For a moment or two Lizzie did nothing. Then she extracted a handkerchief from her skirt pocket and wiped the tears and blew her nose and said, 'Really?'

'Really.'

'He didn't hurt me. Do you love Greta?'

138

She heard him hesitate before he said, 'Yes.'

'I shall have to make the best of it then.'

'If I thought she didn't want me when I was doing my best, if I thought that she wanted somebody else, I don't know what I would do. Something awful probably.'

'Eddie hasn't done nothing awful yet.' Lizzie raised her eyes to the ceiling. 'Unless he's been sick upstairs on my good mat.' And she managed a smile.

It was midday before Eddie ventured downstairs and by then the house was a much cleaner place and the washing was in progress. Lizzie had been up six hours. It was a warm blustery day, perfect for the job, and she was out the back hanging up the wet clothes. She came in to find her husband standing shame-faced in front of the fire.

'I'm sorry,' he said.

'Oh, it's nothing,' she said. 'Some pit lads do that every Saturday night. Some of them do it every night and with less cause. I've never met one that had never done it. Was that the first time?'

'No, I used to get drunk a lot and fight too. I was good. Nearly as good as Armstrong.'

'And then you started going to chapel?'

'I had a brother. We went drinking on Saturday nights and one night some farm lads got hold of him and smashed his head in and he died. He was all I had.'

'Didn't you have any family?' Lizzie said, wondering what on earth they had talked about before now.

'No. There was a home. I don't remember anything before that.'

'Oh, Eddie, I didn't know. I didn't think. But you had your aunty.'

'She wasn't my aunty. I came down from Newcastle to find work the week they were going to put her out. We made a bargain.'

'Eddie Bitten! Don't you ever tell nobody owt?'

'You didn't ask.'

'I'm sorry. Was that where the girls were?'

'What girls?'

'The girls who taught you things.'

'No. It was a boys' home. There were women, then and later. Some women like boys.'

She put her arms around him and hugged him.

'I'm hungry,' he said.

'Let's have some dinner then. It isn't much because it's washing day but–'

'What about the washing?'

'It's done. It's all out on the line. We don't all lie in bed, you know. I'll just tidy up and then–'

As she started past him Eddie caught her around the waist with both hands and brought her back to him. When he leaned over and kissed her she put her hands up to his neck and gave him her mouth.

Seventeen

*T*hat summer Kate was invited to the Nelsons' house for Sunday lunch. Her aunt was so pleased about it that had Kate found any pleasure in the invitation it would have been spoiled by the gushing and fussing, but the truth was that she didn't want to go, though it shouldn't have mattered what she did on Sunday afternoon since now she had no alternative entertainment.

Kate had heard a lot of gossip at the pit recently about Jon and Greta. At first she had not believed it. The gossip caused Jon to be involved in several fights, notably one with his brother-in-law, Rob Harvey, in which Jon reduced him to a state where he needed his friends to carry him home. Jon never spoke to Kate now or went anywhere near her. She cried and cried. She hated Greta Armstrong as she had never hated Lizzie and she was horrified that Jon could do such a thing. Greta was so beautiful, and worse still was beautiful in a way that Kate had always wanted to be. She didn't like to think that Jon was doing something sinful but it didn't make Kate want him any the less. She missed him, she wished that she could just talk to him, and finally she began to hate him.

Mostly, around her, the men were careful in what they said, but Kate had sharp ears and had more than once heard scraps of conversation to the effect that Jon was 'putting Greta on to her back' as they called it. The words were so crude and the idea was so repellent that even on the occasions when she did see Jon Kate couldn't think of a thing to say to him. Not that this was often but he fought so frequently and missed so many Mondays that he was in the office from time to time being told that if he didn't mend his ways he would be sacked. Kate didn't understand why her uncle hadn't got rid of him by now. Plenty of other men had been dismissed for similar offences but when she questioned her uncle all she heard was that Jon was a good miner.

Kate had the feeling that he would not survive long in a society which did not forgive those who broke its rules. He had all the instincts, she thought, of a lemming.

The Sunday that Kate went to what the pitmen called 'the big house' she was, for the first time, the only guest. She was overawed by the silver, the china, the huge dining-table, the uniformed servants, when there were no other guests to take attention from her. She wondered whether the Nelsons always ate so formally and whether they could ever enjoy a meal. There were hideous pictures on the dining-room walls and Charles's mother made the sort of conversation which Kate couldn't bear, about clothes and fashions and styles. She thought the house was especially gloomy that day and had a strange atmosphere. Charles showed her the library. Usually Kate liked libraries but this one was cold and echoing in spite of the sunshine outside. There were huge globes in the corners, and rigid-looking chairs, and ivy tapped against the windows.

He also showed her a small sitting-room at the back of the house where the previous owner's daughter had spent much of her time.

'I think she was mad,' he said. 'Had some very strange notions apparently. She refused to marry an eligible suitor and became a Roman Catholic. From then on she spent most of her life in here. She used to have tantrums, I believe. Odd.' Kate didn't think it odd; she thought living in such a depressing house and having such boring companions would be enough to make anybody eccentric.

She was obliged to stay for tea but afterwards when she reached home she went off by herself to the village, saying she must have a walk to clear her head. She went to see Lizzie. Eddie would be at chapel by now and Lizzie made her welcome. Lizzie was pregnant. She had confided as much to Kate as soon as she found out. Kate was flattered by this and also by the knowledge that Lizzie had of recent times found a new affection for the man she had married. Kate wasn't surprised; she liked Eddie Bitten very much. She looked forward to the birth of the baby with excitement and curiosity. It surprised her that for all her lack of domestic talents she liked babies and children.

She knocked on the back door and when she gained no reply walked in and found Lizzie sitting by the fire engaged in a strange occupation. She was feeding a book to the fire one page at a time. She looked up when she heard Kate but didn't stop, and said only, 'I'll make you a cup of tea in a minute.'

Books were sacred to Kate. She stared in fascinated horror.

'My goodness,' she said, 'what is it?'

'It's a poetry book that Jon gave me. Greta Armstrong's expecting.'

'Oh God,' Kate said, plumping down on to the nearest chair.

The fire was bright with paper for a short while and then went back to its usual burning.

'She's as round as a barrel. I never thought he'd do something like this.'

'Oh, I don't know,' Kate sighed.

The other girl looked sharply at her.

'What do you mean, you don't know?'

Kate knew that she was on dangerous ground here.

'What do you think it feels like when the person you love marries somebody else?'

'I didn't want to marry Eddie.'

'No, but any woman who was thinking about marrying would marry Eddie.'

'The thing is that Eddie's very nice to be married to,' Lizzie admitted. 'If I'd met him first it would be different.'

'If Jon had been able to marry Greta–'

'But Kate, he isn't. What is he thinking about?'

'What men usually think about, I expect,' Kate said.

'He'll never ever be allowed to forget it, you know. Never. Nobody will speak to him or anything.'

'Maybe he thinks it's worth it to have Greta and to have a child. It's the only way he's going to do that, after all.'

'Do you think he loves her very much, Kate?'

'I suspect that he doesn't love her at all,' she said frankly. 'I think he's going to love you for the rest of his life. I wish things had been different; I'd have married him myself.'

Lizzie stared at her.

'What a thing to say.'

'Why?'

'You couldn't marry a pit lad, Kate, it's beneath you.'

'Jon's only socially beneath me. Intellectually I think he's as bright as men get. Not that that's saying a great deal. And I think he could be educated socially, don't you?'

Lizzie laughed.

'You shouldn't talk like that,' she said.

'No,' Kate said wistfully. 'Lucky Greta Armstrong. I wish I was pregnant.'

'Kate!'

She laughed then too but she said, 'Is it nice?'

'What?'

'You know.'

Lizzie blushed.

'You talk about things that other people don't, and you shouldn't.'

'Why shouldn't I? I think Eddie must be very nice, and you're lucky, and you're pregnant too. My life is very pointless; all I have is my office.'

'You like your office.'

'I'd like to have babies *and* an office,' Kate said. 'I hate Jon. I hate him so much I don't think I'll ever forgive him for being so awful.'

Lizzie's mother came to stay. Harold had asked if she and Eddie would take her for a while because she was getting on Enid's nerves, and while Lizzie understood and didn't blame Enid for that she didn't want to have her mother living with them. She was ashamed that she didn't and Eddie said straight away that of course they would have her, but it wasn't that long since she and Eddie had discovered how much they cared about one another and she didn't want it spoiling. She knew that it was selfish but she also knew that now she truly belonged to Eddie.

Her love for Jon was damaged because Greta Armstrong was pregnant. Even though they lived so near Lizzie tried to avoid him. She did not want to go on caring for somebody who had behaved so wrongly, and if she didn't see him much it was easy to pretend that she didn't care at all.

Her marriage improved day by day. Eddie's interest in the pub had gone and quite often he stayed at home when he should have been at chapel events. He liked to sit by his fireside, to read and talk to her and take her to bed, and she was happy there with him now. Theirs had become a peaceful household. Eddie cared for her and he showed it. He was easy to live with. He was not temperamental or awkward. He didn't stop her from doing what she wanted to do. It became everything that mattered, their relationship. She knew that marriage to Jon could not have been better than this.

After her mother came to stay she and Eddie slept downstairs in the big bed. It was easier than having to worry about her mother hearing what they said when they went to bed, or what they did. They wanted some privacy. Her mother did not complain. She liked Eddie, and was very pleased that Lizzie had married him. To her mother Eddie could do no wrong now that Lizzie was pregnant, but it was not the same with her around. They couldn't talk or laugh the same over meals, or kiss each other in the kitchen or sitting-room, and Lizzie got a lot of talk about how spotless Enid's house was in spite of the children. Her mother talked a lot about the twins too. Lizzie got tired of that. And her mother objected to her frequent walks on the beach. Lizzie took no notice of that. Her mother didn't dare object to her reading now since it was a way that Eddie passed his free time, but as Lizzie got bigger and more tired she became grateful for her mother who had no objection to housework, to staying up the odd time for Eddie, to making meals, and she knew that her mother was looking forward to the child coming so she tried to create no dissent in the household. She did the best that she could.

One cold morning Eddie came back wet from the pit. There had been a roof fall which let in sand and sea water.

'Nobody was hurt,' he said, 'but the boss came down and stood around and had a good look. He said it wasn't from up top but maybe some old workings.'

'Would he know? He hasn't been here that long.'

'It would be on a map, wouldn't it?'

Jon and Eddie were still working together but they didn't talk.

'Nobody talks to him,' Eddie said. 'I only work with him because we keep up with each other and it makes things easier.'

'Jon once told me that he liked being around you because you reminded him of Alf.'

'Who's Alf?'

'His brother. He died down the Vic.'

'Don't make it any harder, Lizzie. I need friends in the village.'

'Doesn't Jon?'

'It's his own fault,' Eddie said.

'It isn't his own fault at all. When Alf and Sam died, Jon had to keep Greta.'

'He keeps her all right.'

About two months later Mrs Armstrong came shame-faced and crying to Lizzie's door.

'I need some help,' she said. 'Greta's bad and her mam's no use. Will you go for the doctor, Lizzie?'

She did and came back with him in his horse and trap. She would have enjoyed the journey in other circumstances. The doctor was new and young and chatted to her. He had given her lots of advice about her pregnancy on the way, about rest and what she should eat. When they got there Lizzie didn't want to go into the Armstrong house. She went home. She felt sick, wondering about Greta. When Eddie came in off the foreshift she told him.

'What if she loses the bairn, Eddie? She lost the last one and wasn't supposed to be able to have more.'

'How am I supposed to know?' he said roughly, then washed and changed and went out as he rarely did. After he had gone she itched to go next-door and eventually went.

There was a big fire burning in their kitchen and Jon was sitting in front of it, alone. Lizzie stopped short as she stepped down from the pantry. She hadn't seen him alone for months. He was very thin and his eyes were dark with concern.

'I wondered how Greta was. I went for the doctor.'

'Yes, my mam said. Thanks. She's not very good.'

'I wish – I wish things had been different.'

'Aye.'

Lizzie didn't stay. She couldn't think of anything to talk about.

Two days later on the Sunday afternoon Greta died. The baby boy was dead too. Lizzie's mother came in to tell them and for the first time Eddie told his wife not to do something. She was not to go next-door. When he went off to chapel that evening Lizzie could not keep Greta and the dead child from her mind and she thought grimly that next-door did not include her sand dune. She went off there alone in the evening shadows and found what she had known she would find. Jon was alone, dry-eyed. His face was blank and as she clambered down into the sand he got up and moved back like someone who had no right to be there.

'You have to leave the village, Jon.'

'I can't.'

'You don't have any choice.'

'I can't,' he said again. 'I have to look after my mam and Greta's mam.'

'You're never ever going to belong here again. Nobody will ever forgive you.'

'It doesn't matter.'

'It matters to me.'

'You've got Eddie and there'll soon be a baby.'

Lizzie thought about the child he wouldn't have now and as she looked at him she realised for the first time that he really had loved Greta. She made as if to go to him and he moved back again.

'None of it's anything to do with you. Go home.'

'Jon—'

'You've got Eddie to think about. You can't go sneaking around while he's at chapel. Somebody will see you.'

'I want to help.'

'You can't. There's nothing anybody can do now. Go home and forget about it.'

He made her go. She got back just before Eddie and was ashamed to tell lies.

Lizzie's baby was a little girl, Mary. Mrs Harton was very disappointed. Lizzie was in agony for two days and after it her mother said, 'All that effort for another lass!' But Eddie could not disguise his delight and fell asleep many an evening that winter with the baby on his chest.

Lizzie was surprised at how soon she felt well. The other women said that her baby was easy because she soon learned night from day and would sleep for three or four hours right from the beginning. Best of all her mother declared that when Lizzie could cope she would go back to Harold and Enid because they had the twins and Enid was finding them a handful. Within a month of the birth Lizzie was doing more work than she had ever done and enjoying herself. She found the company of other young women in the village who had small children, and especially spent time with May. Lizzie knew how lucky she was. Rob seemed to feel no responsibility towards his family. He drank his pay. He was out nearly every night and lost a lot of shifts through drunkenness. Sometimes, Lizzie knew, May had bruises on her though not where they would show. May was unhappy as Jon had known she would be, Lizzie thought, but she couldn't tell him. Lizzie was beginning to feel very lucky being able to go back to the peace and Eddie.

May was pregnant again that spring and Lizzie was pleased, not just because she knew that May wanted another child and put up with her husband's closeness for that reason, but hoping that another child would take from her the deep sorrow she had felt at the death of her first baby. Also it would mean that their children would be near in age. In her silliest moments Lizzie dreamed of them growing up and loving one another as she had thought that she and Sam might have done.

Her own little Mary grew rapidly in the months which followed.

Sometimes Lizzie saw Jon going to work as she saw Eddie out if it was the backshift. They never spoke and Jon was always alone. Greta's mother reputedly had not spoken to him since Greta died and Mrs Armstrong began to spend a lot of time at May's once May and Rob got a house of their own which they did early that summer. Lizzie hoped that May's having her own home would also increase her happiness though she doubted it since May had confided that her mother-in-law was fond of her and looked to her and it was Rob who had wanted to leave his parents' house.

Jon went to work and came back. What he did the rest of the time Lizzie had no idea because he never went anywhere. The women of the village were kind to Nellie, Greta's mother, and to Mrs Armstrong. Everybody said it was not his mother's fault that Jon had turned out so badly. Some said he was exactly like his father had been. Lizzie's mother said with some satisfaction that she had always prophesied he would do something dreadful and now he had and wasn't she pleased that Lizzie had had enough sense to marry a nice young man like Eddie!

Greta's mother died when the warm weather came. People said that her heart was broken because of what Jon had done to Greta. Lizzie wished that she did not notice how often Mrs Armstrong was not at the house, how often she slept at May's. Mrs Armstrong said that it was because she was worried about May and wanted to help with the hard work in the house so that her daughter could take things easy and maybe this time the baby would be all right. Lizzie privately thought it might have had something to do with the fact that Rob did not hit his wife or lose his temper as often when his mother-in-law was about.

Lizzie woke up every night and thought about Jon alone, and when she couldn't bear it any more she suggested to Eddie that maybe Jon should come to see them one Sunday. Eddie laughed.

'Is that meant to be funny?'

'He can't go on like this, Eddie, it isn't right. His mother isn't living there any more. He's completely alone. People can't live like that and we can't let him.'

Eddie got hold of her arms.

'He's never coming into this house again. Do you hear? And if he so much as breathes in your direction, I'll kill him. Don't argue with me.'

She didn't argue. Another week went by. That Sunday morning Lizzie could bear it no longer. Mrs Armstrong had not been near all week and Jon had gone to and from the backshift in isolation.

Eddie went to chapel and Lizzie went out of her house, down the lane and in at his back door. It was a dark and rainy day and warm enough to be without a fire but usually in pit houses the fire was kept on for cooking and hot water. In the kitchen the fireplace was clean as though there had been no fire there for days, and although the house was not dirty it was obvious to Lizzie it had had no woman's touch for some time. There was a neglected air, a film of dust on everything, and a silence which bothered her.

She ventured into the front room. The dark day and the rain made the empty grate look especially cheerless. Things were gone from here, ornaments, jugs, as though Jon's mother had moved out for good. Lizzie heard a soft noise behind her and turned around and he was there. She was surprised when she saw him. She had thought all those months of grief and misery would show but they didn't. He looked just the same as he had always done. Lizzie didn't know whether to be pleased that he had survived so well or angry because he looked unaffected by what had happened.

'Now,' he said lightly.

Lizzie couldn't think of a thing to say. She had worried for nothing apparently. She was cross with herself for coming, cross that she had lain awake in the middle of the night for his sake.

'I just . . . I just wanted to see you.'

Jon nodded as though this was an everyday occurrence.

'Right,' he said.

'You could leave. Your mam isn't here any more, is she? You could go.'

'It's nowt for you to concern yourself about. You have a baby.'

'I'm so sorry, Jon.'

That defrosted his gaze. He nearly smiled and then Lizzie wasn't sorry that she had been brave and gone to him.

'You shouldn't be here,' he said gently. 'If anybody found out–'

'That's not very nice,' she said.

'It's not meant to be nice. You stay out of here.'

Even as he took her by both arms to ease her from the room she leaned forward against him and kissed him. He let go of her as if she was burning him but she had her arms well around his neck by then and, although Jon tried to stop her, she printed three or four kisses on his face before he fended her off, and then she opened the back door and ran.

That evening Harold called around to Jon's house and asked him if he would go for a drink. Jon hadn't seen anybody but Lizzie all day and he was grateful to Harold but didn't want to go. Harold persuaded him. To Jon's surprise Eddie was there, drinking with Ken and Rob. They had obviously been there for some time, laughing loudly and talking. They didn't speak to him and Jon didn't say anything. He listened to Harold talking as he got the beer in and then he gradually became aware that the laughing stopped and somebody moved and when he looked up Eddie was there, looking at him.

'I hear my wife came round to see you today,' he said.

Jon didn't know whether to confirm or deny this but decided that he wasn't going to get her involved. Eddie had already hit her once.

'No,' he said.

'What?'

'No.'

Eddie got Jon by the lapels of his jacket and eased him to his feet.

'You're a liar, Armstrong. Your brother-in-law saw you.' He glanced at Rob who nodded. 'What did you do to her?'

'Nothing.'

Harold tried to intervene here. Eddie glared at him.

'I don't believe you,' he said to Jon. 'Come outside.'

'I didn't do nothing,' Jon said flatly.

'Now.'

'Oh, no. Look, Eddie—'

Eddie hauled him out so Jon went. Nobody followed immediately. It was getting dark and it was raining hard. Jon felt quite sick. They had been friends. He accepted now that they were friends no more, but he couldn't bear this and he couldn't hit Eddie.

'What do you think I did?'

'I don't know what you did but after the things you've already done I think you'd do anything you wanted.'

'No.'

'You play by different rules to everybody else. And who told you you were welcome here?'

Jon shook his head.

'Nobody,' he said.

Eddie hit him. Jon wasn't expecting it. Afterwards he could never work out why. After all that was what Eddie had got him out there for. It just seemed to Jon that Eddie wasn't ever going to hit him, that deep down Eddie cared too much about him for that; Eddie was like Alf had been. Eddie was very much like Alf in fact – that was what Jon had liked about him. Eddie wasn't going to hit him, not really. He was just angry. Jon had still been working out what to say when Eddie hit him. He didn't want Eddie to think he was doing anything to hurt either him or Lizzie because he wouldn't. Eddie should have known that and Jon was going to explain but couldn't. He wasn't going to let Eddie hurt him for something he hadn't done. And then Eddie knocked him into the wall and it was quite a long way behind him.

That was when Jon realised how angry Eddie was and that it was not an instant thing. Eddie was like a pot of water on the fire, which had started off from cold and come slowly to the boil. It had been coming a long long time and now it had happened. Jon was surprised too at the way that Eddie hit him because Eddie had been drinking. It didn't seem to affect him. It was so efficient. Jon went into the wall. There was a distinct crack and a blinding pain in his left arm and all Jon could do was let his body slide down the wall. The pain took all his concentration. He caught his breath over it again and again. The ground was cold and wet and comforting.

'Get up.'

Jon would have loved to obliged him but he couldn't somehow. By then Ken and Rob and one or two others were there. They helpfully pulled Jon on to his feet, regardless of his arm so Jon kept his eyes closed and his lips tight against the pain. They put him up against the wall and held him.

'Go on, Eddie, give him a bloody good hiding,' Rob urged.

'You bastards, you leave him alone,' Harold said, coming forward, but they stopped him.

'You've got no mind for your sister,' Rob said to Harold. 'You know what he's like with women. Look what he did to his sister-in-law.'

'Let go of him,' Eddie said.

'But Eddie–'

'Let go.'

Eddie couldn't see for rage. Looking at him, Jon could tell. He had the gravest desire to slide back down the wall again. It was raining harder now. Eddie went on hitting him and Ken and Rob kept pulling him back up again and Jon thought of all the good times that he and Eddie had had before everything went wrong, drinking tea in Eddie's aunty's house with all Eddie's aunty's posh furniture, of shielding Eddie from the others when he first came to the village because he knew that Eddie didn't want to fight anybody, of the talk and the laughter. The rain was coming down very heavily now and it seemed to Jon that Eddie was going to kill him. He didn't really mind now so very much. He could hear Harold Harton cursing through the rain. The knuckles on Eddie's hands were bleeding hard.

Eddie didn't understand why afterwards he remembered what everything looked like, the way that Jon didn't seem able to fight, the hopeless expression in his eyes, the white line of pain around his mouth. And afterwards, when his knuckles bled from the way that they had met Jon's face and body, Eddie didn't know how many satisfying times, Jon closed his eyes; they were bruised almost to shut anyway. Eddie watched him crumple down into the road and lie still. Rob and Ken watched but when he didn't move Rob kicked him a couple of times and they walked away. The only thing lifelike about Jon was the blood on his face and shirt. Only Harold was still there. Eddie stood with Jon at his feet and the rain poured down.

Eighteen

*K*ate and her uncle and aunt had been invited to the Nelson house. Kate didn't want to go but there was no use in her protesting. Her aunt was flattered, and though she knew her uncle would have much preferred to stay at home he was obliged to go to his employers for a party.

They stayed the night. Kate was admired. She didn't care about being admired, the whole thing rather bored her, especially since Charles Nelson danced with her several times. Kate had, for some months now, done her best to discourage him but it didn't seem to work. He even called in at the mine office on any pretext. Kate punished him by talking to him about the pit. It seemed the only way to get rid of him.

They stayed until late on Sunday and then set off for home. Kate was full of relief and everything was well until they reached the village. They had to go past the miners' rows to get home and there was a crowd of men gathered in the dusk. It was raining hard by then and Albert had no intention of stopping but Mr Farrer insisted.

As they heard the approach of the horse and trap the men scattered and Kate had a clear view of what happened after that. Two men were left there. One of them hurried away immediately and, as her uncle jumped down and went over, the second man walked off quickly too. Kate could see somebody lying on the ground. Albert held the reins. Her aunt protested at the interruption and Kate got down and went slowly across.

Even in the bad light she wasn't deceived. If somebody had told Kate the day before that she would have been upset at seeing Jon Armstrong hurt she would have denied it. She thought that he had done unforgivable things, but now she saw that she had been wrong. He was still and there was such a lot of blood. Kate was horrified. She got down into the road on her

153

knees. Her uncle looked carefully, felt for a pulse.

'He's not dead, is he?' Kate croaked, her throat was so dry.

She thought her uncle would make a funny remark because Jon was all right but he didn't.

'No, but he's in a bad way. Go with Albert and fetch the doctor.'

'But he's lying in the rain.'

'He doesn't know it and I daren't move him. Go on.'

Kate went. The doctor came and they took Jon back to their house so that he could be looked at properly, and after that the doctor said he wasn't to be moved any more. Kate wasn't very happy about that. If Jon wanted to get himself beaten unconscious why couldn't he have done it somewhere more discreet? she thought irritatedly, and during the few days which followed pretended that he was not in the house. Not that it made any difference. Mrs O'Connor reported that she had never heard anyone talk less. Kate thought it hardly surprising that Jon appeared to have lost the art of conversation.

Even when he started to get better Kate didn't go near. It was a full week before she asked Ellen about him.

'He doesn't do nothing,' she said, putting an untouched dinner tray on to the kitchen table. 'He doesn't say nothing and he doesn't eat nothing.'

Mrs O'Connor looked regretfully at the uneaten food. Kate ventured upstairs. The room where Jon was lodged was pretty. There was sunshine beyond the window but he couldn't see it because he wasn't turned that way. He was turned in towards the wall and was motionless. He must have heard her, she thought, but he gave no acknowledgement. Kate sat down on the bed and waited for him to turn over. Nothing happened.

'How are you?' she asked briskly.

'I'm fine, thank you.' His voice was level and polite.

'You didn't eat anything. How do you expect to get better if you don't eat?'

He didn't answer that. Kate went round to the other side of the bed and sat there. It was difficult to see Jon's expression. He didn't look at her and his face was badly bruised.

'What happened?' she said.

When he didn't answer she said, 'I was there with my uncle. Were you fighting?'

'No.'

'What were you doing?'

'Nothing.'

Mrs Armstrong had been a frequent visitor to the house during the past two weeks and May had been with her more than once. Kate wondered if Jon had talked to them.

After another week Jon was well enough to get up and said that he wanted to go home but Kate's uncle wouldn't hear of it.

'I don't want any injured men down my pit,' he said, 'and if you go home you'll be back at work in no time.'

Kate thought that she understood her uncle less and less, especially when at work she questioned him and he said abruptly, 'I like the lad.'

She was astonished.

'You like him? After all the trouble he's caused?'

'You don't like people for how good they are,' her uncle said. 'Besides, he isn't fit to go back to work, in body or in mind.'

Her uncle, she thought, was at least unpredictable.

Eddie had gone home with bleeding knuckles and an uncertain temper. Lizzie met him at the door and knew before a word was spoken what had happened. She was only glad that the baby was upstairs sleeping because anything could happen now.

'Why?' she said.

'You went to him.'

Lizzie lowered her eyes.

'After what he did, you went to him.'

'He did no worse than you've done. It wasn't his fault Greta and the baby died. He lost me and then he lost them.'

'Don't you talk about it in my house. He as good as killed her.'

'He did no more to her than you've done to me. Did you think of that when I was having the bairn? That I might die, that I was in pain the like of which I didn't know existed. Did you care for any of that? No, of course you didn't. You'd had what you wanted.'

Eddie lifted his hand but she stood there.

'Yes, go on,' she said, 'and I'll take the bairn and leave and never, ever come back. If he's badly hurt you needn't think there'll be a soft word between you and me from now until hell freezes!' And she walked out. She went to Harold's, hammered on the door, and when he opened it she rushed into the kitchen where her mother and Enid were cuddling a twin apiece.

155

'What happened? Is Jon hurt?'

'If he is, Miss, we all know whose fault it was, don't we?' her mother said. 'Going around there! You had no right.'

Lizzie ignored her.

'Is he hurt?'

'Yes,' Harold said in a low voice, coming in after her.

'Bad?'

'Yes.'

'So where is he?'

'At Farrer's.'

'What?'

Harold walked her back out of the house. Lizzie let him.

'I tried to stop it. They wouldn't let me, and don't you go thinking you can go up to Farrer's and see him. Try to do the right thing for once. It was partly you to blame. Whatever were you thinking about?'

'I don't know,' she said miserably.

'You go up there and your marriage is finished. I've never seen Eddie like that. He nearly killed Jon.'

'Didn't Jon do anything?'

'He got hurt too fast.'

'I want to know. Will *you* go to the house?'

Harold hesitated. 'Aye, I'll go, but promise me you won't do owt more? Eddie's bigger than me.'

Jon sat by the window looking out over the garden. He had been at the Farrers' for several weeks now and had stopped asking if he could go home. He was sitting there every day when Kate came back from the office. He had nothing to say. She sat with him while her aunt busied about, telling him everything that had gone on at the pit that day though he made no remarks nor asked any questions. He went back to his room before dinner and afterwards Kate went upstairs and read to him. She didn't know whether he liked her reading since he didn't say anything.

One Sunday afternoon they were sitting together in the drawing-room, her uncle and aunt having gone for a walk, when she heard the sound of a horse outside.

'Oh no,' she breathed, 'it's Charles Nelson.'

Ellen trotted in with the news and Kate had no option but to invite Charles into the drawing-room to sit with one of his hewers. The funny part was that Jon was wearing a dark suit and, dressed by Mrs Farrer, was indistinguishable from anybody else. Charles took him for a gentleman, frowned at seeing an intruder, but came over to shake his hand. Jon got up and walked out of the room.

Charles did not seem inclined to leave. His father had died some time back and now he was more arrogant than ever, Kate thought. When her uncle and aunt came back, Aunt Rose invited Charles to stay for dinner. When Charles had finally gone it was late but on her way to bed Kate slipped into Jon's room. He wasn't in bed but standing by the window with his hands in his pockets, as he might at home.

She went to him.

'Are you going to talk to me?'

'You shouldn't be in here.'

'Goodness me. A remark! No, you're right, I shouldn't.'

Jon's eyes flickered.

'He likes you a lot.'

'I thought I was safe,' Kate said, leaning back against the wall, 'you know, in the office. I never see anyone but the men and the officials. I felt safe there. I like it. My uncle and aunt try to make me go places all the time.'

'What sort of places?'

'Oh, you know.'

'I don't.'

'Dances and parties and things. I don't like it. I like the office. I like the papers and the figures and the work and being part of things. I like the mine.'

'You must be the only person who does.'

'I wish I could go to classes and learn engineering.'

'Useful for you, engineering.'

'Why shouldn't I? I should be able to learn it, shouldn't I, if I want to?'

'I don't see why not.'

'My aunt is convinced that Charles Nelson is going to make me an offer. He can't. I'm not good enough for him socially though I'm far too good for him in every other way. I have no background. I thought it would matter to him but it doesn't seem to. I talked freely to him when he came to the office. I didn't know. I didn't understand.' Kate folded and unfolded her hands as she talked.

'He's very rich.'

'That's why I thought I was safe. He could have anybody, not one of his manager's nieces. I mean, I know that I'm fairly passable but I'm not startling, and when he's there I daren't even wear a pretty dress. What am I going to do?'

'You're probably the only girl in the county who isn't after him. That's got to be more interesting than anything else.'

'Do you think that's it? I'd rather die than marry him. My aunt has asked him again for next Sunday. You will still be here, won't you?'

'I don't think so, no.'

'You can't go and live back there, Jon.'

'Yes, I can.'

'But why?'

'Because I choose to.'

There was silence at Lizzie and Eddie's house and it was not the kind of silence which blew over in a few hours, but went on for days. Lizzie worked. She looked after her child, cleaned her house and saw to Eddie's clothes and meals, but she didn't speak to him. Eddie went to work and came back and tipped up his pay every fortnight and did not complain about anything. He went to as many events at the chapel as he could and Lizzie was glad to have him out of the house and she suspected that he was glad to go.

When Eddie came back with the information that they were to have a lodger she was startled. And it was obviously not good news to him; his grey eyes were alight with temper and his mouth was grim.

'We've never had a lodger before,' she said. Plenty of people did.

'Armstrong's losing his house and moving in with us,' Eddie said.

'That's not funny.'

'Farrer called me into his office especially to tell me. His mother has taken Greta's lad and gone to May's, and Armstrong is no longer entitled to a house.'

'Didn't you object?'

'Yes.'

'Doesn't Mr Farrer know what happened?'

'I expect he knows very well.'

No more was said on the subject. On the Friday of that week Jon came home. Lizzie watched him hover in the back lane before he walked in at her gate and up her yard. She flew to the door, looking him over carefully, dragging him in by the sleeve and saying, 'You are going to be all right?'

'Yes.'

'Does your arm hurt?'

'No. Where's Eddie?'

'On the backshift. Mr Farrer turned out to know more tricks than a monkey, didn't he?'

Lizzie made tea. Jon cuddled Mary, the baby.

'Do you like babies, Jon?'

'Not when they look this much like Eddie.'

She didn't laugh.

'I don't want any fighting.'

'You tell him.'

'Don't worry, I will.'

Meanwhile there was the weekend to be got through. Eddie slept late and Jon went out. When he came back Eddie had gone to the chapel meeting and when Eddie came back Jon had gone – Lizzie didn't quite know where but he made sure it was late enough when he got back that Eddie and she would have gone to bed.

He had brought nothing with him but his clothes and two boxes of books. Rob and May took the furniture. On the Sunday Jon went there for his dinner. He came back at teatime and Eddie was again at chapel but when he came in at seven Jon was lying on the sofa in the front room with Mary asleep on him.

Eddie picked up the child, pushed her into Lizzie's arms, and as Jon got up he hauled him on to his feet and against the wall. There he put one arm under Jon's chin.

'You keep your mucky hands off my bairn. You're only here because Farrer says you are. You have no rights.'

Jon said nothing. He didn't even look at Eddie.

'You don't touch my wife or my bairn. Get it?'

When Jon didn't answer, Eddie hauled him away from the wall and pushed him back hard against it.

'Get it?'

'Yes.'

In the silence which followed Mary started to cry and when Eddie let go Jon went upstairs and didn't come down again that night.

* * *

The week which followed was less than comfortable for everybody. Since they were on different shifts, Lizzie had to get up at all hours. Jon told her not to bother but she was concerned about how silent and thin her lodger was. He rarely ate and never again sat with them. When Eddie was in the house he stayed upstairs out of the way. When Eddie wasn't in to meals Lizzie made sure that Jon ate what was put in front of him.

'It's good food and it had to be paid for,' she said.

'I don't want it. I never said I did,' Jon objected, getting up.

'Sit down.' She tried to play on the way that Jon had been brought up. 'Sit down. We're having a meal.' He sat down and ate.

Jon had been back at work about a fortnight when he had a visitor. For the first time Lizzie thought that Kate was dressed up especially to come calling. Mostly she didn't care what she wore. Her dull brown hat turned her hair to gleaming fire and she had tan leather gloves on her hands. She wore a coat which few people could have worn, very dark against her creamy skin. She made Lizzie feel dull. It was Sunday afternoon and since Eddie and Jon were both at home Lizzie was quite relieved to be rid of Jon for a short time when Kate suggested a walk; though Lizzie thought she was likely to die of curiosity at not knowing their conversation.

'I'm not going to the beach, mind you,' Jon said as they set off.

'I don't mind where we go.'

They walked up the country roads.

'Isn't Charles Nelson visiting today then?' Jon asked.

'I cried off. I told him I thought I was getting the 'flu.'

It was a cold day and after an hour Jon stopped beside a gate.

'Haven't we walked far enough?'

'I want you to go to college.'

'Oh, not again, Kit.'

'There's no reason why you shouldn't. You could take a special course to be a mine manager, do examinations. You could do it standing on your head and then come back and teach it to me.'

'No.'

'What are you going to do? Live with Lizzie and Eddie forever? It must be a wonderful arrangement. How does he like it?'

'He loves it, and so do I.'

'It must be so comfortable for Lizzie too, you and Eddie likely to kill one another.'

'Shut up, Kit.'

'You're such a gentleman,' she said.

So Jon took to his books and began to work. There were whispers in the village that it was all because of the boss's niece, that Armstrong was trying to better himself so that he could marry her.

'What does he think he's doing?' Lizzie's mother said one afternoon when Jon was at work and Eddie wasn't.

Eddie laughed.

'Kate marry Jon when the mineowner's after her? Very likely.'

'She's a nice lass,' Lizzie said.

'If she is she'll have nothing to do with the likes of him,' Mrs Harton declared.

It wasn't long before Jon was called into Mr Farrer's office and it was after hours which meant Kate wasn't there; only the boss. He looked a more severe man than the one at whose dinner table Jon had sat for the last few days of his time there.

'I've got something to say to you, Armstrong,' he declared, standing in front of the stove.

'Yes, sir.'

'My niece is a very headstrong girl. I'm regretting that I ever let her come here to work. My wife said that no good would come of it and now . . . now it seems that you have abused my hospitality.'

Jon didn't know what he was talking about.

'No, sir.'

'Yes, lad, you have. She sees you, doesn't she?'

'Sees me? She doesn't see me–'

'Don't lie.'

'I'm not. What I mean is . . . I've started going to classes – mining engineering – and you know what she's like. She wants to learn so I teach her.'

'You teach Katherine engineering?'

'Yes, sir.'

George Farrer smiled.

'All right, lad. I know what she's like. But if it's ever anything more than that I'll come down on you like a ton of bricks.'

'It's never going to be more than that,' Jon said. 'I'm never going to feel like that again. I just want to work, that's all, and she wanted to know.'

'I don't think Katherine will have the need to learn mining engineering, Armstrong, not for much longer. I think she'll soon have too many other interests to occupy her time.'

Nineteen

Kate was happier now than she had been since her father died. In fact, that autumn, she thought she was happier than she had ever been. Jon worked hard between classes and the mine, but she saw him frequently and he was a good teacher. She worked too; she looked after her uncle at the office but she also read and studied and kept up as the weeks went by. She was in and out of Lizzie and Eddie's house -- sometimes three times a week -- and even though her uncle knew what she was doing he did not seem to mind and her aunt said nothing. They knew nothing however of the happiest times of all -- Sunday afternoons, sitting in Lizzie's front room by the fire. Kate felt that she had come home, listening to Jon explaining in his sing-song accent the things he had learned. He learned things very quickly.

Sometimes when they needed a break they went walking across the fields and Kate knew that she felt more for Jon than she had felt for anyone except her father and this was different, in some ways it was even better. A plan had begun to form in her mind. Jon would do well if he was given a chance, if he had a woman around him who was the right one. Jon would be a mine manager and maybe even more.

Kate liked walking with him; he was kind. He treated her as if she was special. He gave her his arm if the walking was difficult. She liked being with him better than anything else in the world. She liked going back to sit by Lizzie's fire and have her produce tea, coffee cake and sandwiches. Kate felt as though this was the home she had never had. She felt at peace here.

The peace in the Bitten household was dearly bought. Things were changing. Several times when Eddie had goaded Jon about Kate, Lizzie could see all the old signs of temper in Jon. She knew that Eddie couldn't see them but more than once she had got in front of Jon just in case while he

163

lowered his eyes and backed off. It was hard work making sure the men were not together too much. Sometimes the pit office slipped up and they were on the same shift. Lizzie worried about that but after a while it seemed to be better when they were and she knew they had once worked well together. Perhaps it would happen again. In the meanwhile Jon's temper was uncertain. She tried to talk to Eddie about it but he only laughed and said that if Jon wanted another good hiding he was quite happy to provide it.

They went on like that and the weather grew colder. Jon was out as often as he could be. If it was wet he sat upstairs, but when it became too cold either to spend much time outside or upstairs he sat by the kitchen fire with a book. Lizzie had dreaded this happening but to her surprise Eddie said nothing. He even began to address the occasional remark to Jon though it was never what she would have called conversation. They were now almost always on the same shift which made things much easier from her point of view and as the weeks went by she began to feel almost relaxed. Kate's presence helped and Lizzie encouraged her to come to the house because Eddie would not have done her the discourtesy of being rude to Jon in front of her. She lightened the atmosphere because she was there so often, she was so involved in studying, so enthusiastic, and she made them laugh together sometimes. Eddie started to take Jon's presence for granted though Jon was very cautious and quiet and did nothing to upset him.

The day came when Charles Nelson arrived at the Farrer household just after the big Sunday meal so that Kate was not able to go to Lizzie and Eddie's. Her aunt and uncle knew only that she went walking on Sunday afternoons so thought this no great loss. When Charles suggested that he should walk a little way with her they seemed to think that this took care of the problem.

It was the longest Sunday afternoon of Kate's life. Charles was in good temper and paid her a great many compliments. All she could think was that she wouldn't see Jon. She thought of him waiting for her in Lizzie's front room, of his conversation, the promised walk, and she wondered whether Lizzie had made chocolate, coffee and walnut or orange cake. Orange cake was Kate's favourite just at present so Lizzie usually made that. If Kate closed her eyes she could smell the cake warm from the oven. There was always the smell of baking in their house on Sunday afternoons. Kate longed for it so much that she ached.

The following day she caught Jon as he went on shift and tried to explain hastily. She saw the other men's grins but he didn't seem to notice.

'It doesn't matter,' he said, 'there's plenty of time.'

'Tomorrow night?'

'If you like.'

Kate didn't get to go the next Sunday or the one after that because Charles Nelson turned up on both occasions, and on the second Sunday when they went walking he kissed her. She didn't know what to do. She had never been kissed before. She had badly wanted Jon to kiss her the last time that they had spent Sunday together.

Jon and she had gone walking in the woods. It was a magical afternoon, growing cold. There was not even a whisper of movement among the frosted trees and it was late so that the shadows were dark in the woods. The grass was stiff with ice beneath her feet and as the afternoon grew late there were pigeons and the flutter of their wings. Jon had put both hands on her waist to lift her over a stream. Their conversation seemed to bounce off the trees and when she laughed the sound went on and on in the woods. It was very cold by the time they reached home. The kettle was singing on the fire and Lizzie had just finished icing an orange cake. It was all shiny on top like something from a children's party. Her happiness would have been complete if Jon had kissed her.

She didn't believe it when they told her. It made her feel as she had done after her father died, like there was an earthquake all around her. She was frightened and hesitant and wanted to go back, only there was nowhere to go back to.

'Marry Charles Nelson?' she said.

'Isn't it wonderful?' her aunt said, beaming at her. They were sitting in the drawing-room. It was the following Saturday evening. 'He has officially asked your uncle for your hand. When I think of all the young ladies he could have married! Quite frankly, Katherine, I don't know why he chose you because you must admit that you don't try very hard. Look at that dress. Where's your new jonquil one?'

'I don't know.' She had spent that afternoon studying in her room.

'He's coming to dinner tomorrow, you'll be able to see him then. You can wear your new dress.'

'But I'm going out.'

'Don't be silly, Katherine.'

'I'm going out. I don't want to see Charles Nelson. I don't ever want to see him,' said Kate and fled.

They let her go but in the middle of the evening her uncle sent Ellen to fetch her. Kate went downstairs to her uncle's small study where he worked and read and fell asleep. His study was his retreat. He was standing in front of the fire now.

'Shut the door, please,' he said, and when she had done so he turned around looking gravely at her. 'Katherine, you're very young. I'm afraid you're going to have to let your aunt and me make this decision for you. You will never receive another offer like this. I must say that I'm agreeably surprised because you know men don't usually care for women who behave as you do.'

'How do I behave?' she said, surprised and offended.

'You're far too fond of your own opinions and ideas. It isn't what a man looks for in a wife. But never mind, that will sort itself out when you're married.'

'I don't want to marry him.'

'No, I'm aware of that. It seems to me – you may correct me if I'm wrong – that you've formed an attachment to young Armstrong. Now I've nothing against the lad but let me say this to you. He's proved what kind of a man he really is and a girl died because of it, so even if Charles Nelson had not offered for you I would have had to stop the friendship with Jon. It isn't suitable. He says there's nothing in it . . .'

'You talked to Jon about me?'

'Yes, I did, some time ago.'

'He likes me.'

'I daresay he does but he's a pitman and pit people have strange ideas. They keep to their own kind.'

'That's not true. I'm accepted among them.'

'Has he ever indicated to you that it was more than friendship?'

Kate thought for a moment and shook her head.

'No,' she said.

'Precisely. I want you to promise me that you won't see him.'

'Why?'

'I want you to promise. If you don't I'll dismiss him. Do you understand?'

Kate stood there and said nothing. She had not realised until that moment how Jon saw her. Now she did.

'Tomorrow,' her uncle said, 'you will see Charles Nelson and you will say everything that is proper to him. You won't go back to the office and you won't go again to the village. I've engaged another clerk to take your place. You will behave properly and I don't wish to see you in a mended dress again. Now go to your room.'

The upshot of that was that Lizzie found Kate on her doorstep the following morning in the middle of the washing. She wasn't best pleased to see her – the house was a mess – but when she saw the red eyes and the promise of more tears she left her washing and sat Kate down by the fire and gave her tea while she poured out the story and cried some more.

'What am I going to do?'

'I don't think there's anything you can do. You don't have anybody to go to.'

'Is Jon on the foreshift or is he in bed?'

Lizzie was for once glad that her lodger was out.

'He's at work.' She hesitated for fear she might offend Kate and then said, 'You can't involve Jon.'

Kate looked at her through tears.

'He'll lose his job, you know he will,' Lizzie said. 'He doesn't care about you, Kate, not like that. I don't think he's capable of it any more, not after what happened to Greta.'

'There's nobody else to help me. Jon will if I ask him.'

'I'm sure he will but you *can't* ask him. Don't you think he's had enough trouble?'

Kate dried her eyes and blew her nose and drank her tea.

'I won't be able to come here ever again.' When Lizzie began to protest Kate stopped her. 'I won't. You were right. My uncle's already threatened to dismiss Jon and it isn't fair of me to involve any of you. Will you tell Jon? I don't want him to find out through gossip.'

'I'll tell him,' Lizzie promised.

She did so that evening over a meal.

'It's not much of a surprise,' Eddie said, 'I just think it's a bit strange myself. If I was rich I'd have a blonde.'

Lizzie knew that he meant it lightly but it felt as though he was referring directly to Greta. Eddie finished his meal and went off to his chapel meeting, and as it was a wet evening Lizzie knew that Jon would retreat behind his books so she didn't give him the chance. She said, 'Hold Mary while I clear up. She's cried most of the day.'

Jon hesitated. He had never done so since Eddie told him not to but Lizzie dumped the little girl on him and went back to the table so he didn't have any choice.

'What do you think about Kate's marriage?' Lizzie asked.

'Same as Eddie. I think he's mad to marry her.'

'Do you? Why?'

'He'd be better off with somebody from his own class and with a little bit of style. Somebody who wouldn't argue with him and ask questions all the time.'

'I thought you liked Kate.'

'I do like her. I'm not Charles Nelson, am I? She's gone through a lot and she doesn't like living with her aunt and uncle. I don't quite know why, I think they're nice people, but she was brought up by her dad. It makes her different from other lasses.'

'Are you sorry she's marrying him?'

'I'm sorry because she doesn't want to but you never know, it might work out. I just wish she wasn't marrying the pit owner; we won't be able to be friends any more.'

Lizzie comforted herself because she had been right about Jon's feelings for Kate but could not banish from her mind the image of the girl sitting crying by her kitchen fire.

All day and every day it was fittings and lists. There was the wedding dress for a start which was so beautiful that it made Kate shudder. It was white silk taffeta, the skirt lined with stiffened muslin. The bodice was trimmed with deep cream silk bows and fringes. There was also a huge wedding veil of net with tiny patterned flowers. The dress was so elaborate she felt as though it swamped her, and so heavy that her body ached. Her face peeped out fearfully and unflatteringly from the white veil.

There were going away clothes and clothes for mornings and for evenings and for nights. There were hats and gloves and shoes and boots, and interminable things to organise for the wedding. Her aunt enjoyed every moment of it once Kate had stopped crying and protesting. She got together with Charles's mother and they had cosy afternoons over the teacups deciding who should be invited and how many bridesmaids there would be.

Kate's one escape was riding. She could not even talk about the pit any more. Her uncle did not mention it in her presence. She missed the office and the work and the comings and goings of the men. Most especially she missed Jon, like a hungry person missed eating. At first she questioned Charles but since he took little interest in the pits himself he could not provide any answers and only laughed at her.

She took Dolly to the beach and galloped for miles, hoping to catch a glimpse of Jon. She did not care when her hair came down, she did not care that the days were cool or that the tides crashed high up the beach. She only wanted to be alone.

Charles sent her flowers, bought her expensive gifts – a diamond ring for her finger, ear-rings to match, bracelets and necklaces. He showed a great deal of interest in what she wore. He liked to know what she would be wearing, what the colours would be and the styles. He made suggestions to her and liked to present her to his friends so that they could admire her beauty. Kate was beautiful in her fine new clothes; even she knew it.

He didn't touch her. Kate was glad of this, she was relieved, she didn't want to be touched. He was always telling her how beautiful she was but he liked her to wear Fuller's Earth to cover the freckles. He lavished on her all kinds of clothes and insisted that she wore different outfits: two, or sometimes three, times a day. Worse still, his mother was to live with them at the big house, though Charles had tried to persuade her otherwise, and since she ran the house successfully Kate realised that she was to be left with nothing to do.

There was a holiday at the three pits on the day that Charles and Kate were married. It was early summer by then. They went off to the continent for a long holiday and the men went back to work.

When Kate came home it was almost Christmas. They had been away for six months. It felt like a lifetime. Charles's mother hugged her and welcomed her back and it was worse than Kate had thought it would be. She spent most of her life surrounded by other women who talked of nothing but fashions and children. There were lunch parties and tea parties and dinner dances. It being the shooting season there were people to stay and weekends or even weeks away. Sometimes Charles went alone. She was glad of that. There were dances and suppers and long, long evenings spent listening to other people sing and play the piano, and there were the nights when Charles didn't come to her and the even longer ones when he did.

Kate went riding in the mornings early but had to wait for the light. Her mother-in-law questioned the rides.

'My dear, what if you were to miscarry?' she said.

Since Eddie had hurt Jon Lizzie had not let him near her, and it was a long time. At first she hadn't cared, she would have run away rather than let him near, and after Jon came to live with them Eddie was so awful to him that she didn't regret the decision, but there was an uneasy peace in the house now. Often she looked up and found Eddie's grey eyes watching longingly after her, and often, she knew, he didn't sleep. Also, Lizzie wanted another child. Mary was beginning to grow up. She wanted another baby.

She knew that if Eddie had been a different sort of man he would have forced her long before now or even hit her except that Jon was there. Eddie endured her coldness. He did everything he should: he went to work and never missed a day, he was good with Mary, he didn't drink or shout, he wasn't moody. If it had not been for Jon's presence Lizzie and her husband would have been reconciled long before, she knew, but Eddie could not bear Jon's presence and because of that Lizzie kept herself turned away from him.

Eddie knew that as far as the pitmen were concerned Kate had been Jon's fancy piece. As Rob remarked to Ken, 'It makes a change, Charles Nelson getting one of Armstrong's cast offs.'

That winter when she came home and was seen about riding Dolly the talk began again, and one Wednesday as they were sitting having their bait Rob regaled them with a description of what Kate had been wearing the previous afternoon when he saw her and how being married suited her. The older men would not take part in such talk and the ones who went to chapel, like Eddie, ignored it. Jon sat by himself. A lot of the men still didn't speak to him and Eddie thought he must have got used to it because he rarely spoke at work or indeed to Eddie at home, unless directly addressed. Rob wasn't satisfied.

'He was a bit of a step up for her from you, wasn't he, Armstrong? Was she any good then?'

Jon didn't reply as Eddie knew he wouldn't but Rob still wasn't happy.

'Was she as good as Greta?'

Jon came to his feet so fast that Eddie didn't have time to stop him from hitting Rob, but Rob's friends were there, Ken and two others, and they pitched in and held Jon down. Eddie didn't sit there and make a decision. He took on the other two and left Jon to handle Rob and Ken. There wasn't much space for fighting but it didn't take long now that the odds were better. He and Jon still didn't speak on the way home but the atmosphere was lighter.

Eddie hated his marriage. It was like it had been at first, and Jon being the cause it was difficult not to hate him too. The meals were always on the table, the clothes were clean, the water was hot. Lizzie did not complain when he went out though there were only so many places to go when it was cold and dark and Eddie had run out of them. He sat by the fire and read in the evenings.

He knew that she was never going to forgive him for what he had done to Jon and he was never going to forgive himself because it had ruined what little of his marriage there was to enjoy. He would never break Jon's hold on her affection, he could see that now. She was going to love Jon Armstrong without rhyme or reason for the rest of her life and he had only made things worse with his ridiculous jealousy. He wished he could understand how she felt and why. He did the best that he could. He worked hard, he asked nothing. He lay there in the darkness at night, wanting her, despising himself for wanting a woman who didn't want him. The hunger bit at him, drove him out of his senses, until he couldn't think of anything else. He tried so hard to control his body and night after night he lay listening to her breathing, taking in the sweet smell of her. Sometimes she turned over and her body brushed against his, or she leaned over when she was getting his dinner and he saw the sweep of dark hair brushed away from her neck. He thought about what it was like to kiss her neck, to touch her softness, and knew that this was the payment for what he had done to Jon. They made him feel that only he was guilty and it was not true. Greta had not extinguished the feelings between them; they were always there.

It was true that he could have forced her. Many a man would have, but he knew that it was not the answer. He could have talked to her perhaps, persuaded her, told her that she was his wife and what her duties were. But he didn't. Then came the evening when they were having tea together and he made a joke – he didn't realise that he was going to – and she put her hand over her mouth because she laughed and was eating cake. Jon wasn't there.

'I'll choke,' she said. She swallowed some tea and coughed and swallowed some more tea and the tears came into her eyes and she had to wipe them and blow her nose. She got up to clear the table and Eddie got up and went over. He took her by the arm and led her up the stairs and into the bedroom and he closed the door.

'What are you doing?' she said. 'Mary's downstairs in her cot.'

'The fireguard's up, the door's locked and she's asleep.'

He took her slowly into his arms so that if she was going to resist there was plenty of time but to his surprise and joy she didn't. She came to him and her lips parted and she kissed him.

Twenty

*I*t was weeks after she had come home that Kate first caught sight of Jon. She knew that the sensible thing was to pretend she hadn't seen him, to wheel Dolly around and go back to the house, but she couldn't. She cantered along the sand towards him and when she got there pulled the mare gently to a halt.

Things were different for Kate now when she came to the village. The pitwomen no longer invited her into their houses and the pitmen doffed their caps and retreated respectfully. She hated it.

She knew how much she had missed Jon during those endless months but her heart had not ached nearly as much as it did now when she saw him. She'd thought that he would somehow look different or that he would act like the other men had and she knew that she couldn't bear it, but he was just the same and instead of greeting her politely and taking off his cap looked her over and said, 'Well, don't you look a treat?'

Kate knew that she did. She wore a green military-looking riding habit and a tall hat with a matching ribbon. Her hair was out of the way under a net but she knew it was almost fire-coloured against the green hat.

She glanced down at herself.

'Think how many wages this wretched outfit would pay. I hate it. I have five more in different colours. It's dreadful to wear; it's boned up here and I have a hundred petticoats under it. Oh dear,' she looked at Jon. 'I'm not meant to talk about petticoats. I will keep on forgetting.'

She chatted so that her eyes would not fill with tears that she didn't want him to see. She held out both arms.

'Will you help me down?'

Jon steadied the horse and lifted her down and Kate looked up at him. She thought he was the best sight in the world.

'How are you, bonny lad?'

Jon smiled at the endearment and said, 'I'm fine. How are you?'

'Don't ask.' Kate took the reins from him and they walked a little way. She looked anxiously at Jon. 'Are you still studying?'

'Yes.'

'I hoped you were. I didn't dare come to the house but I've ridden my horse on the beach every day this week thinking that sooner or later you must be on the early shift and out walking in the afternoons.'

'It's not much weather for walking,' he said.

'Will you help me?'

'With what?'

'Studying, of course. I've missed such a lot.'

'What?'

Kate knew by the way Jon looked at her that he couldn't believe what she was saying.

'You've got to help me, Jon. I have to see you.'

'Don't be daft,' he said. 'You're married now.'

'What difference does that make?'

'Does your man think your studying mining engineering is a good idea?'

'It's nothing to do with him and anyhow, he's away. He's gone to Scotland to do some shooting. I want you to come to the house.'

'What?'

'Will you, and bring your books? What about tomorrow?'

'Kit, I can't.'

'I know that you think I'm asking a lot but there's a big balcony outside my room and—'

'Hey!' Jon caught hold of her by both arms and shook her gently. 'You aren't listening to me. I can't do it.'

Kate could feel the tears now in her throat.

'But you have to do it, Jon.'

'What do I have to do it for?'

'I can't come to your house. You have no stable.' And she smiled and blinked hard.

'Look, Kit, I can't. You know I can't. You're not you any more, you're Charles Nelson's wife. You're married, and not just to anybody. Even if you were living in the village I still couldn't, but as it is . . . Kit, you're the mineowner's wife.'

He let go of her. Kate stood looking down, threading her gloves through her fingers and trying hard for control.

'You don't understand,' she said. 'I can't go on any more like this.'

'Any more like what?'

'Like this.'

'But you have everything. Look at you.'

Kate swallowed hard at the tears.

'Maybe you would give me a hand back up?' she said, and when he had she said a hasty goodbye and went off as fast as her tear filled eyes would allow.

There was something about her room that Jon didn't like, but at first he couldn't see what it was. It was late. Half a dozen times he had told himself not to do this but the image of her bravely not crying came unbidden to his mind every time. She never cried, at least he had never seen her. He thought that he had seen few people as desperately miserable as Kate had looked that day. It wasn't altogether a surprise but some part of him had, up to now, refused to think that Charles Nelson would make her unhappy. After all the man had wanted her, had pursued and married her. If it wasn't to make her happy then what was it for?

She was ready for bed by the time Jon slid in at the window, and she was alone. She wore stuff you thought you could see through, only you couldn't. It must be very dear, Jon thought, such rich colours, greens and creams, and flowing all the way to her feet. It was, he felt sure, the kind of garment which women wore for men, but since Charles was away and she had not been expecting him perhaps it was just what women wore to bed when they were married to rich men. Kate didn't look quite right in it anyway; she was thinner now than she had been even when they first met when she had come north after her father died. Her eyes were big with unhappiness and her cheekbones stood out. Her hair was brushed out and loose. Jon hadn't realised that it was so long. It made her look very young.

When she saw him her expression changed and after that Jon wasn't sorry that he had walked a long cold four miles arguing with himself.

The room was very big and it led into other rooms which were lit with lamps and obviously belonged to her. There was a bathroom, she showed him, all done in greens and blues so that it looked like the sea, and a sitting-room with long narrow sofas which she said were very uncomfortable. There were books, lots of them, and chairs, and there were rugs the like of which he had never seen.

'I think Charles's grandfather brought them back from the Middle East,' she said.

The rugs had birds on them and intricate patterns and were woven in vivid colours. The bed was huge and high and four-postered and looked like bliss to sleep in. Jon imagined Charles there and put the thought immediately from his mind. There was a writing desk. He sat her down there and showed her diagrams and notes and the work that he was busy doing and she asked questions.

There was food too. A bottle of wine and daft little sandwiches cut into diamond shapes. When they stopped working she sat him in a big chair by the fire and gave him a plateful of sandwiches which turned out to be smoked salmon, so she said. The wine, which was white, tasted strange and wonderful to Jon, like summer: butter and sunshine. She asked him which books she could borrow and poured wine generously and sipped a little herself and smiled happily at him. Jon was almost content and then he knew what it was about the room that he didn't like. It was the fact that the colours in the room matched and blended perfectly, even down to the clothes which she wore.

'Where did you go when you went abroad?' he asked.

'Lots of places. We went to Paris. We went to Rome and Florence and Venice. Rome has lots of statues and things, and ruins. Florence is very pretty and Venice . . . the houses are all crumbling there. Charles bought me lots of things everywhere we went. Chandeliers in Venice, you know, Venetian glass. And mirrors, ornate mirrors.'

'Charles likes to buy things?'

'Yes. Charles likes colour. He likes me to wear pretty colours and be surrounded by them. I have lots and lots of dresses. He likes to see me in them. He likes to look at me. Says that he can spend hours looking at me. Except for the freckles, of course. He says I would be perfect if it wasn't for the freckles, that they spoil the perfection. He says . . .'

Kate was fast losing control of herself, Jon could see. Any minute now she was going to get up and run out of the room. And she did. Only as she got up and tried she fell over the hem of her nightdress. He was already on his feet and caught and steadied her. If she had been any other lass he knew she would have broken down and cried, but she didn't. Her whole body shook but nothing happened, as though she had been in control of herself for so long that she didn't know how to stop.

'What does he say, Kit?'

She made a strangled noise in her throat and tried to free herself. Jon put both arms around her and drew her against him, and from the safety of his arms Kate managed, 'That I'm cold, that I'm like one of those statues we saw. There were hundreds of them, Jon, in the churches in Venice. Marble. Dead. Like my father.'

'It's all right,' he soothed, and he stroked her hair.

'My father fell over on to the table and died. He was eating, we were having supper together, just like we did every night, and he was talking to me. And then all of a sudden he stopped and leaned over and . . . I should have done something. I didn't know what to do. I was alone with him. There was nobody. There was nobody.'

'You couldn't have done anything. It was his heart. Didn't you tell me that the doctor said nobody could have done anything?'

'He was all I had. He was the only person. When I was small I used to wake up in the night and think that he had died and I was alone. And now I am. It's like a nightmare. I can't wake up from it and I'm so frightened.'

Jon picked her up and put her into bed, then he took off his boots and jacket and lay down with her and cuddled her close.

'Have I told you about it before?' she said.

'No, not much.'

'Nobody asked me what it was like when I came here. Nobody talked to me about him. I wanted to talk about him; it was all I had left, but my uncle and aunt . . . it was just as if he had never been.'

'Tell me about him then. What was he called?'

'Jonathan.'

'Was he? Like me?'

'Are you? I assumed you were called John.'

'I think my mam must have been having a religious phase. You never know. If she hadn't got over it our Alf could have been Hezekiah and then where would we have been?'

Kate smiled against his shoulder.

'I don't believe there ever was anybody called Hezekiah. You made it up.'

'Maybe. I can't remember now.'

'Do you miss Alf?'

'All the time. That's the thing about grieving. People say you get over it but you don't. The loss goes on getting bigger.'

'Did you love Greta?'

'Yes.'

'That's why you don't have another girl, isn't it?'

'I don't want that ever again.'

'I know. People said that my father should have taken another wife but he didn't, even though he was alone all those years. I'd rather have what you and Greta had, and my father and mother, than live a long time and be miserable.'

'Is it that bad?' he asked her softly.

Kate took a deep breath.

'He tells me what to wear, what to do, what to say. He tells me what to think – at least he would if he thought I had any ideas, any thoughts at all but he doesn't, you see. He's been brought up to believe that women are very poor creatures. I think a lot of men are like that. My father brought me up to believe that people should be educated in a way that brings out whatever is best in their minds, but Charles thinks that women are for ornamental purposes. Oh, and for breeding, of course. Do you think I'm ornamental?'

'I think you're worn out. Go to sleep.'

'Aren't you on the early shift?'

'No.'

She closed her eyes against him and said, 'I shouldn't have asked you to come here. I'm sorry. It was selfish of me but I couldn't think how else to manage.'

'It's all right. I want you to study hard this week. Is Charles back on Saturday?'

'Not until Sunday.'

'All right. I'll come on Saturday.'

'No.'

'Don't argue. Go to sleep.'

Lizzie had had a bad night with Mary and had sat for most of the time in front of the fire which had obligingly come to life under her skill with a poker. The light came dull and grey and Mary finally slept, hot no longer. Eddie had slept. Jon, she knew, had not come home. The door was still unbolted.

Not long after dawn she heard his footsteps up the yard and he softly opened the door.

'Well,' she said, 'good morning.'

Jon closed the door and looked at her. Lizzie was wearing a long nightdress, with a shawl over her shoulders and her hair neatly braided. She looked straight back at him and said, 'What time do you call this?'

'I don't know. What time do *you* call it?'

'I call it staying out all night.'

'When did you turn into my mother?'

'I don't remember, but I know you. You can't help but cause problems. Don't do something awful. Please, Jon.'

'Nice nightie,' he said.

'Don't do that.'

Jon only smiled and he went across and kissed her on the cheek and said, 'Goodnight.'

The following Saturday was a wet foggy night. Jon was soaked. He let himself in like before, got even wetter in among the grass and the trees. She opened the window for him when he reached the balcony but it was different from before. She was dressed for a start, her hair was up and her clothes were formal. Jon took off his cap but she made no comment about the way that the rain was dripping off his hair on to his face and neck. She complained about the state of the books even though Jon had wrapped them up, and sat down immediately and began reading.

He ventured to the fire, took off his boots and jacket and left her to read. He sat there before the blaze, drying out with his hands up to the flames, and she went on reading.

'What time does he get back tomorrow?'

'Not until late. There's a meeting at the Victoria early in the week. Something about some water. My uncle is concerned, that's how I know. My aunt mentioned it. It's the only way I get to know anything. My uncle is insisting that Charles takes a look, though how that will help I can't imagine since he knows nothing. Is it very wet?'

'It's like a sieve,' Jon said. 'In some parts people are working in four inches of water. It's a popular spot is that, and it's getting worse.'

'Why?'

'I don't know. Your uncle pretended that nothing was happening at first and of course the market for coal's risen and he's being pressed into producing more and more, so less and less is being left where it should be. There are a lot of roof falls where there never were, or they're heavy where they were slight. It makes things risky. I'm considering getting out.'

Kate looked sharply at him.

'Getting out?' she said.

'There's nothing to keep me. My mam stays with Rob and May.'

'But where would you go?' she asked.

'I don't know.'

'And what about this?' She indicated the books.

'I could find somewhere else near Sunderland or Newcastle and carry on. It would be nice to be in a pit where I didn't have to worry about how well I swim.'

'I didn't know it was as bad as that. You're the only friend I have.'

'We can't be friends, Kate, you know that. We're too far apart. It would only make trouble. I can't keep on coming here like this. You know it as well as I do. Somebody will see me, somebody will find out, and then what?'

'I know. I shouldn't ask you, especially after last time when you were so nice to me. You mustn't keep on being so nice to me. You're all wet. It must be like being at work for you.'

She went off downstairs and came back quietly with a tray. Jon built up the fire and they sat around and ate and drank. Kate swallowed two glasses of wine and then said, 'I know it's very selfish but I don't want you to leave.'

'If anybody finds out I've been here I'll have to leave anyway. You can't hide things in a small town like this.'

She looked appealingly at him.

'It's no use doing that either,' Jon advised.

'Doing what?'

'Behaving like a woman.'

'I *am* a woman.'

'Kit, I swore after Greta that I wouldn't hurt a woman again, and I won't.'

'You're not hurting me. Only if you leave.'

'That's a fine argument.'

'Oh,' she said, exasperated, 'you're like a block of wood.'

'I don't think Kate's very happy,' Rose Farrer announced to her husband over the breakfast cups.

'Isn't she?' George put down his newspaper. 'I don't know why. She has everything a young woman could ask for.'

His wife fidgeted over the tea and bread and butter.

'Every time I go she's either out on that horse or poring over some books I don't understand. It isn't natural.'

'Things will change when there's a child,' George said. 'They always do. It takes time to get used to things. They haven't been married long yet. Give it a chance.'

'And yet she's started coming to the village a lot. I told her she must think of her position but she only laughed.'

Kate was often in the town. She hated being Mrs Nelson. She wished that she was Miss Farrer again. She hated going back to her uncle and aunt's house. It reminded her of how much happier she had been then, of the office and the summer and of reading to Jon during the evenings when he was hurt.

The weather was bad and though she waited several afternoons in the sand dune where she knew he sometimes went to read, Jon didn't appear, so in the end Kate let herself out of the house through the back gardens in the evening and walked four miles through wet fog.

She was terrified that somebody would see her and wore a long cloak with a hood, not realising that it made her even more conspicuous, but the night was dark. It was not much better in the village but she tiptoed up the back lane, counting the number of houses, aware of each breath.

There was a lamp burning in Lizzie's kitchen. Kate hovered beyond the back door and then the cold drove her down the yard and in at the door. She didn't bang on it. In the knowledge that pit people rarely locked their doors, she lifted the sneck and walked in. She clashed the door after her and because it was dark she stumbled over the step between the pantry and the kitchen. She thought she had never seen as welcome a sight as the kitchen fire. To her dismay Eddie and Lizzie were both there and when they heard her they looked up, Lizzie from where she was rocking a cradle by the fire and Eddie from his book. Jon was not there. Neither of them spoke.

'I want to see Jon,' she said.

'He's in bed. He's on early shift,' Lizzie replied. 'What are you doing here?'

It should have been a relief to be spoken to normally – so many people in the village didn't treat her like that – but Kate was offended.

'I came to see Jon. Will you get him please?' She raised her voice.

'No, I won't. He has to go to work at three.'

'I want to see him. I've walked all the way and I'm not going until you let me.'

'You're supposed to be a respectable married woman. How can you do this?'

'I need to see Jon,' Kate insisted.

There was a slight noise from the stairs and he appeared, sleepy-eyed and hastily dressed, with his hair all over the place.

'What the hell's all the noise?' he said, pushing back his hair with his fingers. And then he saw Kate.

'You've really done it this time,' said Eddie.

Jon ignored him. He went on looking at Kate with disbelief.

'What on earth are you doing here?'

'I haven't seen you in weeks. I'm tired of waiting.'

Eddie clicked his tongue over this.

'If we don't stop raising our voices our neighbours will know exactly what's going on,' Lizzie said. 'Sit down, Kate, and I'll make you some tea.'

'I don't want any tea.'

'Go through into the other room and I'll bring it.'

Kate knew that Lizzie's front room would be cold.

'No,' she said.

'Do you think we're going to like being on the street?' Eddie said to Jon. 'Why can't you just go out and find yourself a wife, like other people do? It's always other people's wives with you. This is number three.'

'You lied to me,' Kate said. 'You told me you were my friend and then you didn't come back.'

'How could I?' he said.

'You could. I've spent hours sitting in that blasted sand dune with my horse, waiting for you.'

'Kit, we've been through this again and again.'

'You're frightened of Charles, that's what it is.'

'Don't be daft,' Jon said. 'And don't you bloody well start to cry or I'll give you something to cry for. You married him.'

'I wasn't given any choice.'

'Plenty of lasses around here would give their eye teeth for what you've got. You've never done a decent day's work since you got married and you're waited on hand and foot.'

'Do you think I want that?'

'All you ever think about is what *you* want. What about other people? What about us? You'll get us thrown out of here, and for what? You selfish little bitch.'

In the time that she had been married to Charles Nelson he had said and done many hurtful things to Kate but he had never, ever called her a selfish little bitch. For the first time now she saw where she was and who she was and who Jon was. Her thoughts went no further before she tried to hit him and he grabbed her almost off her feet. She cried out and then Eddie was in the way, properly in the way, right in the middle, shoving her free and holding Jon against the wall, saying, 'You wallop her and we're dead, sunshine.'

'I wasn't going to,' Jon said tightly.

'No? You're a better man than me, Armstrong.'

That was when Kate knew what she had done, how low she had sunk that she would endanger their livelihood. She turned and would have run out of the house. Lizzie stopped her.

'You can't go back tonight. The fog's thick and it's bitterly cold.'

'I have to.'

'Kate, if you freeze to death in a hedgeback it isn't going to help at all. You can sleep in the front room. Eddie, go and put the fire on.'

'I shouldn't have come here. I'm sorry.'

Lizzie went upstairs to find her a nightdress and Eddie went through to put down the bed and she was left with Jon.

'You have an awful tongue on you, Jon Armstrong, but you're right. Living at the house you forget how people really are. I didn't mean to . . .'

Jon went over and pulled her roughly into his arms.

'It's all right,' he said, and then he did what Kate had wanted him to do for so long. He kissed her. She wasn't expecting it and it wasn't gentle. That didn't stop her from closing her eyes and lifting her face and giving him her mouth. When Eddie came back in Jon let go of her and Lizzie came down with the nightdress and showed Kate into the front room and closed the door, looking meaningfully at Jon. She went off upstairs.

From the front room, eyes shut in memory of that kiss, Kate heard Eddie say softly, 'You're out of your mind. When he finds out you're carrying on with his wife, he'll have you murdered.'

'I knew I could make you happy if I tried hard, Eddie,' Jon said.

Twenty-one

*K*ate dreaded the nights. She dreaded them so much that they spoiled any
pleasure she might have felt during the days. She spent more time with
Jon. Even though the weather was cold they met in Sam and Lizzie's sand
dune when she could get away, and when he was not at work or classes. She
had to walk, she didn't want Dolly to take cold.

Charles gave her instructions that she was not to go riding near the beach
or go to the village so in the end Jon had to come to her. They talked about
work and studying and nothing much more. He was businesslike. There were
no more kisses. Kate didn't know what to think. She had enjoyed the
meetings in the sand dune when she had been able to get away but that was
over. She worked hard at her studies at the house but she hid her books from
Charles and the servants.

One afternoon Charles came back unexpectedly early from a shoot and
found her studying in her room.

'What are these?' he said, fingering the books.

Kate had tried to hide them but he pushed her out of the way. He frowned
and picked them up one after another, and he laughed.

'What do you think you're doing?' he said. 'Do you think these are
suitable reading for my wife? Where did you get them?'

'I sent for them – to Newcastle.'

'Kate, you don't listen to me. You're my wife. I'm tired of you hiding
away in your room with the door locked or riding your horse for hours on the
beach. I understand that you've been to the village several times lately. It's
not your place to go there – the miners don't like it and neither do their wives.
Your place is here with me, helping my mother and being polite to friends in
the afternoons. What are you going to wear to dinner?'

'The – the pale yellow.'

'Good.' He took her chin in his hand and smiled. 'No more nonsense, eh?'

He picked up the books as though he was going to take them away but Kate objected.

'I don't believe you heard me properly, Kate.'

'I want the books. I'm not doing any harm.'

'I think it is harmful to fill your head with nonsense. I'm afraid I must insist. You're neglecting your duties as my wife and it won't do. You'd better ring for your maid, and quickly. Dinner won't be long.'

'Kit, those books cost me everything I had.' Jon was sitting on the end of her bed. It was Saturday night. 'What did he do with them?'

'I don't know. I can't find them and I've looked all over the house. I'd replace them for you if I could but I have no money.'

'None at all?'

'He said that if I was going to spend it on things like that I shouldn't have any more.'

It was very late. There had been a dinner party at the house that night. Jon had sat in Kate's room for a long time, reading a novel by the fire, concealing himself when she came back and the maid helped her to undress and brush out her hair. When the girl had finally gone Kate secured the door and Jon came out of her small sitting-room.

'I'm sorry,' she had said, and then she told him about the books. Jon said nothing more about them. He didn't want her more upset than she was.

'Maybe he'll come to your room.'

Kate shook her head.

'He was very drunk. He had to be helped to bed. It isn't just the books, Jon.'

'What is it then?'

She couldn't tell him. She couldn't let him know that her husband had been to her room every night that week until she felt sick at the very idea that not just Charles but anybody might lay hands on her again. It was not that Charles hurt her physically; his love-making, Kate thought with a cynical smile, could hardly be termed as such, there was no love about it. His mother or Charles or both of them, Kate wasn't sure, had decided that it was high time there was a child and so Charles did what she was sure his mother would term 'his duty'. Kate had never been anybody's duty before. She had never

186

loved Charles Nelson, she had never wanted him in her bed, but she thought that if he had been kind, if he had tried to teach her how to respond, there might have been some hope for their marriage. But he didn't kiss her. He didn't hold her or stay with her or talk to her or sleep in her bed. She was there for use and for show. He bought new gowns for her. He cared about how she looked and acted as his wife and that was all.

She hated Charles so much by now that she had to steel herself when Jon was in her room because he too was a man. Not that the two could in any way be confused. Even when Jon had called her names and laid hands on her nobody could accuse him of being unkind. Charles, through neglect and indifference alone, was cruel. Yet it was almost more than Kate could do now to tolerate Jon's presence for what he could teach her. Sometimes she hated Charles so much that it encompassed the whole of mankind, sometimes she could hardly breathe in his presence for hatred of him. And of her uncle for making her live like this. They had treated her like a toy, like a doll, as if she had no thoughts or feelings at all.

'Do you want me to go?' Jon said now.

Her throat was full of tears but she shook her head.

'I'll just sit here and tell you everything I can remember about the class the other night,' he offered.

Kate nodded. She could bear that as long as he didn't come any nearer. He went on sitting on the edge of the bed and she sat in an armchair by the fire and she closed her eyes and listened to his voice. It was straight information, Jon was good at that. He made it so that she could understand exactly what he was talking about. Information held no threat, no personality. It was safe.

Lizzie made no secret of the fact that she disapproved of Jon's friendship with Kate. She didn't try to stop it but she said privately to Jon, 'They should never had made her marry him. She was a different lass when she was in the office, always smiling and with a word for everybody. Why couldn't they let her alone? Look what they've done to her. She's spoiled and petted and self-centred, and has no more sense than to carry on with one of her husband's miners.'

'I'm not carrying on with her,' he said.

'Is there another name for it?' Lizzie replied sharply. 'Everybody in the village knows. Mary has more sense than you, Jon.'

'I'm not doing nothing.'

Lizzie looked patiently at him.

'You spend a lot of time with her.'

'I'm just helping her, that's all.'

'I remember once you saying to me that no lad ever did owt for a lass for nowt back. Do you remember that?'

Jon smiled.

'All right. So I like her. She's different.'

'She's Charles Nelson's wife.'

'She didn't want to be his wife. They made her do it. People shouldn't have to do things like that. She's not happy.'

'If you were going to look to every lass in the village who isn't happy you'd have a full-time job,' Lizzie said. 'It isn't just that.'

'No, it isn't. Kit's different. She feels like family.' Jon looked at Lizzie. 'I'm not going to let him hurt her. He married her because she didn't want him.'

'Why should he have done that, Jon? He could have had anybody.'

'Because he's like that,' Jon said loudly. 'He has money and power and he's a bastard. His father was the same.'

'Well, I don't see where it's all leading except trouble.'

Charles Nelson rarely went away that winter as though he sensed there was something wrong. He came to Kate's room nearly every night. Worst of all he seemed to like doing so which he never had before. Each night he spent more time over it until Kate felt so sick at the thought of him that she couldn't bear it. Several times she pleaded tiredness or headaches which stopped Charles, and then he realised that these were only excuses. Kate grew to hate his disregard for her feelings. The days that winter passed in dull routine, and only the meetings with Jon and her rides on Dolly were any distraction. Otherwise it was all hateful to her.

Charles bought her nightwear for her birthday in the spring and thereafter insisted on seeing her both in and out of it. There were parties and dances during April and May which she was obliged to attend. She endured it all as best she might. Sometimes Charles was so drunk that he didn't come to her room, but mostly he drank just enough to put him into what was, for him, a good mood. Kate came to hate the smell and taste of alcohol.

One night in the middle of May he went upstairs and found the door locked between their rooms. He shouted and banged until she opened it.

'Why did you lock it?' he said.

'I didn't realise it was locked. I'm tired, Charles, I was about to go to bed.'

'I can see that. You're always about to go to bed, aren't you?'

'Please, Charles, not tonight.'

'Why not tonight?'

'I don't think I can.'

'I'm sure you can.' He went over to where she sat at the dressing-table. She was wearing some things he had bought her, satin with thin straps, ginger-coloured. Kate hated them. It was the kind of clothing she imagined kept women wore but then, what else was she? He slid his hands over her shoulders and Kate came quickly to her feet, trying to get out of the way.

'I'd like to be alone tonight.'

'But that wasn't the bargain,' Charles said, his gaze warm on her. 'I married you, little nobody that you were, and gave you everything you wanted.'

'Everything I wanted?' she said in astonishment. 'I didn't want any of this.'

'How can you be so ungrateful? You have everything any woman could possibly want – a beautiful house, good servants, clothes, jewellery, carriages. You never have to lift a finger. You don't even brush your own hair. The least you can do is to give me a son. Come over here.' Charles indicated the bed. Kate stayed by the dressing-table.

'No,' she said.

Charles walked across to her and slapped her face. She cried out and put up her hands in self-defence and he got hold of her by the hair and dragged her across the room. She stumbled and began to cry. When they reached the bed he knocked her down on to it with his fist. She cowered away but Charles held her down.

On the first occasion that they had arranged to meet Jon didn't think too much about it when Kate didn't turn up. He thought that she had not been able to get away because of some social event or because of Charles, but when she hadn't turned up in almost a week he walked over to the house on the Saturday night.

It was a balmy night, good enough for mid-June. It was light and warm and quite late. He thought that unless Charles and Kate were out or had guests she should be in her room by now, and sure enough there was a lamp burning. Jon hesitated, making sure that he could see no one else before he slid in at the window. She was sitting up in bed, reading and didn't seem to hear him.

He said, 'Kit?' quietly so as not to shock her, and she dropped the book and gathered up the covers against her and stared. She said nothing, even when he quietly closed the window and went across and then Jon could see why. Her face was covered in dark bruises. He sat down on the edge of the bed.

'Oh God,' he said. 'Is this because of me?'

Kate shook her head.

'He wants a son. I'm not pregnant.'

'Does he think knocking you about's going to get you pregnant?'

'No.'

'What then?'

'I didn't want him to touch me. He's not . . . he's not kind. He never has been. At least he seems not to have been, I don't know. Maybe it's always like that.'

'No.'

'When I refused he hit me, and then he . . .'

Jon wanted to take hold of her and comfort her but she had moved so far back and pulled the covers up to her chin that he didn't. 'You can't stay here, not now.'

'What am I going to do? I have no money.'

'You have to leave.'

'How can I?'

'Haven't you anything you can sell?'

'Some jewellery. But I have no one to go to, nowhere to go.'

'You could go away with me.'

'You?' Kate's eyes widened. 'I can't do that to you. I've done enough to you already. This is your home.'

'I've got nothing to stay for.'

'It wouldn't be any use. You don't understand. Charles forced me. I don't think I can bear to be touched.'

'It doesn't matter about that. I'm not going to leave you here for it to happen again. Come over here a minute.'

'I can't.'

'Come on. Just a little way. I'm not going to hurt you.'

Kate ventured forward a little and Jon drew her very gently against him.

'You don't know what it's like,' she said. 'You're a lot bigger than me and when we quarrelled . . .'

'I'm never ever going to hit you, Kit, and I'm never going to hurt you. I promise.'

The next day when he and Eddie and Lizzie sat down together for their Sunday meal, Eddie looked across the table at Jon and said, 'So, and how was the lovely Mrs Nelson last night?'

'I'm going to take her away.'

Lizzie looked up from where Mary was sitting on her knee and said, 'Jon, you can't.'

'I don't have any choice. He knocked her about and then he . . . he forced her.'

Lizzie stared. Eddie said, 'The bastard!'

'Hasn't she got any family she can go to?'

'Nobody, and even if she did he'd bring her back. I don't know why he wants her. It's as though he wants her because she doesn't want him. I don't understand it. It's so cruel.'

'Where would you take her?' Eddie said.

'America.'

'And where are you going to get the money for that?'

'Jon, she's been gently brought up,' Lizzie said. 'You can't expect her to live like we do.'

'What for?'

'Because she's not used to it.'

'She used to look after her father, sort of.'

'She'll hate it.'

'Well, at least I wouldn't treat her like he does. Do you know what I'd like to do to him?'

'It wouldn't work, Jon. Look at how she lives now. I don't think you should run away with her. Kate's life isn't your affair. If you leave here with her you'll never be able to come back.'

'That'll be a loss to both sides, won't it?' Jon said. 'I've got a bit put by and she has some jewellery which is hers.'

* * *

191

That evening when Eddie went off to chapel Lizzie and Jon took Mary and went for a walk on the beach.

'Do you think America's like this?' Lizzie asked.

'The east coast is supposed to be a bit like this in parts.'

'You'll never be able to come back.'

'I don't have any life here.'

Lizzie stopped. Mary had fallen asleep on her shoulder. They were way up the beach where the sand was soft. She sat down now and took off her shawl and laid the child carefully down on it.

'You could have,' she said, 'there are plenty of other pits. You don't have to stay here. You could marry a nice lass and have a family. There's no reason why not. You've got that used to looking after people that you feel obliged to do it. There's no reason why you should look after Kate.'

'What am I supposed to do, leave her there? Is that what you want me to do?'

'All your life, ever since your dad died, you've looked after other people. Kate's not your responsibility. You don't even care for her, not like you cared for Greta. You can't marry her. What if she gets pregnant?'

'If I take her away, people won't know we aren't married.'

'You'll know it, and in time it would probably matter very much. These things do. You should marry somebody who would look after you. That would make a nice change. Kate won't ever look after you, not properly; she hasn't been brought up to. I can just imagine how she kept her father, and you wouldn't like it. You're used to pit women's ways, women who can manage a house and make you comfortable. Kate's not like that. She's airy-fairy, all opinions and politics. She should've been a man. You're entitled to your life, you know, Jon. You're entitled to some happiness in it and a lass you want, a lass you've chosen. You haven't ever had that.'

He sighed and lay back in the sand and closed his eyes.

'I don't believe America's any better than this for all the fine talk about it, and if Kate wasn't so selfish she wouldn't ask you,' Lizzie said.

'She didn't ask me. I offered.'

'Well, you would, wouldn't you? I wish you'd never laid eyes on her. One of these days you're going to get through a fortnight without making a mess of something.'

Jon opened his eyes and laughed.

'She's determined to have you, that's all,' Lizzie said.

'Oh, yes, I'm such a catch. And she got her husband to badly use her so that I'd take her out of it!'

'She could have gone by herself.'

'You don't want me to leave, do you?'

'Of course I don't want you to leave. That doesn't mean I don't want you to marry a nice lass and be happy.'

'I always want what I can't have. I'm just taken that way.'

'Do you remember the poetry book, Jon?'

'What poetry book?'

'The one you gave me when I went to work at the house. I burned it when you got Greta into trouble. I sat down and burned it page by page.'

'That's not very surprising. Anyroad, you couldn't have married me. Look how I've turned out.'

'You wouldn't have if we could have got married.'

'And what about Eddie?'

Lizzie looked down at the sleeping child.

'Do you think she looks like him, Jon?'

'She's the spit, poor little soul.'

Lizzie laughed and thumped him.

The bruises were fading. But although they were beginning to go the look in her eyes was the same, that scared look. She stood back a little as Jon closed the window. He stayed where he was and gave her time to get used to him there.

'Are you still keen to run away?' he said.

Her eyes lightened a little.

'I was beginning to think that you'd had second thoughts or didn't really mean it,' she said. 'I thought we might go to London. I know it well; at least I used to.'

'I've never been to London.'

'Charles gave me quite a lot of jewellery before we were married and some since. I could sell some of it. I could go into Sunderland tomorrow.'

'No. I've got enough put by to get us the train to London and we could sell it there where it's less likely to be found.'

'You do mean it?' she said.

Jon went to her.

'I mean it. We'll go away and never come back.'

'That's what I want, to get as far away as I possibly can.'

'When?'

'What about Monday? I have some money which Charles gave me to pay a bill. I didn't pay it. It'll be a start and it would be a good day. My uncle and Charles have planned to inspect the pits this week and they're starting on Monday.'

'Charles down a pit?'

'Uncle George persuaded him that he must. He's going to inspect the Victoria first. We could leave in the early afternoon when they're gone.'

'You can't bring much with you, mind, and wear a shabby dress.'

'I don't possess one.'

'Something dark then and a hat that covers your hair. The less people notice the better. We'll stay overnight in Newcastle and get the train on Tuesday morning.'

Kate sighed happily.

'I only wish I could bring Dolly,' she said.

That week Eddie and Jon were on the nightshift. It was Monday and Lizzie was busy washing. There was tatie hash for dinner, the meal left over from the Sunday dinner with chopped potatoes and onion, all together in a little water and salt in a pan on the stove so that it could bubble away for a while and later be eaten with dry bread and sprinkled with vinegar. Lizzie was glad that it was such a busy day because she didn't want Jon to leave and nothing she could say would make any difference. He and Eddie got up when the washing was almost done and, to her satisfaction, blowing out on a clear day in the back lane. They all sat down to eat together; nobody said much.

'What about all them books?' Lizzie said.

'I can't take them. Don't you want them?'

'Oh Jon, I wish you wouldn't go. You don't have to. Things will get better. Don't go just for her sake.'

Eddie said, 'Lizzie . . .' and she got up and walked out. The day was no longer as fine as it had been but the first lot of clothes was already dry and she had just started unpegging them when Jon came out to say goodbye. He scooped her into his arms before she had time to protest any further.

'Don't go, Jon.'

'I have to.' He kissed her cheek and then her hair. 'I'll be late.'

'Please. I'd give anything that you'd . . .'

And then the pit siren went. Lizzie turned cool at the sound, even though her mind registered Jon close beside her and Eddie in the kitchen. She let go of Jon, seeing the horror dawn in his dark eyes. And then she remembered that Harold was on shift and went cold. After a minute or so Eddie came running out of the house. Jon kicked aside the bag at his feet, Lizzie picked up Mary from the kitchen and they all made for the pit head. Jon didn't even hesitate though Lizzie knew that for him it was the ideal time to leave; nobody would see him. She thought of Kate waiting for him, and thought of Harold and Rob and Ken and the others, and she wound the child inside her shawl and followed the men down the lane.

Twenty-two

Kate had awoken early that morning, feeling excited and worried. She didn't want to leave her warm bed until she discovered that outside was a clear bright sunny day. Deciding what to take was not difficult since Charles had made the decision to buy most of her clothes. She could cheerfully have left them all behind. She looked around her room and thought that she would never see it again and was glad. She would never look out of that window over the gardens, never speak to anybody here, never see any of it after today. Her only regret was Dolly and she went out as soon as she could get ready and went for a last ride with the mare, taking her down to the water's edge near the village.

She glanced in the direction of the houses and thought of Jon and what he would be doing, getting up, making ready. She wondered whether he would be sorry to go. She spent a long time talking softly to Dolly before going back up the yard without a backward glance. She had already packed most things the night before and hidden the bag. She even ate some lunch and made conversation with Charles's mother, marvelling at how calm she felt. His mother always had a lie-down after lunch so Kate was able to creep away upstairs and change and then she let herself out of the house.

It was so easy. Nobody saw her go, nobody met her on the stairs or in the grounds. The weather was no longer fine. The day was beginning to turn dark then, the sky had gone thick and grey. The bag was heavy. Kate had stuffed all her jewellery into it, the little money she possessed and one or two favourite dresses, some underwear, her silver hairbrushes – she thought that she might be able to sell those – and a likeness of Dolly. She wore some of her jewellery around her neck under her dress but none on her hands or wrists or in her ears because that would have drawn attention to her. As she let herself

197

out of the house rain began to fall. It was cooler. She hurried away down the road to the appointed place well beyond the house and away from the village and there she stood, waiting.

The rain came down heavily. Lizzie stood with May and Enid, Mrs Armstrong and her mother. Enid was crying. May's round face was set. She had her baby girl in her arms. Lizzie thought that May had been much happier since Esther was born though Rob had not cared to make a secret of the fact that he was disappointed the child was not a boy.

'I don't want our Jon to go down there, Lizzie,' May said, hugging her small daughter to her. 'He's all my mam's got left. Can't you talk to him?'

Lizzie thought that Mrs Armstrong's affection for Jon was particularly well-hidden these days since she never saw him but it wouldn't do to argue now. She went over to where Jon, Eddie, Mr Forrester the agent, Williams the under-manager, the deputies and a crowd of other men were standing, talking. She touched Jon's arm and when she finally gained his attention drew him away slightly.

'Why don't you just go?' she said. 'It can't make any difference.'

'With a whole shift of men down there, including your Harold? Harold's done a lot for me.'

'Can't you keep out of it?'

He looked at her as though she was mad.

'Jon, your mother's lost two sons down there already.'

'Aye, that was a Monday and all,' he said grimly.

'Jon -' But he turned away from her and went back to the discussion.

Lizzie walked back to May.

'What's happened?'

'I don't know. I didn't ask. I don't think I want to know.'

'Do you think Rob's dead, Lizzie?' May said.

'Of course not,' she said.

'Sometimes I wish he was – only not like this, if you know what I mean.'

'I thought it was better since your mam was there?'

'It is, that's why she stays, but I feel so awful about it. Our Jon shouldn't be with you – not when him and Eddie get on so badly.'

'They aren't as bad as they were.' In fact, Lizzie thought, she had a feeling Eddie didn't want Jon to leave though he hadn't said so. She went on standing there with Mary in her arms. It was good to have something to hold on to, even better to watch the two men she cared about and to know that they weren't down there. She wished with all her might that Harold would be all right. The rain was getting so bad that the light was going. She couldn't believe that it was the same day she had woken up to. It had been so bright and clear. Her washing would be soaked through now, hanging limply across the back lane.

There was a sudden commotion at the pit head and the cage came up and in it were half a dozen men. Amongst them were Harold, Rob and Ken. May said nothing but she went over. Enid gave a little cry and ran, and Mrs Armstrong and Lizzie's mother both smiled. Lizzie was so glad that she wanted to go to Harold and hug him only she couldn't. All these years she had taken for granted that Harold would always be there. There was nothing special about him except that he was her brother. She realised for the first time then how she would have felt if she had lost him, if he had never come back out of that black hole. Harold and Rob and the others stayed, and Lizzie waited and waited, and as she did so many other people gathered. Her mother and Enid went back to their house, taking with them the children, including Mary, out of the rain to the fire and some food.

As Lizzie stood there she saw Kate arrive. She was walking rapidly. Lizzie would have stopped her if she could have because she came straight across to the men who let her through quietly when they saw who she was. She went to Jon and to Lizzie's relief said the right thing.

'What's happening? Where's my husband?' Her voice was full of dismay. Mr Forrester drew her aside.

'There's been an accident, Mrs Nelson. Part of the mine has flooded. I think you had better go to your aunt.'

'I want to speak to Jon Armstrong,' she said, turning from him. The men went quiet, looking sideways at one another. 'Is it going to be all right?' she said.

Jon led her away from the crowd, Kate clinging all the time to her bag.

'What's going on? What's happened?'

'There's been a flood,' he said grimly, 'a bad one.'

'But Charles is down there, and my uncle!' She let go of the bag and took Jon's arm instead.

'Yes, I know,'

'Is Charles dead?' Her face was ashen.

'We don't think so, no.'

199

'What do you mean, you don't think so?'

'Well, the part of the Vic where most people were working was fairly high up and Williams thinks that because of the water in the shaft some parts could be all right so don't go getting upset about it. It'll probably work out. It'll just take time.'

'Why?'

'Because we can't get them out the regular way. Harold and Rob and a few others were working near the bottom of the shaft and they got out but it's flooded deep now.'

'But there is another way?'

'Yes, probably.'

'If that's so then what are we doing here? Mr Williams knows what he's doing, doesn't he? They can get experts. Why should we wait around for Charles and my uncle to find out what we're doing? Let's go now while we have the opportunity.'

'I can't do that, Kate.'

'I waited and waited. I'm soaked through and I'm frozen,' she said in a low agitated voice.

'I know. I'm sorry.'

'Why didn't you come?'

'How could I? You're not thinking properly. You're cold and upset.'

'Don't treat me like this, Jon. There's nothing to stop us now. It's the perfect time.'

'We can't.'

'We won't get another chance and Charles will find out. You know he will.'

'Kate, this is a pit community. I can't walk out now.'

'You don't care about me at all,' she said. 'If you did you'd come. There's no need for you to stay here; there are plenty of other people to help.'

'It could have been me down there if it had happened a few hours later.'

'But it didn't, did it? And you wouldn't have been there anyway. If you don't come with me now I shall be here for the rest of my life and I don't think I can bear it. I'll have to stay there and put up with that – that monster for the rest of my days. I'll have to put up with his neglect and his bullying and his drinking and the way that he . . .'

'I'm sorry. I have to stay.'

'You're going to go down there, aren't you?' she said, staring at him.

'If it'll help. If I can.'

'You're really going to do it?'

'Don't you care about the men at all, not even your uncle?'

'Yes, I care, even though he forced me to marry Charles.'

'He could be dead.'

Kate stared.

'But you said . . .'

'I said probably, but we can't leave until we know that they're all right.'

'And you'd risk your life for them?'

'It isn't for them. There are other people down there, people I care about.'

'They don't care about you, you told me. After what happened to Greta.'

'I can't help that. I have to do what seems right to me.'

'Please, Jon, don't do it. There are other men. Please.' She began to cry. People were watching. Lizzie, who had come over, put an arm around her, picked up the bag and slowly walked her away.

'He'll get killed,' Kate said. 'He'll die down that wretched pit.'

The rain had stopped. Back at the house Lizzie looked despairingly at her sopping washing and sat Kate down by the fire while she went to her mother's to collect Mary. Then she gave Kate tea and tried to make her eat what was left from the dinner. Kate wouldn't eat but sat nursing the cup in her hands.

'I said a lot of things to Jon that I shouldn't have said,' she admitted finally. 'Awful things that I didn't mean.'

'It doesn't matter. He'll understand.'

'Will he? If Charles and my uncle don't come out I'll never forgive myself. I thought Jon would do anything for me; I didn't think about them. I shouldn't have gone to him like that. What will people think? Only I waited and waited for him and then I grew so cold that there was nothing to do but come here. Do you think Charles will be all right? I don't want anything to happen to him, not like that. I just don't want to have to live with him, that's all.'

Lizzie put more coal on the fire. Kate sat staring into its flames and the evening wore on. The pony and trap had been sent to take her to her aunt's but she wouldn't go.

'I think you should,' Lizzie said.

'Mrs O'Connor will stay with her.'

Later still Lizzie put Mary into her cot and they rescued the half-dry washing from the back lane. It would all have to be done again tomorrow, Lizzie thought regretfully. They walked back to the pit head when Lizzie's mother offered to look to Mary again. It was a cool clear night, the stars low and plentiful and stark. The ground and buildings and fields were shadowed and the pit head stood out in the darkness strangely, almost grotesquely, Lizzie thought.

She thought of that morning. How odd that such a bright clear day could hold disaster. Why was there never any indication? She supposed that if there was it would not be called disaster, it would not be so serious or so awful. How could such a lovely night hold death in it? She tried not to think of such things. She tried not to worry about Eddie and Jon. She wondered whether Charles Nelson was alive.

The tears began to roll down Kate's cheeks. Lizzie put an arm around her. There were fires lit at the pit head, braziers with the flames leaping out of the sides. There were lights, there were people. Their talk seemed to echo in the night. Many were still there though some, women with small children mostly, had gone back to their homes. She took Kate's arm and they walked back to the house. Lizzie kept both fires going and prepared food. It was almost morning when she heard the yard gate. She flew to the back door and out into the cold yard and Kate ran after her.

When Jon saw Kate he stood still.

'What are you doing still here?' he said. 'You should have gone to your aunt. She'll be by herself.'

'Mrs O'Connor will be there.'

'Mrs O'Connor has a husband and family.'

Lizzie heard the harsh intake of Kate's breath.

'How dare you tell me what to do?'

Lizzie would have stopped Jon but she knew how tired he was.

'And what about Charles's mother? How do you think she feels? You could have gone back there.'

'I'm never going back there,' Kate ground out, and she flew up the yard and into the house.

'Well done, Jon,' Eddie said, clapping him on the shoulder.

'She was worried about you,' Lizzie said. 'She wanted to be here when you came back.'

'Oh, hell.'

Kate was standing by the kitchen fire.

'What about Charles?' she demanded the moment they were inside with the door shut.

'Nothing yet.' Jon turned wearily to Lizzie before he sat down by the comfort of the kitchen fire. 'How's your Harold?'

'Grand. My mam came over before.'

'And Rob and all?' Eddie asked. 'It would be Rob and Ken.'

'Even God wouldn't want Robbo,' Jon said.

'Kate, would you like to go and sit in the front room?' Lizzie suggested. 'The fire's burning up lovely in there.' And she shoved the girl in that direction and closed the door after her.

'Two fires?' Eddie said.

'I suppose you want to take your clothes off in front of the pit owner's wife?' Lizzie said in a low voice.

'It doesn't bother me,' Eddie said, undressing as he spoke.

'Well, it would bother her. She's a lady. And be nicer to her; she's cried her eyes out. What if Charles Nelson's dead?'

'He isn't,' Jon said. 'The water only got into certain parts of the pit; it came in below some areas and a lot of the men were working above it. And Nelson and Mr Farrer were above it, we think.'

'How many men are trapped?'

'About fifty. He's probably going to be all right.'

'You can tell that to Kate when you've got changed.'

Jon went through to Kate to tell her that the food was ready and found her sitting dejectedly by the fire.

'I'm sorry,' she said. 'I didn't mean to say all those awful things to you at the pit head.'

'What awful things?'

'About going away. I know that you think I'm stupid and spoiled and selfish, but I'm so frightened. I thought you wouldn't come back. I thought if I left here I'd never see you again. If you die down the Victoria, I'll never forgive you for it.'

Jon smiled at her and put his arms around her.

'It'll be all right,' he said. 'Come and have something to eat and I'll tell you what's happening.'

'You'll get Charles and Uncle George out?'

'It's just finding the best way to get through to them.'

'And after that, when you've got them out, we'll go away?'

'Yes.'

'Promise me.'

'I promise. I'll get Charles out and then we'll go.'

'Even if people talk and Charles finds out, no matter what happens?'

'No matter what happens,' he said.

They went back into the kitchen and sat down to eat. Kate chased the food about her plate with a fork. Then Lizzie cleared the table, Eddie put down the bed in the front room for Kate and went upstairs. Lizzie gave Kate her best nightdress and closed the front room door on her.

'Do you really think Charles Nelson's still alive?' she asked Jon softly as he banked down the fire.

'He's too good to die,' Jon said sarcastically.

'You have to get him out. She'll never forgive herself if you don't.'

'We're going to try as hard as we can,' he said, before he went upstairs.

The next day brought people to the village: those who would help, the curious, the interested, and the newspaper people. All to see the pit which had trapped not just fifty miners but the mine manager and, most importantly of all, the mineowner. It rained hard that day, which didn't help, while the debate went on at the pit head to find the best way of helping the men who were trapped. If they had water it was known that they could live many days without food. It was thought that there were large quantities of oats in the dry sections of the pit because that was where the horses were kept.

Old shafts were visited in the hope that some new route would be found, some place from where it would not be too far to reach the men. It was decided as quickly as possible that an old shaft from the next pit, the Isabella, might be the best way in. The shaft was opened up and work began.

From the beginning there was plenty of help and those who could not help stood around, watching and waiting. The first morning Lizzie prepared food for when the two men should come home and then she banked down the fire. She and Kate walked to Lizzie's mother's where they had left Mary and then went to the pit head to see what was happening. Lizzie had stopped trying to persuade Kate either to go home or to go to her aunt's. Either she would not or could not go.

After the decision was made to try and reach the men through the old shaft, the rescuers spent long hours trying to make progress to reach the trapped miners. Lizzie didn't know when her men were coming back or whether they were but she said nothing to Kate. Rescuers were sometimes killed or injured. She knew that Kate had more knowledge of mining than almost any other woman but she voiced no fears so they did not frighten one another. Lizzie loaned Kate her clothes. They were so plain and ordinary that she looked strange in them at first, out of place. They were working clothes not meant to flatter. At first Kate seemed almost unconcerned about Charles and her uncle but she became more worried as the hours passed.

When the two men came back they were too exhausted to eat much. As the second and third days wore on it seemed to Lizzie that their mood changed to sheer doggedness, especially Jon's. Lizzie privately did not believe that Kate would ever see either her husband or her uncle again, and she could see by Kate's face that the other woman was beginning to think the same, in spite of the way that the men talked optimistically and went on with their task.

Kate played games with Mary and read to her and entertained her so that Lizzie could get on and she let Kate help in the house. She showed her some basic cooking skills and set her to clean the brasses to keep her mind off things.

'How did you get by in London if you couldn't cook?' she asked.

'We went out to eat and to people's houses and people made things for us and . . . I don't know. We just did. And we used to buy cooked food.'

Lizzie thought this strange but if Kate was going to look after Jon she needed to know how to. She shook her head over Kate's lack of essential knowledge. She had never made bread or kept hens or cooked meat.

The men were not there much even after four days, just a few snatched hours for food and sleep. Jon kept saying that they would get through, that it would be all right; Eddie didn't say anything much; and Mr Forrester talked to the newspapers about geological faults. Lizzie imagined over and over again what it was like when millions of gallons of water came through what had seemed like safe walls and ceilings, a monster awoken from the depths of the ocean, snarling and raging and hurling itself upon them.

Few had had any chance of getting out of the way. The water flooded in so quickly, smashing out of its path everything which stood there. A small number of men had been near the foot of the shaft and were brought to safety, the water almost to their necks. Within a short while the pit bottom had been flooded to a depth of many feet and there was no way out for the trapped miners.

* * *

On the fifth day Jon and Eddie came back almost at midnight. Kate and Lizzie were sitting by the kitchen fire. The men came in slowly and quietly and Lizzie could tell the minute she saw Jon that it was over. Eddie glanced at her but he didn't look at Kate. She got to her feet and stood, staring.

'He's dead, isn't he?'

'Yes.'

It ranked alongside a couple of others as the worst moment of Jon's life. It was up there with listening to his brothers die down the pit, telling Lizzie that he couldn't marry her, watching Greta die, passing out at Eddie's feet. It was way up there. He would have given a lot not to have to come home and tell her that he couldn't get Charles out of the pit. Eddie had had to drag him away from the rescue area.

'I have to, Eddie, man,' he had said.

'You can't. Howay, Jon, it's over. You'll get yourself killed and all. Then where will we be?'

Worn out as he was, Eddie persisted. Jon tried to shake him off.

'I can't go back there without him.'

'Don't talk soft. It isn't your fault.'

'I promised her.'

'You'll have to unpromise her then, won't you?'

'I wish I'd been there.'

'That would have helped a whole lot, wouldn't it? You bloody stuck there and all. Just be thankful.'

'Oh God, Eddie, I can't go back there and tell her.'

Now by the combined firelight and gaslight he watched her face, the crumbling of her hopes.

'You found them?' she said.

'No, we couldn't get through. The gases exploded. We had to come back.'

Kate stared and Jon remembered that it wasn't like telling any other lass. She knew a bit about it.

'Then he might still be alive?'

'No. There was too much gas. It isn't possible.'

'You don't know that.'

'I don't know but the experts do. There's no way.'

Jon listened to her silence. He knew that he had to keep on saying that, no matter what, so that she would believe it.

'You can't let him die down there like that. 'You can't let him!'

'There's nothing more anybody can do,' Jon said.

'He could live for days,' she said, face full of horror. 'He could live for weeks, knowing . . . No! No, you've got to go back there and get him out. You've got to. You've got to!'

'We can't.'

Kate looked so coldly at him.

'If my husband is dead, officially at least, then I own the pits and I can order that work goes on to get them out.'

'Yes, you can, but it won't do you any good and it will endanger the lives of the men who've tried so hard to get them out. You have no right to do that when the people who know what they're talking about tell you there's nothing more to be done. You'll have to accept it.'

Kate stared woodenly at him for a few moments and then she said, 'I want to go home.'

'In the morning.'

'No, now.'

'Well, I'm not taking you. I'm worn out.'

'I'll go by myself.'

Kate went off into the front room to collect her belongings and Lizzie followed her inside and closed the door, standing back against it.

'He said they'd come out,' Kate said.

'Oh, Kate, that's not fair.'

'You don't understand.' She picked up her bag and looked straight at Lizzie. 'We can't go away now. I hate Charles. I hate him so much. You can't think what it's like when a man does that to you, and not just that, when he humiliates you in every possible way. He took everything away from me – my chastity, my freedom, my sense of identity . . .'

'Be that as it may, it isn't Jon's fault.'

'I didn't want Charles to die, I just wanted to go away from here and never come back. We can't do that now. Do you know who I am? I'm the mineowner. It's almost funny really.'

'Don't go tonight, Kate. You're hurt and shocked and tired. Go to bed.'

She managed to persuade Kate and then went back into the kitchen where the men were hungry. Eddie went to bed afterwards but Jon lingered by the fire.

'Do you want to see her?' Lizzie asked softly. 'I think she's sleeping.'

'No, I don't want to see her.'

'You'll feel a lot better in the morning.'

He shook his head.

'I don't care about Nelson, he was a bastard, but I don't want George Farrer to die down there like that, or the others. I'm so tired of it. I hate the Vic; it takes everything.'

'Come on,' Lizzie said. 'You did all you could. It's finished. There are clean sheets on your bed.' She took hold of his arm and led him to the stairs and Jon sighed and went up. She had thought that Eddie would be in bed and asleep but he was standing by the window, the curtains drawn back, the window open. Lizzie went over.

'What?' she said.

'He wasn't going to give up, you know. He didn't want to tell her. It's just as well they aren't going away; they're not exactly suited, are they?'

'I don't suppose it matters any more.'

'What do you mean?'

'Kate doesn't need to go away now. She has everything and when she wakes up in the morning she'll realise it. And then maybe Jon will find a nice lass and marry her.'

'I hope so,' Eddie said. 'It would be a change for him to do summat right.'

Twenty-three

*K*ate stood by the window in her aunt's drawing-room and thought how strange everything was. When she had first arrived in the north she had thought it a big room. It looked tiny to her now.

'How long will it be before the Victoria can be used again?' she asked as she turned around.

Mr Forrester looked hard at her.

'It could be many months. It could be a considerable time before the bodies of those men, including your husband and your uncle, can be brought out.'

His voice was cold with disapproval. He was wrong, Kate thought. She was sorry. She was sorry that her uncle had died even though he had forced her to marry Charles. She was sorry that Charles was dead too, even though he had married her for his own selfish reasons and treated her afterwards with a good deal less affection than he reserved for his horse. But she was a lot sorrier that fifty good pitmen had died.

'We must see to it that the men who worked in the Victoria are given work in one of the other pits. Is that possible, Mr Forrester?'

'It may be possible for some of them. There is a good deal to sort out. There are all kinds of legalities . . .'

'I'm aware of that. I'm also aware that the Victoria men are going to be put out of work and that there are going to be many widows in the village. I want nobody put out of a house and I want proper financial provision for them and their dependants.'

'That can't be done immediately, Mrs Nelson, because of the legalities.'

'I think you'll find that I have talked to the bank and that money will be made available until the legalities are settled.'

209

'You're an unnatural girl, that's what you are,' her aunt burst out. 'To think of such things at a time like this, with Charles and your uncle dead.'

'Somebody has to think of them. Somebody has to take the responsibility,' she said calmly. 'I'm only being practical.'

What her aunt didn't know was that practicality was the only thing left. Kate couldn't eat or sleep or read or concentrate on anything. She didn't know whether the men *were* dead and still could not convince herself.

But her aunt acted first over one thing. When Kate went down to breakfast one morning soon afterwards Rose was brisk.

'I've told Albert that we shall need the horse and trap. We're going into Sunderland to order some new clothes.'

'New clothes, at a time like this?'

'It's called mourning, Kate,' Rose said severely.

She said nothing. Her aunt wanted to believe that the men were dead so she could begin the process of grieving for her husband. Her aunt was lucky; she, like most women, knew nothing of mining. She believed what she was told. She thought that her husband had died before he had suffered in mind or body. Kate had wanted to believe that, but she didn't, not fully. She didn't want to lie awake night after night thinking that men she had despised or hated, men who had done her wrong, men who had driven her away, were going to die horrible lingering deaths. All she wanted was to run somewhere, far away, and never come back, with a man who was kinder to her than anyone had been since her father had died. She couldn't go now, she couldn't run away, shut any of it out. She had to face it all. She got ready and went into town with her aunt, wishing she didn't have to spend time that way. She despised her aunt's ignorance, her accepting mind, and envied her the peace.

When Kate first saw herself in black – and the clothes were expensive, finely cut and in good material – she was astonished at how she looked. It turned her hair to flames and her skin to cream. In her green eyes there was the brightness of anger. The dresses hung perfectly, they were so full and so carefully stitched, the jet ornaments like black tears.

When she suggested that she ought to go back and live with Charles's mother, her aunt cried.

'How can I stay here alone?' she asked. 'I have never lived alone.'

'Then come with me.'

'I don't want to leave the house.'

'The house belongs to the mine,' Kate pointed out as gently as she could, 'and when the water is drained from the Victoria there will be a new mine manager.'

Her aunt stared uncomprehendingly.

'You can't mean to re-open it?'

'Certainly I do. There's a lot of coal down there. Have you any idea how much it cost to sink that pit and what we've paid since to keep it going? It would be a waste and worse than that, if I didn't make the mine safe again and work it, the men will have died for nothing. What do you want, Aunt, a monument?'

Kate knew the moment that she started this little speech that it was wasted, that her aunt – a chemist's daughter – had no understanding at all. She knew how to be a wife, how to conduct the day-to-day running of a home but she had never ventured into the realm of ideas and it was too late now.

'You can make your home with me.'

It felt strange saying the words. For the first time she felt older than her aunt; she felt as though she was the adult and her aunt a rather large child who had to have everything explained and pointed out. It was hard work. She arranged for Rose's belongings to be taken to the big house and for her aunt to have some rooms of her own so that the three women would not be obliged to live too closely, but it was not easy. Charles's mother did not say much but she was offended at the invasion. The will had been read, however, and everything would soon belong to Kate so there was nothing that she could do.

Kate felt no triumph at her own wealth and power. She was rather nervous of it though she tried not to let this show. And she had never liked Charles's mother, who seemed to think shopping a good occupation for a woman. Kate lay in bed at night and imagined herself far away with Jon Armstrong, maybe even as far as America, living in a cosy house, lying safe in his arms during the dark nights, making plans with him, running some kind of business, perhaps even having a child, doing the normal everyday things which women did – including shopping. Reality was waking up alone, angry, with nowhere for that anger to go.

They were like crows, dressed in black. Three widows all living together, Kate thought, with so much in common and yet nothing.

For a long time after the accident she saw nothing of Jon. She had made sure that he and Eddie were taken on at the Isabella but she did not feel as though she could go to their house without good reason, and so the time wore on – and then she found the reason. She had been making plans and decisions and she needed to talk to him. She could have called him to the office but she didn't. She went to the house.

It was Monday again. Kate thought that she could grow to hate Mondays. Lizzie's kitchen was full of wet washing because there had been rain at midday and Kate could see immediately that the other woman was horrified to see her. She stuttered a greeting, blushed for the state of her kitchen, moving the clothes horse from around the fire while apologising and offering to make tea.

Kate could have cried. She did not understand how, having lived with them for a few days, she could have forgotten that routine was important to the pitmen's families and that whatever happened Lizzie would wash on Monday which was consequently the worse possible day to visit. Lizzie's days were filled with men coming in and going out and needing clothes and baths and food and comfort so that they could do their difficult job. Kate envied her that. There were no men in her own life, no comings and goings at the house which seemed to echo with emptiness. She envied Lizzie her work, her life, her child, and especially her men. She recognised too that it was her changed status that so embarrassed Lizzie now.

'I didn't come to make a nuisance of myself. I just wanted to see Jon and it seemed easier to come here. I've missed you all.'

Her protestations made no difference. She had imagined she and Lizzie sitting around the fire with the child, drinking tea and eating cake and being the same, but it was not like that.

The kitchen was steamy and smelled of soap. Mary cried and Lizzie walked up and down with the child in her arms while Kate drank tea she didn't want. She wished she had not come. The two men came in off shift while she was there. Eddie regarded her in silence as he stepped into the kitchen. Jon looked her up and down.

'Black suits you.'

Kate was so grateful that his manner towards her had not changed she could have hugged him.

'I want to talk to you.'

'What, now?'

Kate didn't misunderstand. He was dirty, tired and hungry.

'What's wrong with now?' she said, shouting above Mary's crying.

'Go into the front room,' Lizzie said. 'There's no fire, mind you.'

Jon shut the door. Even then Mary's screams came through clearly.

'Monday's not a good day for visiting,' he said.

'Monday's not a good day for anything. I've been busy.'

'Yes, I know.'

'How's the Isabella?'

'It's dry.'

She smiled at him.

'You've done a lot,' he said.

'Do you think I have, Jon?' She was eager to hear someone she respected tell her that she had got something right. Mr Forrester and her mine managers thought that most of her ideas were mad. They were too polite to tell her this but Kate never felt more like a woman than when she was in their presence, trying to achieve something.

'More than Charles or his father ever did.'

She was encouraged.

'I want you to help me.'

'Me?'

'Yes.'

'How?'

'I want the Vic back,' she said. 'I want you to get it for me. And after that I want you to manage it.'

'That's a tall order. I'm not an expert.'

'I have the experts. I also have Forrester and old Williams. I want somebody on my side. You'll be qualified soon to manage the mine and I want you there. You can have the mine manager's house; you can move in any time you like.'

'Kate, it's only theory I've studied. I don't know anything about managing pits.'

'And what else are you going to do – stay down and hew coal until you're too old? Then what? Sort out the rocks with the old men? Hewers grow old quickly. You've been down there a long time. What are all the books for? What's the learning for, Jon, if you don't intend to use it?'

'I do intend to use it, but not here.'

She stared at him.

'Not here? Where are you going?'

'I don't know yet.'

'Oh, I see. So you're only here until you qualify, is that it?'

'That's it, yes.'

'Don't you want to work for me, even if you could have the Vic and the manager's house and good money? You won't get better. You haven't any experience of managing or engineering. It would take you a very long time in the real world to get that far. You're not very old yet. Don't you want the Vic?'

'It won't be mine. It's yours. Everything here's yours. I'm not going to die down there like Charles and Alf and Sam and my father. You don't understand. I hate that pit. It's taken from me everything I've ever cared for.'

'Don't you want to better yourself and the Victoria?'

'No, I just want to get out.'

'It isn't going to be like that any more, Jon. There will be fair wages and good housing. I'm going to have model pits. You'll have Mr Forrester to help you, and old Williams. He knows all there is to know. Please, Jon, I need you here. I'm just a woman to them. I need somebody to help me, somebody I can talk to, somebody who won't discount my ideas immediately because I'm female. Somebody who doesn't think I'm stupid. Every time I move they fight me. Please.'

'If I stayed, everybody would say it was for what I thought I could get.'

'Isn't that why anyone is anywhere? I can't run away now. You can't think how often I've wanted to. I have to stay here and face everything and talk to men who think that mining is a rich man's hobby. And Mr Forrester who tries to baffle me with figures, and old Williams who tries to confuse me with technicalities. You and I could learn to run the Vic together. We'll have lots of help.'

It was dinnertime the next day and Jon had told Lizzie.

'I suppose now you'll have to learn to ride a horse?' she said, banging plates down on to the table.

'What for?'

'That's what all posh folk do.'

They were in her kitchen and she was laying the table with her back to him, being unnecessarily energetic. Jon went up behind her and got hold of her and turned her around. She still clutched a fistful of cutlery.

'Would you rather I went away?' he said.

'You didn't even say you were thinking of going.'

'Did you want to know?'

'No, I didn't and I wanted to hear this even less. You'll make a mess of it.'

'I could hardly make a worse mess of it than letting it flood and drown everybody.'

Eddie came in then and, looking from one to the other, said, 'Something up?'

'As though enough hadn't gone wrong,' Lizzie reproached.

Eddie looked enquiringly at Jon and he laughed when Jon told him.

'You needn't laugh, I want you to come with me.'

'And put up with you telling me what to do?' Eddie looked thoughtfully at him. 'Are you going to go and live at Farrer's house?'

Lizzie put the dinner on the table.

'Will you come and keep house for me then?' Jon asked her over the noise.

'Certainly not. I've got my own house.'

'You and Eddie could have nearly all of it. All I need is one room and my dinner. It's a nice house and we could have help.'

'People would say I was getting above myself. Anyway, Eddie wouldn't, would you?'

'Is there a billiard room?' he asked.

'It's Farrer's house, Eddie, not Nelson's,' Jon said with a grin. 'You don't play billiards, anyroad.'

'I might,' he said.

That Sunday when Kate called Lizzie was just washing up after dinner. Jon asked Kate if she wanted to go for a walk. She had come early in the afternoon for just that reason and they went in the same direction as they had done on that special misty Sunday afternoon so long ago when she had wished he would kiss her. She tried to pretend to herself that nothing had happened in between, that Charles had never married her, that the Victoria had not flooded. It was almost autumn. The grass was long in the wood, covered with leaves, and the days were cooler and shorter. Kate wished that she could relive that day and the days with Jon back then which had been some of the best times of her life. Finally, when they stopped on the edge of the wood, she said, 'So, have you decided?'

'Yes. I'll take the Vic and I'll do the best that I can, but I want Lizzie and Eddie to come too.'

'Does she want to?'

'No.'

'Isn't that going to be awkward?'

Jon smiled.

'Unlike you, my petal, Lizzie is a pit wife. She'll go because Eddie wants to go. Anyroad, she hasn't seen the house yet.'

'You like to make her happy, don't you?'

'It's always been one of my first considerations.'

'Are you going to call me "your petal" in the office?'

'No, Mrs Nelson.'

'You don't like mining, do you?'

'It's a dirty, dangerous, insane way of making a living. I think it's the hardest thing there is. It's bad enough for men.'

'I like it,' she said.

'Yes, well, you don't go down the pit.'

'But I intend to,' Kate said as she set off walking again.

Twenty-four

*W*hen they went to see the mine manager's house, Lizzie loved it. She had told Jon repeatedly that she wasn't going but Eddie insisted and then she saw it. It was nowhere near as big as her only experience of big houses, which was the Nelson's, but much better, she thought. It was a big square building with big square bedrooms, a huge white bathroom, and a garden for Mary to play in. There were sea views from the top windows, the downstairs rooms were light, the front ones looking out over the neatly kept garden. There was no comparison with the pitman's cottage where they had lived until now.

'You should get married and have a family of your own,' Lizzie objected stoutly as she and Jon explored the garden. 'There's no reason why you shouldn't now; less reason than ever. There are plenty of nice lasses in the village. You could have anybody you want.'

'Look at all this fruit,' he said, stepping past her into the orchard. 'Apples, pears, plums. We'll have to pick them or the wasps will get them.'

'Will you listen to me a minute?' Lizzie said, following him.

'What?'

'Eddie and I are having another bairn.'

Jon went pale.

'It'll be all right,' she told him. 'Lots of people have half a dozen children. Besides, Eddie wants a little lad.'

'And what if you don't have one? Is it going to be another and another?'

'Come on, Jon. You like children.'

'I don't like women having them.'

Lizzie smiled at that.

'It's the only way that I know. You should have some of your own.'

217

'No.'

'You could marry and bring up a family here and be happy. There's no reason why you shouldn't.'

'There's a very good reason. I don't want to.'

'And what about Kate?'

'I never loved Kate.'

'You were going to run away with her.'

'That wasn't because I cared about her, it was for a future.'

'You could have a future here.'

'I don't care about the future any more. Being in mining, there isn't a lot of point. I'll make do with now.' He looked anxiously at her. 'Don't you like the house?'

'I like it,' she said. 'If you change your mind, Eddie and I will find somewhere else.'

Lizzie thought of the new baby. She thought of the extra room. That night when she and Eddie were in bed she said to him, 'Do you want a lad?'

'I don't mind.'

'I thought you did.'

'It would be nice.'

'What about the house?'

'The garden would be nice for the bairns,' he said, 'and there'd be a lot more privacy.'

Mrs Farrer had left some furniture, the things she had not been especially fond of. These included books for which she had no use, bedroom furniture, rugs, curtains and the odd chair. The day that they moved Lizzie's mother came over to help; Mrs O'Connor had been recruited as well as a girl from the village – not Ellen, who had married a lad from the bottleworks and was expecting her first child.

Lizzie was very excited, she felt like lady of the manor with so much help, and when everything was arranged to her liking she set to in the orchard, picking then bottling fruit and making jam. Mary ran about all day and played. The house seemed so huge but they took to sitting in the kitchen, just as they always had in the evenings, because it was too much trouble to take everything through into the dining-room and Lizzie objected to having people to help.

'Servants!' she said.

'They'll be well paid,' Jon protested.

'I don't like having people in my house.'

'You can't do it all yourself with Mary to cope with and another on the way. Try to be sensible.'

'Well, I'm not having people here at night. We'll eat in the kitchen. Will you mind that?'

They were in Jon's office which had been George Farrer's study.

'Since when did I get so high and mighty?'

'You probably will in time,' Lizzie said, glancing around her for dust.

Kate encouraged her aunt to ask her friends to the house but Rose seemed dazed. She was late for meals and ate nothing. She was vague and tearful and did not want to see anybody. Charles's mother had her own friends and made no effort to help Kate's aunt. She went visiting. Kate was only glad that she was out of the house most of the time.

Kate couldn't understand why she felt so bad about everything when her marriage had been so awful. She felt guilty for what she had done and had tried to do, and lonely with only the two older women to talk to. She thought of Charles and shuddered, and thought of her uncle and was sorry, in spite of what he had done. She tried to be kind to her mother-in-law because she had been left penniless and was now obliged to be polite to Kate. The nights were endless and if it had not been for Dolly and the work her days would all have been the same. Kate got so thin that winter that she had to put pins in her skirt waists.

When the legalities had been sorted out and it was established that she owned everything, she set to work on the pits. She wanted the Victoria draining so that the bodies of the men could be brought out. She wanted the other two pits to work more efficiently. To the horror of the managers and officials Kate went to work every day. She asked questions, she read, she went down the pits to see what they were like – something she had wanted to do for a long time – and she learned and worked. She was very glad that she had asked Jon to help – and that he had insisted on bringing Eddie with him. It was like having a bodyguard. And although it felt to Kate as if Jon contradicted everything she said, he did it in private and so she could flounce out of the office as many times as she liked and slam the door in disagreement. But he never made her feel as though he was doing it because she was a woman. Also he and Eddie never ganged up on her the way that the other officials did. Eddie was more inclined to take her part. Kate liked him better and better as the days went on and she enjoyed the wrangling in the office, the discussions that sometimes went on well into the evenings. She liked the dark nights, the way that the horse and trap came to the office for her, and being in the middle of everything.

She made plans to build new houses so that the widows of the men who had died down the pit wouldn't have to move out. She made schemes so that they and their children would be looked after. Jon approved these in theory though he usually had different ideas as to how they should be done, whereas Mr Forrester clucked his tongue and told her that it was expensive and unnecessary and that the village people would think she was indulgent. Also he did not like Jon. Kate would not have been pleased if he had.

She never went to their house. Everything was businesslike, and it was grim to begin with: the draining of the pit, the recovery of the men, the discovery that the poisonous and inflammable gases which had driven back the rescuers had eventually killed the men. It was assumed that the gases, replacing escaped air, would have found their way through to the trapped miners and, although the men would not have been able to hear anything, they might have thought that they were soon to be rescued. They would have been given fresh hope when there was none. Jon vainly tried to keep this knowledge from Kate and she wished afterwards that she had not known. Often when she lay alone, awake in bed at night, she thought of him coming back telling her that Charles could not be brought out and of how she had resented his judgement and the judgement of other people. He had been right.

She thought again and again of the men hurrying to escape, of the rushing water behind them, of them seeing the water which was cutting them off from escape and the way they must have felt during the eleven or twelve hours that the water was filling up the lower workings and gradually the higher ones. Many of the men had drowned. There were partially eaten dead horses and some candles left unused in the dry parts of the pit where the men had died. Kate knew that Jon had been relieved to discover that what he had tried to make her believe was right and that the would-be rescuers had been driven back by gases which had probably killed the men.

At one point Kate had been told – though not by her new manager – the bodies lay so thickly scattered that it was difficult not to tread on them. In another place the men had made a small shelter. Eight bodies were found there. A horse which had been tethered to a pit prop had partially gnawed away the prop in hunger. Fifty-one bodies were recovered that winter, recognised mainly by their clothes. Kate didn't sleep well at all.

She found to her dismay that she had become socially acceptable and was asked everywhere. Being richly widowed Mrs Nelson was quite different from being poor little Kate Farrer. Her company was sought by the coalowners around her just as much as when she had been married. They asked her to their houses in the evenings. She met again many of Charles's former friends, including William Dove and his wife Claudia, envying them their happy marriage and their children. Mr Dove owned several pits along the Durham coast and also inland. There was also his friend Samuel Marshall who seemed to Kate very astute though they never talked to her of pits. She was left to the mercy of Claudia Dove and Lilian Marshall, and the talk of their children and their homes. She also met the shipyard owner, Joseph Moorhouse. He was now a widower and paid Kate particular attention, but she could not pretend to enjoy going out though her aunt and mother-in-law urged her to. She didn't want to go. Kate's favourite occupation was to spend most of the evenings sitting by the stove in Jon's office at the Victoria, drinking tea with him and Eddie and discussing the day and making plans for the future. When she went out socially all she could do was stand back in amusement while men who would not have spoken to her when she was unmarried did everything they could to gain her attention. It was all very boring since things had not really changed in that they paid her compliments and expected her to know nothing of business. She went for the sake of her aunt and Charles's mother who needed to go out, but what she really wanted was to be asked to the mine manager's house where Lizzie was big with her second child.

Jon had asked Doctor Ingalls who lived two doors away to keep an eye on Lizzie and from time to time he had called to see how she was. Lizzie had never had such an easy time. They had a girl called Rose to help in the house in spite of Lizzie's protests, and Mrs O'Connor insisted on preparing the meals. Either of them would take Mary if Lizzie wanted to go out, but there was suddenly nowhere to go. She went to chapel events at first with Eddie, but it was difficult. People did not treat her the same and she increasingly found that she could talk more easily to her neighbours than her old friends.

Her mother came for Sunday dinner, with Harold, Enid and the twins. Jon's mother came too with Tommy and May and May's little girl, Esther.

One afternoon in early March Jon had come home in the middle of the day for some papers, stopped for dinner and stayed working in the office at the house for some time afterwards. He ventured into the kitchen where Lizzie had been about to bake. There was no good smell from the oven or evidence of work. She was sitting on the settee. Jon went to her, looking anxiously into her eyes.

'Are you in pain?'

'Yes.'

'I'll go and get Ingalls.'

'No. No, not yet. There's nothing he can do. It'll be wasting his time.' She grabbed his hand, squeezed hard for a few moments while she held her breath, and then let go.

'Do you want to go and lie down?'

'No, I want to walk about.'

He helped her on to her feet.

'Are you sure?'

'Yes.'

Jon stayed with her and every short while she stopped for the pain.

'Let me go and get Ingalls.'

'It'll be hours yet, Jon. Stop worrying.'

The time between the pains grew shorter until she didn't want to walk about any more. Jon carried her upstairs and then ran back down. His mother and May were just coming in.

'Thank goodness,' he said, 'I thought you were never coming!'

'Has she started?'

'Yes.'

'It's early,' his mother said as she went upstairs. He went to see whether Doctor Ingalls was at home.

At teatime Eddie came back. Jon couldn't eat, couldn't even sit still. He walked the office floor. Eddie went in there with his cup of tea and closed the door.

'It was all right last time,' he said.

'Was it a long time?'

'Two days.'

'Oh God. I hate this. I hate it. Why does it have to be like this? Didn't you ever think about it when . . .?'

'Don't be daft, man, of course I did. She's my wife. I do care about her,

222

you know. She was the one who wanted another bairn.'

Jon gave him one look and went out into the freezing garden for some air. May put the children to bed but nobody else slept. In the early hours of the morning the baby was born and Eddie went upstairs to see his son. When they had all seen him but Jon, Eddie went into the garden.

'Are you still out here?' he said.

Jon didn't reply. He was standing on the lawn. Eddie went to him.

'She's all right,' he said. 'Are you going to go in and see her?'

'It's your baby. You go and see it.'

'What's she going to think? Everybody else has gone and said how beautiful he is.'

'He probably looks like you so he can't be very bonny,' Jon said.

Eddie chuckled.

'Howay.'

Jon went inside and closed the door quietly. The room was tidy. The baby was in bed with her but he didn't even look at the child. He sat down on the bed and Lizzie smiled at him. Jon leaned over and kissed her on the forehead and on the cheek and pressed his cheek against hers. Lizzie put one hand into his hair for reassurance.

'I'm fine,' she said, 'I told you I would be. There was nothing to worry about.'

'I couldn't bear it if anything happened to you, I just couldn't.'

'Nothing's going to happen to me. But something's going to happen to you if you don't tell me my son's the most beautiful baby on earth.'

Jon scrutinised the baby.

'I don't know about beautiful,' he said. 'Are you calling him Edward?'

'Are you taking my name in vain, Armstrong?' Eddie asked as he walked in.

'Not if I can help it.'

'I want to call him Francis.'

'It's a good name,' Jon said.

One Saturday evening Jon was very restless. He and Eddie walked outside on to the lawn after they had eaten. Jon was silent.

'What's up?' Eddie enquired.

'Nowt. I just wish I could go to Fraser's for a pint, that's all.'

'You can't.'

'I know.'

'I can't either. I promised myself I wouldn't drink no more after I brayed the hell out of you. Anyway, the others wouldn't like it if we did. You can only be a boss or a worker.'

'Let's go for a walk. We could call in and see my mam. Rob'll be at the pub.'

It was the middle of the evening by the time they had wandered through the village down to the pit rows. They walked up the back lane and into the yard behind May and Rob's house. There was silence inside the house though the fire burned brightly. Jon called up the stairs though not too loudly in case Esther was asleep. His mother came to the top of the stairs after a few moments.

'Oh, it's you, our Jon,' she said. 'Just a minute.'

Jon and Eddie stood by the fire and a minute or two later his mother came downstairs with Tommy by the hand.

'Well,' she said, 'isn't it nice to see you. Will you have some tea, Eddie?'

Something wasn't right, Jon knew. He knew his mother's moods and it seemed to him she was avoiding his eyes.

'I'd love some,' Eddie said, settling himself by the fire.

Jon eyed his mother carefully.

'You've been crying,' he said.

'Crying? Of course I haven't. One of my eyes runs, that's all. I've just been out the back for some coal.'

'Rob should do that.'

'He's out. May said to tell you that she's not coming down. She hasn't been too well lately.'

Jon looked at her until his mother met his gaze.

'He's brayed her up, hasn't he?'

'No. Jon . . .'

He was halfway up the stairs by then, the stair rods clattering. He burst into the room. May was lying on the bed but she sat up and the little girl, startled by the noise, began to cry. May's face was dark with bruises and they were shiny with tears.

Jon saw his sister as she really was for the first time in years. Her eyes were frightened and her mouth was resigned. The plumpness was gone. She looked worn and tired. May looked just like her mother had when their father was alive. It all came back to Jon. He glimpsed himself in the mirror above the dressing-table and saw Tom Armstrong on a Saturday night, dressed in a good dark suit to go to the pub, tall and slender and good-looking with that black hair and those bright blue eyes that had driven the lasses wild. His father had liked other women. Jon knew he had gone with them even when there was no money in the house for anything but necessities. How long had he looked exactly like his father? Always? He wondered whether there had come a time when his mother had said to his father, 'I don't care about you like I did, not any more,' and whether it had been after that his father had somehow gone adrift because there was nothing left to hold on to. Or was it just that his father had looked into a mirror and seen what women saw, and liked and used that power?

May was holding the little girl against her fearfully. Jon thought of Kate and how Charles had treated her. What kind of hatred was it that did such things to women? He thought about being very young and of how big his father had been. He was bigger now than his father had been. He thought of trying to stop his father from hitting his mother in the kitchen late of a Saturday night, and of his father hitting him with a belt. He thought of the night when he was big enough to stop his father, of his mother's silence and his father's humiliation, and of May crying because sometimes when their father came home drunk he seemed not to know the difference between her or her mother and more than once had laid hands on her and Jon had had to stop him. He thought of his mother and May going through this again but quenched the anger because of his sister's frightened eyes and thin body. How had she got like this and why had he not seen it happening?

'Sweetheart . . .' He sat down on the bed beside her, took the child from her. The little girl had recognised him now and stopped crying. 'Why didn't you tell me?'

'I couldn't,' May said, sobbing. 'I married him.'

Jon put the child down and drew May near.

'Don't cry. You're not stopping here any longer.'

'He's my husband.'

'I don't care if he's God Almighty. He's got no right to treat you like this. Get your things.'

When May stopped crying, Jon took the little girl and went downstairs. He handed the child to his mother.

'Eddie, will you take them up to the house?' he said and, deaf to his

225

mother's protests, was out of the back door and halfway down the yard before Eddie caught up with him.

'Hey, whoa! Whoa! Just a minute.'

When Jon didn't stop, Eddie got in his path.

'Don't get in my road.'

'It's me, all right? Just wait a minute. Where are you going?'

'I'm going to Fraser's to find him.'

'You can't. You can't just walk in there. The men'll all be there. You can't beat up Rob and expect them to listen to you at work.'

'You can see what he did to my sister, the bastard! He's had it coming a long time. I should have sorted him out years ago. Now I'm going to do it.'

'Leave it. Look, I'll go.'

'Get out of my road.'

'Come on, Jon, be reasonable. You can't start a fight in Fraser's.'

Jon pushed him aside.

'Just stay out,' he said.

But Eddie went after him. Jon walked straight through the village and into the public house where he used to go so often, and where he knew he would find Rob and his mates on a Saturday night. Jon paused momentarily in the doorway and then he saw Rob and he went over and pulled his brother-in-law out of his chair, much to Rob's surprise. Men moved quickly out of the way. Jon didn't even take Rob outside. he didn't say anything, just hauled Rob on to his feet and then knocked him across the room. Table, chairs and mugs slid and rolled on to the floor and broke. Ken went to help and Eddie got hold of him. When Ken objected there were more scattered tables and jugs. Beer slopped over on to the floor.

Rob got up, cursing, with a half broken jug in his hand.

'Come on then,' Jon urged him softly, 'come on.'

It was the middle of the morning when Kate arrived. Lizzie was busy making the dinner. Eddie was sitting sideways at the kitchen table. He looked pale and had a black eye.

'You weren't at chapel. I thought I'd drop in.'

'Have a seat,' Lizzie said. 'I'll make some tea.'

Kate looked at Eddie.

'It's true then. You did break up Fraser's and get drunk. I didn't believe it.'

He didn't reply. His wife looked scathingly at him.

'Oh, you can believe it,' she said. 'Came back at some ungodly hour waking the entire neighbourhood, about as respectable as the store horse.'

'Give it a rest,' he said.

'I've never been so ashamed in my life. We come to live in a nice neighbourhood . . .'

'It wasn't my fault,' he objected. 'I tried to stop him.'

'Is May here?' Kate asked.

'Yes, and the bairns and Jon's mother. They're in the front room.'

Lizzie went out and called, 'Jon, if you want some tea you'd better come and get it. This isn't a waitress service.'

Jon looked worse than Eddie. He peered narrowly at Kate and accepted his tea, pulled out a chair near Eddie and sat down.

'I hear you had a very interesting Saturday evening,' she said.

'It made a change.'

'And do you think it befits your position as manager of the Victoria to behave like that?'

Jon sipped gratefully at his tea and then looked at her.

'It's a nice bonnet, Kate, but do you think red is really your colour?'

'You're not funny,' she said.

'What did you want me to do, pat him on the head?'

'Did you have to break the place up, fight with half a dozen of your own men and get drunk?'

'It seemed a shame to leave just then.'

'And you think you can just walk back in tomorrow morning and be the manager again?'

'What is this, Kate, the sack?'

'No, of course it isn't. I just wish that you would behave differently, that's all. Forrester didn't want you and Eddie there to begin with. We'll never hear the last of this.'

'They're not fit to feed the ponies,' Lizzie said. 'I don't know what people will think.'

'You've got to learn to control your temper, Jon,' Kate reproved. 'Why couldn't you just bring May here and be done?'

'Because he deserved it.'

'That's a fine, responsible attitude.'

Jon looked hard at her.

227

'I thought you'd understand. What wouldn't you have given to have somebody stop your husband knocking you about?'

'Charles is dead,' she said stiffly.

'It couldn't have happened to a nicer man.'

Later that day Lizzie was sitting with the baby beside the fire. May was upstairs with Esther and Mrs Armstrong and Tommy were baking scones in the kitchen. Eddie had gone to bed to nurse his eye and his hangover. Jon came and sat down beside her.

'I'm sorry,' he said.

'So you should be.'

'I didn't mean to land you with everybody.'

'Oh, I don't mind that. I just wish we'd known what Rob was doing. I'll like having May and the baby and your mother. But you should be sorry for drinking and fighting and getting Eddie involved, and for forgetting who you are.'

'I am.'

'You look it.'

Jon smiled at her.

'You look so lovely when you're cross.'

'Even last night when I shouted at you?'

'I think I was too drunk to notice you shouting.'

Lizzie handed the baby to him. 'If you got married you could have children.'

'No thanks.'

'What for?'

'There's nobody I want to marry.'

'What about Kate?'

Jon laughed.

'She wouldn't marry me. There's no reason why she should marry anybody now, especially after the way he treated her.'

'She was going to run away with you.'

'That was desperation. She's got everything she wants now.'

'Not everything,' Lizzie said, nodding at Francis.

'I don't want that,' Jon said, 'not after Greta. You don't know what it was like, losing her.'

'Don't you have any feelings for Kate?'

'Yes, but she owns everything now. That changes it.'

228

'She must be very lonely. It's awful for her stuck in that house with his mother and her aunt. Why don't you go over and see her?'

'After this morning?'

'Especially after that.'

Jon thought this was a good idea and he decided to go to the house that evening and talk to Kate. It was such a novelty to be able to go up to the front door instead of sneaking around on balconies. It was strange, he thought, how things altered.

A little maid answered the door and ushered him into the hall. It was huge with a staircase which almost flowed out of it and a kind of glass dome at the top which made it very light. Jon stood there for a minute or two while the little maid ran upstairs and then she came back down again and led him up there and into a library. It was the biggest room that Jon had ever seen, lined with books from floor to ceiling and its windows were the length of the walls. A fire burned in a huge grate and there were damask-covered easy chairs. There were oil paintings on the walls, Venetian scenes, lots of water and buildings and bridges in pale colours. There were two globes in the room, one at either end, and huge rugs on the floor. But Jon didn't notice anything of this. There were two people in the room. One was Kate and one was a man who Jon didn't recognise. Kate looked extremely pretty. She was wearing a black dress with tiny touches of cream and to Jon's astonishment it was the most feminine thing he had ever seen in his life. To the office she wore serviceable clothes. This was intricately patterned within the material and well-cut, with so many yards of material that it hung perfectly. The dress flattered her when she didn't need flattering, accentuating the copper glow of her hair, the hazel flecks in her green eyes and the golden sheen of her skin.

The man was older than Jon, perhaps as much as forty, and when Kate introduced them Jon had to stop himself from staring. Joseph Moorhouse was a shipyard owner and Jon had heard of him; heard how badly he paid his workers, how ill he housed them, how lowly he treated them, but Jon managed a flawless accent and a polite interest in what he was saying, while another part of his mind wondered what Kate was doing entertaining such a man. Joseph Moorhouse made his excuses and left but Jon could see the sparkle in Kate's eyes when she came back from seeing him to the door. Jon thought of how well-dressed the man was, how rich and well-connected. He came from a landed family, a family with a name, a background – he was as good as titled, his father was a lord.

'So,' Kate said, as she came back, 'what can I do for you?'

Jon couldn't think for a minute.

'Have you known Mr Moorhouse long?'

'Not long. He just called and then he stayed to tea. He should have left hours ago. Have you walked all the way here? Would you like a drink?'

She ordered wine even though Jon said he didn't want anything. She poured it herself and handed him a glass. 'I didn't mean to shout at you this morning. You've been very good for the Vic. I had this impression that you'd got hurt and when I could see that you weren't it made me angry. Isn't that ridiculous?'

'Do you like Joseph Moorhouse?'

'A little. He's from one of the first families,' she said. 'His father had the title and his mother had shipyards. They have a thousand acres and a house . . . oh, you should see it, Jon! And they have glasshouses. He brought me flowers to fill the house and fruit to last all week. He has a library three times as big as this.'

'You've been there?'

'Oh, yes, several times.'

'I thought he was married.'

'He was. She died about two years ago.'

'He's quite old.'

She laughed. 'He's not much past forty. He and Charles were friendly. He used to come to our parties. His wife never came, she was always too ill. You haven't touched your drink.'

Jon had been staring down into the dark red liquid in his glass.

'I have to go. I've got some work to do for tomorrow. Am I forgiven?'

'Yes, of course you are. I'll order the carriage for you.'

'No, don't. The tide's down. I'd like to walk.'

It was late when he got back. Lizzie had gone to bed but Eddie was still about. He had just made tea and poured some for Jon. They sat at the kitchen table.

'How was the boss, did she spit you out?'

'Joseph Moorhouse was there.'

'Moorhouse? What, the shipowner?'

'That's him.'

Eddie looked across the table at him.

'What was he doing there?'

'Laying siege to Kate, I think.'

'Successfully?'

Jon nodded.

'He's such a bastard he makes the Nelsons look like farm cats,' Eddie said. He didn't often swear and only when he and Jon were talking on their own. 'I thought she was looking a bit pleased with herself lately. Do you think she's going to marry him?'

'Yes.'

'If she does, you and I are out of here the following day. He treats his workers really badly, Jon, and she'll never stand up to him. You could do something about it.'

'What?'

'Marry her yourself.'

'Very funny, Eddie.'

'You could. She always fancied you.'

'Oh, yes, with my background and family and money.'

'You don't want to marry her, do you?'

'How would you like to marry the boss?'

'It's worth considering,' Eddie said, 'or are you going to marry somebody else?'

'I'm not going to marry anybody. No woman is ever going through childbirth again for me. Never! I swear it before God.'

He got up and went over to the fire.

'It wasn't your fault.'

'Whose was it then?'

'Things don't have to be somebody's fault all the time.'

'It was. You don't get used to it, Eddie, when people die. Your life turns into a kind of subdued nightmare. You go to bed and you dream badly and then you wake up and it isn't any better. And you have to go on pretending that things are all right. You pretend to people every day of your life. But I caused it. She was so bonny, all blue and gold and laughing. When she died she was . . . all swollen up and in the kind of pain I've never seen before. I never want to hear it again. Never. And the baby was so tiny. It never breathed. My son.'

Twenty-five

Kate and Jon quarrelled over the sacking of Rob. She insisted that Rob's treatment of May was no good reason.

'It's totally illogical,' she said, 'he was a good worker.'

'It wasn't meant to be logical,' Jon said.

They were in his office which had been her uncle's. It was a cold wet day. The fire burned cheerfully.

'What was it meant to be then?' Kate said from where she sat behind Jon's desk. Jon lounged by the window.

'A total misuse of power, something the Nelsons have always been good at.'

'All the more reason for us not to be.'

'Why?'

'You'd already beaten him. He was a good worker and it was nothing to do with his work.'

'I don't care.'

'The union cares.'

'And you mind what the union thinks, you a good capitalist?'

'The fact remains that you had no right to sack him.'

'Don't tell me what my rights are, Kate. I'm the manager. I got rid of him.'

'So, every time you don't like a man you're going to finish him, is that it?'

'No, that's not it.'

'Good, because I really do want some men to work down my mines regardless of whether you approve of their personalities. There are plenty of people around here who don't like you, but I employ you.'

'That's because I'm good.'

'So was Rob Harvey. I hope you take the point?'

'No, I don't take the point. I'm the manager. Why can't you let me manage without interfering?'

She came to her feet.

'I am not interfering.'

'Kate, I can't breathe without you getting in my road. I'm perfectly capable of running the Victoria. I don't need you to nursemaid me.'

'You are offensive.' He didn't answer. 'I suppose you know that he's disappeared?'

'Good riddance.'

'Nobody saw him leave. His mother is frantic. He's May's husband. Does she even know about this?'

'I have no idea.'

'But you know?'

'Am I supposed to be concerned? He's been a waste of time since the day she married him. In fact he's been a waste of time all his life. She's having nothing more to do with him as long as I have the strength to keep him from her, and I neither know nor care what happens to him. Now I have a lot of work to do, Kate. Do you mind?'

She would have marched out of the office, slamming the glass door so that it shuddered, but when she got there she stopped, changed her mind and turned.

'All right. You do make a good job of it mostly, and I don't interfere mostly, but I care about the men and their rights.'

'I care about them too.'

'Very well then. I want you to find him and take him back on.'

'That's totally unreasonable, Kate, and you know it.'

She would have hauled open the door then but that he had moved closer. He put his hand flat down on it so that it wouldn't open.

Kate turned to him.

'You had no right to take it personally,' she said. 'If we sacked every man who beat his wife or his children or drank or had some serious fault there'd be nobody left save the Methodists – and then perhaps not all of them. Personal faults do not make good or bad workers.'

'I am not taking him back on, and if you insist on Rob's being taken on at either of the other two pits I will go down and haul him out of there and send him on his way in a less than perfect condition.'

234

'You'll take him back on straight away after he's found,' Kate said, but her voice shook slightly.

'No.'

She would have left the office after she had finished speaking but Jon had her trapped with his hands either side of her on the door. Eddie was usually there when they had discussions; Kate was sorry he was not there now. Jon was never as angry as this.

'I have to go.'

'You're not going anywhere until this is sorted out.'

'As far as I'm concerned, it is.'

'I am not taking on a man who beat my sister, and I'm not going to see him taken on anywhere else around here.'

'Fortunately it isn't your decision,' she said, and tried to get past his arm. Jon pulled her back.

'Every time we argue you walk out of here and slam the door. I'm surprised the glass hasn't shattered. Let me put it to you this way. The minute you employ Rob Harvey, I will walk out of here.'

'That's totally unreasonable.'

'It may seem unreasonable to you, Kate, but that's it. Now if you walk out of here and slam that door again, I won't be responsible for my actions.' And Jon let go and moved back and glared at her.

Kate didn't even look at him again and she didn't shut the door at all.

Kate was having a spring party and had insisted that they should all go.

'She doesn't mean it?' Eddie had said, dismayed.

'You, me and Lizzie.'

'But we've got a new baby,' Lizzie said.

'You could leave him with May and me,' Jon's mother said, 'it wouldn't hurt just for a few hours.'

'What am I supposed to wear?'

'The eternal cry,' Jon teased.

'I'm not going to no party,' Eddie said.

'I don't think no is an acceptable answer.'

'I'm a pitman, or is she asking everybody from the mine?'

'No, just us.'

'Whatever for?'

Jon grinned.

'I can just see you with all the local business people, Eddie.'

Eddie groaned.

When they were by themselves he said to Jon, 'I suppose Moorhouse will be there?'

'Sure to be.'

'So why us?'

'I don't know.'

In the evenings now Jon began to teach Eddie what he knew and had started making him go to classes.

'Are you wanting to turn him into a boss?' Lizzie asked.

'He'll do it. I did. Are you going to wear that frock for Kate's party?'

They were sitting by the fire in the sitting-room. Lizzie held up the blue dress.

'If I can get into it by then. What do you think?'

'There doesn't seem to be an awful lot of it at the top.'

'No, there isn't.' Lizzie looked critically at it. 'I've been on ages making it. Cissie Ingalls says ladies wear dresses like this in the evening. I'll go and see.'

She ran upstairs and came down a short while later wearing the dress. Jon stared. It had a very low neck and tiny sleeves off the shoulder.

'Has Eddie seen it?'

'Not yet. Do you think it's too much?'

'No, I think it's too little.'

'What, I'm too fat?'

'No . . .'

'What then? Don't just sit there, tell me.'

'Well, it's . . .'

May came in then from washing the dishes. Her eyes widened.

'You're not going out in that? You'll get your death. It shows all your shoulders and . . . everything.'

'It's meant to,' Lizzie said, losing patience.

'It's indecent,' said May. 'Eddie'll never let you wear it.'

Later that evening in the privacy of their bedroom Lizzie put on the dress and did a little twirl.

'Well?' she said.

Eddie didn't say anything, he just looked.

'The other women will be wearing dresses like this. Cissie told me.'

236

'Are you sure?'

'Positive.'

'It'll not be much of a party then.'

'What do you mean?'

'If they look as bonny as you in them they'll never get there,' Eddie said, grabbing her and putting her down on the bed.

Lizzie didn't really want to go to the party. She didn't dance, she had never met rich people before and couldn't understand why Kate had invited them, but Kate wanted her to be there so Lizzie put aside her objections and went.

It was strange and rather pleasant to go to the house as a guest, and a welcome one. Kate came out and hugged her in the hall. She, to Lizzie's relief was wearing a dress similar in style to her own but it was black and white and had a good many flounces with tiny sleeves low down on her arms. Lizzie thought back to seeing other young women at similar parties at the house with music and dancing and elaborate food. She thought how unhappy she had been then, envying them so much, and now she had everything. There was champagne. She didn't mind that she didn't know any of the people. It was the perfect finish to her evening when Eddie asked her to dance.

He had said to her only a fortnight before, 'Do you think there'll be dancing?'

'Do you know how to dance? What a dark horse you are, you never told me. Will you show me?'

Now, after a glass and a half of champagne, she was very happy with him there on the dance floor.

Jon hated the party right from the minute he got there. He talked to Kate's aunt and was introduced to Mrs Nelson. He didn't drink much. He knew that he didn't like sherry, the champagne wasn't to his taste and there was no beer. There were a lot of young women about, either throwing him encouraging glances or pointedly ignoring him, and in the end he avoided them by going outside. He had been there for about half an hour, standing away down at the bottom of the gardens where there was a summer house, when a voice behind him said, 'I've been looking for you. There are a dozen girls in there who would love to be asked to dance.'

'I don't know how.' This was a lie, Lizzie had insisted on teaching him.

'I could show you.'

'No thanks. I don't think it's my sort of party.'

'It wouldn't be, would it? There's no beer and nobody to fight with. Couldn't you try to be a gentleman, just for once?'

'I think there are enough gentlemen in there.'

'You don't like my friends, do you?'

'I don't know them.'

'And don't want to.'

'Well, I can see Joseph Moorhouse and that's enough for me!'

'And what does that mean?'

'I can't talk civilly to people like that, Kate. They break other people's backs for their own pleasure and comfort. They owe too much. How can you make friends with them?'

'Just because they're successful?'

'You call that successful? Because they're rich? You didn't used to think that was success. At one time you were happy enough with people who could think.'

'That was before I left London,' she said coolly. 'I had to make my way here.'

'So does everybody, Kit, but not by walking all over other people.'

'I think you're very rude,' she said. 'You come to my party and then you won't be nice to my friends.'

'Coming to your party appeared to be in with my job. Your friend Joseph Moorhouse keeps his workers in slums, in houses where you wouldn't keep your pigs. He pays them so little they can hardly live, and when they try for better wages he starves them like your husband used to.'

There was a cold silence and then she said, 'That's not true. How dare you come here and think you're better than people who have education and civility and grace?'

'One day,' he said, 'those people in there won't own any of the pits. The pitmen will live in decent houses with proper facilities and their children will be educated. They won't have to go down into that black hell every day in the foulest conditions not knowing whether they'll come back so that people like that can drink champagne. It won't be like that any more.'

He turned around and started to walk away and she shouted after him. 'Jon! Come back here.'

He stopped.

'I mean it, Jon. Come back.'

He turned around and looked at her and then walked slowly back to her. When he reached her Kate took a step backwards but he got hold of her by the waist and pulled her to him and kissed her. She put the heels of her hands against him but her mouth betrayed her. Her lips were warm. She tried to move backwards but he put his hands flat on her back so that she couldn't. She made her fingers into tight fists against his chest but it made no difference, and when she tried to turn her mouth away he put one hand into her hair. Then he let go abruptly and she lost her balance and sat down in the wet grass.

'Goodnight,' Jon said, and left.

Lizzie found her crying in the conservatory.

'There you are,' she said. 'They're serving the supper. Everybody's wondering where you are. Whatever's the matter?'

'He does it every time! He makes me say things I wouldn't normally say, things I don't mean. Does he have to be so rude, so . . . Why can't he behave?'

'Never mind. Come and have something to eat. It'll make you feel better. Here.' And Lizzie gave her a handkerchief. 'Why are you so wet?'

'I suppose you think it was nice to walk out of Kate's party?' Lizzie said the next morning, which was Sunday. It was a bright day and everyone else had gone to chapel while she prepared the dinner, except for Jon who had just got up.

'It was nicer than having me strangle her,' he said, pinching meat off the joint as she set the dish down on the table to turn it over.

'She cried her eyes out.'

'Good.'

The baby began to whimper in his cot beside the window. Jon went over and picked him up and he stopped.

'You'll spoil him,' Lizzie said. 'He thinks the whole world belongs to him.'

'I don't like to hear him cry.'

'I have other things to think about besides him.'

Jon sat down in the rocking chair and cuddled the baby.

'Do you think Kate will marry Joseph Moorhouse?' Lizzie said. 'He's very rich and he hardly left her side all night.'

'I have no idea.'

Lizzie put the meat back into the oven and lifted the lids and prodded vegetables.

'Kate is coming to dinner,' she said.

'Oh, she's not, is she?'

'There's no reason why you shouldn't be nice to her.' She tapped him on the head with a fork. 'Are you listening to me, Jon?'

He got up and dumped Francis in her arms.

'I am not going to marry her.'

'I should like to know why not? If you don't she'll marry that awful man, and then where will we be?'

'I am not going to marry a rich awkward self-centred little bitch like Kate.'

'Jon!'

'I'm not going to marry her. For the last time.' And he walked out of the kitchen.

When the others came back, Kate with them, Lizzie gave them coffee and told Kate what a wonderful party it had been.

Lizzie liked Sundays best; she liked having everyone around. Her mother and Harold and Enid and the twins were there too. She liked to have the house as full as it could be. Jon's mother and May had done the vegetables and set the table and her mother had brought two enormous trifles. They helped with the final preparations; Eddie stirred the gravy, he said it was his big contribution. Jon was not there. Lizzie found him in his office. She went in and closed the door and waited until he stopped writing and looked up.

'I'm sorry,' she said. 'I did think there was a time when you liked Kate a lot.'

'I do like her a lot, at least when we're not at work. She pushes me around.'

'She must be very brave,' Lizzie said, and Jon grabbed hold of her and tickled her. When she broke free she said, 'The dinner's ready. If you'll be nice to Kate I won't mention marriage again, I promise, even when Joseph Moorhouse sacks us and we have to camp outside.' She ran out of the office before he could catch her.

They all sat down to eat. Lizzie kept Jon and Kate well apart. She wondered if Kate did care about Mr Moorhouse, if perhaps she was attracted to his kind of men, rich and powerful? Lizzie hadn't liked him at all and though she had once had the feeling that she and Kate liked the same kind of men, now she wasn't certain. He had seemed so sure of himself and paid Kate lots of attention. He didn't dance with anybody else and when she danced with other men he stood back against the wall and watched her. Lizzie wondered whether part of the attraction for him was the pits. Kate, she thought, would always have that problem; not being certain whether men cared for her or her money.

Kate took the baby from her so that she could eat and Lizzie thought how nice it would be if she had been married and they could have had their babies together.

There was beer which Kate drank only a little of, there were half a dozen vegetables and a big piece of beef and lots of Yorkshire puddings. They had risen high and golden so that they could be filled with little ponds of gravy. Afterwards there was a treacle pudding and then tea. Kate insisted on helping to clear up. May and Enid helped too. Mrs Armstrong sat by the fire with the baby in her arms and the children around her and talked to Lizzie's mother.

Half an hour after Kate had left in the early evening Jon was in the kitchen when he saw her ride back into the yard. She pulled on the mare's mouth as she never would have done. She was white-faced and looked agitated. He opened the back door and went to her as she halted the mare and burst into tears. Jon lifted her off the horse. She clung to him.

'Jon! Jon!'

'It's all right,' he soothed her.

'What is it?' Lizzie asked as she came outside with Eddie. 'You're not hurt, are you?'

'No, it's – it's not me. It's . . . in the wood.'

'What's in the wood?' Eddie asked.

'Somebody. Lying there. I think . . . dead.'

Lizzie led her inside and Jon went off to find the local police. When they came back one constable questioned Kate as to exactly where the body was and then two of them went to investigate. They were gone a long while and afterwards Jon took them into the office. Lizzie and May and Kate were in the kitchen when Jon came out of the office. He went to May and sat down beside her and said quietly, 'They think it's Rob.'

'Is he still alive?' May's voice quivered.

'No. He's been there quite a few days.'

She put her hands over her mouth.

'It was just with the weather being so nice and Kate taking another way home that they found him.'

'Has somebody killed him?'

'They don't think so. They think he fell and hit his head, but they don't know yet.'

'I expect he was drunk,' she said. 'He always was.' She looked down and then straight into Jon's eyes. 'I can't pretend I'm sorry, not after what he did, but it is a shock.'

'Yes, I know. Stay here. I'll go with them and make sure it's him.'

Kate stayed to tea though nobody ate anything much and after that Jon offered to take her home.

'What about Dolly?'

'You can come for her tomorrow. We'll look after her.'

She made no further objection. They went a little way in silence and then Jon asked, 'What made you go that way? There isn't even a proper path.'

'I don't know. It just looked so pretty.'

'I'm sorry about last night.'

She said nothing to that. When they got to the house the groom took the horse and trap and Jon went inside with Kate who promptly offered him sherry.

'No, thank you,' he said, looking around the empty drawing-room.

'Would you prefer some wine?'

He said that he would and they sat by the fire.

'He's asked you to marry him, hasn't he?'

'What?' Kate looked guilty.

'Lizzie said he never stopped looking at you all night.'

Kate looked down into her wine and then said, 'Yes, he's asked me.'

'And have you said you will?'

'Not yet.'

'I thought you wouldn't want to marry anybody after the way Charles treated you.'

'So did I.'

'But you've changed your mind?'

'It wasn't like that. Joseph knows everybody. It's interesting being with him. He goes to all kinds of places and meets people, and when I'm with him people treat me as though I'm worth talking to and being with.'

'And eventually you'll be "your ladyship"?'

'I don't care about that much, but yes, it would be nice.'

'Isn't he a very difficult man?'

Kate laughed. 'I never met a man that wasn't.'

'What about me?'

'You? You're impossible.'

'When?'

'All the time. Ruthless.'

'I am not.'

'No? If we had kept Rob Harvey on at the pit he'd probably still be alive.'

'You don't know that.'

'No, but I think it and so do you.'

'I don't care.'

'Exactly.'

Jon was silent for a few moments and then he said, 'If you marry him, do you think he'll let you go on as you do now?'

'Maybe I won't want to.'

'What does that mean?'

'I don't know exactly. All I know is that it wouldn't be anything like being married to Charles. Joseph is much older and treats me differently to the way Charles did. He's a man of the world. He won't want me to do anything that I don't want to do. He'll look after me and respect me. Joseph's not like Charles was. He really cares for me.'

'Does he?'

'Well, he doesn't need to marry me for my money, if that's what you mean. He has plenty of his own. He has told me of his regard for me and I believe him.'

Jon and Eddie sat by the office fire later that night. Jon told Eddie the news and watched his expression change to anger.

'She wants her head looking at,' he said. 'How has he managed to get that far with her when her marriage to Nelson was so terrible?'

'Flattery, I suppose. She has some idea that because he's older he's going to treat her like a china doll. Maybe because Charles treated her so badly she needs a marriage that stops at the bedroom door. I don't know where she got that idea from but I couldn't very well argue with her.'

'Maybe he put that idea into her head, if she's told him anything about Nelson?'

'Maybe. I didn't think Kate wanted looking after but it seems that she does and she thinks that somehow marriage to Moorhouse would protect her.'

'From what?'

'I don't know.'

Lizzie opened the door.

'Aren't you coming into the sitting-room with everybody else? It is Sunday night and May has had an awful shock today.'

Nobody spoke. She came in and shut the door.

'What is it?'

'Joseph Moorhouse has asked Kate to marry him,' Eddie said.

Lizzie sat down on the nearest chair.

'I thought he might have. Did she tell you herself, Jon?'

'No, I asked her. She says that he has great regard for her.'

'He has great regard for her money, you mean!' Eddie said.

'Eddie, that's not fair,' Lizzie protested, 'Kate's bonny.'

'I'm not saying she isn't but you've got to look at it from another point of view. She was a penniless little nowt when Nelson married her. What Moorhouse sees is money – and pits. No man in his right mind would take her on except for that.'

Lizzie stared at him.

'Eddie, that's awful!'

'It's true though. You don't want your wife at work. You want her at home with the bairns making the dinner.'

'Some men might not.'

'When?'

'She says he's strong-minded and clever.'

'He's strong-minded all right,' Eddie agreed.

'She has to marry somebody,' Lizzie said.

'What for?'

Lizzie gave him a long-suffering look.

'What else is she supposed to do, sit at home and knit?'

'She won't be comfortable with him; he'll take everything off her,' Eddie said.

Lizzie looked directly at Jon.

'You do care about her,' she prompted him.

'You said you wouldn't mention it again.'

'Things have changed.'

'Yes, they have. When I asked her to go away with me she was Charles Nelsons's wife. She wasn't rich, she didn't have things the way she wanted them, like now.'

'What's the difference?'

'The difference is that I'd be rich, that I'd own the pits as far as the pitmen were concerned. I can't do that.'

'Whatever for?' Lizzie shot back. 'Don't you think that's better than letting Joseph Moorhouse have them? Do you think the people around here would prefer that? You understand the pits and the people. We don't even know if he cares for her at all. What if he treats her badly? He could be marrying her to get his hands on all this and everybody would suffer. Kate, for all her spirit, would never stand up against Joseph Moorhouse, you know she wouldn't. He'd have her under his thumb in no time and then where would we all be? She's always liked you a lot.'

'That was before we worked together.'

'You're in no position to be proud, Jon,' Lizzie said, and walked out.

Lizzie asked Kate to tea on Wednesday and when it was over Jon said he wanted to talk to her and they went into the office. He shut the door.

'It isn't about work,' he confessed.

She gave him a surprised look.

'Oh?' She smiled at him. 'I thought you lived and breathed the Victoria, Jon? Has something gone wrong. I must say May looks the happiest I've ever seen a new widow – except for me perhaps.'

'It's about Joseph Moorhouse,' he said, trying to look squarely at her and not managing very well.

'I'm seeing him on Friday.'

'Are you angry about last Saturday?'

'It wasn't the nicest way I've ever been treated, but then I wasn't very nice to you. Neither of us likes to back down.'

'You know when we were going to run away?'

'Yes.'

'Did it matter to you that we couldn't have got married?'

'I didn't think about it. I just wanted to go.'

'Kate, I don't want you to marry him.'

'I know. You made that perfectly plain on Saturday. You don't like my friends and you think Joseph in particular is some kind of devil. But he's not. He's a good man and he's kind to me. He's older, of course, but it takes time to make money.'

'So you are going to marry him?'

'Yes. I'm telling him on Friday.'

'Don't marry him, Kit.'

'What?'

'Don't go and marry him.'

She hesitated and then said, 'But I want to. You didn't really think I'd turn down an offer from a man like that?'

'I thought you might. Please, don't marry him, Kit. You'll regret it every day of your life, and it'll be hell for everybody here.'

'I don't think it's any of your business.'

'You could marry me.'

'You?' She stared and Jon didn't flatter himself that it was with joy or delight. 'Whatever for?'

He didn't know and couldn't think.

'You don't care about me,' she said. 'You're just trying to get what you want, as usual. I'm going to marry Joseph Moorhouse and you can go to hell. You thought I was going to hand over control of the pits to a man you despise, that's all. You're wasting your time. All you care about are your friends. Lizzie in particular.'

'Lizzie in particular?'

'You love her, Jon. You'll love her until you go to your grave. You took the mine manager's job because of her . . .'

'No, I didn't.'

'You even moved her into the mine manager's house.'

'What's wrong with that? Eddie will make a manager in time. He's good.'

'And who did you think you were going to be? Lord of the manor?'

'No, honest, Kate. I didn't mean Eddie could have the Vic.'

'I didn't think you did. You wouldn't give the Victoria to anyone, and that's the reason we're here. You don't want to lose the pit. You're frightened. You think if you get this wrong now I'll put you out. But it's lonely being on your own in a house like mine with two older women, and Joseph can see past my money. He sees me. I trusted you with the Vic

246

because you'd proved what you would do, but when it came down to it the Vic mattered more to you than I did.'

'That's not true.'

'Yes, it is. You wouldn't come away even though you thought it might be to your advantage because of your precious Victoria. You almost died down there with your brothers, but when Charles and my uncle and the other men were stuck down there you risked your life for them. One of these days they're going to bring your body out of there.'

'Obviously not a day too soon,' he said.

Kate stared at him for a few more moments and then she choked on tears and ran out. Jon winced as the door slammed.

Twenty-six

*T*hat summer Kate became officially engaged to Joseph Moorhouse and was seen about with him everywhere socially. Lizzie did not invite her to the Victoria manager's house on Sunday mornings or for tea, and Kate had the dubious satisfaction of having Jon argue with her no more. She dreaded going to the Vic at all but he did his job so well that she didn't need to. Old Williams had died the previous winter and afterwards the pit ran even more smoothly so that Kate could not delude herself about Jon's abilities. She divided her time between the problems of the Isabella and the Catherine. Jon was always there, late and early, week and weekend. He didn't speak to her unless he had to, and he had to less and less. Kate knew that he went down the Victoria a lot and shivered for what she had said to him.

There was a depression that summer. The men were put on short time. At the Isabella a hewer died when a large piece of coal struck his head. At the Catherine a boy of fourteen died when a pony rolled on him. At the Victoria things went on as usual in spite of the short time.

Jon and Eddie were at home more often. Eddie began in the garden, digging and planting and tidying up. Jon helped when he was there. May had an admirer, a local farmer. She had gone there for eggs. That summer they had more eggs than they knew what to do with because he was always calling and using the excuse. They gave the eggs to other people because times were hard again in the village.

At the end of the first week in July Jon came back from work one hot day and everyone was outside. The children were playing, Eddie was weeding around the roses, Lizzie was sitting on the lawn. May had gone to the farm and Mrs Armstrong was in the village visiting friends. Jon sat down. The children fell on him and he played rough and tumble with them until Lizzie brought tea. They sat down and ate cake and then went off to play. Eddie came for a rest.

'There's going to be a party at the house,' Jon said.

Eddie looked at him.

'What is she doing having a party when we're all on short time? Some people have hardly got enough to eat.'

Kate was 'she' in their house now, in spite of Lizzie's objections.

Jon looked at him.

'It's for the pitmen and there's to be five per cent more on the wages from the beginning of the week.'

'That means we have to go up there and be nice to her?'

'It wouldn't hurt the pair of you just for once,' Lizzie chided.

There had been a big party when Kate became engaged to Joseph Moorhouse but no one that they knew had been invited. The party for the pitmen and their families was to be a picnic lunch, as Kate called it, and afterwards there would be a small dance in the evening which the managers and officials and their wives were expected to attend. Eddie and Jon had not wanted to go but Lizzie insisted.

The picnic went off well; it was a gloriously hot day and the food was plentiful. The children played games and there was music.

Jon managed to get through the entire day without speaking to Kate. That evening Joseph Moorhouse arrived.

She introduced him to Jon and Eddie. Joseph looked hard at the two miners before he smiled.

'We've met before. Kate's told me a lot about you since then. She says that you have a great deal of ability. Frankly I think the fact that you were a pitman must influence you unduly when it comes to a dispute.'

'You mean he's soft?' Eddie said.

Jon looked at him.

'I am not,' he said mildly.

'You're like horse muck,' Eddie replied.

Lizzie, who was standing nearby, glared at him. Kate could see the look of amusement in Jon's eyes and didn't hold out much hope for the conversation.

'I don't like your methods,' Joseph Moorhouse said. 'I think you indulge your workmen.'

'He does,' Eddie said, 'something fierce.'

'I'd like to dance,' Lizzie said loudly.

'I'll bet Mr Moorhouse is a good dancer,' Eddie said.

As Kate watched Joseph Moorhouse lead Lizzie to the dance floor, Jon turned to Eddie.

'Don't you think Mr Moorhouse's velvet collar suits him?'

'I think he looks a treat in it.'

Kate, colour high, took in both of them with one look.

'You should be on the stage,' she said, 'as a pantomime horse.'

'Well done, Kate,' Jon said. 'Want to try again?'

'I'd like to dance. Lizzie said you've got quite good at waltzing.'

She liked waltzing with him for all kinds of frivolous reasons. Firstly he did it well, secondly he was tall, and thirdly it was good being so close with his arm around her waist. Stupid that it should matter.

'I wanted you and Joseph to be friends,' she said.

'That was asking a lot, wasn't it?'

'I suppose. You might have given him a chance.'

'What for?'

'I think it was very small-minded of you to behave like that.'

'Do you?'

'You could stop being clever and asking questions every time you reply. It's hardly very polite.'

'The week after you marry him I'm going to be looking for work. Why should I be polite?'

'That's not true. I wish you wouldn't go down the Vic quite so much, Jon.' She had been aching to say this to him for weeks now and out it came. 'It isn't necessary, you know. My uncle hardly ever went down and you know that the men don't like it.'

'I like to make sure everything's right. I don't ever want a flood or a roof fall or a man hurt again that I could prevent.'

'You can't take care of every eventuality.'

'I like to try.'

'I know you do. I had a dream the other night that you were hurt. I said awful things to you. Do you remember?'

'I'd hardly forget asking you to marry me, would I?'

'You didn't want to marry me. You just didn't want me to marry Joseph.'

'Don't you think I want to own the pits, Kate?'

'I think you'd rather die.'

When the music stopped they were near the double doors which opened on to the garden.

It was one of those rare balmy summer nights. Kate knew that she ought to get back to Joseph but she didn't want to. Until tonight she had not regretted her engagement. Joseph was received everywhere and he looked after her. He was to her, she knew, like a father. She did not have to think or do anything when she was with him, and it was so comforting after all this time of having to watch out for herself. He was gentle with her too; so far he had confined his kisses to her cheek and the back of her hands. She had been grateful for the safety at first after Charles's brutality. She liked the luxury too, servants to see to her every need, her wishes fulfilled the moment she voiced them. Joseph did not insult her intelligence as Charles had by telling her what to do but she was careful to ask nothing about the shipyards in case he thought, as her uncle had once said, that she was unwomanly.

She didn't feel unwomanly tonight with her shoulders bare and her hair dressed so that the faint rustle of wind in the trees in the garden touched her neck.

Joseph had paid her a great many compliments about her dress which was in a colour few women could wear, her dressmaker assured her. It was almost ginger – not the offensive colour of the underwear which Charles had so liked but a soft spicy-coloured drift from which her shoulders rose creamily.

Jon had said, 'Nice frock, Kate.'

They walked slowly across the grass and she thought of that first day when she had fallen from her horse and he had, without any fuss, made sure that she was not hurt and had caught the horse. That was the day I fell in love with him, she thought. She glanced at him. He wasn't really any different, he didn't look like someone who kept hundreds of men safe each day, he was so tall and dark and immaculate beside her. Perhaps, she thought, he only looked that young because Joseph was so much older. Kate liked him still in spite of the way they had quarrelled so fiercely at work and the shocking way that he had asked her to marry him because he had wanted to save the pits from Joseph's influence. She was quite certain that Jon didn't love her, that he had loved no one in his life but Lizzie Harton and Greta – but not in that lasting way – and that when it came down to it he would do anything he could to save Lizzie one moment of pain. She thought back to Lizzie dancing politely with Joseph in the ballroom and realised that Jon had done very well by Lizzie in spite of the problems. She had married a man whom Jon cared for, a good man, and he had made sure that when he bettered himself Lizzie was there too. But he had been good to Kate too and she knew it. Joseph had been kind to her since she had been rich and widowed but Jon had tried to help when her marriage had been so difficult. Yet he had broken impossible promises. Kate thought when she met Joseph that he would not break his promises, but then he would never have to make such choices and she did not delude herself that Joseph would even have noticed her when she was Kate Farrer.

I'm not in love with Jon any longer, she thought as they walked further and further away from the house, I have Joseph now to take care of me and that is so much more important, so much more lasting.

'Will you sell the house when you get married?' he was asking her.

'I expect so. I've never liked it. We've set a date for Christmas.'

'We won't see you any more after that.'

'Why not?'

'I've had an offer from William Dove. He's losing one of his managers soon.'

'How did that happen?'

'He came over to see how we were running the place and liked what I was doing at the Victoria.'

'You'd move?' Kate said.

'When Eddie gets his qualifications he might be able to help him too.'

'What about Lizzie? You've never been away from one another before.'

'We were when she was at your house. It felt like a million miles at the time.'

'Lizzie's been so kind to me. When I think of the things I said about her the last time we quarrelled.'

'You didn't say anything about her that I can remember, or is the fact that I love her a stain on her character?'

'You do love her?'

'I also love May and my mother, and I loved Greta, and . . . in a funny way the Victoria.'

Kate laughed.

'The Victoria's not a woman, Jon,'

'She is to me, rather like you; quarrelsome and unpredictable and . . . I don't want to leave her ever.'

'You won't have to.'

'Yes, I will. The day that you marry I'm finished here.'

'I don't want that. I want everybody to be happy the day I get married. We're having a very big wedding,' she said, and then remembered the mansion on the Tyne, the huge marble fireplaces, naked marble figures, the endless dark rooms and the garden which fell away from the house in a series of jagged rocks. When she stayed there were always a dozen people to dinner; men like Joseph talking business, but not like she and Jon had talked about it. Not safety and new houses and better working methods, but money and deals. They had talked about their workers merely as numbers. The women were older than she was, middle-aged matrons done up in jewellery and expensive clothes which did not hide their lined necks and thickening waistlines. Their opinions were their men's. Even their thoughts were not their own.

She and Jon had walked a long way now, the music from the ballroom was faint. There was the summerhouse, door open because it got the heat all day. It was painted green with gold roman numerals telling the time rather like a sun-dial all around the outside. It was one of the prettiest things about the garden because it would turn around to follow the sun, being on circular runners. The sun was gone now but the light had not faded.

'The last time we were in the garden you were awful to me,' Kate said. 'You pushed me into the grass. I was soaked.'

'I didn't push you; you fell.'

'A fine distinction considering how you were treating me.'

She stepped into the summerhouse. It smelled of summer flowers and old wood. It was not a place for unhappiness and she knew now how very unhappy she had been. That unhappiness was some way from her; she could see past it, breathe freely.

Jon followed her inside. The summerhouse was smaller with him in it, Kate thought, but she didn't mind. She felt safe. Joseph had put a ring on her finger; it was several diamonds shaped like a flower with a round stone in the centre and petal-shaped stones on the outside.

There was a big sofa. She sat down there.

'I suppose we ought to go back,' she said, 'but it's too nice an evening to be inside. Joseph will be wondering where I am. Couldn't you be nice to him, Jon? I want you to run the Vic. If you -'

'No.' He wasn't even near her but she almost felt the snap in his voice.

'Why don't you open your eyes, Kate? He's not a man like your father or your uncle even if you wish he was. He'll rule you – and well – and he'll take the pits from you. You thought you were unhappy with Charles Nelson. It'll seem like a picnic compared to Moorhouse, and don't think I'll be there to help you this time because I won't.'

'That's not fair . . .'

'Fair? Who told you it was going to be fair? And what evidence have you? Your mother died and left you, and then your father. Your uncle gave you up for some idea that being rich would make you happy. And for God's sake, you actually still believe it! How can you be so stupid? Charles Nelson beat and raped you, and now you haven't the sense to stop a bastard like Joseph Moorhouse.'

'Joseph hasn't touched me, and you have no right to talk to me like this,' she retorted, getting up.

'Well, somebody should before you drag us all down with you. You have a moral responsibility to your miners not to put them into the hands of a bastard like him, but you can't see it. You think he's bloody Santa Claus!'

'I'm going,' she said, unable to stand any more of Jon's temper.

'Yes, go on, get out. Go and marry him. You deserve to be miserable, you pathetic little bitch!'

Kate had rarely thought that Jon was bettering her verbally but she knew that mostly it was because he kept to being a pitman and didn't say what he really thought or how he thought it.

'I love him,' she said.

'No, you don't. What do you know about loving anybody? All you've got to go on is Charles Nelson and he wasn't capable of it. Moorhouse is going to love your pits, don't delude yourself. It's your money he's after, not you.'

'What an awful thing to say,' she said breathlessly.

'He's made love to you then, has he?'

'Of course he hasn't.'

'Of course? What's he doing? Containing his passion?'

Kate was trembling now. She didn't trust herself to leave. She didn't want to stay.

'Joseph cares about me.'

'No, he doesn't. He could have plenty of raving beauties; women who are less intelligent than you and who would therefore revere him. You don't

255

really do that, not when you're using your mind. You want to because you think he's like your father. He even looks a bit like him, doesn't he, Kate?'

She had to concentrate on her breathing.

'No,' she said.

'It's not that you're beautiful, it's just that you're beautiful and rich. He's a gatherer. He gathers money and businesses and capital. He'll do very well out of you.'

Kate badly wanted to cry but knew that she had to get out. She eyed the open door. The smell of wood and flowers was repugnant to her now. She couldn't breathe. She fought with the tears and made for the door but he caught hold of her around the waist as she had wished so many times that he would and he brought her back to him.

'Let me go.' Kate wanted to fight with him but couldn't because of all those walks in the wood on Sunday afternoons when he had never touched her except to lift her over a stream or steady her when she stumbled.

He said urgently against her ear, 'Oh, Kate, I wish you wouldn't. If he was different it would be all right. There are a lot of good men and if he was one of them . . . Give him up, Kate, please. You can't care about him or you wouldn't feel like you do about me.'

'I don't feel anything about you,' she said.

'Don't you?' And when she looked up at him he kissed her.

They could have been back in Lizzie and Eddie's small pit cottage on the evening when she had ventured out in bad weather because she had not seen him in so long and badly wanted to, in the days when she was married to Charles. It was the same kiss. Kate forgot the party, became deaf to the music. She couldn't remember Joseph or where she was.

Jon closed the door and drew her back on to the sofa. Kate realised then what he was doing. She said, 'No, Jon, don't,' but he didn't take any notice. He kissed her all over her face and hard on the mouth and then her throat and neck and shoulders.

Kate had sometimes thought about what the first night of her marriage to Joseph would be like. She imagined that he would be polite and considerate and kind and that somehow he would erase from her mind the way that Charles had treated her. It had never occurred to her that something else might happen.

It was like a different world there; the music muted, the shadows, the sweet smell of summer flowers and old wood, and it was quiet. He kept hold of her and went on kissing her and his fingers found the fastenings on her dress.

He loosened the top and pushed it down to her waist then put his hands on her warm breasts and pressed kisses and caresses everywhere.

Even in the early days with Charles Kate had not felt like this; warmed through as though it had never happened before. It was so different to her. She was on fire, cold, helpless, reluctant, frightened, exhilarated. There among the cushions he put his hands under her skirts, and among the flounces and frills and lace and underskirts he reached accurately and took down her drawers. Charles had insisted on her wearing nothing but expensive underwear which he would remove slowly until she was naked. That to Kate was being a wife. This was what the young pitmen privately, Kate knew, called 'giving her what for', removing what was necessary to reach what you wanted. Charles would have taken her then but Jon didn't and it was for Kate a novel experience to want to be taken and to have to wait as though she was expected to take part here rather than have something done to her.

It soon became clear to her that her husband had never loved her, perhaps not even liked women at all, because Jon kissed and caressed every part of her as he slowly took down her dress and her petticoats.

She was almost crying by then. She still didn't believe it. She felt like this was happening to somebody else, only she knew that it wasn't. Part of her wanted to stop Jon. The other part of her was greedy for him. She was conscious of him just as she had been that first day on the beach; his hair black and straight and shiny, his blue eyes warm now with want, his mouth intent and his smooth young body which he was easing out of his clothes.

'Jon . . .'

'It's all right. I'm not going to hurt you.'

He was close again, he slid his hands under her.

'Jon . . .'

He was so gentle with her, his hands and mouth and the slow soft words, that when he took her Kate's eyes widened. It was too late to pretend and she had forgotten how Charles had not once made her feel like this in all the nights they had spent together. Her fingers clasped handfuls of his open shirt. Her body fought for nearness until she was crushed against him, and then Kate thought insanely that he was no different here than he was at work. Just as Charles had been cruel and insensitive in everything he did so Jon was now making certain that she didn't stay frightened and cold and reluctant; it wasn't just a taking or even a mastery as Kate's previous experience had led her to imagine. He persuaded a level of response from her such as she hadn't known she possessed. She felt afterwards as though she was in some kind of shock. It was rather like drinking too much wine. She lay there among the wreckage of her clothes and smiled idiotlike into his eyes. She could hear the music but it was much too far away to be of any significance.

'I didn't think it could be like that,' she said. 'Was it like that with Greta?'

'Yes.'

'What, always?'

'Yes. I mean it was always different but it was always good.'

Jon stroked her hair and then put an arm around her and Kate was content to lie there for a while thinking of nothing but gradually she realised, there against the warmth of his body, that she had not been allowed to touch Charles. She ran her hands over Jon's back in experiment, waiting for him to tell her not to, and when he didn't she grew bolder and even kissed him. Encouraged she kissed him all over his face and then grew shy and stopped. Jon drew her down on top of him.

'Come on then,' he said softly.

It was late. Kate was suddenly aware of it. The music seemed further away than ever. She sat up. Her clothes were strewn on the floor. The party was going on without her. She should have been there. Perhaps even now Joseph was searching for her, wondering where she was. How long had she been here? Neither broke the silence in the summerhouse until she turned and looked at him and realised that he was not the man she had been married to or the man she was planning to marry and said, 'I have to go.'

'Not yet.'

'Now. Before now.'

He looked so young without his clothes. He looked like the pit lad he was, his hair in his eyes and his eyes darkly wistful. He said, 'Don't leave me,' and he put one slender hand on her hip and kissed her gently. She twisted away. He kissed her all the way down her spine but she got up. He reached for her, drew her back to him. He cupped her face and kissed her, put his hands into her hair and on to her breasts, and she said, 'This isn't right.'

'Isn't it?' He looked vaguely surprised. 'Well, you're the clever one. You tell me what to do.'

'I have to go.'

'Oh, not yet.'

'Jon –'

'Go on, give us a kiss.' And he rolled her over on top of him and held her to him.

Kate was suddenly very angry with the young woman in the summerhouse and how she had behaved. It could not possibly have been the same person that she was. There in the velvet darkness she had been deliciously happy, being pleasured like never before. She was the giggling type, Kate thought in disgust, so young without any problems or any responsibilities, and he was like Charles could never have been. He was the pit lad that she had met on the beach and so admired the day that she fell off Dolly. All she had wanted was to be with him and to have him treat her like this.

It was dark in the summerhouse now and she could hear the music playing again. She got up and felt for her clothes and began putting them on with as much speed as she could.

'Don't go,' he said again, moving towards her. Kate stayed out of reach.

'It's late and they'll be wondering where I am. I have to.' She tried vainly to fasten the buttons on her dress.

'If you come over here I'll do that for you.'

She didn't answer but went on struggling and he got off the sofa and went to her. The enormity of what she had done was just beginning to reach her but she turned her back and he did up the buttons for her while her eyes filled with tears and her throat got a lump in it that was a hundred per cent misery. When the buttons were done up he slid his arms around her waist and put his mouth to her neck and kissed her.

'I wish you wouldn't go,' he said.

'I must. Joseph will come looking for me. Where are my shoes?'

'Kit –'

'Find me my shoes.'

He did so and when she had put them on, he said, 'Will I see you tomorrow?'

'No.'

'When?'

'I don't know.'

'Kit –'

She turned and opened the door and ran.

259

Twenty-seven

*K*ate had been invited to London to stay with Joseph's family. She had never been so relieved to accept an invitation. Going back to the party had been unreal; smiling at her guests, seeing Joseph and waving across so that he would think that nothing strange had happened. When he came to her she told him that her dress had been badly torn where someone stepped on it and had had to be repaired.

'You were a very long time,' he said gravely, and Kate nodded and agreed.

It was with relief that she found Eddie near her asking her to dance but when the music began and she was in his arms she discovered that that too was a mistake. Kate fell over his feet without any excuse because Eddie was a good dancer. She apologised, saying that she thought she was rather tired. Eddie said it didn't matter.

She had never been so glad to end a party, to watch people leave when it was so late that the light had begun to filter into the sky once again. Joseph was inclined to linger.

'I love the summer,' he said. 'We should have organised things better and been married in the summer.'

When they had all gone Kate ventured down the garden to the summerhouse. The door was still open. She half-expected to find Jon there waiting, but it was empty. There was no evidence of their lovemaking. Kate had thought that somehow there would have been; it was as though it had never happened, as though it was some kind of dream, and she thought that perhaps it was better that way, that real life held no room for passion like that. She smelled the flowers and the wood. She stepped inside. It was all shadows.

Everything was changed now, she thought. She had been so sure that she

261

wanted to marry Joseph and now that certainty lay in ruins. She knew very well that there was no tenderness in Joseph's nature, she had not asked for any, nor thought that she would ever want such a thing again. She had thought that Charles had destroyed any desire like that.

She thought of those first nights of her marriage. If he had shown even a little of the kind of passion that Jon had given her then her marriage would have been at least a partial success, but he never had. Kate thought that nobody knew how awful such a beginning to marriage could be. Even when Charles had beaten and raped her it had not been in some way as savage as his wild contempt for her chaste, virginal body when he first uncovered it and took her. It had been almost casual, a brief invasion and a curious humiliation.

She thought back to the night and wished for the hundredth time that it had not happened. She had schooled her mind against such things. Her body she had thought already well chastened but it was not so, she saw now. The lad from the pit cottage had taught her that long ago and now . . . now she would have to begin all over again. She sat down on the old sofa and then lay down and cried.

Lizzie and Eddie went home.

'But where is he?' Lizzie objected. 'He's been missing for hours. He'll have to walk.'

'Just leave it.'

She looked sharply at him.

'You know where he is, don't you?'

'No, I don't.'

'You know where he was.'

He didn't answer her. Lizzie pestered him. They didn't go to bed; she made some tea. Their garden was full of warm light. She took the tea out to him and they sat on an old wooden bench.

'Something could have happened to him.'

'He's probably just gone for a walk.'

'A walk now? Whatever for? Are you going to tell me what happened or aren't you?'

'I don't know what happened. Will you be quiet? You'll waken people up.'

'The last thing I remember was when he was dancing with Kate. After that

I didn't see her for ages or Jon at all and when she came back . . .'

Eddie yawned.

'I'm going to bed,' he said, 'the bairns'll be up and about shortly. Did you look in on Francis?'

'Yes, he's still sleeping. He looks lovely when he's asleep.'

'That's because it's the only time he shuts up.'

Lizzie sat there a little while longer. She was as happy now as she had ever been in her life and she suspected that happiness. It was like an accident waiting to happen. Things were too good; Eddie, the bairns, the lovely house with its garden. She had the feeling that Joseph Moorhouse was hovering somewhere just beyond that happiness and that by Christmas it would all be over.

As she sat there Jon came in through the garden gate, something no one ever did. They always used the back yard.

'Jon. I was worried about you. Where have you been?'

'Just on the beach.' He sat down beside her but didn't look at her.

'Would you like some tea?'

He shook his head.

'Didn't Kate look bonny?' Lizzie said. 'Joseph Moorhouse is so middle-aged. He's as bonny as an old gnome. How can she marry somebody like that?' She looked anxiously at Jon. 'You and she had another row, didn't you? There's nothing you can do about it, Jon, nothing at all.'

'Except move.'

'You won't like managing another pit.'

'I don't have any choice. I'll take my mam and the bairn. May won't come now and you and Eddie won't be able to have this house, but after he qualifies he'll get a pit.'

'I don't suppose he will,' Lizzie said. 'Maybe a better job but not a manager's job; not for a long time.'

'I'll get him in. I'll talk to Dove. Don't worry about it. He has influence with other people and fingers in other pies.'

'You won't like leaving the Vic.'

'It's not leaving the Vic that bothers me, it's leaving you and Eddie and the bairns, but maybe it's time. You've got so many people around you.'

'I like it like this. This is the best it's been since . . .'

'I know, he said. 'I'm going to bed.'

Lizzie followed him but as she snuggled in against Eddie's warm back she heard the baby move and then begin to cry, in a low voice at first and then as nobody took any notice in a wail.

'Oh no,' groaned Eddie, 'I'd just got to sleep.'

Lizzie leaned out of bed, picked up the child from his cot and drew him in with her.

'Is he wet?' Eddie asked wearily.

'No, he's just hungry.' And she put the child to her breast and listened to the silence.

'Thank goodness,' Eddie said, and went to sleep in the peace which followed.

Kate's trip to London had been planned weeks ago and she had never been as glad of anything. She wanted to get Jon out of her mind. She thought also that she could somehow recapture the way she had felt when her father was alive; that in some street or road she might see a glimpse of the way things used to be. She had heard that when people lost those they loved and went back to the old places there was still an essence of them, a feeling. She badly wanted that now.

The London to which she went was not the London she had known and to her initial dismay she was not the same person. Joseph's town house was in the very smartest area of the city, nowhere near the place she had lived. His father and mother were there and they were kind to her. It soon became obvious to Kate that Joseph's father was dying. He was grey-faced and frail though they all denied that he was ill. When Kate made the longed-for visit to the square where she had lived in the early years with her father, she discovered that there was no evidence that he or she had ever been there. London life went on all around her but nobody recognised the shabby girl who had cared so much in the well-dressed lady who found nothing but tears in the old street. She did not know whether the tears were for her father, Joseph's father or the life that she had lost. There was nothing to do but return to the splendour of the dying man's house.

Joseph was unconcerned, as though no one had ever or would ever die, but Kate could see that this was because he did not believe that anyone who mattered to him could ever die. His mother even gave a big party for Kate while they were there though she protested, and, except when she went to bed or when she awoke in the dawn, Kate forgot about Jon and everything connected with the pits, confident that if anything went wrong he would see to it.

She went shopping and bought new clothes; she attended parties and musical evenings; she did all the things that she had once despised and was introduced into high society. It was a life so entirely removed from the one which pit people led that the north-east became unreal to her. She put it from her mind.

The women around her spent thousands of pounds a year on clothes. They wore so many jewels that sometimes they could hardly walk and had to have footmen waiting behind them with chairs. In the town house the lace on the sheets and pillows was sumptuous and people there did not regard their servants as people. How much less would they think of the miners? The pits meant only money to them.

Kate was there six weeks. Joseph's father did not die, he even began to look a little better; and as for her own father – when Kate left London for the second time she knew that there was nothing of him left in the city where he had spent his life. Except for her it was as if he had never been.

The first part of the journey north had no effect on her. She thought that her trip had done her good but as she drew nearer to the life that she had made for herself it seemed so dismal and so ugly that she wished she could have stayed in the south where life had been so easy.

She did not go to the pits immediately. She stayed at home where she could make herself believe that even here she could be comfortable, but it was not so. The pretty little kitchenmaid cried with the toothache and irritated her and Kate took her to the dentist and thought what a wretched girl she was. But on the way back when the girl was in pain no more and thanked her so profusely Kate knew that she was still her father's daughter and could not ignore even a hurt dog in the road, nor see any person in pain, and she tried to be glad of that.

The early autumn was rainy and foggy and grey. Kate huddled by the fire. She had reports from the pits and there, from the Victoria, was Jon's bold black handwriting. She didn't go. She found herself not quite well, as though she had enjoyed herself too much in London, and she tired easily and fell asleep over the teacups.

She didn't want to go riding or see anybody. She wanted to refuse the outings which Joseph had planned. Her aunt had been to Scarborough to visit her newly-widowed sister and had come back feeling better, and Kate had taken Charles's mother to London with her so both the older women were happy that autumn. They helped her with her wedding plans and often, as Joseph's father grew frailer, spent weekends with Kate and Joseph at his big house in the country where both older women blossomed in the new and interesting company.

The wedding was planned for just before Christmas. Joseph, finally acknowledging that his father would not see the spring, voiced a wish to be married quickly so that his father could see him happy. Kate had no quarrel with that.

She told no one that she felt unwell. She was often dizzy, she was continually tired, her breasts were sore, her monthly bleeding had stopped – but it was not until the second morning that she was quite violently sick that the truth dawned on her and even then she could not believe it. She lay in bed long after her usual time. The hot tears coursed down her cheeks and she wondered why this should happen *now*, from half an evening spent in a summerhouse, when if this had happened during the early part of her marriage to Charles it might have been the saving of it.

This child, if it lived, this pitman's child, would inherit everything the Nelsons owned and had worked for. Kate found from deep within herself a longing that Jon was dead, and then she revoked it. She had a suspicion that to wish a pitman dead was to condemn him, and she had done that once already with Jon and spent many a dark dawn praying not to be paid out for her wickedness.

That evening when she was sitting alone in the library – her aunt and mother-in-law had ventured out to a small dinner with people Charles's mother had met in London – Jon came to the house. Kate was half-inclined to tell him that she was not at home, which she wouldn't have been if she had felt better, but she was curious. Curious to see again the young man she had not been able to resist a full three months ago. And when she saw him, even though she was angry, and even though he stood in her library, cap in hand, like the pitman he was, she could see why. There had been no man in London who looked better to her critical eye, and even though Kate badly wanted to hate him, she found it impossible.

'They told me you were poorly,' he said.

'It's nothing.'

'You haven't been to the pit. Kit, look, I . . .' He stopped. The clear blue gaze came to rest on her face and he said, 'I'm sorry about what happened;

266

I didn't mean for you to be hurt. I couldn't tell you . . . you went . . . It was just that you looked so bonny that night and I . . . I haven't held anybody in my arms in such a long time.'

This was the very last thing that she wanted to hear.

'Forget about it. I have.'

'I just didn't want you to think that I was trying to get in your road.'

'That you might have done it on purpose?' She shot him a look that would have melted ice. 'Do people do things like that on purpose to save their beloved pits? I didn't think it of you, Jon, not for a second. I thought you were devastated by my loveliness.'

He didn't say anything to that. She wasn't surprised.

'Did you have a nice time in London?'

'I had a wonderful time, thank you.'

'They say that old Moorhouse is dying.'

'Yes, I believe he is, and Joseph wants his father to see us married before Christmas.'

'You are going to marry him then?'

'Did you think that an hour in the summerhouse would make the difference?' It was a low blow, she thought even as she said it, and his silence confirmed it.

'I thought you weren't coming to the Vic because of what had happened.'

'Really?' Suddenly Kate was very angry with herself. She couldn't believe that she had actually given herself to this man. He was nobody. He had been born in a pit row and was only now a mine manager because she had persuaded him to study and then made him manager. He was never going to be a man like Joseph, somebody with money and influence and friends. He was just a tall, good-looking pitboy. 'Why on earth should I do such a thing?'

'I don't know, I–'

'You didn't find my ear-ring, did you?'

'What?'

'I lost it. I thought I might have left it in the summerhouse. Diamonds, to match my engagement ring.'

'I didn't find it,' he said.

'No, well, I didn't think I'd be that fortunate. Perhaps it was in the garden or when I was dancing. Did you want me to come to the Vic especially? Is there some kind of problem?'

'No,' Jon said, and went home.

When he had gone Kate sat trembling by the fire. What would he do when he found out that she was pregnant? He could hardly ask her to marry him again. She shook her head to try and rid herself of the thought. Somehow, if she tried, the problem would go away. She might even miscarry, plenty of women did. She thought of Greta and shuddered. She wished that she could have her London time over again, when she had enjoyed herself and cared for nothing. Here in the dark gloomy house it felt as though she would never be happy again.

That summer Jon had been so quiet that often Lizzie didn't even know whether he was in the house, though he was rarely at home. She'd expected that things would get better when Kate came home but it didn't seem to make any difference. He spent more and more time at the pit.

'Are things going badly?' she enquired of Eddie one drizzly Sunday morning when Jon wasn't there again.

'Not that I know of, why?'

'He practically lives there.'

'Maybe that's why things are going well.'

'Don't get clever, Eddie Bitten. What's going on? I thought over the summer that he was missing Kate when she was away, but she's been back weeks. Has he seen her?'

'Just that once when he went to the house.'

'Don't you two ever talk about things?'

'Just work.'

Lizzie had to visit her mother in the village to hear the rumour that Kate Nelson was expecting. Enid and Lizzie and her mother sat around the fire one afternoon and Mrs Harton gravely reported the news.

'She can't be,' Lizzie said. 'Rich folk don't go on like that.'

Enid was inclined to giggle. 'Wanted to make sure of him and his money and his title,' she said.

'It can't be right,' Lizzie protested.

'My sister, Bet, has a friend who works at the house and says she's got morning sickness. It's not something you can hide,' Enid said sagely.

Lizzie went home and tried to tell her husband but his only reply was that she shouldn't listen to gossip.

In October Joseph's father died. The funeral was a huge affair in

Newcastle on a wet dark day. The leaves blew about the churchyard, the paths were slick with rain, and Kate wished even harder that she could be back in the summer with the old man so kind to her in his sumptuous London house. In some way it was like losing her own father all over again. She wept so much that Joseph had to keep an arm around her shoulders as they walked away from the grave.

By the carriage, where the horses tossed their heads in the downpour, he looked tenderly into her eyes.

'I never thought to see you display so much compassion,' he said. 'You're so good, and I can't tell you how glad I am to have you here with me. You'll be a comfort to my mother when we're married, and more than that to me. When I first met you I have to admit I didn't think I could ever care this much for any woman, but I love you, Katherine.'

That evening when Kate came home she knew that she had to tell Joseph she couldn't marry him. It was cold and the rain had ceased. He warmed his hands by the drawing-room fire and as Kate joined him there, he turned and said, 'I'm afraid this means we'll have to postpone the wedding. I'm sorry, my darling.'

She looked at his tense, white face and knew how hard the day had been for him. She felt what she thought was the first real stirring of love for him, but she had been putting this off for such a long time and couldn't do so much longer.

'Yes, I know,' she said. 'Joseph, I'm sorry. I know that losing your father . . . I know what it's like, but I can't put off saying this for much longer. I can't marry you.'

He stared at her from hurt, tired eyes.

'Can't marry me? Katherine, you *have* to marry me. I never, much as I loved Mary – God rest her soul – felt about her the way that I feel about you. You're so kind and beautiful and . . . Is it because of today? I know that I'm a good deal older than you and will probably die first but–'

'It's nothing to do with that,' she said.

'I thought that you loved me?'

'I think I do, though I feared I was incapable of loving anyone again. I have a worse self, Joseph, a self you haven't seen and wouldn't wish to.'

'I don't know what you're talking about,' he said. 'You're a very fine young woman. I don't care what you are. I love you and I want to marry you.'

'You aren't listening to me, Joseph. I'm not going to marry you, not in a while, not in a few years, not ever.' She pulled off the diamond which he had given her. It glittered coldly as she held it out to him.

'I can't accept it.'

'You must.'

Lizzie had quite enjoyed her afternoon spent in the garden. It was a week later and just as she had thought the warm weather was over for good back it came. It had been one of those rare warm October days which are better than summer. She had swept the last of the leaves into a pile and set fire to them. There was no wind. The grey smoke spiralled upwards. Francis was sleeping peacefully inside with Jon's mother listening as she knitted by the fire. The other children were playing in the garden. It was afternoon. The sun was sinking magnificently into evening and Lizzie was content. She thought that she might take a walk on the beach before dark if she could spare the time, only she probably wouldn't have a chance – early evenings were the busiest time of day, with a meal to cook, the children to bathe and put to bed, and the men coming home.

As she stood her husband stepped out of the house into the garden. He had just got home. He came over and looked into her eyes and kissed her. Lizzie tried to read his face.

'What?' she said.

'Kate has broken off her engagement.'

'She hasn't?' Lizzie stared into his handsome grey eyes. 'But how could she? I mean . . . You don't think he's treated her badly, do you? What about the baby?'

'I don't know. It's just talk so far.'

'But she can't do that. She can't bring up a bairn on her own; she has to marry him. Maybe the boot's on the other foot.'

'What for? He'd marry her. It gets him an heir even if it isn't what you'd call respectable.'

'I don't understand it,' Lizzie said. 'I would have thought he was a stickler for propriety.'

It was so late when Jon came home that everyone except Lizzie had gone to bed. She was dozing in a kitchen chair by the fire and awoke with a start when he opened the back door.

'Jon, is that you?'

'Who else would it be?' he said, as he closed the door behind him.

'Have you had anything to eat?'

'I just want to go to bed.'

'Not on an empty stomach,' she said, and gave him tea and sat him by the fire and then sat down with him, watching him from her rocking chair as he ate.

'Did you hear about Kate?' she asked.

'Yes.'

'And?'

Jon looked narrowly at her.

'I never see her.'

'But her engagement to Joseph Moorhouse?'

'Maybe she's just come to her senses.'

'If she's expecting, why isn't she going to marry him?'

'It's just talk. Are you going to let me eat in peace or not? You should be in bed anyroad. You don't have to wait up for me. We're not married.'

Jon never said hurtful things to her. Lizzie stared at him and then suddenly realised the truth. Jon stopped eating.

'Why don't you leave me alone?' he said.

'You can't let her sort it out by herself.'

'There's nothing to sort out,' he said flatly.

Lizzie knew that she had gone too far. In one minute he was going to be on his feet and losing his temper, and if he ever laid hands on her he and Eddie would kill one another.

'But Jon—'

'Will you let me alone?'

Lizzie fairly ran out of the kitchen and up the stairs. Eddie was sitting up in bed as she groped for the door in the darkness and came in where there was a light.

'He says Kate's bairn's nothing to do with him.'

'Well, if you believe that you'll believe anything.'

'Jon wouldn't lie to me.'

'Why not? He's busy lying to himself.'

Eddie lay down again. Lizzie went over to him and sat down on the bed.

'He wouldn't.'

Eddie looked hard at her.

'You know, don't you?' she said.

'No, I'm just not daft, that's all. The night of the summer do they went off to the garden and were gone ages. Some people might think that means they had a long talk about marigolds.'

'Eddie, she was engaged to a rich clever man, a man who owns a great big country house, has a big house in London and all. He has shipyards, he has houses and carriages, and most of all he has a title. What lass in her right mind–'

'She wasn't in her right mind. If you're in your right mind when I get hold of you I'm not the right man, am I? Joseph Moorhouse can have all the houses and shipyards in the whole world but Kate fancies Jon. Always has done.'

'But if Jon–'

'It's been a long time since Greta died.'

'Poor Kate,' Lizzie said.

Kate's aunt and mother-in-law were so disgusted with her that if they had had anywhere to go they would have gone. As it was they contented themselves with staying away from her as much as possible. She had never been as lonely in her life. She couldn't ride Dolly because she didn't want to fall and hurt the baby; she couldn't go out because people had heard the rumour and stared. Even the servants were strange with her. She was quite alone with nothing to do except get bigger and contemplate a disastrous future. Her friends had deserted her. She couldn't sleep and she couldn't eat and there was no one to tell her that rest and food were important. In her mirror she saw the shadows like bruises under her eyes, the hollows in her cheeks. Except for the baby she was thinner now than she had ever been. It was as if Joseph Moorhouse had not existed, as though that wonderful summer in London had never been. She was left alone in her disgrace.

Eddie gave Jon a couple of days before he went into the office at the end of the working day. They talked about the problems of the pit and when things were sorted out Eddie said, 'I'm away for my tea. You coming?'

'Not yet.'

'Can I say summat?'

'I wouldn't.'

'Pretending it isn't happening isn't going to make it go away.'

Jon glared up at him since he was sitting and Eddie was standing at the other side of the desk.

'I suppose you think I can go up there and ask her to marry me again?'

'You took her out to the summerhouse and bloody well gave her what for!'

'One night,' Jon said, coming to his feet.

'Let's just say you're unlucky then, depending on how you look at it.'

'What does that mean?'

'It can't be Joseph Moorhouse's, can it, or there wouldn't be a problem? You can't leave the lass to bring the bairn up on her own.'

'She's not a lass. She owns everything.'

'That's the whole problem, isn't it?'

'She doesn't want me.'

'She's not exactly spoiled for choice, is she?'

'I can't go and live there and be the boss. I can't!'

'Better you than Joseph Moorhouse.'

'It's not just that.'

'What then?'

'What if summat happened to her, Eddie?'

'Summat did happen to her,' Eddie said dryly. 'You.'

Twenty-eight

*J*on had wanted to walk to the house but before he was halfway there he regretted the decision because rain began to fall heavily. He was glad of the weather, it matched his mood. He had a grave desire to kill Kate. He didn't want to marry her, he didn't want to know about her condition, he didn't want to see her. He wanted nothing at all but to go home and crawl into bed and forget everything. He thought of her in that ridiculous dress at her party, thought of her pretty face and her creamy body. How could she possibly be having a bairn?

He was soaked to the skin by the time he got there and the rain hadn't soothed his temper. He was kept waiting on the doorstep while the water dripped off him and then ushered as before upstairs into the drawing-room where a big fire blazed. Kate got to her feet as the door was shut after him and Jon's temper died away.

She was a different lass to the one at the party. She was like a scarecrow. Her eyes were huge and it was as if somebody had punched her under them. Her cheeks were hollow and her lips pale. Her hair, which was dull, had been scraped back unbecomingly. Little wisps of it escaped across her ears. She was very thin indeed. She wore a dress of dark green. She didn't look pregnant, she looked ill.

'Oh, Kit, why didn't you tell me?' he said, and if she had given him a fragment of encouragement, a look or even a word, it would have been all right. Kate turned glitteringly cold green eyes on him. They were the only thing about her which was lively.

'This is not how I planned things,' she said.

'I'm sorry.'

275

'Do you know how I felt when I had to tell Joseph that I wasn't going to marry him?'

'Am I being blamed for this?' Jon said. 'Weren't you there? Oh, I see. It's my responsibility. How many nights have you sat there blaming me?'

'There's nobody else,' she said steadily.

'There's you. Anyroad, it isn't going to make any difference. We only have one thing to sort out – whether we're going to get married or not.'

'I don't want to marry you.'

'You can please yourself. It's either me or nobody.'

'You're glad about that, aren't you?' she said. 'That was what you wanted.' And after a moment or two she turned on him a thin shuddering back.

Jon closed his eyes at his own stupidity and tried again.

'Kit, look, you can't do this by yourself, even if you want to.'

'I'm ruined,' she managed.

From the other side the dam broke, tears rained, but when Jon put a hand out to her she moved further away. He waited but when she had gained control of herself again she said, 'Do you really see yourself here with my aunt and Charles's mother and the servants?'

Jon winced. He thought of the mine manager's house, of the bairns tumbling about, of his mother, of Eddie to talk to and May singing and the garden. He thought of his comfortable bed and his office and the meals, the bread-making, the jam tarts and coffee cakes, the kitchen fire and coming home no matter how late, knowing that the woman of his dreams would be dozing by the kitchen fire waiting for him.

'All right,' he said, 'I don't know what you want me to do. Do you want to bring the bairn up on your own?'

'No. I can't. It wouldn't be right.'

'But you won't marry me? You've got me there, Kit.'

'I didn't say I wouldn't. I said I didn't want to.'

'And do you think I want to marry you?' he said.

She turned around, her face ravaged with tears.

'Why shouldn't you?' she said. 'It's the only way you're ever going to be anything.'

Jon wanted to hit her so much that he put his hands into his pockets. He was not going to be Tom Armstrong even to suit Kate because then he would not be able to forgive himself for what he'd have done to her.

'I'm going home now,' he said steadily. 'You can make the arrangements. You've got nowt else to do. How about Christmas?' And he walked out.

Lizzie kept going back through to the kitchen thinking that she had heard him come in, but he hadn't. She and May put the bairns to bed and then she sat with Eddie and May and Jon's mother by the sitting-room fire. Mrs Armstrong was quiet. Jon was in disgrace with her. Then Lizzie heard him, or thought she did, and ran through into the kitchen, regarding with dismay the dripping figure beside the door.

'You didn't walk back in this. You'll take your death!'

She took his cap and coat and Jon pushed off his shoes and went upstairs. When he came back dry and changed Lizzie had given cups of tea to the others. She handed him one. He didn't reach for it, didn't even sit down; he just stood by the fire with his hands in his pockets and said nothing.

'Are you getting married?' she said, unable to bear the silence any longer.

'Yes.'

'It'll be a good thing. You need a wife and bairn. Soon?'

'Christmas.'

'That's nice.'

'She's so thin and so hurt. I didn't . . . she looks awful.'

'You'll have to look after her then, won't you? Drink your tea.'

Jon lifted the cup to his lips, swallowed gratefully and then looked at her.

'Brandy?' he said.

'It's for the cold,' Lizzie said stoutly.

They were married in time for Jon to see snow at the big house. It was the time that Kate had planned to be married but she went through the ceremony in a daze, thinking that she was asleep and that any moment now she would awaken and be back in that happy time in London. But she didn't waken. She was obliged to take her youngest pit manager home with her and give him her seat at the head of the table. Most galling of all was the way that he looked so at home there in his new expensive clothes, his shiny straight hair expertly cut. Neither her aunt nor Charles's mother spoke to him but he either didn't notice or didn't care, Kate thought, and that very first evening he said that he wasn't having the servants standing around while he ate so Kate was obliged to dismiss them. She hadn't the nerve to argue with him – or the energy. It had been one of the worst days of her life. She imagined how different everything would have been if she had been married that day to Joseph Moorhouse. She thought of the celebrations, of going away on honeymoon, of not being fat and noticeable and humiliated. She wanted most of all to run away.

When the servants had gone she voiced her objection and Jon said flatly, 'I'm not going to make polite conversation while I eat because other people are there.'

'And what kind of conversation are you going to make?' she asked furiously.

'I don't know, but I don't want it repeating in the village.'

'Good servants don't gossip.'

'Rubbish!'

'You would know.'

'Yes, I would,' he said, and ate his dinner. Kate was so angry that she couldn't eat hers.

The evening was not over. Later, when Emma was brushing out her hair, Jon walked into her room. Kate had somehow expected that he would not do so until he was invited but then reasoned bitterly she had been around gentlemen for too long. He was not going to do anything of the kind.

'Aren't you going to sleep next-door?' she said when Emma was safely gone.

'No.'

'I'm pregnant,' Kate said ridiculously.

'I had noticed.'

'That would stop a gentleman.'

'Would it? Whatever for?'

She turned away, hands shaking, and for the first time in months remembered how Charles had come to her room nightly and how he had treated her.

'I don't want you here.'

There was a short silence during which nothing could be heard but the crackling of the fire.

'What did you think this was going to be like?' Jon said.

'I don't know.'

'Come over here. Come on, I'm not going to bite.'

When Kate did so he sat her down on the bed. He sat down with her and looked into her eyes and said, 'We're married now. I can go and sleep next-door if you want me to, and behave like the mine manager, go to work every day and be polite to you at mealtimes – if that's what you want. I'm not Charles Nelson, I'm not going to do anything awful to you.'

'I've never slept with anyone else in my life,' she said shakily.

'Didn't Charles sleep with you?'

'No.'

'Not ever?'

'That's not how middle-class people go on.'

'It doesn't sound to me as though they have much idea,' Jon said. 'It's nice to turn over in the night and have somebody there.'

Jon had never made love to a reluctant woman before and he wished both during and after that he had behaved like the coward he was and gone to bed. It was just so awful. He did everything he could to make her respond and she lay there like a block of ice and let him. She was like somebody blind and deaf. He had never experienced rejection before. He thought about Greta, her laughter and her warmth and her arms around his neck, and thought that never again would he put himself through that. He called himself such names afterwards.

He didn't stay with her, but got himself out of the room and into the next room and stood against the door with his eyes closed, listening to her sobbing into the pillows. He couldn't understand why he had tried when she so obviously didn't want him there. He had wanted to prove to her that he was not Charles Nelson, that he cared about her, that he could be gentle and kind and it would be all right, but it wasn't. Jon had hated himself before over Greta for different reasons but the feeling was the same. He went to bed and lay there looking up into the darkness, wishing things could be any way but this.

He didn't come back to dinner the next day or the one after that until it became a pattern, and though Kate had made sure that the connecting door was locked and had locked the other door after her there was no need. She lay in bed and thought from time to time that she could hear him moving around next-door but he was a pitman, used to thin walls, and made little sound.

Every day Jon got up with the servants and went to the pits and every night he came back very late and had a tray in his room. It was, Kate thought, rather like having a lodger. He was still officially the manager of the Victoria but in fact Eddie was doing most of the managing and Jon was in general charge overall.

Kate wondered what it was like for him to come back to no woman waiting for him. She knew that the servants did not accept him because he had, what they called, 'got her into bother'. There was no open hostility, there could not have been, but there was an atmosphere.

Kate waited for him to do something that she could criticise, but he was never there to be criticised. He worked on Saturdays and Sundays, and her aunt and her mother-in-law, neither of whom ever spoke to him, said that they thought it was too much that he should work on the Lord's day. But Kate didn't see Jon to talk to him and she thought that even if she did it wouldn't make any difference. In the end she went to the pit to see him.

'You could come home and eat like civilised people do,' she said. Jon had a big office there now which Kate was privately impressed with. He had rescued the room from storage purposes and in a matter of days turned it into a comfortable place where he could meet the mine managers and officials. The windows on one side looked out over the pit head and on the other was the tantalising track to the beach. The day that she called a roaring fire blazed. She was seated in a comfortable chair and given tea by one of the clerks. If Jon was a visitor at the house, she was certainly regarded as one here, she thought. Jon didn't answer her remark about civilised people though she knew now that he could very well have asked what was civilised about going back to eat with people who didn't speak.

'I'm just trying to sort a few things out,' he said.

'And how long will that take?'

'A week or two.'

'You haven't forgotten about the servants' dance? I've asked the tailor to call on Friday.'

'Ask him to call here. I'm busy.'

As she went home two men arrived and Kate recognised them. They were coalowners: William Dove and Samuel Marshall. They had been friends of the Nelsons. They greeted Jon warmly, smiling and chatting. Kate was so curious that when Jon came home that evening, a little earlier than usual, she knocked tentatively on the door between their rooms and when she heard his voice opened the already unlocked door. Kate was surprised when she walked in. He had changed nothing in the house but he had in the three rooms which had once been Charles Nelson's and were now his. All the clutter had gone, most of the paintings and ornaments, half a dozen small tables. Now it was neat as never before. Charles had been brought up to be a gentleman and threw his clothes on the floor for others to pick up and was generally untidy, but here nothing was out of place. In the bedroom a low fire burned. By the bed there were books. In the small sitting-room the fire was bigger and the long sofa which had stood under the window was gone. In its place was a writing desk and chair and there were other comfortable chairs and a good many books in bookcases which Kate had never seen. Charles had rarely used this room but Jon obviously did.

'You've changed everything,' she observed. 'Where did the desk and the bookcases come from?'

'The attics. Mrs McArthur found them and had the other stuff moved.'

Kate had not realised that her husband was on such terms with the housekeeper.

'You could have the library,' she said.

'Thanks.'

She wasn't sure whether his reply contained sarcasm or not. She was suddenly conscious of her nightwear even though he wasn't looking at her. The fact that Jon had been into her bedroom plenty of times when she was wearing similar things did not help. Now that they were married it was different. He was dressed. She sat down in a chair across from him and said, 'What did William Dove and Samuel Marshall want?'

'They're hoping to sink a pit a few miles down the coast.'

'And what do they want from you?'

'Local knowledge.'

'Capital?'

Jon didn't answer that.

'It will make money, won't it?' she said.

'I don't know. I expect it will, but it's always a gamble and it takes time and investment.'

'You could have asked me.'

'I don't want your money,' he said. 'I'm only here for two reasons. The first is that you're expecting my child, and the second is that I can run the pits.'

'There is another. I shall want you to dance with the servants on Saturday night.'

* * *

Lizzie and Eddie had been invited to the servants' dance since it was to be the only social occasion at the big house that winter. Kate had written an urgent note to Lizzie and Jon had told Eddie that if they didn't come he wasn't going so they went. It was, Lizzie thought that night, a very different kind of occasion from the one she had attended as a maid. For a start all the women down to the kitchen maids had beautiful dresses. She noticed a pretty dark girl in particular in a rose pink dress. Jon was dancing with her and she was looking up at him and chatting and smiling. It gave Lizzie a little shiver up her spine to see him there so elegant in his expensive clothes, bending his head to catch her words. Their feet matched as they danced.

'Who's the girl in the pink dress?' she enquired of Kate.

'The kitchen maid – one of them. I bought material for them for Christmas and had it made up. What do you think?'

'I think it's a very nice idea.'

Eddie danced with Mrs McArthur. Lizzie danced with everyone who asked her. Kate wouldn't dance. Her aunt and mother-in-law stood about looking lofty. The supper was as sumptuous as anything Lizzie had ever seen, and there was champagne, but the best part of her evening was watching Jon persuade the other kitchen maid to dance with him. She was a plain fat little girl and Lizzie was convinced that she had never danced a step in her life, that no one had ever paid her a moment's attention or asked her before. She stayed in the corner at the beginning, in the shadows. Kate had had made for her a very becoming pale straw-coloured dress which flattered her. Lizzie watched Jon find her, persuade her, saw her downcast eyes and confusion, but he got to the very edge of the dance floor where it was still rather shadowed and taught her to waltz, and since it was the last dance before supper he took her arm and led her in and looked after her and suddenly she wasn't plain any more. Her cheeks were blushed and her eyes sparkled and she laughed.

'Goodness,' Kate remarked, as she and Lizzie sat down together. 'I think Jon's made a conquest.'

'Are you very unhappy?' Lizzie said.

'You don't think I wanted to *marry* him? I'm just like every other woman he meets – I couldn't resist him. And at what cost.'

'You wanted to marry him once.'

'That was when I knew nothing about marriage. Now I know everything.'

'He can't be as bad as Charles,' Lizzie protested.

'I don't know. I never see him. He works every day. He should have married the Vic.'

'Don't you eat together?'

'He doesn't come back for meals.'

'When does he come back?'

'At night, late.'

Lizzie frowned at her.

'Don't you see him then?'

'No.'

'Not ever?'

'No.'

When it was very late Lizzie danced with Jon. They danced well together because she had spent a lot of time teaching him after Eddie had taught her, while May played the piano amidst much laughter. It seemed such a long time ago. Jon didn't talk to her now, or anyone else she suspected, and while they danced he was silent and held her very lightly as though he had no right to touch her. Lizzie wished there had been some other way than marriage between him and Kate; it was obviously not working.

'Things don't have to be like this, Jon,' she ventured finally.

'Like what?'

'If you could put Greta from your mind you might learn to treat Kate like a wife. There's no reason at all why she shouldn't have half a dozen children.'

Jon's face, she thought, was all horror.

'It's perfectly normal,' she said firmly.

He stopped dancing.

'You're pregnant again, aren't you?'

'Yes. Don't stop in the middle of the floor. People are looking.' But Jon had already walked off and left her.

Lizzie pretended that nothing had happened; she didn't call out but went after him with difficulty through the crowded room. It was ten minutes before she found him in the library. She was irritated that she had not thought of this at first. She closed the double doors and went to the fire where he was standing.

'I like children, I want lots. Tell me what's wrong with that?'

'Nothing.'

'Then why did you walk off the dance floor? It wasn't very nice of you.'

Lizzie put a tentative hand up to his shoulder. Jon responded as though she had hit him.

'Don't touch me,' he said, and drew away sharply.

'You didn't seem to mind when we were dancing.'

'That's different.'

'How?'

'It just is.'

'If you're going to get upset every time somebody's pregnant–'

'Oh, so you're just somebody now.'

'Jon–'

'Go away. Go and dance with your husband.'

'Kate loved you once, you know she did.'

'No, she didn't. I was just a way out, that's all. Now she thinks I've trapped her so that I can have the pits.'

'That's not true and she knows it. Can't you be nice to her? Why don't you go and ask her to dance? You haven't spoken to her all evening.'

They went back to the ballroom. Kate was smiling and talking to Mrs McArthur and her own personal maid but when she saw them she came across.

'Dance with me, Kit,' Jon said, 'just once.'

'I can't. I'm too fat and too tired.'

The music ended and Eddie left the parlour maid and came over to them.

'I've had enough,' he said to Jon. 'Don't you know when to offer a man brandy and cigars?'

'You don't smoke cigars,' Jon reminded him.

'I'm trying to cultivate rich tastes, man. Howay, let's out of here.'

Jon led him off to the library and gave him brandy. Eddie declined the cigar and took his glass and chuckled.

'What's funny?' Jon said.

'You and me and all this.'

'I'm glad you like it.'

'Oh, come on, Jon, it can't be that bad.'

'I hear your wife's pregnant again.'

Eddie looked narrowly at him.

'Aye. I can't think what's doing it.'

Jon said nothing.

'That was meant to be funny,' Eddie pointed out. 'I don't see why you

284

have to take it personally. It's nowt to do with you, your wife's pregnant too. What was that, an immaculate conception?'

'You're as sharp as hell these days.'

'I spend too much bloody time with you,' Eddie said. 'It's not for you to complain.'

'I wasn't–'

'Yes, you were, and I'll tell you this for nowt, Armstrong, she's mine. She's been mine for a long time now in a way that she was never yours, and if you've got owt else to say about my wife I'll take you outside and give you a good hiding.'

It was a moment before Jon looked at him.

'On my own lawn?'

Eddie didn't answer that.

'Do you want some more brandy?' Jon offered.

Eddie put down his glass.

'It tastes like cough mixture,' he said.

It was late when Kate went to bed. She sat in front of the mirror and looked at herself and slowly realised that there was no way she could get out of her clothes without help and it would be wrong to ring for the maid when it had been their dance.

She had long since stopped locking the doors to her bedroom and did not pretend that Jon was in bed because his light always burned long after she was. It was to Kate quite comforting to lie in the almost darkness and know that he was next-door. She went tentatively and knocked but there was no reply. Softly she opened the door.

'Jon?'

She went through the bedroom into the sitting-room where the fire still burned brightly. Jon was lying on a sofa in front of it. He was asleep. A book had fallen on to the floor. Kate didn't like to waken him but she was feeling very uncomfortable in her clothes.

'Jon . . .'

He opened his dark eyes, looked vaguely at her and then sat up.

'You should have gone to bed,' she said.

'Are you in pain?'

'What? Oh, no. I can't get out of my dress and I don't like to call Emma. She's probably gone to bed anyway.'

Jon got up.

'I don't see how it comes off,' he said.

'It's all hidden around at the back. Here.'

'Right.'

Jon had difficulty with the tiny buttons. Kate waited patiently.

'There. Does it come over your head?'

'I can manage the rest.'

'It's all right, Kate, I'm not going to touch you.'

'I can manage. Thank you,' she said, and swept out.

She did have difficulty with the dress, there was so much of it that it was heavy and cumbersome. When she was finally undressed and in bed she was exhausted and that was why she cried.

Twenty-nine

*A*fter that, as far as Kate was concerned, the rot set in with the female staff. She began to regret having had a servants' dance. Mrs McArthur took to staying up every night no matter how late Jon was so that he had a hot meal when he came home. Sometimes that winter he stayed at home on Sundays. He would not go with Kate to chapel but they ate Sunday lunch and she knew very well that the kitchen maids and the parlour maids pushed to be where he was. When Jon was at home the fire was built up twice as often as necessary and if he sat on his own in the library they were always interrupting him with offers of tea and cake and coal and wood, and Kate could see why. Jon wasn't a gentleman, he had no idea how to treat staff. He talked to them and made jokes in that light teasing way he had done with Kate when they met, and the maids came out of the room smiling and glowing. The atmosphere eased.

Down at the stables the head man went with Jon to buy a horse, and because he had been consulted he was pleased and taught Jon to ride that winter. They went out as soon as it was light so that more often Jon was later going to the pit and was in to breakfast. Because neither her aunt nor Charles's mother came down to breakfast – they preferred to eat in their rooms – Kate had Jon to herself.

During the final month of her pregnancy she was so uncomfortable that she couldn't rest. She didn't want to eat, she couldn't walk far without tiring. She lay down every afternoon but the baby felt so heavy that she didn't sleep.

One night she awoke when it was dark and cool. The fire had almost gone out. She lit the lamp and then lay still. Jon was knocking softly on the door.

'Kate, are you all right?'

'I'm fine.'

'Can I come in?'

'Yes.' She wasn't sure about this but didn't know how to refuse. 'You're still dressed,' was her first remark.

'It isn't that late. Is there something wrong?'

'I'm just not comfortable. Are you working?'

'I'm finished. Here.' He pulled out the pillows from behind her and plumped them. He also put one at the side of her and Kate was reminded that he knew about things like this. He poured her a glass of water and when she had drunk it he told her to lie down and tucked her in. Kate hadn't been tucked in since she was a little girl.

'Shall I build the fire up, or are you hot?'

'No. I like to see the flames on the wall.'

Jon went over and put coal on to the fire, not too much, just sufficient so that the flames broke free.

'Is that better?'

'Yes, thank you.' He sat down on the bed and pushed a stray lock of hair out of her eyes and then he bent over and kissed her on the forehead.

'If you want anything just shout. Goodnight.'

'Jon . . .'

'What?'

'Nothing.'

There was more and more to do. Jon liked it that way. The manager of the third pit, the Catherine, had been ailing for some time and things had not been running as they should though the officials were mostly good men and did what they could. Jon had itched to have the Catherine for Eddie and the Victoria for himself so when the manager conveniently died he didn't appoint another even though Kate objected.

He appointed a relatively new man called Josiah Smith for whom he had a great respect to manage the Isabella. Jon also spent a lot of time with Dove and Marshall overseeing the sinking of the new pit. Sometimes in the evenings they went to Marshall's house in Sunderland. It was to Jon rather like the mine manager's house had been. Samuel Marshall's wife was a bonny lass. She kept a good table and sometimes Jon and Samuel and William Dove sat around the fire there and talked about the new pit and made plans for a fine new model village. Jon had realised that a familiarity with pit life was a good starting point for his ideas and Dove and Marshall seemed inclined to let him do what he wanted in the way of design, though they laughed over the idea of cottages in triangles with ashes and rubbish at the back and a green at the front for the hanging out of washing and a place where the bairns could play. He did get them to agree to big cottages with two rooms each up and down, blue slate roofs, and coal delivered daily, refuse and ashes removed at the same time.

Sometimes Jon went to see Lizzie and Eddie but although Lizzie invited Kate and him for Sunday dinner, Kate kept refusing so that Jon felt he couldn't go. He hated going back to the big house because although it was April the nights were cold. By the time he got home there was a chill on the place and it was full of shadows and lonely corners. The trees around the house made strange creaking noises, there was a small dogs' graveyard not far from the house and it was silent except for the wind. Mrs McArthur had stopped waiting up for him because he got later and later and he had told her that he would eat before he came home. More and more often he went to Samuel's comfortable Sunderland home.

One night that April when he had spent some time at the new sinking and even more time having dinner with Samuel and his wife he came back very late to find lights on in the house. Nobody said anything at the stables but when he reached the stairs Mrs McArthur came slowly down to meet him.

'Mrs Armstrong took bad this afternoon,' she said.

The baby wasn't due for a fortnight. Jon would have run up the stairs but she stopped him.

'We couldn't get you.'

'Is the doctor here?'

'Been and gone, sir. Sent his apologies. He had another case to go to.'

'Is she going to be all right?'

'Yes, but he'll be back first thing in the morning. He left a nurse with her.'

'The baby?'

Mrs McArthur shook her head.

'Dead?' Jon said.

'I'm sorry. Mrs Armstrong took a bad fall.'

'How?'

'She tripped over her skirt hem at the top of the stairs. We did send for you, sir, but by the time we'd been all the places you'd been and were meant to be . . .'

He had told no one where he was going for once, and it was impossible to explain. He felt guilty about being with Marshall and Dove, it was not his work but an indulgence. He liked being in on a completely new pit, seeing his ideas taken seriously, having men of ambition and influence seek his company. He had become, Jon thought with a shudder, a coal owner. He might even enjoy the kind of parties which he had once despised where the talk was of the use of money and somewhere in the background was a wife like Lilian Marshall with shiny blonde hair and a generously curved body who would give you more to do in bed than read books. Also, Jon knew that Lilian reminded him of Greta. He had found himself staring longingly at her pretty face, blue eyes and rounded curves, and remembering what it was like to turn over in the night and reach for a woman like that. He thought of Greta's laughter and her kisses. She was the only woman who had ever belonged to him. Lilian soon noticed. Jon had apologised but she only laughed.

'Are you proposing clandestine meetings in the afternoons?' she said.

'No.'

'What a relief. I wouldn't know how to refuse and Samuel would be bound to find out.'

Jon found himself telling her about Greta. They spent most of one evening sitting by her fire while he poured out the story as never before. He had thought Lilian might be shocked but she wasn't. She was rather like Kate, Jon thought, she was more educated than most women. Now he was ashamed for the time that he had spent with these people.

Worse still when he ran up the stairs and reached Kate's room the nurse was just coming out and closing the door behind her.

'Mrs Armstrong has gone to sleep,' she whispered. 'The doctor gave her something to help.'

For the first time in his life Jon went off to the library and reached for the brandy, but he put it down again. If Kate should wake in the night he would never hear her that way. But she didn't waken. He was the one who stayed awake until the daylight arrived, standing by the window wishing it was summer, wishing it was anything else, wishing the long-awaited light would come or never come, and when it did he heard the nurse, the murmur of voices in the room next-door, and ventured to the connecting door and opened it.

The nurse looked up.

'You can come in. She's awake now.' And she went out by the main door and left them.

All night Jon had known what he wanted to say, the words had been rehearsed in his mind. Now he couldn't think of anything. His mind gave him constant replays of Greta in pain, Greta dying, of the dead child and the way he had held her, and afterwards. There was nothing worse than afterwards. He would have gone through all the rest a million times to stay well clear of that. It came back at him now, all that crashing guilt, the loss, and the way that his life had been emptied out like a tin bath after washing.

'Where were you?' she said.

'At Samuel's house.'

'Oh, yes. Not at work or at home or anywhere you might be reached. But then I should have known. Lilian Marshall and her pretty blonde hair. You could at least ask what the baby was. You could pretend to be interested in something other than your work and Samuel Marshall's wife.'

It was Harold who came to the mine manager's house. He often came with his family to Sunday dinner but rarely alone. Eddie and Lizzie were sitting in the kitchen. It was the middle of the evening. He came to the back door and Lizzie ran to meet him, fearing the worst.

'Jon's wife's lost the bairn,' he said immediately, and when his sister ushered him inside he told her the details that he knew without embellishment and then looked at Eddie. 'He's at Fraser's.'

'What?'

'If somebody doesn't go and get him out he's going to be to carry.'

'He can't go to Fraser's, not now.'

'He doesn't seem to know that.'

Eddie thought at first that Harold had been mistaken, that Jon wasn't drunk. He didn't look it. What he did look was completely out of place like never before. Eddie stood in the doorway and knew it instantly. Even when Jon had been a mine manager there had been something of the pitman left in him but there wasn't now. He was sitting by himself and the place was unnaturally quiet, the pit men all grouped well away from him. He was sitting on a bench by the fire and he was wearing what even Eddie knew to be a very expensive suit. His hair was shiny clean under the light and fell forward like wings to hide his face. It was Saturday night and every man in the room was done up dog's dinnerlike, but Jon made them look scruffy.

Eddie had the feeling that not only did Jon not realise that he shouldn't have been there, but he was hardly conscious of where he was. He didn't move, even when Eddie went over to him. Harold hovered in the doorway. He had been convinced that Jon would get into some kind of fight. Eddie sat down on a bench across the table and Jon looked at him. Eddie knew that if they had been strangers he would have said that Jon was on his first drink. His eyes were clear and steady and so were his hands but Eddie wasn't deceived.

'Now then,' he said.

'Now.'

Eddie looked up.

'Tom, let's have another jug here,' and when the landlord complied he swallowed his beer slowly. Jon said nothing. 'You been into work today?'

'Of course.'

'You have any problems at the Cath?'

'No.'

Eddie got stuck there and so launched into a short monologue about Lizzie and the bairns while the beer in the jug went slowly down. When it was empty he said lightly, 'The supper's ready. Are you coming?'

'No.'

'Lizzie's made lots. It's pot pie.' He knew it was Jon's favourite. 'Howay.'

'No, thanks.'

'It's getting late.'

Jon looked up. 'Tom, bring us some more.'

Eddie caught the landlord's eye and shook his head. Jon glared at him.

'You keep your Methody ways to yourself!'

'I think you've maybe had enough. Come on, let's go.'

'I'm not going nowhere.'

Eddie put his hand on Jon's arm and even as he did so knew that it was a mistake. Jon came to his feet and brought Eddie with him and he knocked him the length of the room. On the floor, hurt and dazed, Eddie called himself names and cursed. The men retreated. They knew full well, Eddie thought, that they weren't dealing with the mineowner any more. Jon was Tom Armstrong's son and they weren't going to get in the way. Harold helped Eddie to his feet.

'Come outside,' Jon said.

'I don't want to come outside, thanks,' Eddie said, examining the pain in his face.

'You wanted to before.'

'No, I didn't want to before.'

'Yes, you did. Said you were going to kill me.'

'I'm beginning to think I should have done. You're bloody well blind drunk. I'm going home. I've had enough. I promised Lizzie I wouldn't let you get into a fight, and now look.'

Eddie walked out with Harold close behind him but Jon followed them and when he got them outside he started on both of them; Harold first which Eddie knew was sensible because Harold hadn't much skill, and after he had put Harold on to the road he would have gone for Eddie again but that for the first time that Eddie could ever remember Lizzie came running up the street, saying as she reached them, 'I knew this would happen.' She surveyed Eddie's face and Harold who was bleeding and turned on Jon. 'There's no call for this,' she said. 'Just look at you. You're drunk.'

'I am not.'

'Oh, yes you are. I've seen you drunk plenty of times. You're forgetting yourself. You're forgetting who you are.'

'I wish I could.'

'Lizzie, leave him alone,' Eddie advised softly.

'You have no right to come here and behave like this.'

'I have no right to come here at all, that's what you mean.'

'That's exactly what I mean! You don't belong here any more and when things are bad it isn't right of you to go on like this and even worse to hurt your friends. Eddie came to help and so did Harold, and what did you do?'

'What did I do?'

'You had no right to treat them like this.'

'I don't seem to have many rights, do I?'

'Lizzie, he's absolutely out of his mind. Leave him,' Eddie said.

'Yes, leave me,' Jon said. 'You've got Eddie and Eddie's not drunk. Harold's not drunk either. You would have thought with them not drunk they could have left me alone, wouldn't you?'

'You're a disgrace.'

'Yes, I know. I'm not fit. You told me. I remember. I'm not fit to feed the ponies. I need another drink.'

'No,' Lizzie said immediately, and grabbed hold of his arm as Jon started to move away. 'Come home with me.'

'I can't.'

'Of course you can, Jon.'

'Do you know Lilian Marshall?'

Lizzie looked wildly at Eddie.

'Lilian looks like Greta,' Jon said. 'She has the bonniest hair in the whole world.'

When Jon awoke he was in his room at the mine manager's house and it was full daylight. For several delicious moments afterwards it seemed to him that he was the Vic's manager again, that he belonged here, that the marriage to Kate was a dream, that he was back at the happiest time of his life. And then he saw the expensive shoes which Lizzie had placed side by side on the floor beside the window and he remembered.

He lay there knowing that he should have a bad hangover, but he didn't, and thinking that it was Sunday and that he would have to face his mother and May and all the others, but there was nobody about. When he got up the house was silent. His watch declared that it was mid-afternoon. Jon bathed and found his clothes washed and ironed and his suit pressed. He dressed except for his jacket and wandered downstairs. It was a cold bright windy day and to his surprise from the kitchen window he could see Lizzie hanging out clothes. He went out the back. She was alone.

'Where is everybody?' he said.

'Eddie's at work. Your mother and May have gone shopping and taken the bairns.'

'At work?'

'It is Monday.'

'What happened to yesterday?'

'You decided against yesterday as I recall. Your father used to do that apparently; get blind drunk and miss a day.'

'I'm sorry.'

'Sorry?' Lizzie stopped hanging out the washing and turned around and looked at him. 'You knocked Eddie down in Fraser's, you did the same to Harold in the street. How we got you home I just don't know, and who in God's name is Lilian Marshall? Really, Jon. My mother was right – you're as like your father as it's possible for a man to be.'

'That's not true,' he protested. 'I haven't done anything.'

'I don't know how you dare!' Lizzie said, and would have stormed off into the house except that Jon caught her by the arm just above her elbow and she turned and smacked him so hard over the face that he let go. The clothes billowed like sails in the cold wind. He hated the smell of them; had done ever since that Monday that the pit flooded. And it was Monday when Alf and Sam had died. He hated Mondays, everything always went wrong. And what he hated most about it was the way she looked at him.

'You don't love me any more, do you?' he said.

'No, I don't love you, I love Eddie. As far as I'm concerned you're just the pit owner now. You're just like the rest of them.' And Lizzie turned and walked into her kitchen and this time he let her.

Thirty

*K*ate thought a great deal about her dead child and cried a good deal as
well to begin with. She wished everything different. Jon had left and
not come back for three days, and having driven him away she wanted him so
much that when he came back she wouldn't speak to him or see him. She
remembered how she had not wanted to be pregnant, how she thought it had
ruined her life, and now she felt as though her life was ruined because the tiny
girl had not survived. Her arms were so empty. Charles's mother and her
aunt and the servants were kind to her. Kate went nowhere at first, she tired
easily and could not be bothered to see anyone, and Jon came home less and
less, sometimes not for four or five days at a time. She did ask him once
where he slept. He said, 'At the pit. Where else?'

She didn't ask again. When she began to feel better she started riding
Dolly again. She even saw one or two friends but she didn't go to the pits and
didn't ask Jon anything about them. The only thing they had discussed was
money for the continued sinking of the new pit and since Kate was convinced
that it would be a profitable adventure she supplied the capital. They didn't
discuss the details. He started to tell her about his plans for the new housing
but Kate dismissed him, saying she wasn't interested, and he didn't offer to
tell her anything again.

The early summer came. Kate got better. She ordered new clothes.
She walked about the garden giving various instructions to the gardeners.
She went shopping. She gave a dinner party and among the people she
invited were William Dove and his wife and Joseph and Lilian Marshall.
That evening she watched Jon with Lilian but he behaved just as he
always did with women. He was gentle and made her laugh. If anything,
Kate thought, there seemed more to worry about with Claudia Dove

297

who smiled into his eyes very warmly indeed.

Jon and Kate began to socialise in just a small way. They went out to dinner and at one such party she overheard two men in the hall, as one said to the other, 'If you didn't know better you'd take Armstrong for a gentleman, in spite of his accent.'

'Plenty of gentlemen have had to marry a woman for her money,' the other said, and laughed.

Kate didn't laugh, she went home seething, and if Jon had been at home long enough for her to release some anger in his direction, she would have.

She found herself wanting to have another child. At first she denied the feeling but as the weeks went by, the more she denied it the worse it became. It seemed to her that there were children everywhere she went: babies in their mother's arms, older ones playing in the street, pregnant women, families going home together. Kate, in spite of her friends and her aunt and her shopping expeditions, became lonely and she waited for Jon to come home though he rarely did. She began to notice more and more when he was not there. If she planned to have people to the house he came back; if she expressed a desire to go out or accept an invitation he did. On Sundays sometimes, but only at her request, he was there for dinner. She felt as though she had to ask him for everything, but he never refused. At night he came home late and went to his room and worked, and Kate lay in her bed and cried. One Sunday when Jon had gone to chapel with her at her request – they had met Eddie and all the family there and she had felt even more the need for a child – she asked him to take a walk in the garden with her after lunch and Jon, as usual, complied with the request. Conversation appeared to be beyond him though. He answered in monosyllables to everything she said. He could talk to other women, she thought, but not to her. Finally she stopped trying to make light conversation and stopped inside the rose garden where there was a wooden bench in the warm sunshine. It was a perfect July day. Here she sat down. Jon sat with her.

'I want to talk to you,' she said.

'I gathered that.'

Kate had meant to lead into this conversation but now that she was faced with it she couldn't think of anything but, 'I want a child.' He said nothing. 'I don't want to go through my life like this. Other women have children. I want them.' Still he said nothing. Kate wanted to throw something or hit him.

'It's not something you can order,' he said softly, 'it's not like a shop. It comes of people living together naturally.'

'I know what happens,' Kate said through her teeth.

Nobody said anything more. That night she found her plainest nightgown, it was all she could bear somehow. It was white with buttons down the front and she wished herself thousands of miles away. Emma brushed out her hair and plaited it and left, and Kate waited. The line of light under the door assured her that he was there but after fifteen minutes or so Kate was so nervous that she was ready to go to bed and forget all about it when he quietly opened the door and slid into the room. He was dressed as though he had almost forgotten and Kate didn't pretend to herself that he wanted to be there. He looked her up and down strangely, she thought, and neither said anything. It was worse than the conversation of the afternoon. Kate had left only one lamp burning low. She was grateful somehow for the lack of light. He wasn't fully dressed, as though he had been working hard and had gradually shed jacket and tie and shoes and undone several buttons of his shirt.

She sat down on the bed and he sat down with her and reached for her but she was so nervous by then that she drew back and turned her face away. She couldn't help but think of her wedding night when he had tried to persuade her to go to bed with him and she had thought it her duty. Jon was not the kind of man to be deceived just because he got what he wanted and this was just as bad because she wanted so much to have a child but didn't want him here any more than she had done then. She tried to will her body towards him but she couldn't. She made herself turn to him, made her body endure his hands and mouth, felt his fingers tremble on the buttons of her nightdress – and just when she thought that it was going to be all right, just when she thought that she was going to be able to bear it, he stopped and moved slightly away and looked down and said, 'I can't do this.'

In all the time she had been married to Charles Nelson there had not been a problem of this kind. Whatever the hour, whatever the circumstances, Charles had never said that he couldn't. It was the first time that Kate realised that perhaps men couldn't always. She thought it was a sort of automatic response like pressing a button. She sat up and looked scornfully at him.

'What do you mean, you can't?'

Jon had put off going into her room for as long as he could and when he couldn't put it off any longer he had gone. There a shock awaited him. This

299

was not the Kate of the seductive, almost diaphanous nightgowns. She looked like Greta had at bedtime, with her hair plaited and her nightgown plain. For seconds together his heart sang and it was easy. He gathered her to him, his body and his mind remembered her and rejoiced. He knew that she would come to him as she always had done, laughing, eager, full of kind words and long kisses. Only she hadn't. It was like having a doll that was rather like Greta. She turned away and the light fell on her hair and it was the wrong colour. She was smaller and more slender and her body was anything but eager, and suddenly he couldn't remember what to do and the more he tried the less it worked.

'I can't,' he said.

'Why can't you?' Her voice was full of scorn. 'I told you, I want a child. You're my husband. You're a man, aren't you? You gave me a child before, easily.'

'That was different. You wanted me then.'

Kate had never been deliberately cruel to anyone in her life but she knew that she was in danger of it now.

'I didn't feel any different,' she said, 'it's you. You made me want you that night. Why can't you do it now? You've done it before, lots of times. You made Greta want you, didn't you?'

'I didn't have to make her want me.'

'But you know how to. You must know how to. You did it before.'

'I loved her.'

'You couldn't possibly have loved her. You couldn't have loved anybody quite so stupid.'

There was silence. It was a very long silence indeed. It was long enough, she thought, to fall right into it and never come out. She had inflicted damage and she knew it.

'If you could make love to her for no good reason, you can make love to me for the sake of a child. Greta had nothing but her looks. They would have faded as she grew older and you wouldn't have wanted her after a while.'

Jon got up from the bed.

'You're my husband,' Kate objected, but she let him walk out because she was humiliated and on the verge of crying.

They avoided each other all week. On the Friday evening Jon had been invited by Samuel to go over some business details but when he reached the

300

pretty house in Sunderland Lilian opened the door, looked dismayed and said, 'Jon! Didn't you get his message? Samuel had to go out. Come in.'

He went into the hall and through into a cosy room which was Lilian's for writing letters and reading. Sunlight played on the walls.

'He had a last-minute business problem. He was certain you would get his message. I am sorry. Would you like some tea?'

Jon said that he would, and because Lilian said it was the servants' night off he went through with her and sat at the big kitchen table while she made the tea. It was pleasant sitting there, the children in bed and the house silent. Lilian chatted, Jon half-listened and drank his tea.

'So,' she said finally, 'has something gone wrong at the mines?'

'No, no more than usual.'

'But there is something wrong?'

'No.'

'You didn't laugh at my funny story. Are you angry that Samuel isn't here?'

'Of course not.'

'How's Kate?'

'Fine.'

'It must have been dreadful for her, losing the baby. I realise lots of women have miscarriages but I know how desolate I would have felt.'

'She wants another,' he said.

'That's perfectly understandable. It may take a while of course.'

Jon got up abruptly from the table. He went and stood beside the kitchen fire. It reminded him rather of the fire at home when he was little, with the ovens on one side and the boiler on the other, and the warm smell of food which never quite left the little pit house and which was only in the kitchen in Lilian's more prosperous place. He remembered being very small and crying over something, and his father so big and so frightening, leaning over and saying, 'Are you a lass? Well, are you?'

'No.'

'Only lasses cry. You stop it this minute or I'll give you the wrong end of this belt.'

He had never cried again. Even when Greta died there was nothing to relieve the hard knots of guilt and misery. Lilian had come up behind him and now she placed a tentative hand on his arm.

'Can't she have any more, Jon?' she said quietly.

'She doesn't want me.'

Lilian gave a small cold smile.

'Darling, she must be the only woman of your acquaintance who doesn't.'

'Don't, Lilian.'

'No, I mean it. Have you done something?'

'Of course I have. I got her pregnant. She wasn't going to marry me.'

'Or you her? Don't you love her?'

'I don't know. I thought I did once but after Greta died I didn't want anybody. I certainly didn't want anybody having my bairn. Now she wants a bairn and we're married and she thinks it doesn't matter how we feel. There was only Greta, you see, and she always . . . she always . . .'

Lilian took him into her arms. She brought his head down on to her shoulder and stroked his hair. He fastened his arms around her.

'Oh God, Lilian, I want her back so much.'

'I know, but you can't. Can't you try and be nice to Kate?'

But Jon was looking at her golden hair and blue eyes and pale milky skin, and when she looked up at him he kissed her long and slowly on the mouth. Lilian kissed him back. She put her fingers into his hair and then she let him go.

He trudged up the stairs when he got home, not having eaten and not hungry and not wanting to see anybody – least of all Kate, who appeared at the head of the stairs.

'Where have you been?' she said.

'Work.'

'Oh, really? At the Victoria?'

'I went to Samuel's house afterwards. We had a meeting.'

Kate waved a paper in her hand.

'What's that?' Jon said.

'It's a note which came for you just after you left the mine apparently. It was brought here. Eddie thought that perhaps you had called in here first. It cancels the meeting. I thought I had better open it since you weren't here, in case it was important. So where have you been?'

Jon walked past her and along the hall.

'Drinking tea with Lilian.'

'You didn't think of coming home to dinner?'

'No.'

'Perhaps you'd like something now.'

'I wouldn't.'

'Why did you lie to me?'

Jon stopped.

'Because I knew you would make a fuss, because you hate Lilian.'

She laughed.

'I don't hate her. I just don't quite understand your fascination with her. You're sleeping with Lilian Marshall, aren't you? You see her in the afternoons and sometimes in the evenings when you don't come home to dinner.'

'I'm not sleeping with her,' he said.

'You must be sleeping with somebody and it isn't me and it could hardly be Lizzie and it most definitely couldn't be Greta, could it?'

Jon turned around and got hold of her. He dragged her the length of the hall. At first she didn't say anything and then she began to protest and try to stop him. She dragged her feet. She even began shouting at him in spite of the fact that there might be servants, though he didn't see any. He opened the door of her bedroom and pulled her in there and slammed the door. He didn't listen to the voices that told him Charles Nelson had treated her badly. He put her down on to the bed, put one hand into her hair so that she couldn't turn away and then he kissed her. She tried hard to get away, she tried to kick him, she squirmed as if she was on a hook but pinning her down was not difficult, she was so slight. Even then she tried not to let him touch her lips but Jon held her.

He was too angry to go back to reasonable civilised behaviour. He pulled off the necessary clothes. Several of the little pearl buttons on her blouse didn't withstand the handling and got lost in the bedcovers. Her underwear was made of better stuff and even when he treated it with disrespect it didn't tear. She started to cry and then to cry out until Jon hoped very much that the walls were as thick as they might be because she had come alive in his arms and was cursing him as freely as anyone he had ever heard. That, he thought, was the problem with letting a woman near a pit: she picked up bad habits. By the time he remembered Charles Nelson the bed was a wreck and down in the middle of it by the light of one lamp Kate's face was shiny with tears and white with rage and her eyes were lit. Her slender body was almost naked and she was shaking. She had stopped fighting with him by then so he stopped pinning her down but still held her lightly.

'There's always been somebody else,' she said, lips quivering. 'First it was Lizzie and then Greta and now Lilian. And in between times it was the pits, the Isabella and the-the Catherine and the-the bloody Victoria. Never me. It was never me.' When he didn't reply she said, 'Are you going to let go?'

'I don't want you thinking I'm Charles Nelson here. Do you want me to do this or not?'

The tears spilled again. It was like a never-ending supply, Jon thought.

'Well?'

'I want a baby.'

'You never give up, do you?'

He was still too angry to be gentle with her and there didn't seem any place for tenderness so he just got on with it, but it was better than he had thought. She really did want him and it was such a relief to watch the distress go from her eyes, to feel the way that her body instinctively reacted to him. But even so he couldn't tell whether all she saw behind her eyes was the image of the dead child and the way that he had not been there. She didn't know how difficult it was to go on as though only the future mattered when he could remember so clearly Greta's coffin going into the ground, knowing that the tiny child was in there with her, and even more clear and even worse now was the little dead girl. Kate had blamed him for that. You could, he thought now, only take so much of it. After a while the blame was more than you were when all you really wanted was just to bury your face against somebody and not to keep having to face the mornings and the nights. The days jumbled past and you were out of step with everything.

Here was another responsibility. She was all warm against him now, all soft and responsive, even though he was doing this less tenderly than he'd ever done it in his life. He was too bitter to be nice to her, she was just a spoiled little bitch who wanted a child, and then he remembered what she had said. 'It was always somebody else. It was never me.' Well, it was her all right now. She was helpless, making small pleading noises in her throat. He was actually getting this right, knowing that she wasn't Greta, not deceiving himself any more. He just couldn't get rid of the anger but she was past caring about anything but what he was doing to her, no matter how. She didn't remember about wanting a baby, he knew, she was like liquid against him, she was golden in the lamplight and her hair had turned to fire.

Thirty-one

*W*hen Kate awoke the next morning, for the few first moments she felt wonderful and she reached out one arm. Then she remembered the night and opened her eyes. It was a lovely late-summer morning. She looked across at the other pillow and tears welled up into her eyes. She thought of how badly she had treated Jon during the past few days and of how he had treated her last night. Jon was not Charles Nelson. She had not thought so even for a moment that night and did not confuse them now. She had never felt for Charles what she felt about Jon, angry, frustrated, jealous and wanting to hurt him badly because she was hurt about the baby and Lilian Marshall and the way he never came home. She got slowly out of bed and put on a wrap, went into his room and the bed was empty. That was when she remembered that he had said he was going to the office. It was late, well after ten, he would be long gone. She thought about going after him to explain, to see him, but knew that she couldn't. She would just have to wait here until he came back that afternoon. She went over and over the night and after a while she couldn't bear the house any longer so she had Dolly saddled and rode off to the mine manager's house.

Tommy, Sam's son, was a big lad now and was outside with some of his friends. He was going fishing. It was a bright clear morning without a cloud, promise of a hot day. Mary was playing in the garden and when Kate ventured into the house Lizzie was there in her kitchen as usual with little Francis. The house was as spotless as ever and Kate wondered why she had let things get so wrong, and then knew. She had always been jealous of Lizzie Harton, the woman her husband couldn't marry. She wished it wasn't like that because she liked Lizzie better than any other woman she had ever met. They could have been such good friends, she thought.

305

Uncertain of her reception, she hovered by the door.

'I just wondered how you were.'

'Oh, Kate, I'm so glad you came. The kettle's just on.'

The kettle, Kate reflected happily, was always just on in Lizzie's kitchen.

'Take our Francis, will you?'

She sat down with the small child on her knee. He looked exactly like Eddie.

'Your children don't look like you at all,' she said.

Lizzie laughed.

'I know,' she said, 'and I'm going to go on having them until one does.'

'How are you?'

'Tired. Fed up.I've had enough of this one, I wish it was over, and then he has to work Saturdays.'

'Yes,' said Kate.

She liked holding the small boy on her lap. He was so warm and cuddly and he smiled and dimpled at her. She thought of how old her baby would have been now. Lizzie poured out tea and said gently, 'You'll have other bairns, you know, lots probably 'til you wish differently. Sometimes I wish mine away.'

'I suppose Eddie looked like this when he was small,' Kate said.

'Isn't he a picture?'

'You quarrelled with Jon, didn't you?'

'Yes.'

'Badly?'

'Bad enough. Men don't know what it's like to lose a bairn. I mean, I know it made him think of Greta but . . .'

'I thought he had another woman,' Kate said.

'With Jon there's always been another woman.'

'Yes, but the other woman was always you, until Lilian Marshall.'

'Kate–'

'Lilian Marshall looks like Greta would have looked if she'd lived. She's got golden hair and blue eyes.'

'Did he go to bed with her?'

'I don't know. The trouble is, you see, that he treats everybody alike. He makes every woman in the room think that he wants to go bed with her.'

'Even your aunty?'

Kate laughed.

'I hope not!'

'I do know what you mean but he doesn't do it on purpose. His dad was like that but worse. He used to take advantage.'

'I want you to make it up with him,' Kate said.

'Kate—'

'Please. You're the only woman he's ever really loved in his life. It's making him so miserable. He has no interest in anything.'

'That's not true. He loved Greta very much, and he loves you.'

'I want you to make it up with him,' she said, 'so that we can all be friends like we used to be. He hates not seeing you. It's almost as bad as being married to Charles.'

Jon had got up early in a black mood and had gone to the office. He didn't want to feel guilty over Kate. In vain did he try to rationalise. He called her names in his mind and told himself that she had wanted what she had got, but he was still unhappy with himself for behaving nearly as badly as Charles Nelson. He opened the window on one side and looked out over the pit yard until Eddie walked in.

'Now, sunshine,' said Jon.

Eddie didn't say anything for a minute and then he closed the door after him.

'Look, Jon, I'm sorry if I dropped you in the clarts last night.'

'How do you mean?' he said, leaving the window.

'I sent the message to the house with Fred Hobson and he said you weren't there and that Kate opened it.'

'Yes. So? Is there any tea around here? I want to go down the Vic and I'm not doing it without tea first.'

It was late afternoon when they eventually inspected the Catherine. They had left it until last because there were just small problems with the other pit but rumblings had been reported down the Cath. It seemed like a good time; there was nobody in the way. The men were finished for the weekend. Jon had almost as much love for the Catherine as he had for the Victoria. He didn't know why. It was as hot as hell down there; you were conscious of each breath.

It was big enough at first – as big as a room, the main roadways – and then it was down to low and narrow, harder still for tall men, desperate for

307

anybody who worried about small, narrow places. You had to keep ducking down every few yards, minding your head. It smelled like an empty oven, a typical low-seamed Durham pit. Down to the first level with Eddie's reassuring voice behind him, though he didn't know why it should have been reassuring, full of bloody complaints. He was used to that. Eddie was a perfectionist, that was what Jon liked about him. Well, one of the things. Eddie would not neglect a pit, would look after the men and the officials, and this was his pit. It was as dear to him as his wife and bairns. Jon liked that too even if it meant listening to his grumblings all the way along the first level, tunnels leading off here and there. Eddie knew the plan of the pit off by heart in his head.

The new workings were on the eastern side of a geological fault and were fairly straightforward. The main A seam was straight with two-foot-six seams in galleries off. It was very much like the old pit had been really, until the fault had halted proceedings forty years before.

They went down to the second level, Eddie not complaining by then, just making general remarks, checking here and there, stopping now and then, holding his lamp close to the side. There was no visible evidence of trouble down there even though they went as far as the slope which led up to the old level to where the old pit was blocked off.

Then he paused, listening.

'Summat wrong?' Jon said.

'No. I just thought I heard . . . I don't know.'

'Ghosts?'

Eddie looked at him like he was an idiot.

'No, just–'

He didn't finish what he was going to say. All of a sudden there was a tremendous bang. It was the loudest thing Jon had ever heard; it pained his ears and shook the floor and the walls and the ceiling, and then the whole world caved in and after that there was nothing.

When he came to he thought he was dead and then it was his nightmare over again and he thought, You can't fool me this time. I'm going to wake up in a minute and the bonny lass with the golden hair and the white nightgown is going to take me into her arms and then I'll stop screaming. Only he wasn't screaming, and when he opened his eyes properly there was a lamp still burning and he remembered that he had put the lamp down.

He wasn't in any pain, he wasn't hurt. He was able to get up. To one side everything was just as it had been. To the other there was a solid wall of fallen rock. Eddie was nowhere to be seen. Jon shouted his name a couple of times and in response there was a faint groan, at least he thought it was a faint groan, from within the rock. It made Jon think of Sam and Alf and he knew now that Eddie meant as much to him as Alf had ever done and maybe more so he turned his lamp down low, got hold of the only pick they had and started digging.

He didn't think about anything beyond getting Eddie out but it was hard work and the time went by and he seemed to make no progress. Worse still the groaning stopped and he thought then of having to go back and tell Lizzie that Eddie had died. The work was hard and long and went on forever and after a while it occurred to him that even if he did get Eddie free it would only be to die of thirst down there, but he went on trying until at last the solid rock gave way to Eddie's leg and then more of him and Eddie came to cursing more violently than Jon had ever heard him. When he was free it was obvious to Jon that he was badly hurt.

'Don't you die on me, you bastard! I'm not going back there to tell her she's a widow.'

'I'm not dying,' Eddie said, voice quivering with pain, 'and don't you call me a bastard. I'll kick the shite out of you.'

'Not with that leg you won't.'

'It hurts.'

'What's the other one like?'

'I don't know.'

'Can you walk?'

'Don't be stupid. Anyhow,' Eddie opened his eyes, 'there's nowhere to walk to.'

'Do you think it's bad?' Jon said, his gaze following Eddie's to the solid wall of stone.

'I don't think we're going anywhere,' he said.

'We could try.'

'What, the fall?'

'No, walking somewhere,'

'I said. There isn't anywhere. This is it. This is yon end. There isn't anything past here.'

'Are you sure?'

'Who's the manager?'

309

'All right, I'm just asking. We can't just sit here.'

'Jon, I've got a broken leg.'

'Are you sure?'

'Will you stop saying that? It hurts like merry hell, it's broken.'

'Then why are you holding your arm?'

'Because it hurts.'

'Is there anything that doesn't hurt?'

Eddie closed his eyes and a single tear ran. Jon left him there. He picked up the lamp and went some way along.

'There are other tunnels along here, Eddie.'

'They don't go anywhere. They stop not far on and we're way past the upcast shaft. Anyhow, they'll have somebody digging shortly.'

Jon came back to him and put the lamp down. He sat beside it.

'You want to rely on somebody digging us out? It's Saturday afternoon. There's nobody there.'

'They must have heard that noise in Sunderland. Anyroad,I can't move. I wish you'd sit down.' This because Jon had got up again. When he came back he did sit down. He looked at Eddie.

'I think we should try moving.'

'I can't.'

'I think you're going to have to. If it was a big fall – and it sounded that way, didn't it? – if it was, they'll never reach us. We don't have any water, we're not going to last. You want to die down here?'

'If they don't reach us we're not going to make it anyway.'

'It might take them too long.'

'Jon, I keep telling you. I know this pit, I have the map up in my office. I know it forwards, backwards and sideways. There's nowhere to go from here, nowhere that leads any place, not from this level.'

'Nowhere from here up to the top level?'

'No.'

Jon sat down, sighing.

'She told me I'd die down the Vic. I love to prove people wrong.'

'Who told you?'

'My beloved wife. At least she'll be able to marry Joseph Moorhouse.'

'Yes, let's look on the bright side,' Eddie said. 'My baby is due this week.'

'Don't worry, somebody'll marry her. She's the bonniest lass in the world.'

310

'I thought Lilian Marshall was the bonniest lass in the world?'

'Who said?'

'You did when you were drunk that last time.'

'I have to get you out of here. Lizzie'll never forgive me otherwise.'

'You won't know,' Eddie said comfortingly.

At the surface Kate was remembering who she was. It was an interesting process. One minute she had been a married woman with a faithless husband who had spent a good part of the previous evening forcing himself on her in her own bedroom, feeling sorry for herself, drinking tea in another woman's kitchen; and now she was standing at the pit head and she was the mineowner. She had never felt as sick in her life, morning sickness was nothing compared to this, and beside her Lizzie was big-bellied and grey-faced and Kate would have told her to go and sit down if she hadn't known her so well. Josiah Smith was not her favourite man; he had been Jon's choice. His wife was a meek little woman and now Kate knew why. He tried to ignore her, he and Forrester, clustered together with the other officials.

'What's happened?' Kate demanded.

'There's been an explosion and I've had men down. There's a bad rock fall. Your husband's down there. Aye, and Mr Bitten. You can go home and wait.'

'I shall do nothing of the kind. Have you got men down there digging?'

'Not yet.'

'Then get them down,' she said. 'Now.'

Lizzie was standing a little way back. Kate gave various other instructions just so that Josiah Smith would know who was in charge and then she walked Lizzie up the yard to Jon's office and ordered tea and sat her down.

It seemed strange to her that only hours before Jon had been there. There were papers on the desk and an empty teacup.

'Don't worry,' she said now, 'I'll get Eddie up, and that bastard I married.'

'Oh, Kate, don't use language like that, somebody will hear!' And Lizzie started to cry.

Kate got down beside her.

'Nobody can hear,' she said. 'Drink your tea.'

'I've got two children, and one on the way. If anything happens to him I don't know what I'll do.'

311

'I'm not going to let him die down there,' said Kate, hoping that she sounded confident. She thought back to the night before, the anger between Jon and her, the violence, the sweetness of the kisses and his body so smooth and young. She thought of him buried under stone and turned away from Lizzie in pretence of pouring more tea. She thought of how much she hated him. She hated the way he had never loved her, the way that he could make her want him, the way he had in the end gained everything and now perhaps lost it all. She hated to think of him dead; he couldn't leave like that, as though it was all over, like walking out of a theatre in the middle of a performance. She thought of him putting her down on to the bed. She wanted to talk to him so badly that she actually parted her lips to say something, as though he could hear.

Lizzie was holding her cup in shaking hands, slowly spilling hot tea over the sides on to her fingers. Kate took the cup gently from her and as she did so Lizzie's tears ran and ran. Kate put both arms around her.

'I'm so frightened. There's nothing past Eddie. There's nothing past him. I love him.'

'I know.'

'I never thought I would. I thought I'd want what I couldn't have for the rest of my life, but I don't. I told Jon.'

'You told him?'

'It wasn't fair. It wasn't right. How could he go on thinking that he meant as much to me as the man who I'd married and given myself to and had children with? Eddie belongs to me, I love him. Why should I pretend otherwise?'

'And you quarrelled with Jon then?'

'He got drunk and hit Eddie and seemed to think he could have whatever he wanted, and I wasn't having it. I don't care about him. I don't care what happens to him—'

'Shh. That's not true either.'

Lizzie hid her face against Kate's shoulder.

'Oh God, Kate, what if he's dead. I was so awful to him!'

In the end Jon persuaded Eddie to move. There was no sound of any digging, of any kind of help. They couldn't go back, there must be tons and tons of stone in the way. Jowling – knocking on the stone with the pick – brought no response from any rescue party. They could go up the slope before them. It was blocked off, of course, because it was the end of the new workings but at least the air might be better – give them a chance to live longer until a rescue party had a chance to reach them.

When they had to stop again for Eddie's sake, Jon wondered again how bad the roof fall had been and estimated, as he was sure that Eddie must by now have estimated, that it was very unlikely they would get out. He began to wonder casually what it was like to die of thirst and reasoned that with a bit of luck the gases would be so bad long before then that it wouldn't matter. His thinking was getting less clear. All he really wanted to do was fall asleep. Eddie seemed already asleep and it would be so easy. He even thought he saw the golden-haired girl through the shadows which his lamp cast upon the walls. He could see Alf's slow smile as he had not seen it in years and remember the cradle which he had made for Greta and Sam's children. He dozed and there she was in his arms, giving herself to him freely like no one had done before or since. The most tragic thing in his life had been the most precious, the purest. He opened his eyes and reached out and there was nothing but the heat and the faintly sickening smell. He could hear Lizzie saying to him, 'I don't love you. You're just the pit owner. You're just like the rest of them.'

He touched Eddie gently on the shoulder.

'Are you dying on me?'

'No.'

'All right. We're going to get out of here. You're going to move.'

'I can't.'

'Your wife is having a baby. You have three children to keep. You're going to move.'

'I'm in too much pain.'

'You're going to die else. Then you won't be in pain any more and don't think you'll be in any bloody heaven either because you won't, because you'll have given in. Now come on.'

It was slow; each breath hurt Eddie, Jon knew. He had to almost drag him and they had to stop a lot because it was so hot and narrow and Jon was so thirsty now. He tried not to think about that but it was hard, the sea above and maybe even rain. And when they stopped Eddie was too exhausted to talk but after a while he said, 'You know, Jon, when this seam was opened up it wasn't so far away from the old pit, the original one.'

'Do you know anything about it?'

'Not much. There aren't any plans, it was all years ago, but I checked it and when they opened this seam it was running a bit close to that. They had to be careful. Forrester knows about it.'

'Oh, well, that's a big help, Forrester knowing.'

'Maybe he'll remember.'

'And get us out? How's he going to know where we are or where the old pit connects, if it does. Does it?'

'No.'

'Are you sure?'

'You're doing it again.'

'Sorry. You want to go on now?'

'No.'

'Come on then.'

That night Lizzie went into labour. Kate wasn't surprised. Back at the mine manager's house she paced the floor like an expectant father and in between went to the pit head half a dozen times through the night to see what was happening.

The rescuers went on digging but all they could see in front of them was a solid wall of stone. The pit wheel stood out against the night sky. Kate shed no tears. She spoke tersely to Josiah Smith and then went back to see how Lizzie was. The night was not dark; it was warm and there were stars. In the dawn she heard the child's cry as she walked into the house and when the doctor had come downstairs and said she could go up she went to Lizzie's bedroom and sat on the bed and took the baby into her arms. He seemed so tiny.

'Dear me,' she said, 'I don't think you're ever going to turn out a child that looks like you. He's the image of his father. You are there when it happens, are you?'

'Oh, Kate, you're so coarse,' Lizzie said, smiling.

'I can't go any further.'

'You don't have a choice. Come on.'

'Jon, I can't.'

'Yes, you can. Don't give up on me, you bastard.'

'I wish you wouldn't call me that.'

'Why not?' Jon said, dragging him.

314

'Because I am.'

'Are you? Well, I had a father, and believe me being a bastard can't be any worse. Every time he got drunk he used to put me over the kitchen table and thrash me until his arm was tired. I was never half so glad of anything in my life as I was the day they brought him out of that bloody pit. I went upstairs and prayed hard that he would die.'

'And did he?'

'Aye.'

'You might give it a go this time,' Eddie said.

Kate spent all the next day at the pit in the pouring rain. She didn't keep to the office; it seemed so cowardly somehow. She stood there in the puddles and wondered what it would be like being widowed again. She tried to be constructive, she made plans. She thought that she would have Lizzie and her family to live at the big house and it would be nice with all the children and Jon's mother, and then she knew suddenly that Lizzie would hate it. She was not the kind of woman to get by without a man. Kate thought, I'll introduce her to society and find her a rich husband and I'll marry Joseph Moorhouse and forget about Jon. And she stood there in the drenching rain and cried.

'Do you think it sounds different here, Eddie?' Jon said, banging the pick against the wall.

'No. Should it?'

'It might.'

'You're imagining it, man.'

'No, listen. Doesn't it sound hollow to you?'

'I wish I'd never put the idea into your head. We're nowhere near it.'

Jon banged the pick off the stone again.

'It does sound different. Listen. It's hollow. Look, sit down there.'

'I can do that.'

'So listen.'

Eddie listened.

'It sounds just the same to me.'

'Well, I don't think it does.' And Jon started in at the stone.

'You're wasting your time.'

'I haven't got nothing else to do with it.'

'We could go to sleep for a while.'

'No, don't.'

'I keep thinking I'm at home.'

'Well, you're not.'

Eddie lay there a long time. Jon knew that he would have been grateful to stay there for what remained of his now very short life expectation. The thirst was a torment, the pit was hotter than ever and he was making it worse with all this activity. It was hard work. He would have given a lot for a drink of water. Eddie was still. Jon wondered if he was asleep. Being asleep would take away all the torment. Being asleep he could conjure Greta's smile as clear as yesterday. He had to keep stopping. It was harder work than he had ever done because of the heat and the lack of water and the feeling that there wasn't much time left, and here he was making it worse than it already was. He hadn't even yesterday to be grateful for, having forced his wife and then walked out and left her on the bed. He wondered what she was doing now? She was probably making plans for the future to marry Lizzie and herself off to rich men and live happily ever after. He got back up again and started in on the stone with the pick and it started to give. He stopped and stared at it at first and then went on and it gave further.

'Eddie! Eddie, look.'

Eddie opened his eyes and Jon went on, not thinking about anything else now, hacking his way through until there was a small hole and then a much bigger one so that he could get through there and drag Eddie with him. He was exhausted by then and sat panting. It didn't look like much progress to him. The air was dank and smelt very bad and he didn't know which way to go. He knew that there had to be a way out but had heard of men wandering around in old pits and never finding an exit and he didn't think that Eddie could go much further. He had grown quieter and quieter. The old pine pit props that the men used to make themselves creaked dangerously around him. Jon badly wanted to give up.

'Come on.'

'No.'

'You've got to.'

'I can't and you can't make me. Leave me, I'm all right.'

'No, you aren't,' Jon said, and dragged him further.

In some ways it was worse than before, the air was getting fouler all the time and it was dusty. There were broken wicker baskets which the lads

316

would have used. Jon wanted to look around him for ghosts. He wondered whether anybody had died down there before. He had to keep stopping more often now and then it seemed that they were getting somewhere, that this was a way up to the first level, that they were making progress. But eventually he was just too tired to go on any further and he sat down beside a silent Eddie and gave in to sleep.

By Monday Josiah Smith was ready to give up. He stood in the yard in the morning sunshine and told Kate to her face that the pit fall had been tremendous and there was no hope of getting Mr Bitten and her husband out. It was, to Kate, a particularly horrible re-enactment of what had happened before, only this time the tall pitlad was not there to tell her the news. He was either dead or dying down her pit just as she had forecast. It was a different pit of course; there was always something to be thankful for. She argued with Josiah and the morning wore on and in her mind she saw him hurt, gassed, thirsty and dead. In the afternoon Lizzie came to the pit head to the scandal of the midwife and the lying-in nurse and when she heard what Josiah was saying she didn't argue. She drew Kate away.

'He's right,' she said, 'you know he's right. You can't expect them to go on forever. There's too much stone to shift and they wouldn't be alive when they were found. Jon's dead, Kate.'

'He isn't. You know he isn't; not unless the fall got him. What do you want me to do? Let them die of thirst down there?'

'What is there that you can do?'

'I don't know.'

'I think you should come home and let the men stop.'

'How can you?'

'Because I was born here. My father's dead, friends, family. You know what it's like.'

'It was bad enough losing Charles, even though he was so awful – but to lose Jon . . . I can't.'

Lizzie went to Josiah.

'Mrs Armstrong thinks you should call off the rescue,' she said,' and so do I.'

Jon dreamed about Lizzie, his sweet Lizzie. She was lying in a sand dune with him and she was laughing. They were days away from their wedding and she was waiting for him and then he was kissing her and it was just as right as it had always been. And then he awoke and remembered and wanted to cry but for the fact that he didn't seem to have any tears. His lips had cracked and his throat was sore. Eddie was still sleeping. Jon didn't know whether to disturb him. Eddie had begged to be left the last three times he had insisted on going on and Jon was a lot weaker than he had been. He debated with himself whether to leave Eddie and then come back but wasn't sure he would be able to find the way back or have enough energy so he shook Eddie awake. This time Eddie didn't even suggest he couldn't go. He didn't say anything but when Jon dragged him away from the spot where they had been sleeping he passed out. He was a dead weight then and Jon hadn't the strength to go much further so he stopped again and sat down. Eddie's eyelids didn't move. Jon pulled him up into his arms and cradled his head.

'Don't die on me, Eddie, please. Don't leave me here. Eddie. Eddie!'

There was no response. Jon got up and dragged him a bit further and a bit further and then he couldn't do any more so he sat down with Eddie and closed his eyes and tried to think of something nice instead of which he was in Lizzie's back yard that particular Monday morning and he could smell the wet clothes and she was smacking his face hard and saying, 'I don't love you.'

Oh God, Jon thought, I could have stood anything but that. And then he suspected what day it must be. It was Monday today. The wet clothes would be blowing about in her yard and he would never see her again.

When he woke up it was somehow not as dark as before.

'Eddie?'

When Eddie didn't answer he shook him. Eddie groaned in pain.

'Eddie, I think I can see something.'

'It isn't an angel, is it?' Eddie said.

'Very funny. Howay.'

'No.' Eddie put a surprisingly strong arm up against him. 'I've had enough. Honestly, Jon. You go.'

'No.'

'Every time you move me I wish I was dead.'

'You will be if you stay here.'

'Look, just leave me.'

Jon didn't listen. He dragged Eddie on and then stopped and let go of him.

'I can see something. Hey, Eddie, I can see something. Look at it.'
He got down and pulled Eddie into a sitting position.
'Look at it, Eddie, it's light.'

Thirty-two

Kate and Lizzie didn't go home, as though their staying on would somehow alter things. They sat in Jon's office and drank tea; at least Lizzie sat, in Jon's chair behind the desk. Kate stood by the window which looked out over the pit yard.

'Widows are invisible, you know, to other people,' she said. 'They don't exist. They're pitied and ignored. Long after Charles died I had to wake up to those letters which came addressed to Mrs Charles Nelson as if even though he was dead I still belonged to him, like I wasn't a person.'

'Was that why you wanted to get married again?'

'I suppose it was. It isn't polite, being widowed. It's perfectly acceptable for men of course. Perhaps we ought to request to be burned as if we were in India.'

'I should go home. The baby will want feeding.'

'Have you decided what to call him yet?'

'Eddie and I talked about it but to be honest I think he thought it would be a girl. I can't call him Florence.'

Kate giggled.

'You weren't really going to call your daughter Florence?'

'Why not?'

'It's hideous.'

'I'll have to ask–' Lizzie stopped short. Kate went over as she got up and put both arms around her. 'I have to go back to the house,' Lizzie said, 'I really must. He'll be screaming his head off by now and Jon's mother . . . How am I going to tell her, Kate? I've been telling her for three days that everything will be all right. He's the only son she has left.'

'At least Eddie hasn't got a mother,' Kate said with a shudder. 'The things

321

you end up being grateful for. Shall I come back with you and tell her?'

'Would you, Kate?'

'Of course I would.'

Being numb, she decided, had some merit. She didn't know how long the numbness would last because it had not been like this when Charles died. She remembered feeling vast relief and some guilt and after a while an immense sense of freedom and relief that she had the chance to do what she wanted at the mines. Power. But Jon had never tried to take that power from her. He had always insisted that the mines were hers and if she had allowed he would have talked to her about them, even encouraged her to go there and take part in what was happening. Perhaps, she thought, if the child had lived things would have been all right. Now there was nothing ahead but a vast desert. She remembered once hearing somebody say that being a widow was like being a bird with a broken wing. That was how it felt now.

She went back to the house with her friend and there Lizzie fed her screaming baby and Kate took Mrs Armstrong off into the sitting-room and told her. She took the news so calmly that Kate was worried but Mrs Armstrong looked hard at her and said, 'I was expecting it sooner or later,' and went off upstairs.

Kate returned to the kitchen. The baby was quiet now. May was putting the children to bed. Kate wanted to put off going home for as long as she could possibly manage it. The idea of going back to nobody but her aunt and Charles's mother made her feel so sick that she was faint. When the baby finally slept she and Lizzie sat by the kitchen fire. The evening grew late and Kate remembered how she had hated the nights when she was alone. However would she go back to her room and not have the line of light under the door or hear Jon moving quietly about in the next room? She didn't think that she could bear it. As she gazed into the fire Lizzie said to her, 'You do love him, don't you, Kate?'

'Yes. Isn't that awful now? He doesn't care for me, you see; he never has done. I was always just there, first in the pit office and then in the way. And when somebody doesn't love you, you want so much not to love them that you make yourself believe it. I hate him because he doesn't love me. He can make me want him and yet he never once said that he loved me. I wish he had. I'd rather have had my intelligence insulted with lies.'

'Had you ever thought about telling him?'

'I couldn't. I just couldn't. He told me that he was with me for two reasons; the first was the child and the second was the pits. You try going to bed with somebody like that. The only thing was that Charles had been so awful to me that Jon was easy by comparison. He didn't hurt me. At least not until Friday night . . .'

'Friday night? He hurt you?'

Kate hesitated. 'No,' she said.

'Did you have a fight?'

'It doesn't matter now, does it? He's dead and you've lost Eddie. Eddie was the nicest man I ever met.'

'Sometimes he was. Sometimes he was impossible. I'd give anything to have him back.'

As she spoke there was a slight commotion outside and Kate saw a carriage pull up.

'Oh no,' she said, 'it must be my aunt coming to take me home. They must have heard.' But as she looked the driver got down and helped a tall dark man out of the door and Kate gave a little scream. 'It's Jon!' she said.

'Don't be silly, Kate.' But she was already out of the back door and through the yard. There she stopped short, thinking she was having some kind of dream. His clothes were torn and his face and hands were covered in coal-dust and blood, but he looked happily at her and grinned.

'Thought you'd have had your blacks on by now, Kit,' he said.

She couldn't think of anything to say, her eyes filled with tears. He pulled her into his arms quite roughly and crushed her to him so that she couldn't breathe.

'I thought you were dead,' she said.

'Making plans, were you?' he said against her hair.

'Oh, Jon.'

Behind her she sensed Lizzie hovering and heard him say flatly over her head, 'He's all right. You didn't think I'd let your husband die?'

They put Eddie to bed. The doctor came. Kate bathed Jon's face and hands by the kitchen fire and when Doctor Ingalls had come down from making his main patient comfortable, he said to their worried faces, 'He'll be fine but it will take time, and as for you, Jon, you should go to bed and be careful of those hands. I'll give you something.'

Lizzie had made up Jon's bed. Kate didn't like to leave him but he was exhausted and she made herself go down into the kitchen.

323

'How's Eddie?'

'He's asleep. I think it'll take a long time, especially that leg. It's in a bad way. He said it wasn't so bad before Jon dragged him out.' And Lizzie smiled. 'Whatever will I say to him?'

'Anything is better than "I don't love you",' Kate suggested.

The next morning, thinking that Jon would sleep for most of the day, Kate offered to go with his mother and the children shopping to give the house some quiet for the two men and Lizzie was left alone with her washing and the baby, whom they'd named Alfred. She was pegging out the last lot when she heard somebody behind her and when she turned Jon was standing a little way off, near the kitchen door.

'Are you feeling better?' she asked.

'Are you trying to make every day Monday?'

'I was busy yesterday. I didn't know about the old shaft in the wood. I never thought about it. It was very clever of you.'

'No, it was just luck.'

'If it hadn't been for you . . .'

'Eddie would have done exactly the same. He was the one who was hurt.'

'Yes, but you . . .'

'I could have left him, that's what you mean? You always think the worst of me.'

'That isn't what I mean. I didn't think the worst of you, Jon. How can you say that?'

'Where's Kate?'

'She took the children out so that the house would be quiet for you and Eddie. Jon, I'm so grateful–'

'Don't be.'

'Jon Armstrong, you . . .'

'Yes? Go on, shout at me. It makes me feel normal, but try not to smack me round the face. It hurts.'

Lizzie hesitated for a moment and then she threw herself at him. Jon caught her just as though she did it every day. She could feel his arms fasten around her. She reached up both arms to his neck and kissed him on the mouth.

'You could have died,' she said.

Jon smiled into her eyes.

'I thought I was never going to see your back yard and all your washing again,' he said, 'and to think I hated the smell of it!'

Kate came back with the children.

'What are you doing out of bed?' she said, finding Jon sitting in the garden.

'I'm fine.'

'Your hands are a mess and you're exhausted.'

'I wanted to talk to you.'

'We can talk later when you're better.'

'No, it won't wait. I treated you so badly.'

'Jon, you're incapable of treating a woman badly, physically at least, I already knew that. I'd had experience. You like women too much to hurt them.'

'I didn't go to bed with Lilian Marshall . . . or anybody else.'

'Jon–'

'Just let me spit it out, please. It all went through my head a hundred times when I was down there. I thought I wasn't going to come out. It was only the thought of you marrying Joseph Moorhouse that got me through.'

Kate laughed.

'I had it all worked out,' she said, 'I was going to find rich men for Lizzie and me.'

'She doesn't want anybody but Eddie.'

'No. I know.'

'I didn't mean to trap you into this, Kit. I don't want you to think that I did it for the mines.'

'I never thought that,' she said.

'Didn't you? The truth is I couldn't help it. I wanted you so much and you were so rich and I'm not – I'm not ever going to be like Joseph Moorhouse, rich and influential and–'

She put her hands on either side of his face.

'Oh, do shut up,' she said. 'I love you.'

'What, really?'

'Really. From the very first moment we met on the beach. You know that. You knew it always.'

'No. Fancying somebody isn't loving them. You just liked the look of me.'

'It's a consideration,' she said.

'Let's go home. I want to take you to bed properly.'

'With those hands?'

'I'll manage.'

It was weeks before Eddie was any better but at last he started going around on crutches and complaining and Lizzie was so relieved.

'Will you stop kissing me?' he said.

'I thought you liked me to kiss you?'

'Not like I'm little Alf and not in front of other people. I'm going back to work.'

'You're not going anywhere.'

'I could go to the office. Jon needs me there.'

'No. And you are never, ever going down a pit again in your life,' Lizzie said, turning away to fold some clothes. They were in her kitchen.

'You what?' Eddie said, and she heard the warning note in his voice and turned. 'Look, it's my job to go down the pit and when I'm good and ready I will, so don't start telling me what to do. Tomorrow I am going back to work.'

'Good,' Lizzie said, turning back to her ironing.

It was autumn and Eddie was hell to have at home and she wanted things to be as normal as possible considering what had happened. She was quite glad to be rid of him the next day.

Just before noon a carriage pulled up outside and Kate got out. Lizzie went out to meet her.

'Let's sit in the garden. Jon's mother is busy in the kitchen,' Lizzie said, and since the day was warm they went around the side of the house to the front and sat on an old bench in the sunshine.

'How's Eddie?'

'He's gone to work. Thank goodness.'

Kate laughed.

'I've got something to tell you.'

'What?'

'I think I'm expecting.'

Lizzie cuddled her.

'I'm so glad,' she said. 'What does Jon say?'

'I haven't told him.'

'Whatever for?'

'I don't know, I just can't.'

* * *

Things had changed at the pits since the accident. Jon was to his men some kind of hero and they were happy to have him and Eddie go drinking with them every Saturday fortnight when they got paid. He and Kate stayed at the mine manager's house and on Sunday they stayed for dinner. The other weekends they socialised. Jon said that if she would give him the one Saturday night he would do whatever she wanted on the other. Kate put him through hell. She accepted invitations to dinner, to parties, and worst of all to musical evenings. She thought that she would never forget a particular night when a young lady was playing the harp. There was on Jon's face an expression of the most excruciating boredom that Kate had ever seen. He didn't normally drink but when he got home that night he went into the library and swallowed what was for him an extremely large amount of brandy, casually saying to her as she watched him, 'Would you like some?'

'No, thank you.'

'You didn't really enjoy it?'

'Well . . .'

'We could stay at home instead of going to these dos.'

'Not so long as you go drinking the other Saturday.'

'Once every two weeks!'

'We only go out once every two weeks,' Kate pointed out, and went off to bed.

Jon followed her. He sat down on the bed.

'Nobody could have enjoyed that, Kate. You just like putting me through it.'

'Yes,' she said sweetly.

'Why?'

'Because you're my husband.'

The lamps were lit and there was a big glass of hot milk on her side of the bed.

'Since when did you start drinking hot milk?' he asked her.

She looked at him but didn't answer.

'Are you going to tell me or am I meant to guess?'

'I wasn't sure. I didn't want to frighten you.'

'I'm not frightened. Don't shut me out.'

'I didn't mean to. There's something else as well, Jon.'

'What?'

'I want to come back to the office. I'm not going to stay here and play tea parties. I want my office *and* babies.'

'Babies? How many do you want?'

'Lots,' Kate said roundly. She put her arms around his neck and smiled into his eyes.

'I'm going to go and see how they're getting on with sinking the new pit on Monday,' he said. 'You haven't seen it yet. How would you like to come along?' ·

'I'd like that. I've been thinking and I've got some ideas about it, you know.'

'Something told me you might,' he said. And he kissed her.